I0554302

Rogan's Robbie

Love Happens in Vegas

Irene King

RW&W

ISBN: 979-8-9854934-0-5 (Print)
ISBN: 979-8-9854934-1-2 (E-book)
ISBN: 979-8-9854934-2-9 (Hardcover Large Print)

Library of Congress Control Number: 2022904219

Book cover by Panagiotis "Peter" Lampridis.

First printing edition 2022.

Published by:

Irene W. King
Renie Writes & Wines
840 S. Rancho Drive
Suite 4-228
Las Vegas, NV 89106

Printed in the U.S.A.

Visit the author's website at www.RenieWritesandWines.com

For email permission inquiries: Renie@RenieWritesandWines.com

Note: *Rogan's Robbie is a work of fiction about a BWWM (Black Woman/White Man) romantic relationship. It contains mature and sensitive themes and situations intended for readers over the age of 18. Reader discretion is advised.*

Contents

To Aunt Joyce and the rest of my girls. You complimented, criticized, and encouraged me throughout the writing process. I love you all!

I wrote my first novel because I wanted to read it.

Toni Morrison

Prologue

ABOUT A DECADE AGO

Palo Mesa High School is located in the Centennial Hills area of Las Vegas. At the time, it was the only local charter high school, and the competition for admission was fierce.

Palo Mesa had been built specifically as a charter school. Because of the donations of wealthy local benefactors, including my parents, the impact on taxpayers was minimal. The school was top-notch in academics and athletics and could, and did, demand the highest caliber students. In addition to a zero-tolerance policy against bullying, academic slackers would quickly find themselves transferred out. It also gave bright students from poorer households or substandard schools an opportunity to receive a private-school caliber education. Because of its high standards, eager students lined up for admission.

Graduating students continued on to top-notch, often Ivy League, colleges and universities, most with scholarships or grants.

That's pretty much how my parents described Palo Mesa and their personal involvement. Yeah. I'm bragging.

I'm the oldest of two children of fairly well-off parents. My folks had been born into the equivalent of the middle-class in their native countries and had worked their way up. Mama's originally from Spain, Dad is from Scotland, and they immigrated to the States together. I'm sure they'll tell me their love story one day. They are still tight. Sometimes overly so, if you get my drift. Get a room.

At any rate, they looked at the school as a way to allow any gifted or talented child an opportunity to get a world-class education without the expense of a private school or the parental limitations of homeschooling. They wanted to offer the same academic opportunities to others that they had worked so hard to get for themselves.

Palo Mesa had the same standard layout as most high schools in Clark County, but it was more sprawling. Its maze-like halls confused new students who regularly got lost. With that in mind, one day I saw a person standing in front of the school map, unmoving. He wore baggy coveralls, an oversized t-shirt, and had coiled hair that brushed his shoulders. I couldn't tell if it was male or female to tell the truth.

"Can I help you? Are you lost?"

"I'm lost," was the reply. The voice was female, but because of its huskiness, it could have been a gay dude, too. "This place is a darned maze."

I laughed and said, "Yeah, I know. I can help you."

The person turned from the useless campus map to look at me. Something inside of me hitched. It almost felt as if my heart had stopped. How corny is that?

The person in front of me was clearly female, and despite her obviously young age, was pretty, in a way. She had caramel-colored skin that looked smooth other than a couple of zits. She had a dimple on her left cheek and full lips upturned into a smile full of braces. Her hair was wildly coily, and her figure was invisible under all the baggy, paint-stained clothes she wore. She had a backpack slung over one shoulder and huaraches on her feet. But what really got to me were her big, light gray eyes that smiled along with her expression. They looked awesome against her dark skin.

"You're new here."

"Yeah. I was just transferred."

"I'm Rogan." I extended my hand for a shake.

"I'm Rob," she replied and immediately started giggling at what I'm sure was my look of confusion. "That's what some of my friends call me. My name is Roberta, which I hate."

Ah. Definitely female.

"You can call me Robbie. That's what I generally answer to."

"Okay, Robbie. You seem awfully young to be in high school," I noted.

"I am," she agreed. "I just turned 13.

"Apparently, I'm a prodigy or a genius or something," Robbie continued. "I'll graduate at 15, so it's not like I'm all that smart. If I were a real prodigy, I'd be graduating college by now," she laughed at her own humor.

Once again, my breath caught. Her laughter was easy and somehow made her dimple stand out. Her gray eyes went silvery with humor.

"I'm already a seasoned artist. I mean the whole articles in magazines, face on TV showcasing young artists on Bravo and PBS thing," she explained in one breath, "and I'm here for the art and academics. Mostly academics."

"Where do you need to go?" I asked. This little black chick was impressive.

"Wherever the Art Department is," Robbie answered, looking up at me.

"I'm an ambassador for the school," I told her with a lift of my shoulders as we started toward the department. "I get to show new people around and answer questions. My father made me do it, but I don't mind." I smiled down at her again. "I kinda like it."

"Why would he make you do it?"

"Long story. He's supporting and contributing to the school, and because it's a charter school, they can use the money. He's making me be a good citizen. It's supposed to build my character. So I'm okay with it."

Robbie was still laughing when we arrived at the Art Department's hallway entrance, and I swept my hand toward the double doors. "Here you go!"

"Thanks, Rogan," she said. "See you 'round!" She waved at me as she opened the double doors into the Art Department hallway and disappeared inside without a backward glance.

I stood in the same spot for long moments after she was out of sight. I was trying to figure out the feelings I was dealing with. I was 18, a senior, my grades were good, and as the soccer team captain, I had both status and female company. While the females consisted of the usual groupie girls who were willing to put out for *any* male member of *any* varsity team, I was more than okay with that. I'd been able to get some play from time to time and thoroughly enjoyed the encounters. I always had a couple of condoms in my backpack. Just in case.

For all intents and purposes, life as a senior was outstanding.

So why had this little girl affected me? She was not even remotely my type. She was on the tall side, African American, flat-chested, skinny, and way too young. Jailbait, even. She was decidedly *not* a blonde. Other than her smile, she had shown zero interest in me either as a jock or the son of a wealthy benefactor. She was just being friendly and nothing else. At the time, I couldn't put my finger on the effect Robbie had on me.

"Rogan!" I heard my name being called and looked up to see Colleen, the slender, athletic blonde I was currently dating, waving and trotting toward me. She was a forward on the girls' soccer team, which meant we had a shared interest in the "real" football, as my folks called it. I grinned at her and gave her a hard kiss as she skidded into me. Yeah. This was more my style.

She looked at me oddly. "Everything okay?"

Even as I nodded, I inwardly shook my head as we jogged to our next class on the other side of campus. I put Roberta on the back burner of my mind. She was a distraction I didn't need or want.

Three months later

"Hello, McDonald. How are you doing?"

Mrs. Green, the school librarian, greeted me in her usual dry style. I'd asked for help in Advanced Euclidean Geometry and needed to sit with a tutor for a while. I was pretty sure that I'd pass the midterms. However, since I couldn't find a study partner, I'd finally put my name on the list for a tutor. Colleen was worse than useless, and my teammates didn't "do" tutoring.

I nodded at Mrs. Green and checked the tutoring pairing list. Ah. There was my name next to *Thornquist, R.* Hm. Swedish. Maybe a blonde. I should be so lucky.

"Thornquist is in the Reference section," Mrs. Green told me. I nodded again and headed toward the area. It was late afternoon and relatively quiet. I stood near the tables and looked around. Several people were there, and a couple looked at me curiously before returning to their books. I walked to the Reference desk and asked the student assistant, "I'm looking for R. Thornquist. Do you know them?" The student nodded and pointed at a solitary figure sitting at one of the tables with his back to us. The hunched posture told me that he was deep into his reading.

"Thornquist?" I asked as I arrived at the table. The head shot up, and once again, I was speechless. It was Roberta. I looked at my paper, then at her, and asked, "*You're* Thornquist?"

Robbie smiled at me and nodded. She waved at the chair next to her and scooted over a bit to give me room to sit.

"Thornquist? Isn't that Swedish?"

"Yes," she replied. "My family history is, well, *complicated-*. Maybe one day I'll tell you about it."

"You're tutoring Geometry? *Advanced* Geometry?"

"The more I know about Geometry, the more I can apply it to my art, especially with my more complex and geometric pieces. Good art is math, and I have to know math. I hate it, but it sticks in my brain, and I can use it practicably."

Well, well, well, I thought. *This little girl is crazy smart as well as cute.*

I inwardly shook my head at that thought and smiled at her. She gave me a metal-covered grin, silvery eyes almost disappearing.

"Now, Mr. Rogan," she chuckled, "how can I help you?"

"I don't need tutoring so much, but I do need a study partner for today," I answered. "I need to review stuff that's going to be on the mids, and I want to make sure it's right. Tell me whatcha know."

She smiled again, opened her book, and took a sheath of notes from her binder. As she began explaining what she had written and how it pertained to the midterms, I realized that I was only half-listening. Once again, I was struck by how mature and intelligent she was and that her face, even with zits and braces, was actually kind of pretty. Her body was lost in another oversized t-shirt, but today she was wearing jeans and Vans. Her boyish figure served as a reminder that she was just a little kid.

I smiled at her as she began going point-by-point over the topics we needed to cover since she was taking the same exam. As she spoke, I found myself drifting, not because of boredom, but because this chick was interesting, and, if I, as a young, masculine, hormone-driven male could use the word, *adorable.*

"Okay, Miss Robbie," I interjected when she took a breath. "Let's start over again. I'm a little distracted today, and I don't think I got everything."

"Okay, Rogie." She smiled. "I get it. No problem."

Rogie. How had she come up with that?

I smiled and paid attention, this time focusing on the subject because I had a date with Colleen later. A date that would most likely require the use of the condoms I just bought.

I need to get this test prep out of the way so I can focus on the real stuff. I smiled to myself, thinking of Colleen's sexy body. *Too bad this one is barely out of diapers.*

Chapter 1

Rogan

"ROGAN! IS THAT YOU?"

I turned around at the sound of the familiar voice and was greeted by my sister Janina who threw herself into my arms. I caught her, and we whirled around together, laughing.

I was meeting Dad on what seemed to be a crucial matter, and I didn't know that Janina would be a part of it. Nevertheless, we grinned at each other as we walked toward the building housing Dad's offices. I draped my arm companionably over her shoulders, happy to see her. When we were kids, we were as thick as thieves, and even though our adult lives had seen us take different paths, we were still close.

"What are you doing here?"

"Dad called me," she replied, one arm around my waist. "He was kind of cryptic about why he wanted to meet me," she continued. "He didn't say anything about you being here."

"Ditto," I answered.

Neither of us was worried about whether there was bad news. He would have told us to prepare for heartbreak if necessary. He had done that when our granddad, his father Hamish McDonald, had died in a work accident a few years back.

When he called me, his voice had been enigmatic but flecked with humor. The fact that he hadn't told me that Janina would be arriving at the same time suggested that he'd have a surprise waiting for both of us.

I looked down at my little sister as we strode across the parking lot. Anyone seeing us together should know immediately that we were siblings. She was the shorter one, taking after Mama. Our hair color was virtually identical, a fusion of the colors of our parents' hair. Dad was originally from Scotland and had the blinding red hair, sky blue eyes, and masses of freckles expected from that country. Mama was from Spain, and her beautiful dark looks with olive skin, nearly black hair, and eyes the color of clover honey still turned heads.

Janina and I sport a hair color that's a vivid chestnut with luminous red overtones. It's a dark red in the sunlight and can look nearly black in darkness. We both inherited Mama's olive complexion. And that's where our genetic similarities more or less part. Janina's bright blue eyes are definitely Dad's, and she has smooth, freckle-free skin like Mama. I, on the other hand, have freckles in places that most people probably don't. My eyes are similar to Mama's in that they are more honey than brown. The difference is that mine are an unusual bright gold, which sometimes leaves people peering into my face just to take a look. I'm used to it by now, but sometimes it could be disconcerting. My eye color had earned me the nickname "Wolf" when I was at UNLV and was also a play on my stalking style of defense when I played soccer. Or the "real" football, as Dad likes to say. Nowadays, I'm occasionally compared to *The Witcher* character on Netflix because of how I sometimes wear my hair as well as my eye color. People who know me no longer notice, and neither do strangers after a while.

At Dad's insistence, I had flown in from Florida for this meeting. I knew it had to be important because he wouldn't have called both of us in just to have a cup of tea. I opened one of the front glass doors and allowed Janina to enter before me. After nodding to the security guy, we walked to the elevators to go to the third floor. The entire floor belonged to Dad's company. Fact is, he owned the whole complex and leased the business office and storefront spaces on the lower levels, but he took the entire top floor in the main building of the complex.

Unlike other major cities, Vegas doesn't have a lot of skyscrapers. Most of the tall buildings are either casinos, some government, hospitals, luxury condos, and of course, the Strat. Double-digit business skyscrapers are a rarity, with most business buildings being six stories or less, depending on location. Can't upstage the casinos!

Dad's Vegas headquarters are in North Las Vegas, located on Camino Al Norte near Cheyenne. It's a little trek from where he and Mama live in Summerlin in Vegas, but the price had been right. Dad is, when all is said and done, a true Scot. He's a Scot who is laser-focused on the purse strings. Frugal. Thrifty. Economical. Cheap. In fact, it's only been in the last few years that we learned that we were wealthy. Not just a little rich or "well off," but actually in the affluent category. We learned Dad had many holdings in a lot of profitable areas. That said, our parents raised us like everyday middle-class kids. Janina and I had worked hard for and earned scholarships, jobs, and careers. Absolutely nothing was given to us just for breathing.

We stepped off the elevator and walked through the walnut double doors leading to Dad's business offices. Rita, Dad's receptionist of about a gazillion years, greeted us enthusiastically by name and waved us back to his office.

A quick knock and Dad's voice invited us in.

Angus McDonald is a bear of a man. Yet, even in his mid-fifties, he commands respect with all who interact with him. He's taller than me by just a hair, and although he now wore some of the stoutness often seen in men his age, he still cut a striking figure. His bright red hair is now muted with strands of silver, but his sparkling, intelligent eyes haven't lost an iota of his omnipresent energy. He'd decided a little while ago to grow his beard long, and except for the fact that he keeps it neatly trimmed, it gives him a Viking-esque appearance.

After giving both of us a generous hug, he looked at us approvingly and grinned as we sat down in the comfortable leather seats in front of his desk.

"Me bairns."

Janina and I looked at each other, rolled our eyes, and laughed. Dad's Scottish accent had muted over the years, and he rarely used the vernacular. However, he would occasionally dip into his history and resurrect the brogue, which he'd bounce between the odd Americanisms.

"I'm glad ye could come," Dad started, smiling. "I have a surprise for each of ye, but I need some information first."

He turned to me. "What are ye plans for the future, son?"

Coincidentally, this was something I'd been thinking about a lot lately. Dad and I co-owned interests in several thriving restaurants in South Beach. I was ready to leave and focus on starting my own restaurant in Vegas. Because I'm a classically trained chef with a boatload of experience behind me, I wanted to work in my own kitchen with Mama. Mama grew up in her family's restaurant kitchens in Catalan and Spain and was a prominent chef in her own right. As a young girl, she'd learned French technique from the best, ultimately completing her formal culinary education at Le Cordon Bleu in Paris.

While in Paris, she met a gregarious young Scotsman who was traveling to different countries to learn the restaurant and hospitality business. He swept her off her feet with his admittedly irresistible charm, and the rest, as they say, is history. Some thirty-odd years later, the offspring of that fateful meeting were sitting in front of their father, talking dreams.

"I want to shed all of my interests in Florida, move back to Vegas, and open my own restaurant here," I replied. "I want a restaurant that will appeal to people who like high-end but who don't necessarily want to pay high-end prices. I want to compete with the Strip restaurants but have a more relaxed environment."

"With ye Mam?" He already knew that I wanted Mama as my Head Chef.

"Yes," I nodded. "I hope that Mama can work with me for a while before she decides to retire, which I don't think she ever will."

Dad chuckled and turned to Janina.

"What about ye, lass?"

"I want to keep learning the hospitality business," Janina replied with a shrug. "I want to experience everything about how a hotel works, how a casino works, and the management part of restaurants."

He nodded in approval. "I have something to show the both of ye," Dad said. "Watch."

Room-darkening shades hissed down to cover the windows, and a video intro appeared on the large display monitor.

"I want to show you what we have and what I can do to help you with your dreams." He reverted to American English, *sans* brogue.

A video began with soft, elevator-style music and a man's soothing, well-modulated voice speaking about the life of Angus Iain Malcolm McDonald, founder and CEO of AIMM International Enterprises, Inc., one of the largest hospitality corporations in the world.

Dad had custom-ordered this video only for Janina and me. It had information that would never be shared with shareholders or other outsiders. The video was, in a word, a tour of Dad's life. A tour of all of the businesses that Dad had invested in or was running. It included interests in hotels and casinos not only in Vegas but included Dubai, Shanghai, Macao, and South

Africa, among others. There were also shares in Mississippi riverboats, ski resorts, and vacation homes. He had interests in or outright ownership of restaurants and chains in major resort corridors. He was a silent partner in the newest NHL hockey team, the Houston Badlands. He was the primary owner of a major liquor distribution company that provided alcohol to businesses required to use distributors for their beverage essentials.

With all of those interests, along with his involvement in real estate development projects, Angus McDonald controlled or had partial control of a conglomerate worth $50 billion. With a B. His personal net worth was $8.5 billion.

I let out a long, low whistle when the video ended. Wow. Janina and I were gobsmacked, as Dad would say. This video showed us that Dad, and by extension, we, including Mama, were rich. Filthily so.

Don't get me wrong. We'd grown up with a lot of the "better things" in life. We had a lovely home located in the same gated tract community as our school friends. They were upper-middle class, but by no means super wealthy. Our cars were regular cars. My first car, which I had to earn myself, had been a used and somewhat recalcitrant Ford F-150, for instance. Nothing spectacular. We didn't have Hollywood-type celebrities over at the house, ever, that I can recall. And Janina and I were expected to do our household chores just like everyone else. Despite their busy schedules, we never had a nanny, butler, or maid. A cleaning service came in twice a month to take care of the details that we missed, and that was about it.

Okay. I admit that the closest things to celebrities we had in our house were foodies, chefs, regular cooks, and the occasional bartender, wine steward, or sommelier. Mama loved to share recipes, cooking methods, and stories with her "cheffy" friends and the workers on the Strip who'd stop by to both share and receive cooking tips. If Dad wasn't on the road, he was in the kitchen with Mama and the crew. I had my own apron and chef's hat in kindergarten, and I learned how to work in the kitchen from my personal step stool. Dad would don his chef's apron and serve as Mama's sous. Toddler Janina would sit at the counter in her highchair, her chubby fingers grabbing bits of food whenever she could.

Essentially, we grew up "normal" just like our friends, without the trappings and pretense of extreme wealth. The only thing that was out of the ordinary was a very discreet security presence at all times. Dad always kept a low public profile despite his gregarious nature. He did little to attract attention to himself or his family. Our modest lifestyle was not unlike Warren Buffet's, and we were better for it.

Dad's a man of standards, frugality, ethics, and character, and had no problems dumping anything that would tarnish his name. He and Mama had been together for over 30 years, and if he'd had any affairs, which I doubted, they were discreet. He was totally in love with her and always showed her, and us, how much he loved his wife.

That said, I didn't see what this discovery had to do with Janina and me. We'd both completed our education, and after my professional soccer career came to a crashing (literally) end, I'd paid my own tuition in culinary school. I also worked with Dad to invest my money in Florida restaurants and real estate projects. Janina worked in the hotels division of Dad's company and proved to be a savvy businesswoman. We were just like the kids of any successful businessman as we learned the ropes.

We'd received little help from Dad and were both pretty much self-made, self-sufficient adults. With the business guidance from Dad, I had a personal worth in the seven figures, and yet I still lived a pretty frugal life. The apple doesn't fall too far, I guess.

We weren't the spoiled offspring that you'd usually see from wealthy parents. Even with all those zeroes that I never had access to, I felt no resentment toward my parents. I was happy and lived a comfortable, if busy, life. I gave thanks every day that my folks didn't raise my sister and me to be spoiled, entitled, self-centered douches. Those I'd met didn't know their assholes from a hole in the wall, and I never liked a single one of them.

"The most important thing to me and yer Mam," Dad continued, "was to make sure that you were decent people. That's why you were raised as close to normal as we could get. I saw too many wealthy parents whose offspring were the Devil's own spawn because they thought the world owed them something just for breathing. I didn't want that for me own kids."

Dad rose from his chair and walked over to his bar. He poured two fingers of Laphroaig Lore Single Malt into some glasses and handed one to Janina and one to me. I inhaled the fragrance from my glass. Smoke. Citrus. Ocean. Peat. Delicious. I took a sip and settled comfortably into the cushy leather chair.

"I have a surprise for both of ye," Dad smiled, blue eyes twinkling, "When you turn 30, you'll each receive two hundred and fifty million dollars."

Janina and I both gasped, stunned at that inconceivable amount of money.

"It's a combination of cash, real estate holdings, bonds, and investments. In other words, it's making money even now. But, before that," Dad continued with an irrepressible grin, "I'm giving you each twenty-five million dollars. Today."

My breath stopped. My brain shut down. What?

"You both have shown me that you are responsible adults," Dad continued, now serious. "And I want to reward you for that. But don't disappoint me. If you do," he said, "I will reduce the amount you're getting at thirty. Please continue to show me how responsible you are."

"Why are you doing this, Dad?" Janina inquired gently, her worried eyes meeting mine. "Is there something that we need to be concerned about?"

Dad laughed heartily. "No, lass, not at all! Just the opposite, in fact."

He looked at both of us, smiling his sunny Scottish smile. "I'm doing this because I *can*. And it will hardly make a dent in me and yer Mam's money. The only thing we ask is that you not be stupid with how you use it.

"Rogan," he continued, turning toward me, "You want to have your own restaurant in Vegas. We'll discuss divesting your interests in Florida. That's not a problem. I know that you want to narrow your focus here, and you have excellent reasons for doing so. If you don't have a reliable accountant, I'll introduce you to my financial firm. I trust them completely."

He turned to Janina. "When I'm old and ready to retire, I want you to have earned the CEO position on your own. If you're successful," he chuckled, "you'll be richer than your brother by a lot."

Janina sent an amused glance my way. I didn't care if she'd be richer. She would have earned every bit of it. My path was a different one.

"And that's all," Dad said. "I just wanted ye to know what I had planned for ye two," he continued, slipping back into his Scottish brogue.

"The only thing ye Mam and me ask is that ye have some wee bairns for us to love. Don't wait until our laps are too old to bounce them on our knee!" Once again, Janina and I looked at each other and rolled our eyes.

A few hours of eye-bleeding paperwork later, Janina and I were still laughing in disbelief as we exited the building. She looked up at me, eyes sparkling.

"So how does it feel to suddenly be a multi-millionaire?" she asked.

"Same as before," I replied. "But I do appreciate the freedom. I'll be able to pour as much money as I need into my restaurant and then either make a profit or have a write-off. I prefer profit. Especially if I want to expand in the future."

We hugged each other before we went our separate ways, Janina to her Lexus LX, and I to my rental Chevy. Dad had given us a lot to chew on. Now that I had the go-ahead from him, I could begin to unwind everything connected to Florida and establish myself in my hometown. Once I bought a condo or whatever in Vegas, I could start looking for a spot to build my dream.

Chapter 2

Rogan

Six months later

I rolled over and dropped my feet over the side of the bed. I stood up and stretched before making my way to the bathroom. Nature called. Loudly.

It was early Monday morning, and today, the ownership of *Chez Dionysius* would officially and legally transfer to me. After months of real estate agents, business plans, permits, inspections, licenses, contracts, *ad nauseam*, the nightmare ordeal known as purchasing a restaurant business in Las Vegas would be over. And the real work would begin.

I did not care. I was happy everything had fallen into place. Truthfully, the process had gone so smoothly that it almost felt predestined. Weird.

Dad and I worked together to free me of my interests in Florida since I had no plans to return for business purposes. Any visits to the Sunshine State would be for vacation and fun only. My interests had either been transferred to Dad or sold outright, which padded my pockets quite nicely. It freed me to pursue my business ventures in Las Vegas.

I'd sold my South Beach condo for an obscene amount of money and returned to Vegas, ready to begin my actual grownup life. All I needed to do was to find a good, off-Strip restaurant location and go from there.

I planned to be fully self-funded, and thanks to Dad and my own hard work, I had the resources to do so. Although I could have done it even before Dad's overwhelming gift. I opted to use my own money and avoid any pain-in-the-ass investors so I could be independent and responsible for my own vision. I didn't want to answer to anyone, and good or bad, my decisions were my own.

I purchased my new condo from a man who was, ironically, moving to Florida, and it was fully furnished. Because it'd been on the market for a while, I was able to get it for less than the listing price. I came in with an all-cash offer which let us close in two weeks. All I had to do was to walk in with my suitcases.

It's a one-story condo with two bedrooms, two bathrooms, a nicely appointed kitchen with, thankfully, a gas range, and a small outdoor patio area. The best part is that it's located in a gated community inside Desert Shores, and its location just blocks from the restaurant is a bonus. On cool days, I could walk there.

"You're up early," Hera what's-her-name, my lay for the weekend, whined from the other side of the bed. This was the fourth time we'd gotten together in about two months, and her welcome had worn thin. She was pleasant enough, but I had a new focus. I didn't have time for someone who was never going to be relationship material anyway.

Hera lived in SoCal, and although she'd no doubt be protesting, she'd be leaving for home in a few. I'd met her at a "giving back" charity function where she'd been there as a plus one with an invited guest. We'd had an immediate attraction, and that night, she was in my bed. She was a pleasant distraction from lotion, my hand, and a warm shower.

"Why do you have to get up now? I think we could have a quickie."

I sighed. No. I wasn't feeling it and she needed to go.

After I'd finally gotten her to leave for California–sans sex–I headed to the restaurant an hour later.

Justin Crews of Crews & Crew Construction, the general contractor for my project, and Paul Garganelli, my project manager, were waiting for me in front of the restaurant. While we shook hands and greeted each other, an Outback drove up and parked close by. Two people, Claire and Augustin Delavigne, stepped out, faces shining.

They were the third owners of *Chez Dionysius*, and after a decade of management, had decided to retire. Even though they were French nationals, they opted to stay in their adopted country and move to Utah. They had purchased a cabin located on a few acres in the center of the state, and they would be "living our best lives!" as Augustin declared. Their grown children weren't in the restaurant business, so they decided that selling to a passionate new owner would be the best way to preserve their reputation.

The financial statements had proven that *Chez Dionysius* had been profitable for the entire tenure of the Delavigne's ownership, and I planned to continue that legacy.

Chez Dionysius was a good luck charm, it seemed, to anyone who owned it. A landmark in the sprawling Desert Shores community, *Chez Dionysius* had always been popular, not only to the locals, but also to the random celebrity, sports figure, politician, or tourist who discovered it.

For me, acquiring this restaurant was like winning the lottery or hitting MegaBucks. I'd always loved it, even from the time I was a child visiting with my parents. And now I was the new owner and ready to begin the renovation.

The five of us walked into the restaurant. The staff was busy preparing for service because until I had all the plans finalized, nothing would change. The staff, the menu, and the hours would remain the same, and the Delavignes were grateful for that.

Augustin called the team together in the main restaurant space near the small bar to introduce me as the new owner. I saw the worry in their eyes and several people exchanged concerned glances. Naturally, they were worried about their jobs.

Time to put them at ease.

"The first thing you're going to be concerned about," I began immediately after the introduction, "is whether or not you'll have jobs. The answer is yes.

"The Delavignes and I have talked at length about the quality of the staff here, and I see no reason to change. We will be shutting down for renovations in a few weeks, but you will all be on full pay. We'll be conducting training before reopening. I'm in a position to ensure that nobody has to worry about their income."

The staff, while relieved, still looked at me with a combination of reassurance and skepticism.

"Give me a break!" I quipped. "I had to sign a contract, for fuck's sake!"

Relieved laughter.

"This is how it's going to work," I continued, "I'll be working side by side with you until the pain-in-the-ass red tape paperwork is completed. I won't be in the front of the house, primarily because, as the chef and owner, I want to see how things work in the kitchen and how everyone works together.

"When we finally must close for the buildout, you'll be on full salary even through training for the new concept."

I stopped and looked at everyone, now very serious.

"Naturally, there are some caveats. I require everyone to have a good work ethic and be loyal to and believe in the new brand. I have a strong work ethic myself, and I expect as much from you. When the new concept opens, you will be among the best-paid restaurant workers in Las Vegas. So of course, I'll work you like a rented mule.

"Some of you may or may not know that I'm a semi-regular on the Food Channel and that I won Top Chef a few seasons back. So my focus on the new concept, whether we're nominated or not, is at the level of James Beard awards and Michelin stars. My expectations are pretty high.

"If at any time you find any of this intolerable, you're welcome to seek other employment opportunities.

"The Delavignes have told me you're the best. And from what I can see from their success, online reviews, and my observations, they aren't lying. I'm hoping you'll stay on board even through the construction."

I stopped to take a breath and to observe the reactions, which ranged from happy to concerned. I didn't see displays of anger. Good.

"All that being said, I'm hoping you'll stay along for the ride. Nice to meet you all."

The staff applauded as I bowed my head. Whispered, excited titters rolled through the group. Also good. They were enthusiastic. And that's all I needed before I won their trust and they won mine.

Chapter 3

Rogan

A WHOOSH OF AIR hit my face when I pushed through the double glass doors and sauntered into the art gallery at Tivoli Square. My best friend, Derrick, had told me about this little gem located in Summerlin, not too far from my childhood home and miles from the Strip. I was searching for works by the artist who'd done the stylized desert watercolor he'd purchased here and was now hanging in his living room. I wanted the artist to do a mural in *Chez Dionysius* now that the renovations had started. The restaurant was an extensive buildout, and it would be a few months before the project's completion.

The gallery represented several artists in its standard exhibits. Each framed painting or drawing was hung on the neutral pale gray walls, with ceiling-mounted track lights painstakingly positioned to illuminate them. Statuary was placed on stands, some with protective plexiglass surrounds. Many of the artists' works were realistic or semi-realistic displays of America's deserts. Others were portraits or body studies. While the primary gallery theme was centered around realistic paintings, abstracts and other styles were on display.

This month, however, the gallery featured an exhibition for Derrick's artist. A section was partitioned to display those works only. I looked at one painting and drawing after the other and knew that this was precisely what I needed. I don't know a lot about art, but I know what I like.

Like the art in Derrick's condo, these works had one thing in common: they were stunning. All of the art, whether larger watercolor pieces or the smaller, mixed-media compositions, were, in a word, spectacular. The completed paintings and the less-complex studies had all been finished with rarely seen skill and attention to detail. Yup. This is what I wanted for my new venture. Hell, maybe even for the inside of my own place.

I focused on a particular piece that looked as wide as I am tall. It was a gauzy interpretation of Red Rock Canyon, apparently a winter view. I had seen this vista in real-time when driving out to Red Rock Canyon, and this artist had perfectly captured the essence of the scene.

Derrick's artist was incredibly versatile, having done a half dozen wine watercolors that caught my eye. Each one displayed a woman's hand holding a glass of varying types of wine with alternating backgrounds. The style was just short of being photorealistic, and every one was just as painstaking as the one before.

Yes. I needed this skill and style in my restaurant decor.

"These are really pretty," Hera opined as I studied the art.

Yes, I know, I thought in answer. The gallery visit was for my restaurant, and I hadn't intended for her to tag along with me. Hell, I hadn't invited her to visit me this weekend at all. She just showed up at my door early this morning, unannounced, uninvited, and unwelcome. I needed to focus, and she was an annoying intrusion on my concentration as she wavered between boredom and inane comments. I had work responsibilities today and didn't have time for her nonsense. I should have sent her away when she arrived.

What I'd intended as a one-, maybe two-night stand had somehow turned into a few nights' stand that stretched over a few months. In fact, during our second time together, she'd gone all porn star on me. Noisy, whipping her hair around, and screaming porn clichés while riding my cock. The only thing I liked about that scenario was the cock riding part; otherwise, it was a surprise and a turnoff. It seemed like fakery. That being said, she had scratched the need-for-pussy itch, and it was time to move on with no strings. Hera's problem was that she didn't seem to understand the "move on" or "no strings" parts.

Don't get me wrong. Hera was pleasant enough, I guess, but not exactly the brightest light if you get my drift. But, to be honest, it wasn't her brains that had initially caught my attention.

The woman was any straight man's wet dream. She had milky white skin that was lightly sun-kissed around her bikini lines.

Her full, collagen-augmented lips could suck the chrome off of a bumper. She had a killer body, even though full of very well-done "work." She had large, surgically enhanced tits, naturally lush hips and thighs, and a Brazilian Butt Lift that complimented those curvy thighs. Top that with big baby blues and long, thick sable hair, she was an undeniably sexy woman.

And that's where the attraction ends.

When it came to conversation, an Einstein she was not. More than once, I found myself rolling my eyes or pinching the bridge of my nose because she seemed to be incapable of following ordinary conversation. Talking to her about cerebral subjects was out of the question. She was as brilliant as a piece of sandpaper and nearly as abrasive. Apologies to the sandpaper.

As I got to know her better, I also realized that she was petty, shallow, whiny, self-centered, entitled, and easily bored if the conversation didn't center on her or contain mostly single-syllable words. She didn't have to use any intellect because, with her looks, she could get any man she set her sights on. Apparently, brains were an unnecessary encumbrance. Despite those lips and her sexual enthusiasm, I was pretty much done. I could go back to lotion and a self-handy in a warm shower for release and not have to deal with her drama.

This time I just nodded and agreed with her. Yes, the art was indeed pretty. And spectacular, and extraordinary, and ethereal. And probably other words Hera wouldn't know. That said, I didn't want to fry my own brain trying to get her to understand anything. It would be a waste of time and patience. She'd be gone permanently after this weekend anyway, so why bother.

I peered closely at one of the paintings to find the artist's signature.

With Love, BTW

Yes! That's the same signature on Derrick's painting. Now I know I'm on the right path.

I walked over to the concierge desk to ask for information about the artist. It was a sheer stroke of luck that the artist, "BTW," was being showcased at the gallery that month, and today was the artist's luncheon reception. Quite a few patrons were examining the featured artist's works.

The receptionist, or whatever you call the person at the concierge desk, a slender, dark-haired older lady, pointed to two women in active conversation. One, a sixty-ish petite woman with graying blond hair, nodded smilingly at the younger, taller black woman whose back was toward us.

"The tall one is the artist," the concierge woman answered amiably. "The other is the gallery director."

I nodded my thanks and began to stride in their direction when Hera caught my arm to steady herself as she walked with me. Although I had told her I'd be doing some heavy-duty walking all day, she hadn't changed out of the bandage dress and platform stilettos she'd worn when she drove here. I was both angry at myself for allowing her to stay and irritated with her for wearing ridiculously inappropriate clothing apparently designed to seduce me. I stopped while she steadied herself and waited until she loosed my arm.

At least she had the sense to look a little embarrassed.

The back of the young black woman revealed a graceful figure. Locs hung down just shy of her waist, and her off-the-shoulder crop top displayed slim shoulders and a willowy waistline. The bohemian-style patchwork skirt she wore draped over her slender hips and hung nearly to her ankles. Her curvy round butt was outlined through the colorful fabric even though the skirt was loose. She wore a slim gold chain around one ankle and her shapely feet were clad in beaded leather sandals. She had just the sort of hippie vibe you'd expect of an artist. "Free spirit" jumped into my mind and made me smile.

The gallery director found my eyes through the groups of patrons as I approached. She was about five-three and wore her blond hair in a severe bun that highlighted the halo of white around her hairline. She had few wrinkles for an older woman, and despite her austere appearance, wore a congenial expression. She nodded toward me as she whispered something to the young woman facing her, and the artist turned to greet us.

Holy hell, what a stunner!

She was about five-seven, model slender, with skin the color of whiskey. Her locs were pulled back to showcase her face, which was animated and friendly. She had a nearly flawless complexion, plush lips, and high cheekbones. A single dimple on her left cheek almost completed the picture.

But what had my breath hitching and knees buckling were her eyes. Impossibly large and framed with full lashes, their exotic slant was almost enough. Ice-and-silver in color, they would have been arresting in a white woman, but they were breathtaking against her dark skin. If eyes are the windows to the soul, hers were plate glass, showing a vibrant intelligence and a warm, welcoming spirit. Her smile, friendly and sparkling white, hurdled straight to my gut. My whole center was rocked. What was it they called it in *The Godfather*? The thunderbolt? Yeah. I get what that means now. My blood was roaring, and my heart was thundering, threatening to leave my chest and jump straight into this woman's hands.

Yet, there was a tug of familiarity to her face, but I couldn't possibly have ever met this beauty. She was someone no sane man would forget. I felt like an idiot as I realized I was just gaping at her. I can't recall if I was drooling.

The shorter woman saved my dignity by sticking out her hand and introducing herself.

"Hi. My name is Doris Haskell. I'm the gallery director."

It was just enough to shake me out of my stupor. I grasped Doris's hand like a drowning man and nodded like an idiot, dragging my eyes away from the artist to greet her. I turned back to the artist and extended my hand to shake hers.

"Hi, I'm..."

"Rogan McDonald." Her voice was husky yet womanly, and flecked with humor. My heart hammered even more as my cock jumped in my jeans at the sound.

I wasn't surprised that she knew who I was. My acquisition and renovation of the iconic *Chez Dionysius* restaurant had my face and name splashed on several local rags. People recognized me. But there was something about the way she said my name that pulled at some real-life connection.

"Do I know you?" I couldn't believe that I hadn't recognized this woman. How would I have forgotten someone like this? She was gorgeous, sexy, and although far less endowed than my usual preference, I was drawn to her.

"Obviously, you don't remember me," she laughed delightedly. "We were in high school together."

Wait. What? As the high school soccer team captain, I had been quite the jock back in the day and had lots of girls throwing themselves at me. How come I don't remember her? Okay. I will admit that the black chicks weren't exactly flocking to make themselves available to me, but I would have remembered this one. She was beautiful. I was speechless.

"I'm Robbie."

Holy fucking shit.

This was Robbie?

I remembered her as a skinny, shapeless, gawky nerd of indecipherable sex, with wild coily hair, a mouthful of braces, and scattered zits. She had always worn baggy, paint-spattered coveralls and oversized t-shirts. Yes, we'd been in school together, but that hardly counts as a thing. We met when I was an 18-year-old senior, a soccer jock. She was a 13-year-old sophomore art prodigy who'd been accepted into the school to take advantage of the advanced art curriculum and support her academic bona fides. She had been advanced several grades from her middle school into the charter high school we both attended.

Along with being a talented artist, Robbie was also brilliant. She was in the gifted program and had saved my shit academically once or twice. She was the textbook definition of an egghead. No wonder I didn't recognize her. Other than seeing Janina cluck over her from time to time, she would not have been on my radar. Young, braces, shapeless, androgynous, brilliant, jailbait. She'd done absolutely nothing for my burgeoning youthful hormones and therefore was put in the dustbin of my memory. Despite that, I was surprised those incredible gray eyes didn't tip me off.

And now, she was a woman who was tall, slender, friendly, and *stunningly* beautiful.

"*You're* Robbie? When the hell did you grow up?" I croaked.

She replied with a peal of musical laughter. "Quite a few years ago," she chuckled, her voice and smile situating themselves firmly in my crotch. "It took a while. I'm the poster child for late bloomers."

No *fucking kidding.*

We grinned at each other before she opened her arms. "Bring it!" she beamed, and I eagerly stepped into her hug.

I wrapped my arms around her as we rocked back and forth, happy to reconnect. Her slim, warm figure molding into my body felt like I'd just come home. Like I belonged here in her arms. I closed my eyes and inhaled her cologne. Warm and exotic. Just like its wearer. Robbie hugged me tightly, her face and breath warming the hollow of my neck where she nuzzled the sensitive skin. My breath hitched. My skin goosepimpled. I swallowed a groan. We pulled back from each other, and I think we both had the same shocked expression. What in the actual hell had just happened? Where had that heat come from? Her smile went from wide and friendly to open-mouthed surprise.

"Wow," she whispered. We stared at each other, thunderstruck. Something in the universe had shifted ever so slightly. Whatever it was, it made me want to lean down and take her mouth with mine.

Thunderbolt indeed.

Doris chuckled.

A throat clearing sound, and I remembered Hera standing at my elbow. Oh yeah. Dammit. I quickly introduced her to Doris and Robbie as my "friend" Hera. She gave them both a weak plastic smile and what looked like a cold, limp handshake. Her expression was like someone who'd like to use a little sanitizer after touching the unwashed. I scowled my irritation at her.

"So what brings you here, Rogie?"

Rogie. I smiled at the sound of the old nickname.

"I'm here to commission you for some work," I replied, including her and Doris in my glance.

Robbie lit up and gave me a dimple-infused grin. The braces had done their work well. Her grin was even, white, and mesmerizing.

"Really. What kind of work?"

"I'm renovating *Chez Dionysius* and need a mural done."

"Oh! I'd heard the owners were retiring. You're the one who bought it?"

Ouch. So much for my cockiness in thinking she'd recognized me because I was oh so very famous as a prodigal son. Obviously, she either hadn't been paying attention or hadn't cared. That was a nicely placed kick in the crotch of my ego.

"I am."

"That's fabulous!" she exclaimed with a smile. "I don't do murals."

What do you mean you don't do murals? It's work and good money!

Instead, I replied, "It pays well."

"Don't care. I don't do murals. They take forever because I'm overly anal, and the people who commission them almost always turn out to be temperamental divas and or pain-in-the-ass pricks. I'm not interested in that kind of grief. I'm good."

I looked at her, frowning. I had a feeling that I'd just been insulted but couldn't quite put my finger on exactly how. Her eyes were sparkling with suppressed humor even though she was seemingly serious. I scowled at her, and she burst out in another peal of delighted laughter.

"You heard her, honey. She doesn't do murals," Hera breezily offered.

What the fuck?

I whipped around to her, and if my irritation wasn't evident before, it was on full display now.

"This has nothing to do with you," I snapped, my voice low. "This is my business and my concern. And for crissakes, don't call me honey. Where the hell did that come from?"

Hera reddened, crossed her arms sulkily, and pouted. I glared at her for a long moment and turned back in time to see Robbie and Doris exchanging a quick glance. Ugh. Embarrassing.

"I'm sorry," I said, addressing them both. "I'm pretty keen on getting a mural in the place, and I really want Robbie's work. I haven't seen anything else that affected me as much." I smiled at Doris and did everything except roll over and offer up my belly for scratching.

Robbie eyed Hera assessingly. Hera was quietly fuming, her head turned away, not meeting Robbie's icy probing eyes. Robbie then swung her glance to me.

"I can take a look at the job," she replied with a shrug. "But I'm not going to promise anything. There are many conditions for me to do a mural, and maybe you can meet them. If not, then it's a no. You need to understand that I have absolutely no problems giving murals a hard pass."

Doris chuckled. "She's a tough cookie. She's a professional who knows her worth."

Who knows her worth.

Indeed.

Doris continued, "Meet me at the concierge desk in a couple of minutes. Robbie has an appointment..."

"I do?"

"...That I need to introduce her to, and she'll be occupied for at least the next fifteen minutes, half-hour or so. Maybe longer."

I shrugged. I didn't want to leave Robbie's presence, but there wasn't much I could do with her appointment waiting and Hera still around.

"You embarrassed me back there," Hera hissed as we walked toward the concierge desk. "Did you have to be so rude?"

"Did you have to be so presumptuous?" I hotly returned. "What gave you the idea that you could give me an opinion on my business? Something you know nothing about?"

"Well, since we've been getting closer..."

"A few random hookups over the course of a couple of months do not a relationship make," I countered angrily, struggling to keep my voice calm and even. "I told you when this started I wasn't looking for a relationship, and nothing has changed. We are not getting closer. I didn't even invite you this weekend, but here the hell you are."

She pouted, blue eyes rimmed with tears. I was being a douche, but since this was out there, I might as well take care of it now.

"Look. I hate to sound like an old cliché, but it's been fun. Other than scratching each other's itches, I didn't look for this to go any further than a random booty call. If I ever gave any other impression, I'm sorry, but I thought I'd been clear from the beginning. I was only seeing you to nut when needed. Period. That was never going to change, and this is not turning into a relationship. Not now. Not ever. Consider this our last weekend. We are done."

Her teary baby blues turned to red-hot fury.

"I hate you!" And then she stormed out of the gallery, stilettos wobbling.

Alrighty then. That probably could have gone better. I felt like a jerk, but I also felt an enormous, Hera-sized weight lifted.

I waited for Doris at the concierge desk while watching Robbie talk spiritedly to two young men in business suits. They were listening to her attentively, all while giving her blatant looks of male appreciation. She was very animated, apparently describing a job or something because she was gesturing in the air and holding her hands to her bosom. She was oblivious to their male focus. One of the young men stood a bit behind her, appreciating her ass, whose sexy rounded imprint was behind the skirt. His lecherous expression made me want to go over and bury my fist in the middle of his face.

I felt oddly possessive at the thought of them having her attention and possibly spending more time with her. I shook my head. Those alien thoughts had no business in my mind.

Doris reappeared, Robbie's business card in hand.

"Here you go. Give her a call, text her, whatever. You guys can set up a time. I'm not her agent, but I don't mind handing out her cards to serious potential clients."

BTW Arts

Simple, not outlandish. Conservative, even. I wasn't surprised. Robbie had never struck me as someone who'd be over the top. There was a PO Box, a cell phone number, and a web address. The card was off-white with charcoal lettering and printed on heavy stock, pleasing to the touch. Tasteful.

"I'll call her this evening," I said to Doris. "I need to have her come to the restaurant to see the space and give me an estimate, which I'll pay for regardless. If I start the begging and whining process early, maybe she'll show me some mercy."

Doris laughed and looked at me with an assessing expression. "She's only done a few murals, by the way," she explained conversationally. "The jobs were very successful, but she hated the experiences enough that she swore them off for life. The fact that she'd even consider talking to you about it says something about her evaluation of you. But don't think that's an automatic okay. Just a warning."

"Good to know," I replied. I was glad Doris had said something because I was already counting the mural as a done deal, despite Robbie's earlier words. "Maybe she'll feel sorry for me as an old friend and take the job anyway."

Doris laughed, her eyes crinkling at the corners. Her laugh made me smile back at her.

"Don't bet on it. She's just being nice," she chuckled. "And pardon me for being so forward," Doris smiled, moving a little closer and lowering her voice, "but I'm betting you're a little enamored with our artist. I know the look. Most men have it when they meet her. What would your girlfriend think?"

The woman had no filter.

"She wasn't... isn't my girlfriend. And 'our artist' is just a friend from high school. There's nothing there." I nodded my head, even though I didn't believe a word of what I had just said. Neither did Doris.

"Okay." Doris gave a surprisingly youthful peal of skeptical laughter. "If you say so." Her grin told me she knew I was lying. To myself.

"It was very nice meeting you, Rogan McDonald," she smiled as she extended her hand. "I have a feeling we'll meet again."

With a wink, Doris returned to the gallery, chuckling. I took one last look at the young men who were talking to Robbie. One had moved very close to her and was definitely appreciating the sexy outline of her ass. The other dude was quite mesmerized by her face as they talked. His look of warm pleasure as he spoke to her had my blood simmering.

Okay.

Boiling.

What in the actual hell.

Chapter 4

Robbie

SEEING ROGAN AFTER SO many years had been a shock. My high school crush, in the flesh, had shown up at my gallery reception. I don't know how I managed to maintain my cool when Doris pointed him out to me.

He was a grown man, and even though I'd thought he was cute in school, he was now wearing adulthood very well. He'd been a jock, and like many jocks, had his share of wannabe girlfriends and groupies. I was way younger than everybody else, clearly a tomboy, and a nerd of biblical proportions. Flat-chested and shapeless, I hadn't, um, *developed* the way the other girls had because I was so much younger. I think he looked at me as the kid who sometimes hung around, occasionally gave him some help with whatever random academic subject, and that's about it. I'm pretty sure he mistook me for a boy once or twice. I was so busy, though, all I could do was admire him from afar while focusing on my art and academics.

And, yeah, I was a little jealous of those girls who caught his attention, but I knew I'd never be one of them. With my appearance and my age, I couldn't even begin to compete. After all, I was black, had just barely turned 13, and they were pretty much adults, technically speaking.

I hadn't seen him since the party after my high school graduation when his sister Janina and I finished our senior year. The party was pretty big since several families had decided to share a ballroom's expenses at The Venetian on the Strip. It was a huge celebration. Rogan had been there with his current college girlfriend. I had only gotten a brief glimpse of him, and I'm pretty sure he missed me altogether.

Janina was 18 when we'd graduated and had looked after me like an older sister in school. Because I was younger than everybody else, she was literally my only friend. Unfortunately, we'd lost contact after graduation when we pursued our separate goals. I knew she'd gone on to finish her Hospitality Management degree like her brother. I'd gone to the Moore College of Art in Philadelphia at the behest of my very old-fashioned Swedish grandfather.

Morfar, my grandfather, or Papa as I called him, apparently wanted to preserve my virginity until I was middle-aged or so and had therefore insisted that I go to Moore. Even after all these decades of political correctness being almost the law of the land, Moore is still an unapologetically all-female college. I'm more than certain that if there'd been a similar college in Nevada or Southern California, he would have insisted I go there, just so that I'd be under the family's protection and avoid the drooling evil of lecherous young men.

Fortunately, I was determined to finish my studies in less than four years, and Moore provided the atmosphere I needed to do so. Moore's environment meant that boys and hard partying were not a distraction. At least not for me. Even the professors were gruff, talented, mostly married, and totally disinterested in being "friends" with students. They were also subject-focused nerds. Just my type.

Since I had a full ride, a wealthy stepfather who supported me, and college credits before I began, I was able to finish my BFA in about three years. Good thing, because as a Southern Nevada girl, I hated the freezing Philly winters and the stifling humid summers. I graduated *Magna Cum Laude* at the age of 18, and after a summer in the UK and a month in Sweden, I was ready to begin my real life.

Papa worried because of what had happened to Mom, and I get it. He wanted to make sure I was more focused than she had been, and I wouldn't end up with a child out of wedlock by a no-good dude. Like *my* sperm donor.

Even now, I was still pretty detached from men as a whole, which was just fine. Truthfully, most of my guy friends were also hippy-dippy artists like me, and, also like me, were more invested in their craft than in relationships. The others were self-centered assholes who weren't worth the energy. That didn't necessarily mean that they were only into sexual conquests. It just meant they were into themselves far more than they could be into any woman.

But seeing Rogan had stirred something. Not only the happiness of seeing an old friend, but also the pleasure of appreciating a truly fine, as in crazy good-looking, man. A lethal combo indeed.

He was taller than I remembered, probably about six three or so. I'd pretty much finished growing at the age of 14, and I guess he continued. Instead of the softer roundness of youth, he now sported the rugged, muscular planes of a man. His eyebrows were thick slashes of chestnut above long-lashed eyes. His skin wasn't the usual pale ruddiness you'd typically see on redheads, but olive in tone, probably due to his mother's Spanish origins.

Along with her skin color, he'd also inherited her golden topaz-colored eyes that gave him the fierce look of a wolf. His hair was the same luxurious chestnut red color I remembered, except now he wore it long, tumbling in lustrous, touchable waves over his shoulders. His build was athletic without being bulky, and if what I could see from his forearms was any indication, he had musculature to spare.

What made me remember him more than even his hair and his golden eyes were his freckles. Apparently, he'd inherited them from his father, a big, strapping, red-haired, bombastic Scot. The freckles gave his masculine face a gentle appeal. Rogan now wore a super short, reddish-brown beard which showcased his full lips, square jaw, and covered some of the freckles. The freckles looked adorable anyway. I mean, as "adorable" as a hot, sexy, mouth-watering man could look.

He was casually dressed in Levi's, which fit his thick, toned thighs and rounded, muscular calves perfectly. He wore a long-sleeved plaid Eddie Bauer shirt open at the collar and rolled up to the elbows. Scuffed brown cowboy boots and a somewhat battered Australian-style outback cowboy hat completed the picture. My eyes were delighted to appreciate him.

Even though he'd ignored me in school for the most part, it was apparent that he liked what he saw when Doris pointed him out and I turned to face him. I could almost feel the heat of his gaze on me, and for some reason, I immediately knew who he was. That said, I wasn't the least bit surprised he didn't recognize me.

Since we last saw each other, I'd matured a bit myself. I have smallish breasts, a willowy waistline, and slim hips with a curvy butt and thighs. My hair had been a wild bush of curly coils that I sometimes tamed with an elastic band to keep it manageable. I now wear it in locs, each one perfectly sized at about the diameter of a pencil. I was very particular about the look that I wanted, and twisty, uneven dreads weren't it. My loctitian is an *artiste*.

My braces were removed just before graduation, and I loved the resultant white smile. My teeth looked good behind my full lips. The dimple in my left cheek had somehow become more pronounced with age. And even though I'd never reach the height of my mother and grandparents (thanks, sperm donor), I was tallish at five-seven. Because of morning runs in my vintage Vegas neighborhood and occasional days-long drawing or painting marathons without much eating, my figure remained slim. Probably overly so. But as my friend Daria had told me, "You skinny but got a phat ass." I'll take it.

And then there'd been that hug. I had initiated it, thinking we'd do the quick, back-slapping, hey-old-buddy, long-time-no-see type of hug. But something had happened. The feel of Rogan's body against mine had undone me and almost had me swooning in his arms. *Swooning! Me!* What the hell! I was inwardly trembling when we broke the hug, and my panties were damp. Where had *that* come from?

The woman he was with, his "friend" Hera, must have paid for her plastic surgeon's summer home. Could Rogan have possibly found anyone more fake than she was? Her boobs were obviously store-bought, and from the lack of expression on her face, she'd probably been botoxed within an inch of her life. Her butt was sticking out more than any white girl's I'd ever seen. Her lips looked over-filled with whatever they're filling lips with these days and poked out too far from her mouth. Is that what's called duck lips? She could barely close them. She couldn't possibly think they looked natural. Ew.

Her big tits, big lips, and butt lift made her look like an assembly line silicone fuck doll. Her overly tight bandage dress and stilettos were out of place with Rogan's ruggedly casual outfit, and he appeared embarrassed in her presence. For whatever reason, she glared at me and seemed to be incensed by Rogan's warm, enthusiastic greeting and enveloping hug.

I pretty much detested her on sight. It was obvious we had no love for each other.

Some time after Rogan had left, presumably to find his woman, I finished my conversation with the two art auction representatives. One of them, a nice-looking mixed dude with a café au lait complexion and hazel eyes, asked me out on a date. After I declined and sent the two of them on their way, Doris approached me, eyes twinkling.

"I think you have a smitten fan." I looked at the backs of the two departing reps and told her I'd turned down the offer of a date.

"No, I'm not talking about them. It was obvious that they were boys and drooling over you. I'm talking about your old friend from high school."

"*Rogan*? I don't think so. Besides, he's with that rather, um, *overripe* woman," I quipped. "While he may have had a flash of attraction, when he realized it was me, that faded. He remembers me as a shapeless tomboy, not as an actual female. Besides," I deadpanned, "I think he's with his type. Silicone is apparently a requirement of the job. It seems that he hasn't upgraded his standards since we were kids."

Doris laughed at my assessment and shook her head. "I'm telling you, he's thinking about it. Mark my words. And when he makes his move, I want all the deets."

It was my turn to laugh. "I don't think so, but okay."

She had no filter.

The successful "meet the artist" luncheon reception was finally over. I'd made connections, sold a few pieces at fabulous prices, and had promises of upcoming commissions, Rogan's included. I walked through the Village to fetch my minivan from the underground garage. It was the only vehicle I owned, although I could easily afford something fancy. I wasn't into fancy. I was into function. My newish Odyssey did everything I needed, and that was fine. My 40-year-old Econoline had finally gone to big van heaven last year, and I was forced to upgrade. To another van, of course!

After visiting my favorite art supply store and spending too much money, I arrived home a few hours later. I parked under my porte cochère and let myself into the courtyard. I toed off my sandals and left them by the door.

After graduating from Moore, I'd spent late spring and early summer in the UK learning papermaking and taking a short cooking course at Le Cordon Bleu London. Afterward, I'd gone to Sweden to spend a month with Papa's relatives and had appreciated the fact that they leave their shoes by the door, even in the most ferocious of winters. That, along with the Japanese friends I'd made while at Moore, cemented the shoes-at-the-door habit. It only made sense. I mean, why track dirt through your house, right?

My friend Daria was staying with me for a bit while she looked for a new job and her own place. She'd finally left her good-for-nothing piece of shit cheating asswipe of a boyfriend in LA and moved out to Vegas to begin a new life. Her shoes were gone, so I figured she was out doing stuff.

I dropped my keys and small purse on the table by the front door and made my way through the house to the studio to store my purchases, and then back to my bedroom to freshen up. After taking a quick shower, I changed into cargo shorts and a t-shirt. I was heading out to the studio when my phone rang. I picked it up and frowned at the number. It was unfamiliar, but it was local.

"BTW Arts," I answered, "how may I help you?"

"Hi, Robbie. This is Rogan."

My heart, and this sounds so very corny, skipped a beat at the sound of his deep, rich, friendly voice. He'd really turned into quite a man, hadn't he? I grinned into the phone.

"Hi, Rogie! What a surprise!"

"Doris gave me your card, and I wanted to touch base as soon as I could. I have a schedule I want to keep, but before that, I wanted to talk to you one on one to see if we could possibly come to an agreement."

I nodded into the phone.

"That's how I work, so I'm glad you called. Wanna meet for a working breakfast or lunch?" I asked. "Someplace where if it takes a while to get through the basics, the wait staff won't get pissy."

"How about Beerhaus?"

That was perfect. Beerhaus was outside of the T-Mobile Arena right on the Strip, and if we could be there on a day when the Vegas Golden Knights were out of town for the playoffs, we could talk for hours and not be bothered with crazed pre-game crowds or cranky wait staff. Especially on a Monday. The interior was expansive, and we could sit at a booth, a high-top, or even a picnic table. Probably not the bar. It was, after all, breakfast, more or less.

I said as much and agreed to meet him there on Monday when it opened.

After we clicked off, I held my free hand in the air and watched it tremble. Why was I so nervous? I had meetings like this with clients all the time. I recalled Doris's words about Rogan being an admirer and shook them off. It was a meeting with a client who was asking for more than what I may be willing to give on a professional level. All we needed to do was to see if we could come to some sort of agreement.

Nothing more.

Chapter 5

Rogan

I maneuvered my Tesla S into a slot at the parking garage at The Park MGM and walked to Beerhaus. It was shortly before opening, and I had a folder full of ideas and was ready to beg. I hoped my ideas would impress Robbie and that my begging and whimpering would soften her heart. Or, at the very least, not make her throw a beer in my face and tell me to go fuck myself.

Yesterday had been a train wreck. Hera had awakened about 5:00 a.m. and was nastily hungover. When we'd returned to my condo on Saturday afternoon, she'd attacked my bar and got sloppy drunk after we'd had a disagreement I wasn't bending on. Very unappealing.

I took her to a locals' casino early Sunday where we had breakfast in the café. Because I sure as hell wasn't cooking for her. Once we finished and returned to my place, she tried to finagle her way into staying an extra day. I was adamant. She had to go. For good.

Oddly, it wasn't because I wanted to be free to approach Robbie. Far from it. Okay, maybe a little. It was because I was tired. Tired of Hera's physical and sexual fakery, her nonstop whining, her petulant moods, and her immaturity. I'd gotten to the point where I actually disliked her. I had originally planned to have "the talk" later this week over the phone. Let's just say that showing up the way she did and her little "we're getting closer" scenario at the gallery sealed the dealbreaker for me. I was done.

After she left, I lazed around for the rest of the day, feeling like a slacker because I wasn't getting any work done. I really needed to focus on my ideas to present to Robbie, but the exhausting day and a half of Hera drama had drained me.

I walked into the Beerhaus, happy they'd opened the doors a little early. I found a picnic-style table in a far corner and waited for Robbie. At 11:00 a.m., she appeared. Once again, I was struck by her beauty. She wore her signature baggy t-shirt and paint-spattered jeans, which fit snugly over her slim body. As she turned to talk to the hostess, the jeans perfectly outlined her gorgeous ass and curvy thighs. From where I sat, she appeared to be wearing Merrell hikers. She'd done her locs up into a stylishly messy bun at her crown and had a messenger bag slung over one shoulder. When she spotted me at the table, she waved as she made her way through the aisles. I stood when she approached.

"Sorry I'm late," she puffed as she sat on the opposite bench. "My Lyft driver got caught in traffic."

"You didn't drive?"

"Nope! I refuse to pay for parking. It's cheaper for me to take Lyft from home than it is to pay the gouge for the privilege of using their garage," she said heatedly, her face animated.

Okay then. Obviously a sore point.

"I'm hoping you'll have mercy on me," I began, looking at her with my head tilted, batting my eyelashes. From my vantage point, I could see that she wore no makeup save for a rosy lip gloss. She chuckled.

"Mercy? Why should there be mercy? And you can stop the batting your eyes mess. That won't work."

I sat back and smiled. "Because I really want you to do a mural in the restaurant. I knew I wanted something you'd done because a friend of mine has one of your watercolors in his condo. I saw it and it blew me away. I fell in insta-love and came prepared to grovel."

A waitress came over to take our order. I ordered a Big Dogs Lager and Brat, and Robbie ordered a sweet tea along with the specialty Cobb Salad. The waitress took the menus and went to fill our orders.

"So what's BTW?" I inquired conversationally.

Robbie smiled. "Those are more or less my initials."

"But how?" I asked, puzzled. "Your first name is Roberta."

"It is. But while attending Moore, a few people started calling me 'Bob,' which I thought was cute. I guess it kinda fit into my tomboy vibe and all. So I took the B for Bob, and my middle name, which is Thornquist, after my maternal grandfather."

"So what's the W? Did you get married?"

Please say no.

"No. Not even close," she laughed. "Wilkes is my father's last name. After persuading my sperm donor to give up his parental rights, he adopted me, so I legally became Wilkes. The adoption process wasn't finalized until my junior year in high school."

The impact of the surge of relief I felt surprised me. I'm not sure how I would have reacted if she was married. It shouldn't have mattered. She was Roberta Thornquist at school, and I had wondered about the unusual last name for someone with such a dark complexion. I figured it was Swedish, and, let's face it, she didn't exactly look like a typical Swede. But because I had been thinking about other more, um, *developed* girls, I didn't care enough to probe.

"I used the initials BTW to honor my time at Moore, my grandfather, and my adoptive father."

Just then, our waitress came back with our drinks and promised that the food would arrive soon.

"Thornquist is Swedish, isn't it?"

"Yes. My grandfather, my *Morfar*, is Swedish. My grandmother is Ghanaian, a first-generation American. They met on a modeling shoot in Sweden, and apparently, fireworks ensued. They've been together for some forty-six-ish years, give or take. And that was at a time when such a union was frowned upon.

"You have to meet them," she added. "Grams is so patient and long-suffering, and Papa is always worrying about 'his girls,' Mom and me, and Zion, my little brother. Papa's adorable."

Ah. That explained a lot. I'd met her mother once or twice, and if she'd been the cougar type, I would have happily volunteered. She was beautiful, tall, and slender, with Robbie's silvery eyes in a café au lait complexion and tons of dark curly hair.

"So Mr. Rogan," Robbie began with a smile, "what have you been doing with your life for the last, what is it? Eight, ten years?"

I grinned and shook my head. I didn't know if we had enough time to talk about my cautionary tale of a life for the last decade.

"Well," I began, "because we want to be out of here in less than a year, I'll give you the Reader's Digest version."

She laughed that musical laugh of hers that went straight to my heart.

"After Palo Mesa, I went to UNLV on a full ride, both academic and athletic. Technically, I didn't need it with my father being a real mucky muck, but I had earned it. I learned later that Dad donated the equivalent back to the school, so it all worked out.

"During my senior year, we made it to the Final Four, and apparently, I was outstanding because I was offered an opportunity to try out for the Los Angeles Galaxy pro team. I was lucky because it's one of the hardest teams for a simple American college student to be signed onto. I started training with them before I graduated, and I felt on top of the world. For exactly one year."

"What happened?"

"Car accident." I thought about the day that had ended my soccer career.

"I was riding shotgun in one of the fellas' cars. We stopped at a red light, and when he went ahead at the green, another car blew through his red light and hit the front panel where I was sitting. The good thing is the driver had slammed on his brakes, and my teammate had seen him in his peripheral vision and started to turn away, so it wasn't as bad as it could have been. And he didn't T-Bone the car, which would have been the end of me."

Robbie flinched. "Ow."

"Ow is right," I nodded. "Broke my leg. It wasn't a compound fracture, but I required surgery and a metal plate with a rod and pins. It didn't bother me unless I was in a hurry at the airport and TSA had to wand me or if the weather was wonky. You'd be surprised how metal in your body can either get heated or frozen. The cold was worse. So I avoided most summer tanning and almost all winter sports. I was happy when the docs removed the hardware once the damage had healed.

"At least I got the opportunity to participate in the World Cup, even if we got our asses handed to us."

Robbie laughed as the waitress arrived with our meals, fussed around a bit, winked at me, and then left us to eat.

"All of my bills were taken care of, and I received a generous settlement. The other driver was wealthy and had gotten distracted by his cell phone. He'd run the red light, and fortunately for us, there were intersection cameras that got the whole thing on video. He had no defense. And since LA is the litigation capital of the world...well, you can guess the rest.

"Mama," I continued after taking a sip of my beer, "had always hated the idea of me going pro. She was not happy I chose soccer instead of acting on my degree and years of kitchen experience. Still, I had figured I could do that later after I retired from soccer.

Everything worked out for me when I decided to attend the Culinary Institute of America in Napa. I began after I'd recovered enough from the accident. The CIA was a maturing experience."

I stopped long enough to take a big bite of my Brat sandwich. It was dripping with juices and delicious. Robbie was already chowing down on her salad.

"I've been working alongside Mama since about a year after I finished my studies there. They had externships available, which I took advantage of, but ultimately I felt that working in my family's restaurant businesses was where I needed to be," I continued. "I've been her sous chef on and off for the last few years, and I've co-owned restaurants with my father in Florida. The Food Channel and Bravo 'discovered' me, and everything took off from there. I won Top Chef, which put me on the map. I've been a guest judge on several cooking competition shows. I finally decided to open an off-Strip restaurant in my hometown because the casinos' greed was getting to me, even though I was living in Florida.

"About seven months ago, I divested my interests in Florida and moved home permanently to start this restaurant. I feel people should be able to have a fine dining experience that includes good wine without sacrificing the house payment."

I realized I was getting a little heated, but Robbie's gaze was full of warm admiration as she nodded in agreement.

"I get it. That's why I took Lyft here. I don't want to give those bastards any more than I have to, especially since parking for locals isn't even free. So fuck 'em."

I held up my right hand, and we high-fived over the table and burst into laughter.

"We are definitely on the same team," I grinned. Robbie smiled back at me, and I almost stopped breathing. Her silvery eyes were twinkling with humor and affection.

"Speaking of teams, my father is now a sports team owner," I continued after mentally shaking my head and taking another bite of my sandwich. "He is a silent co-owner of the new Houston Badlands NHL team, and they hope to make a splash in the coming years."

"Good luck to him. And I sincerely mean that. Ice hockey is growing like nobody's business, and now that it's far more diverse, it's more fun." She winked at me impishly. "Plus, those skaters are super hawt!"

I grinned back at her, ignoring the blooming jealousy. "That said, the other teams are pieces of shit compared to our Knights," she declared. We laughed and high-fived again.

Damn. I've got to stop this. I didn't come here to have fun. I have business to take care of.

She looked at her watch and seemed to have the same thought.

"I have an appointment at three, and it's almost noon. We have a lot of work to do," she nodded as she flipped open a notepad she'd fetched from her messenger bag. "We're only going to talk about what you want. I will need to see the wall you want to have painted and get an idea of your design preferences and plans. We won't be discussing money yet. But you need to know it'll start at least in the five figures. Anything after that is up to you. Change orders aren't free."

She smiled at me mischievously. "That is if I say I'll do it."

I was okay with that. This would allow time me to get to know her. I hoped I wouldn't always turn into a blathering, drooling idiot in her presence. The money it'll cost me is just an aside because I can easily afford it. And I'm sure she'll say yes.

I watched the top of her head as she bent over the notepad to take notes. Several stray locs came loose from her messy bun and trailed on the paper. My fingers itched to push them back, but she fussed with them and tucked them away.

"Okay, Mr. Rogan. Tell me whatcha want."

A couple of hours later, she was finishing up her notes, nodding in satisfaction. She flipped through the notepad, making corrections where needed and making sure that she could read her own writing.

"I gotta pee and go," she said. "I don't want to be late. But three sweet teas have wreaked hell on my bladder."

She got up from her seat to find the ladies' room. She'd left her notepad, the messenger bag, and her iPhone on the table. Her phone lit up with a buzz, and somewhat by accident, I saw the face that displayed when it rang.

Zion.

Good. That's her little brother. I realized that I would have been crazy jealous if the face of an adult male had appeared. Yeah. I was struggling.

After a few minutes, Robbie returned to scoop up her belongings. "I have to contact Lyft so that I can make it in time."

"I'll take you," I offered. "No need to spend money on a ride if I can take you there. This was my only appointment for the day, so I'm free."

"Thanks, Rogie!"

"Just let me go relieve myself," I told her, "then we'll walk to the garage." After one beer, I'd sucked down a few sweet teas, too.

"Where do we have to go?" I asked her later when we began walking to The Park.

"East. Not too far from Shenandoah," referring to Wayne Newton's famous home. She patted the messenger bag. "I have draft sketches I need to go over with my clients."

I nodded. If I played my cards right, I'd be able to spend the rest of the day with her. And who knows where that might lead.

AS IT TURNED OUT, not much happened, at least not in the way I'd hoped.

Robbie's customers, the Holmens, were brand new transplants from Florida. They recalled a restaurant Dad and I had owned and managed in South Beach and lamented that the new owners weren't as meticulous as we had been.

George Holmen was a tall, angular man with silvering hair and sparkling blue eyes. His wicked sense of humor kept us laughing.

Marjorie Holmen was shorter and rounder, and completely in love with her husband. They'd been married for some 40-odd years and still acted like newlyweds.

Relationship goals, to be sure.

It took no time at all to approve Robbie's concept of the painting she was going to do for them. They were oohing and aahing over every point that she made as she showed them each unique feature for the custom work. I was impressed with her professionalism and her friendliness. After their final approval, we stayed for a while, which allowed me to get to know some of Robbie's clients. They were fond of her, and by extension, seemed to like me as well.

The rest of our time together consisted of Robbie and me getting to know each other. Again.

We went to Chili's on Rainbow, and both of us ordered—what else?—baby back ribs and a beer! It was a quiet Monday evening, which allowed us to shoot the breeze for a couple of hours. After dinner, we each ordered another beer and dessert.

It was nearly closing time when we left, and Robbie looked tired, her bright gray eyes clouded with fatigue. Surprising myself, I realized I wasn't interested in persuading her into letting me spend the night. Don't get me wrong. I wanted her, but it could wait. Since we'd be collaborating about the project and we'd reconnected on a personal level, I wouldn't be going anywhere. Hopefully, neither would she.

I drove into her circular driveway and helped her out of the passenger side. She smiled tiredly at me and gave me a hug and peck on the cheek. She opened her gate and trudged toward her front door, head drooping. She waved at me when she opened her front door and then disappeared inside.

I was a goner, and I knew it. I had just spent the day with the woman who was my destiny.

Chapter 6

Robbie

I APPROACHED THE ENTRANCE to Rogan's restaurant project, and when I stopped at the construction zone tape, I waved down a worker. He was chewing gum and ran his eyes up and down my body before meeting my eyes. Ew. Some people can be such douches.

"Hi," I greeted him, suppressing a snarl while trying to remain civil. "I have an appointment with Rogan McDonald."

The creep looked me up and down again with an expression of approval and interest and then told me I'd need a hard hat. He disappeared inside behind the barrier tape, and minutes later, Rogan came out with a smile on his face and carried an orange hard hat in his hand. The creep followed him and gave me another "I think you're fuckable" look and a slow wink. I scowled, tried not to roll my eyes, and turned to Rogan. Rogan had a white helmet perched on his head above his low ponytail. He was dressed in a flannel shirt, jeans, and black Timbs.

I had dressed in jeans and a baggy t-shirt, my usual non-sexy, no-nonsense work outfit. I wore women's Timbs, and I'd slung my Sony Alpha around my neck. My satchel of supplies included notepads, pencils, a couple of tape measures, pens, and other items I'd need to estimate dimensions for the mural space. Assuming I'd actually take the job.

"I've been thinking about this a lot," Rogan began cautiously, causing my Spidey senses to tingle. "I think just one mural isn't enough."

He studiously avoided meeting my eyes as he said this.

The hell? This was supposed to be a one-and-done. Period.

"And just exactly what does that mean?" I didn't even try to keep the irritation out of my voice.

"There are three walls that would look great with your art. I tried to keep it to a single location, but your stuff is so fucking awesome that I want it everywhere that I can put it." He shrugged. "I finally googled you. Damn, girl."

His eyes reluctantly drifted in my direction as he quirked a small, hopeful smile.

Damn him all to hell.

I avoided being influenced by flattery, but this was Rogan. My immediate reaction was to send him a fuck you middle finger and walk out, but I didn't. I crossed my arms, glared, and remained silent.

At least he had the good grace to look nervous. I knew I was scowling, but what the hell. I hated doing murals because of the work involved. There had to be special materials, ladders, the scaffold I had to drag out of the garage, drop cloths, non-watercolor paints, and time. Lots and lots of time. Oh. And sometimes spray paints. Forgot about that.

"What do you want?" I demanded, fuming.

"I've figured out two walls," he replied, encouraged by my question and not telling him to go fuck himself. "I have an image in my head for the last one, but I need to work on that. So for now, I just need an estimate on two."

I could tell that he was uncomfortable with my response to his "three murals" change. Damn him! I had already told him I don't do murals, and he goes and multiplies it!

Could this tall, handsome man be worried because of me? Good. Let him.

I've worked very hard with a focus on my future and success in a field where my level of accomplishment is hard to achieve. My social life has been shitty, but now I'm almost a millionaire because of my work ethic, art, and savvy. So yes. Bring it on. I can be picky with the projects I choose to work on. I've worked hard to get to a place where I can decide my own options.

And here I was, at his restaurant, ready to work. Or not.

Options.

He handed me the orange helmet, and scowling, I followed him inside.

I had visited the restaurant several times over the years and loved the ambiance. When I walked inside, however, my jaw dropped. I realized this was new. Very new.

Rogan began the tour, starting with the kitchen. He'd completely gutted the old kitchen, tripling its size. New, updated appliances were on order, and a new air handling system would soon be in place. There would be long tables for staff family meals and chef's table service. Black trimmed white subway tile and brushed stainless would adorn (and protect) the walls. He had visualized making a small video kitchen studio and a few seats for invited guests. They would take part in the filming of the cooking episodes. Think Molto Mario, except in white.

The refrigerated wine areas were being updated and modernized. The open racks of wine available to customers would remain, although in a different configuration. He planned to focus primarily on American wines—Canada, South America, and the USA—to best showcase the magic of American food and wine pairings.

Rogan pointed out that he was extending seating along the manmade lake to have extra room for tables and chairs alongside the popular area.

He pointed out the new expansion areas and where some outside sections would be glass-walled in. The walls would encompass the view of the multimillion dollar homes on the lake's far shore and the waterfowl that called the lake home. He had acquired the small business spaces on either side of the original restaurant, giving him more growth options. I was impressed and couldn't wait to see it when he'd completed the project. Murals or no murals, it was going to be spectacular.

He focused on this restaurant being a viable choice apart from the overpriced Strip options. He had the means to ensure that would happen. This project probably didn't endear him to the corporatists in the high-end Strip resorts, but he didn't care. He and his dad were worth millions—at least as far as I knew—and could stand toe to toe against anyone. I became an instant cheerleader.

We walked back to the lobby and looked at wall number one. It was near the entrance, and Rogan turned to me as I dropped my satchel to the floor and fished out a notepad, tape measure, and pencil.

"I think I want something eye-catching by the cash register," he said, vaguely waving his hand. "I don't know what I want other than it has to have something to do with money."

Okay. I jotted down a few notes after I'd taken some photos. It took a while to do the measurements and take a few more pictures, and then I was ready to move to the next wall.

We sauntered through the lobby and over to the wall near the bar area. The crew had demolished the old bar and built a new U-shaped framework next to a small seating area.

"I want something Art Deco and wine or cocktail related," he said. Okay. That could work. I was thinking of feasible alternatives, but I liked his concept. I scribbled more notes and questions onto my pad. More photos. More measurements.

The featured wall was located over what would be private, high-backed booths. This wall, the focus in a separate VIP dining area, would be the showcase mural location. The booth seating promised an intimate and cozy atmosphere. Romantic. Elegant. Stylish.

"I want diners to enjoy their food and wine. So maybe we could have a beautiful woman. Maybe a couple. Whatever. This is the wall I can't decide what I want. Not really."

"So you're thinking that you want people as the mural here," I stated.

"Maybe. I'm not sure, but it seems to be a good start."

"I'll do what I can with the materials and time I'm willing to expend. And if I have a better idea, I'll use it. Otherwise, if you don't like my ideas, I don't know what to tell you."

I decided now was the time to tell him about me, Roberta Thornquist Wilkes, the artist.

"I'm very good at what I do, Rogie. I've been able to command high prices on just my original art. Because of my talent, I've been creating and selling art since I was eight years old. Remember, it's the prodigy aspect that got me into Palo Mesa. I also have side ventures that allow me to do other things as well, including commissions like this one and some mass-market commercial work under a pen name. I've been designing calendars, greeting cards, book covers, you name it, for years.

"We will come to an agreement regarding your and my needs, or we won't have an agreement at all. If you want realism on a mural, you need to know that it will take extra time. Three murals will take me away from my primary projects for at least a month, possibly more. Despite whatever you want to pay, I'm not sure I can afford it."

Rogan sat back on his haunches. It seemed that I'd taken him by surprise. I was more than sure he had no idea about how successful I was and how I'd gotten to the level where I could afford to turn away work. Even high-paying work.

"So, my dear," I continued, "What do you want to do?"

Chapter 7

Rogan

WHEN I ARRIVED FOR our meeting, I eased my Range Rover into the generously sized curved driveway and parked under the porte cochère behind her Odyssey. I gave a long, low whistle. In the daylight, Robbie's home had a beautifully finished exterior and seemed far more expansive than I had expected. I guess living in one of the vintage neighborhoods of Vegas can get you a lot of house.

As Robbie had instructed, I opened the courtyard gate and walked down the brick pathway toward the front door. The courtyard's cover was wrought iron as was the front gate, and there were strings of Edison lights overhead. The walkway was lined with colorful desert plants, all in large terra-cotta pots. The heavy mahogany wood door opened before I had a chance to press the doorbell, and Robbie stood there, a warm smile on her beautiful face.

She wore a brightly patterned patchwork sundress with spaghetti straps tied at her shoulders and a loose skirt that floated to just below her knees. I'd already figured that she didn't seem to be inclined to wear revealing, sexy clothing. Except for her bare shoulders, this dress confirmed that. Her locs were held back in a simple ponytail. She was barefoot with a thin gold chain circling one ankle.

"*Suivez moi, s'il vous plait,*" she drawled as she closed the door and walked toward the back of the house. I followed her down a long hallway past a spacious living room. We went through a set of French doors that led to the back. A covered patio displayed a view of an enormous backyard with a fenced shimmering pool and a separate pool house. The pool house had a porch with chaise lounges and low tables. We went inside using a side entrance door. As it turned out, she had converted the pool house into a world-class artist's studio.

Inside, everything was painted white, and bright sunlight filtered through two large windows and French doors that lined the walls to the pool area. Plantation shutters covered the windows to shut out the sunlight if needed. There was a small but surprisingly well-appointed kitchen at one end. A single door opened to the bathroom and dressing area. Wooden shelves were stacked with art books, painting supplies, boxes of pastels, palettes of watercolors, and jars of colored pencils. Art cabinets with wide drawers that held her specialty papers lined another. A small desk held Mason jars for water and tin cans of brushes. Robbie had rolls of heavy watercolor paper stacked against the same wall. A photography setup with backdrops, lighting stands, and tripods stood in one corner. Next to it was a computer and printer station.

A large kitchen counter-height table topped with a smooth piece of varnished MDF sat near the middle of the open space. Only three large easels stood in the room, which surprised me. I expected more, but what do I know about art. This surprisingly large pool house looked more like a person's home than a pool party place.

I examined some of the artwork hanging on clotheslines or propped against a wall, and I was stunned. While they were in varying stages of completion, they were magnificent. There was a spectacular desert landscape that looked as if something had transported it directly from the Mojave. There were studies of skies, landscapes, and people. But what really caught my attention were the works of wine. These were similar to what I'd seen in the gallery and apparently were her signature style.

One in particular caught my eye. It was a woman's hand gracefully draped around the stem of a glass of white wine. While it didn't have the detail of the landscape paintings, it was ethereal and almost gauzy. The backdrop was a rendition of a very stylized Strip.

Wow. Spectacular!

"I love the glass of white wine," I said without turning around. "I'm amazed how you can get the glass to look like actual glass, and the white wine looks so realistic."

"Napa Chard," she smiled. "It generally has a more golden tint to it than either a White Burgundy, Pinot Gris, or even a Chard from anywhere else, and the background through the glass reflects it."

"You have a good eye."

Her head bowed in acknowledgment of my compliment. "For what it's worth, my works are in private collections, tasting rooms, and small wine museums. The wine paintings are most of my commissions, although I've expanded successfully into other styles.

"This is one of the many reasons I don't do murals."

She turned me around to face her, expression serious. "My smaller paintings have sold for hundreds, but some of my wine works sell for hundreds of thousands of dollars. It's what I'm really, really good at. It's my passion." She paused in thought.

"You haven't seen my body studies. Those take me upwards of 300 or more hours of work apiece, and I've done less than a dozen of them in over two years. Those aren't my bread and butter, so to speak, but they are treasures."

"Come with me." She nodded to the door we'd just come through.

Intrigued, I followed her out of the studio back into the house. We walked down another hallway into a large room converted from a bedroom into a secondary studio. Like the pool house, the walls were white. Plantation shutters covered the windows to adjust the sun's intensity, and the ceiling had large, dimmable LED lights.

In front of me were two nearly life-sized works. One was a graphite of a nude elderly black man sitting on a large shipping crate facing away from the artist and looking over his shoulder. The background was nighttime dark, and the old man's folds on his back and wrinkles on his face stood out in full display. The play of light on his dark skin against the darker backdrop was, in a word, breathtaking. His face was expressionless with just a hint of humor, almost as if he was thinking, *how the hell did I get here?* It was wistful while still eliciting a smile.

I moved close to it, looking at the details on the skin. There were moles and other skin imperfections drawn in photorealistic detail. It was scarily good.

"Damn, girl," I murmured as I slid a quick glance at her. She smiled.

I moved to the next one, which was painted in detailed watercolors. It was a young man who had a towel wrapped around his middle, caught in mid-stride as he approached the artist. His dark hair was wet as if he just showered, and he wore a sexy, satisfied smile on his face. He looked in the artist's direction with hooded, sparkling blue eyes as if they were lovers and held a secret together.

The hammering jealousy that hit me was both unexpected and irrational. What the hell? This was a *painting* for crissakes! I took a long, steadying breath.

They were the only life-sized works in the room. Except for a couple of Art Deco pieces and the two life-size works of the men, all the other paintings showcased the signature woman's hand holding a glass of wine.

"These are commissioned works, already spoken for," she explained, "and when the purchases are completed, I may be able to count my larger works in six figures. Possibly seven." She nodded toward the art. "The last eighteen, nearly twenty months of my life have been spent on these. In fact, I had this room specially renovated to hold them."

We left the room and returned to her pool house studio. "I'm pretty exhausted," she continued, "and I mean bone-deep. When you hear me say that I can't do something because I'm so busy, it's because of works like those. I already have a reputation, and these will put me over the top. My auction works are just as spectacular and will double the value of these."

I was impressed. *Damn.*

"So what will this mean for my mural?"

"You'd better have a good security system or else someone may steal your wall," she laughed.

"Rogan, I've worked hard to get to this point. But now that I'm here, I want to scale back enough so that I can have an actual life. At least for a while, anyway. This has been my toughest and busiest year, but it's also been my most rewarding, both creatively and financially.

"I must be crazy for doing this, but lucky for you, I like you, and I think a mural is a good idea in your restaurant."

I smiled at her, relieved. I'd had no idea that she was this, well, awesome. That Robbie would make time for my project humbled me. I also felt like a dick for acting like an unreasonable, entitled ass. If other people acted the way I did, it's no wonder she didn't like doing murals.

"Let's go over this stuff so that we can get your show on the road." She picked up her iPad, and we started the mural planning tour while sitting at her small table in the kitchenette.

Two hours later, we had hammered out a tentative timeframe and projected costs. Robbie was right. This was not going to be cheap or quick. She was no desperate, starving artist. As Doris had said, she knew her worth and could easily charge market price. The time it took to do the murals would be pulling her away from the work that made her real money. I wouldn't complain. I tried to haggle, but she wasn't having it. She added that she could charge me double, and I'd pay it.

She was right. I laughed in acknowledgment.

Robbie was uncompromising in her requirements. First, she'd hire a small cadre of talented art majors from UNLV who'd work on two murals under her supervision. She alone would work on the showcase in the VIP dining room. I wanted her to do all of them, but she made me an offer I couldn't refuse. Essentially, it was her way or the highway. She didn't have to do any of this, but everything would be on her terms. Period.

Damn. My respect and admiration for her grew.

Robbie stood up and stretched, and it was then I realized she was not wearing a bra under her sundress. I felt myself stir and met her eyes as I stood up to stretch, too. I smiled at her while internally shaking my head.

Was it possible that she was that oblivious to her appeal? She simply threw me a friendly, engaging grin, and we walked back to the house. My hopeful member was praying for the bedroom. Instead, we went into a large, incredibly outfitted kitchen. My inner Auguste Gusteau thrilled at the sight.

The cabinetry was painted a soft blue-gray. Stainless open shelves framed the large window over the brushed stainless farmhouse-style sink. There were only a couple of upper cabinets, which had bubble glass fronts and held wine glasses. All the cabinets and drawers had satin-finished brass pulls. The work surfaces were concrete-colored quartz, and off-white subway tiles adorned the backsplash.

Along one wall, floor-to-ceiling cabinets held everything from small appliances to spices and dishware. Built into the cabinets was a French door oven whose brushed stainless finish matched the other appliances. A tall wine cooler stood near the fridge, and from my viewpoint, looked as if it held at least 300 bottles of wine.

The working island had a 6-burner BlueStar rangetop outfitted with a French top. Overhead was a massive, restaurant-style venting fan. A couple of feet from the cooktop was a small brass vegetable sink. Along the length of the island, six counter-height bar stools stood side by side facing the back of the cooktop.

The island was topped with Carrara Quartzite, a veritable twin of natural marble. Its gray-blue streaks perfectly matched the cabinetry. I ran one hand over the honed surface and, for the second time that day, gave a long, low whistle.

This could easily be a home studio kitchen, I thought. I visualized a video setup in this perfectly designed room. My condo kitchen, while nice, couldn't even begin to touch it. This one had the general vibe I was creating in *Bistro Veritas*, the new working name for *Chez Dionysius*.

"Okay," I told her, "I have major kitchen envy." She chuckled.

I sat on one of the off-white leather stools and made myself comfortable at the island.

"It's only been a month since it was finished," she said, "because when my life settles down to mere pandemonium, I want to spend more time here."

"Who's the dude in the towel?"

She turned to me, confused. "What?"

"The dude in the towel. The watercolor. His expression looked..." I struggled to find the right word. "...intimate. Is he your boyfriend?" I felt like an idiot because I didn't want to name the emotion I was feeling.

"Why?"

Because I'm a crazed wild jealous son of a bitch. And I don't know why.

Instead, I replied, "He looks like he knows you. I was just wondering."

Liar! You want to know who the competition is!

She looked at me, brow furrowed, lips twitching with a suppressed smile. "He's a model. Actually, all of them are models. I need reference photos for painting, and I prefer to do my own photography. I don't have a photographer working for me in Vegas. I know what I want, and I can see it through the camera lens with my own eyes. When the models are here, I'm able to get just the look I want."

"How long do they stay with you?" Yup. There was that weird feeling again. Had this man spent time with her?

"They don't," she replied. "I request a 'type' from a modeling agency, flip through headshots, body shots, or whatever, hire who I need, and they come to the studio. I photograph them and send them home. Sometimes I need a hand model for my wine glass series, and sometimes I need the whole person. It's all above board, with model releases, references, and all the right legal stuff. And just in case you were wondering, there's no intimacy. Not ever. That's unprofessional."

Am I that transparent? Damn.

"The guy in the towel was here with his girlfriend," she continued. "Apparently, they'd had quite the exciting morning before his afternoon appointment. So I had him shower for effect, and she stood at my shoulder while I clicked away. It was so cool. They had real chemistry, and the results were awesome."

I laughed at her humor and wondered at the flood of relief. I was more and more impressed with her and realized that I needed to examine my feelings. This was getting crazy. I don't do serious relationships, which meant I was having a hard time with the sensations roiling inside of me.

"The landscapes require a little more hands-on, so to speak. Red Rock Canyon and Valley of Fire are both my muses in Nevada." Robbie continued, "I will occasionally head to Utah or Arizona, or even some remote places in the national and state parks. Great Basin. Arches. Cathedral Gorge. Even the Red Rock Canyon in California. Usually when I'm at Dad's Central Coast house and can drive anywhere I want. There's so much great scenery that I could choose just one park and make a bunch of showpieces. The desert is so beautiful that it can take your breath away."

"You go out there alone?" I asked, horrified. She does what?

"Always," she replied. "People disturb my quiet and focus, and they babble too much. I don't need or want any pain-in-the-ass running commentary."

"Aren't you afraid for your safety?"

"Krav Maga, brown belt," Robbie replied. "I have the invitation to test for the first-level black belt, but I haven't had time to follow up. I've been too busy the last few months to focus, blah blah blah. Anyway, I can kick most people's asses, even if they have a weapon. That's how I stay fit and how I stay safe. Plus, having a 9mm Smith & Wesson as my backup doesn't hurt, either. I'm not so foolish as to go to what is essentially the middle of nowhere without protection. I've never had any problems, but why be stupid."

While I was trying to unravel my feelings about what she'd said, she placed a cheese board in front of me. Then, pulling off the plastic wrap, she revealed a fully loaded charcuterie and cheese layout.

"I thought we'd have a little celebration," she grinned. "This was to either celebrate an alliance or to mourn a failure to cement an agreement. Either way, I thought that a snack and wine would be suitable whatever the result."

The black walnut charcuterie board had thin slices of Genoa, Soppressata, and Cotto salamis. In addition, there was a ramekin of Nduja and thin, buttery squares of Jamon Iberico, toast points with lardo, Deglet Noor dates, manchego and pecorino cheeses, and other-worldly green Castelvetrano olives. Slices of homemade paté were fanned around a corner of the board. A generous drizzle of truffle honey, a bowl of blueberries, and a pile of Marcona almonds completed the picture. She placed a shot glass of bamboo picks next to the board. My mouth watered. Damn. She can throw down, too. I looked at her, surprised.

"Six-week Le Cordon Bleu course in London," she answered my unasked question.

Robbie grabbed an extra-large bottle of Pellegrino from the refrigerator and set it on the island in front of me. After tossing me a key to pop open the bottle, she padded over to the wine cooler and examined the tags before choosing a bottle of red. Robbie had it opened in seconds with the skill of a sommelier. Grabbing two Riedels from her overhead cabinet, she brought them to the island, sat on a stool next to me, and poured some fruity Santa Barbara Sangiovese in each glass. We lifted the glasses by the stem and toasted to our new agreement.

"Tell me about the old man."

She laughed. "Henry was a doll! He had decided years ago that he wanted to earn some extra money to supplement his retirement. A photographer friend of his talked him into modeling, which he thought was ridiculous."

She chuckled as she deftly skewered a couple of blueberries on a bamboo pick. "He is as busy as he wants to be and is still trying to figure out why people want to see his old ass, as he puts it. He is kind of a flirt, though. Did you see the look he gave me over his shoulder? He propositioned me after the shoot."

This old guy propositioned Robbie? I laughed, not feeling any jealousy at all. I figured that 70-odd-year-old retirees weren't Robbie's type.

"What do you do after you take the photos?" This was engrossing, and I liked what I was learning about her. I loved the animated expressions she flashed as she described her life and her workflow as an artist. I understood why the two poor saps in the gallery were so enamored. Unfortunately, I wasn't much better.

"I always go to my editing software and decide what I want to use. I increase contrast for my graphites and sometimes soften contrast for the loose watercolors. It all depends. I crop out what I don't want and import what I do."

She popped a few Marcona almonds in her mouth and chewed thoughtfully.

"Anyway, after that's done, I run it off on my large printer and use a pencil to finalize details. For instance, if I don't like the way a Utah arch looks, I may change it a bit. Give nature a helping hand, you might say. After that, it's the drawing and or painting. Sometimes I can't decide."

She tilted her head to one side, looking at me with an eyebrow quirked.

"I could do you."

Hope fluttered as heat rose. "Excuse me?"

"I could do you. You have a wonderful face, and under the right light, I can see the possibility of a play of light and shadow. You have great angles, coloring, and eyes, and it would be fun figuring out your freckles."

She nodded, smiling. "After the restaurant is open, and if you have a couple of hours of free time, you have to come over for a photo session. By that time, this job," she waved a hand toward the pile of paperwork we had worked on, "will be done. Everything else is on the back burner till then."

"Okay," I replied. I was both flattered and hopeful. Yes, I'd like to see Robbie do me. In any way she wanted.

Please!

"What are your future life plans?" I asked, savoring a piece of lardo toast.

Robbie smiled. "That's easy. I want to marry Mr. Right, have a boatload of kids, and run my art business on a smaller scale. Maybe teach part-time at CSN," speaking of the College of Southern Nevada, the community college.

"Maybe teach online. Spoil my husband and kids," she continued.

I was a little startled. With her education and success, I never figured that she had June Cleaver aspirations. You learn something new every day.

"You are or *were* an only child before Zion. Your choice of profession is pretty solitary. I never would have guessed that you'd want a big family," I commented.

"Blame Dad and Papa," she laughed. "What you said is pretty true. I had no interest in serious relationships. Then Dad came into Mom's life, and everything changed. He has a big extended family back in Philly, and they embraced me as one of their own. And when I spent a month with Papa's Swedish family of lunatics, I was sold. I knew I wanted to have that kind of bustle and chaos and love in my life when the time was right. Having a bunch of kids might play havoc on my body, but that's okay. It's a price. With love, it won't matter anyway."

She smiled at me as she asked, "What about you? You're already a famous jet-setting TV celebrity chef. So what's your crystal ball telling you?" She swirled her wine and took a sip, one beautifully arched eyebrow lifting in question.

I sat back in my chair at that question and looked directly at her, pondering.

What do I want in my life? My career was set. I'd been fortunate to have been a success in the restaurant business. While my parents weren't famous outside of that world, my mother was an accomplished chef in whose footsteps I happily followed. My father was a successful businessman in the hospitality and spirits fields. The everyday Joe would have no idea who they were, but they may recognize me if they watched food programs on TV. Or maybe not. But what about my future? What about my actual life?

"Rogan?"

"Sorry," I smiled, shaking my head. "I guess I never really thought about my personal future. I haven't thought about settling down and having a family. The fact that I'm even talking about it, though, would make Mama ecstatic.

"I've been too busy for serious relationships. Even so, I'm a serial monogamist because I prefer to avoid complications that could hurt someone. Mainly me!"

Robbie laughed, her eyes sparkling with humor.

"I guess I never saw myself as a husband and father. You'd think I would, especially since I have great role models. And ditto on the crazy extended family thing. Mama and Dad both have families overseas who'll drive you nuts." I shrugged. "I don't know. I may be using the 'too busy' thing as an excuse."

"The 'too busy for a relationship' thing isn't an excuse," she air-quoted. "At least for me, it's the story of my life! I think I told you that those large works cost me at least 300 hours each, and that's only the actual work time. That doesn't include booking the models, doing the photography, working on the photographic drafts, blah blah blah. Which is why the pool house is really my home when I'm focused. No time for dates or mindless fun. Which I sometimes crave. Mindless fun, in my opinion, is way underrated."

After taking a sip from her glass of Pellegrino, she gave a little shrug. "Art is fickle, and you have to strike while the iron is hot. I'm fortunate enough to have this gift as well as a solid work ethic. The fact that people want my works and are willing to pay top dollar for them is a bonus. I'm forever grateful, and I love what I do. I just don't want to die one of those lonely deaths as a shriveled old childless spinster who never saw anything outside of her palette and her cats."

She looked wistful as she continued, "One day, I want to be in love. I hear it's pretty awesome if it's with the right person. That's a direct quote from Mom and Dad. But until I know I won't drive a man crazy with my quirks and nutty schedule, I'm good."

"What kind of schedule do you have?" I asked, inhaling another lardo toast. Damn, these were good. I made a mental note to put these on my brunch menu.

"Gallery exhibits, speaking to associations, some travel, local art groups, stuff like that. When I get the urge, I'll travel somewhere to photograph some inspiration.

"I don't know of any man who'd tolerate me sleeping in another building or even another state while I'm so focused. I just want to get to where my focus can make sense and not be so obsessive. I need balance, and right now, I don't have it."

"The right man would understand your passion and focus," I ventured, treading carefully. "The right man would love you and your obsession. I think that you're not giving yourself enough credit," I said quietly. "You don't even know who could be waiting for you to notice him."

Robbie looked at me, disconcerted. I could almost hear her brain's gears whirring. Our eyes locked on one another's, and hers were turbulent, as if she'd just realized something she hadn't thought of before.

I decided to give her a hand.

Placing both of our wine glasses on the counter, I reached for her hands and stood in front of her. I kissed each one and then dropped them on her lap. I took her face in one hand and stroked her cheek with my thumb. I leaned over to kiss her beautiful plush lips, which were already parting expectantly.

Holy. Fucking. Shit.

Chapter 8

Robbie

After Rogan left, I put my hand to my mouth and touched my lips. Long after his departure, I still tasted him. I crossed my arms over my breasts, and my now-sensitive nipples hardened with just the memory of his gentle suckling and light caress. I still felt the imprint of his erection against my core. And I was still shaking.

Rogan's lips were so soft. So warm. He touched my lips once, twice, and then used his tongue to enter and caress my mouth. My hands shot to his muscular biceps and held on for dear life. My center began to quiver and wobble. I was trembling, as unsteadily as if I were in a rolling earthquake. I never expected this. I didn't even know he was attracted to me. What in the actual hell.

When he began kissing me, I started to gasp and couldn't quiet my moans and whimpers. What was he doing to me? I felt my core melt with a liquefying heat as his mouth went from my lips to my jaw, my ears, my neck. His mouth feathered soft kisses on my breasts through the fabric of my sundress, which caused me to throw my head back and curve my body toward his. He undid the tie at one shoulder. The dress slipped down on that side, exposing a nipple that immediately pebbled in the open air. Next, his lips were softly sucking on it as he untied the other bow so that he could access both. As his tongue swirled on each nipple, I cried out at the unexpected invasion, the intense pleasure, this surreal experience of Rogan McDonald, my Rogie, loving my body.

The feeling was more intense than anything I'd anticipated. My hands went to Rogan's shoulders as he nibbled and sucked on my nipples, and somehow, my legs were opening around him. My body seemed to have a mind of its own as it writhed against him of its own accord. When his lips returned to mine, I opened to him, my tongue eagerly dueling a dance of fire with his. My arms went around his neck as I lost myself in the fervor of his kisses. My brain was going *no no no*, but my body was saying, *shut up brain! We're into this!*

He moved one hand under the hem of my dress and softly stroked my outer thigh before moving between my legs. My breath stuttered at the intimate caress. Then, when he touched the outside of my panties over my folds, I cried out, and my hips rolled against his hand. How had I gotten so drenched?

"Oh baby," he moaned, "you're soaked. For me." His voice had become even deeper and smokier.

Oh god.

He stroked the outside of my panties and then let a finger slip inside the hem to caress my petals and touch my clitoris. I arched with a cry; the feeling was so intense and intimate. So dreamlike. He took my mouth again, this time a little rougher and deeper as he moved his hand to my butt and pulled me against his erection, gently rotating his hips. That movement was too real for me, and I knew I had to douse this thing before there was no turning back.

"No," I gasped. "I can't. Not like this."

He wrapped his arms around me and let my breathing return to normal. I was shocked. Stunned. Shaking. Rogan took my face in both of his hands and gazed into my eyes. His golden topaz eyes were soft, and I detected no anger or upset.

"I've been wanting to do that ever since I saw you at the gallery," he said, his voice still gruff and smoky. "I had a feeling that we'd ignite."

I couldn't answer. More than anything else, I was embarrassed about my over-the-top response. Where the hell had that come from?

"I'm sorry about all the noise I was making," I apologized. "I felt like my body had a mind of its own."

He wrapped his arms around me again and pulled me close. I could feel rather than hear a chuckle rumble from his chest as he kissed my forehead.

"No need to apologize. You had the type of response that every man wants from his woman. You gave me something that no one else has. I found myself responding to you in a way that I've never reacted to another woman. You blew my mind, babe."

His woman.

I decided to address the elephant in the room.

"Your girlfriend wouldn't be happy that you're here with me. Especially doing this," I offered hesitantly, waving my hand in the air between the two of us. The tension in his body was immediate. Ah. I'd touched a nerve.

"She's not my girlfriend," he stated flatly. "She's someone I hung out with for a couple of months for one reason only."

"Hm," I said. I pulled out of his arms and grabbed my dress's straps, and shakily tied them back over my shoulders, covering my now-aching breasts. I found the hair elastic he'd tossed on the countertop and put my loose ponytail back together. I peered at him from underneath my lashes.

"There seemed to be some unfinished business because there was a sexual relationship involved. Even if it wasn't 'that much.'" I took a deep breath and looked unflinchingly into his eyes. "She's pretty even though I think that she's fake as hell, and she's still present in your life. I'm too busy to get involved with someone who has obligations or distractions." I air-quoted "distractions," but there was no question about what I meant. "I decided a long time ago that I wouldn't be 'the other woman,' 'the side chick,' 'side piece,' 'sometime chick,' 'Plan B,' in a triangle, or whatever the current slang is for the one who isn't 'the one.' I have never been, and I'm not going to start now."

I looked down at his large hands, which were resting on my bare thighs. My dress had bunched up, and he was absent-mindedly massaging my skin. Which wasn't helping my scrambled brain at all.

"I've always liked you, Rogan. More than you know. But not even you can shake me from my focus. I know what I bring to the table, and I'm not going to compromise my values for anyone."

He looked at me steadily, unsurprised, and not in the least irritated or upset. He closed his eyes and tilted his head back. My lips twitched to kiss that beautiful column of a neck and lick around his Adam's apple. Nibble the juncture at his shoulder. Oh god. I want this man.

"I could make love to you right now," he began, his eyes meeting mine. "But I'm not going to approach you until my shit is together. It's about 95% there, but you're right. I have to make sure that she stays away. She's gone now, but I'm finding out the hard way that she seems to be a little deranged. She showed up at my condo when I was on my way to the gallery. Uninvited and unwelcome.

I should've sent her back right away, but I didn't feel like a fight. She lives in Southern California, so it helps that she's not local. If she lived here in town, no doubt there'd be a problem."

He gazed at me again, thoughtful. "Plus," he continued, "I want to make sure that you're one-hundred percent on board and that you trust me. I have no room in my life for deception, and I want you to know that. I think you and me could be in it for the long haul."

I nodded. I didn't say anything at first because I was afraid that however he tried to get rid of his personal fuck doll, he'd still be pulled back into her or we'd be caught up in a lot of drama. I'd seen it happen too many times with some of my girlfriends. They'd get involved with a guy who still had his main squeeze around or on hold, and after the girls gave up the goods, he'd go back to the old girlfriend. Or he'd be screwing both of them. Or even worse, he'd be doing both of them and a couple of others besides. And lying to everybody. Hell, it happened to Mom with *my* sperm donor. And it damn near ruined her life. No thanks. Count me out.

I said as much to Rogan, and his eyes widened. He grunted.

"You forget about my mother," he said. "She'd kill me if I did such a thing. She likes you and she'd have my head. On a platter. With garnish."

I laughed. "Well, I'll have a talk with Mama, then," I quipped. "But until then, no goodies from me."

He let out a hoot of laughter, then stopped to give me a look so tender and warm as he stroked my hair that I almost told him to just take it.

Almost.

Chapter 9

Rogan

I DON'T KNOW WHAT had possessed me to kiss Robbie. We had a fun and profitable afternoon, and I'd hit my stride with her. She no longer hated me for sniveling my way into having her take on a time-consuming special project she didn't particularly want to do. We'd connected on a professional level as we talked about the project and our respective careers. More importantly, we reconnected on a friendship level, which I'm sure is the only reason she decided to do my project in the first place. That being said, I found it drew me to her more and more, and definitely not on *just* a friendship level.

And as she sat there, wineglass in hand and looking at me affectionately with those gorgeous, smiling gray eyes, I couldn't hold back anymore. I'd never been shy around women, and I wouldn't allow nerves to take over now. I wanted her and needed to taste her.

When our lips met, it blew my mind. I knew her plush lips would be soft, but *damn*. I don't know why I hadn't considered if she'd respond to me. She did. In spades. Her whispery moans turned me on like I'd never been turned on before. I kissed her over and over again, encouraging her to surrender her mouth to mine. I lost myself in the sueded texture of her locs when I swept off her hair elastic and buried my face in her hair. When I pulled her head back to deepen our kisses, I reveled in the sound of her intensifying moans as I worked my way down her body. And when I loosened the ties of her dress so my lips and tongue could swirl around her nipples, she cried out in helpless pleasure. Her gasping cries and moans went straight to my granite hard cock. I was ready to spill like a 12-year-old having his first wet dream.

Her body responded to every touch. When my hand reached her panties outside of her core, she arched against it, choking off a gasp of surprise. And she was soaked. My fingers went inside of her drenched panties and touched her folds, and she inhaled sharply as her hips rose to meet them. When I pulled her core against my hard and pulsing erection, I thought she would lose it altogether. I was this close to making her mine. All I could think of was sinking into her and losing myself in her sweet heat. I didn't have any condoms with me, but with Robbie, I was very willing to risk whatever consequences may arise.

But then the worst enemy of all men bent on a sure-thing seduction happened: her sudden return to sanity and common sense.

Dammit.

When she said no, I stopped and held her in a caressing embrace until her breathing slowed down to normal. Hell, until *my* breathing returned to normal.

And then she brought up Hera.

Fuck.

But I understood her concern. Hera was, frankly, a beautiful woman. She looked highly fuckable. That said, her tits were fake, her lips filled, her ass lifted, and Botox ensured she'd never have to deal with wrinkles. The good thing was that she used those lips to suck my cock, and she liked to ride. The bad thing was that she made enough noise in bed to make me think she was auditioning for a porno. When you're fucking somebody, you're not supposed to roll your eyes, but I'm pretty sure I'd done so on more than one occasion. Her overdone moaning and caterwauling could soften the hardest of cocks. Several times I'd been tempted to tell her to just shut up and fuck.

Robbie, on the other hand, was very different. Where Hera's skin was milky white and barely sun-kissed around her bikini line, Robbie was all warm caramel and Bourbon whiskey. Robbie's breasts were scarcely a handful of soft mounds with small, rosy brown nipples that pebbled with just a breath and a kiss. Hera's tits were, well, *excessive*, not soft and yielding. Putting my hands on them was like handling a soccer ball with nipples.

Robbie's lips were soft, plush, responsive. Kissing Hera was different, which is an understatement. They always felt as if she had inner tubes inserted into them. The inner tube feeling was great around my cock, but when kissing, not so much.

I'm not one who makes comparisons, but with her fake screaming and eye-rolling theatrics, Hera had never responded to me in a raw and organic way. On the other hand, Robbie's emotionally passionate response was genuine, and I got aroused every time I thought about her. God only knows what may have happened in her kitchen if the 600-pound Hera gorilla didn't exist.

Robbie was exquisite, and yet I understood why she might think I'd prefer Hera's body to hers. It's because she thinks men are shit and prefer overdone women. I'm sure of it.

Robbie was right about my continuing to see Hera. And, thanks to having absorbed my very focused parents' ethics, I'm not the type to have more than one relationship at a time. That kind of stuff is juvenile, short-sighted, and time-consuming. I'd have to make sure Hera was out of the picture if I wanted to be with Robbie, especially considering her mom's history. I don't have time for immature fuckboy bullshit.

Mama had met Hera once, entirely by accident. Because I sure as hell didn't take her home to meet the folks. We'd stopped at a new restaurant on the Strip where Mama worked as a consultant, and I didn't know she'd be there. Mama disliked—hell, *loathed*-—Hera almost on sight. Mama had been polite to her because that's Mama's way, but I got a blistering earful later. Mostly made up of phrases like, "what the hell are you thinking?" and "she's a *puta*. Or can't you tell?" *Puta*, by the way, is Spanish for whore. I think Hera knew Mama despised her because when we got back to my condo, she deep-throated and fucked me all night, depleting me with almost no rest.

We men can be shit.

Spending the afternoon at Robbie's house changed everything. I had to finish this Hera mess I found myself in and not be half-assed about it. While I had allowed Hera to hang around longer than I should have, it was also a conveniently lazy way to date while I conducted my business. After all, I rationalized, I had "needs" that had to be met. Which, in retrospect, was total bullshit. Being wishy-washy and using someone because it was an easy nut was not a way to treat anyone, not even Hera.

We men are shit.

Yeah, even though Hera and I had fallen out at the gallery exhibit, she'd tried to make up for it when we got back to my condo. She knew I was done with her, but she whined, whimpered, and undulated against me as she dropped to her knees. I really didn't want to do anything with her, but my little head and overactive imagination had different ideas.

She somehow managed to wheedle her way behind the buttons on my Levi's, push down the waistband of my boxer briefs, and take my cock in her mouth. What a mistake that had been. I was stupid and let my little head do all the "thinking." I stood, eyes closed and legs apart as her hands and lips on my cock made it easy to fantasize that Robbie's lush mouth and pillowy lips were licking and sucking it. That it was Robbie's soft hands that were gently caressing my balls, and that it was Robbie's mouth drinking in my length. When I erupted, it wasn't into Hera's mouth that I groaned my release but into imaginary Robbie's.

Yeah. We men are *total* shit.

Afterward, I couldn't get aroused enough to have sex with Hera. To be honest, I didn't even try. I let her stay overnight in my bedroom, but I didn't sleep with her. I wasn't interested in getting her off. She'd snuck into my bar cabinet and killed almost half a bottle of high-priced vodka before I took it away from her. I had planned to send her back to California, but she was too hammered to drive. When she eventually passed out, I tried to watch some old movies on Turner's Classics in the living room. I felt like shit because I'd let her blow me. That was a dick move. So to speak.

I got up from the sofa and poured two fingers of Lagavulin, neat, after watching a couple of movies. I intended to sleep on the sectional, knowing I'd probably pay for it in the morning. Even though I had a second bedroom, it didn't have a lock, and I didn't trust Hera not to get up early and catch me in bed while I was sound asleep. Morning wood has no conscience.

After taking Hera to breakfast in the morning and returning to my condo, we had another big blowout. Letting her blow me the day before sent a different message than what I intended. I apologized for not reciprocating and told her having sex wasn't in the cards anymore. She glared at me before screeching and slapping my face. Then she turned on her heel and flounced away, seething.

Yeah. Well.

That probably could have gone better, I thought as I held my stinging cheek and locked the door.

We'd only spoken a couple of times since then. I flatly shut down her demands to visit me, making it clear that I wouldn't even let her in if she showed up again. It was time to put the period at the end of this Hera sentence once and for all.

My mind went back to when I kissed Robbie at her front door when I was leaving. She responded as she had at the kitchen island, arching her body against mine and moaning with pleasure. After we broke it off, she seemed to be annoyed with herself for so quickly losing control. I was happy that she had, although I was careful not to gloat.

Oh yes. This fiasco with Hera had to end so I could focus on Robbie. And for once, my big head and my little head were in total agreement.

Chapter 10

Rogan

I'M HERE!

I texted Robbie when I got to her front door.

Come on in! I'm in the studio.

I opened the unlocked front door and walked through the house to the French doors leading to the back. I was smiling before I even cracked the studio door and was inundated by noise, music, air conditioning, and people.

Robbie grinned in my direction from her position at the photography corner. There were other people whom I assumed were models. Her attention quickly turned back to one of the men and a woman standing in front of the backdrop. So this is how she worked.

Robbie barked orders, and the models changed positions. Then, after photographing them from several angles, they helped her drag a restaurant-style table to the middle of the scene. They sat at the table, one woman holding a glass of wine and a man holding what looked like an old-fashioned glass of scotch. Neat, of course.

One woman had shorter, bob-cut dark hair that swung at chin length. She had large green eyes, a small straight nose, and thin lips. Another wore her reddish hair in loose waves, circa Katharine Hepburn heyday. She had a square jaw, hazel eyes, and fuller lips, and with her makeup in place, she looked very much like the late actress. Both women were stylishly dressed in vintage form-fitting 40s dresses. The fabrics were silky and dropped to mid-calf. They wore chunky heels, which were popular at the time and still looked good now. The long-haired woman held a cigarette holder in one hand.

The men wore 40s style fedoras, dress shirts, vests, suspenders, and pleated trousers. Two other people similarly clad stood in the background of the photos, moving at Robbie's commands. Big Band music provided ambiance. Bottles of Champagne and still wine sat on Robbie's main art table.

It all looked like fun!

I sat on a stool and tried to be inconspicuous while I watched Robbie work. Her locs were pulled up in a high ponytail, and she wore her usual uniform of jeans and a baggy t-shirt. Her feet were bare, and she had a thin gold chain around one ankle. As usual, she wore no makeup, yet her face was shining as she and the models bantered back and forth.

"The Boogie Woogie Bugle Boy of Company B" by the Andrews Sisters blasted through the speakers. Robbie screamed, "dance break!" and she and all the models began gyrating over the floor. I found myself laughing and applauding their antics as they tried to do 40s style shimmying. I whipped out my iPhone and took a quick video of Robbie, surrounded by the models, immersed in the song, and having the time of her life. When the song was done, I gave them a standing ovation while they high-fived each other, laughing uproariously.

"In the Mood" began immediately after, and I stalked over to Robbie, grabbed her hand, and started swing dancing with her. She was surprised at first and then blasted me with a 1000-watt grin before getting into the, well, *mood* of the song. Our bodies perfectly synchronized as we danced, and at the end of the song, I twirled her around before bowing her backward over my arm. The models had been dancing as well, all the while cheering and hooting for us. It was loud, fun, and I laughed harder than I had in what felt like years. I felt buoyant and happy, and, to coin an old cliché, as light as a feather.

"Okay guys," Robbie finally yelled, "I think this is a wrap!"

"This was fun!" exclaimed the girl with the dark hair. "I don't think I've had this much fun at a shoot in ages! Not at any other job I can remember." All the models were smiling and cosigned her statement.

"Can we help you clean up or anything?" one of the male models asked. He was very blond, his face tinged pink from exertion. His blue eyes sparkled with humor.

"No, no," Robbie replied, "you guys were great. I'll get my friend to help me with the cleanup since it's his project." She grinned in my direction as the others waved and excitedly chattered as they exited the studio.

"Don't you need to escort them out?"

"No. They're all great, and I've worked with them before. They like working for me because I pay more than the usual rate. All they have to do is to lock the front door when they leave."

Robbie turned and looked at me, eyebrows furrowed and head tilted to the side. Her smile faded into an unreadable expression. "Go sit on the stool in front of the backdrop," she ordered.

Okay.

I was wearing a regular dress shirt with sleeves rolled up to my elbows, black Levi's, and black Timbs. My hair was in a low ponytail and sunglasses were perched on my head, holding back any loose strands. I started to remove them when Robbie said, "No. Leave the glasses. Take off the band." I removed the elastic and stowed it in a back pocket.

I sat on the stool, and she walked close to me, frowning in concentration. I watched her, raising one eyebrow. She fluffed out my hair, nodded as if she'd made a decision, and walked back to the tripod where her camera was sitting, portrait lens in place.

"Look over toward the window." I did as she asked, and she snapped off a few shots. She continued to give commands as Big Band music played in the background.

"Take off your shirt," Robbie ordered. "I have an idea."

Okay. I'll gladly take off my shirt or any article of clothing you ask, my dear, but it's not going to help tame my libido any. While I unbuttoned my shirt, Robbie rummaged in one of the small closets and took out sheets.

Sheets? This is getting better.

She spread out one sheet on the platform and rumpled it a bit. "Lay down."

Okay, baby. Whatever you say.

I positioned myself on the rumpled sheet. Robbie looked down at me, brows still furrowed. She fluffed out the other sheet and let it parachute over my body. After it settled, she fussed with it until it lay over my hips, leaving my chest bare. And my swelling cock hidden.

"What a great tattoo!" she exclaimed at the wolf tattoo on my chest. "Don't move."

Robbie went over to the tripod and extended the legs. She grabbed a step stool to stand on and adjusted the tripod arm so the camera faced downward towards me.

As she gave directions, I moved on the sheets, first covering myself, uncovering, pretending to be sleeping, turning on my side, and on and on. Finally, after about twenty minutes, she told me I could get up and put my shirt on.

Dammit!

I shrugged back into my shirt while she gathered the sheets, folded them, and returned them to the closet.

After retrieving the camera from its station on the tripod, she looked at the LCD screen, moving unconsciously to the music while "Chattanooga Choo-Choo" played.

She grinned at me happily. "You're really photogenic!"

I am? I never thought so. Even semi-gingers like me were usually relegated to the dustbin of humanity. Add my freckles, hair that readily turned into a frizzy mess with any humidity, and a physique that was on the slender side of muscular, I never considered myself particularly photogenic. Robbie must have seen the skepticism.

She beckoned me to her computer, inserted the camera's SD card, and launched her photography software. She scrolled through a bunch of photos before she arrived at those she had taken of me. I was, in a word, shocked.

The photo of me looking up toward the lighted window when I was sitting on the stool was striking. That was me? She fiddled with a few settings and turned it into a black-and-white image. The light and shadow played on the sunglasses, my hair, and my eyes. Another one had me looking directly at her when lying on the sheets and elicited a gasp. Another photo looked like I was beckoning her to join me. My emotions were smack dab in the middle of my sleeve and reflected in the way I looked into the camera.

"Wow," she whispered.

I knew I'd plant my foot squarely in my mouth if I said anything, but carried on anyway. "I think those are some of the best pictures anybody's ever taken of me," I derped.

"It's going to be so much fun to do you. This is going to be fabulous!"

I groaned inwardly. Yes, I wanted her to do me. I had to get used to artist-speak because it was playing havoc with my libido.

"Why the photos of me?" I asked her. Robbie turned and smiled at me. My heart thudded.

"I told you I wanted to do you," she replied cheerily, "and since you were here and we had lots of time, I figured I'd get some reference photos now. I may do some preliminary sketches before I even start the mural."

This woman was killing me and didn't even realize it.

"Give me a minute," she said as she started printing, abruptly changing the subject. "I have the beginnings of a terrific idea for the main mural. That's why the kids were here."

Kids. They were close to her age, if not older, but she called them kids. I chuckled.

"Take the A Train" started playing in the background. "Why the Big Band music?"

"To fit the mood," Robbie replied. "It works with the theme of the planned murals. That's why I wanted you over here. It's going to take a lot of imagination on your part, but the idea speaks to me, and I know it'll be perfect."

"If it's going to be perfect, then why do you need me here?"

She shot me an exasperated look. I laughed. It took all my willpower not to sweep her up in my arms and lay a big sloppy one on her.

"Because I don't want it to be a total surprise. And your idea, while cute, wasn't quite complete. Mine is better. Which reminds me. I need to get your color scheme information. Last time I was at the restaurant, everything was in construction mode."

"Which it still is," I replied. "The kitchen expansion is all but complete. The outdoor patio has been resurfaced, and the sliding glass walls are in place. We've finished the bar extension and will be grouting and sealing the floors in a few days. Finishing the walls will be next, but I know the color scheme. I'll make sure you get a copy of the final renderings. I don't know why I didn't think of it first."

"Cool!" Robbie looked at her watch, frowning slightly.

"Expecting company?" I asked.

"Sort of. My roommate."

Her roommate? My stomach turned, and my whole body felt like it was hollowing out. Had she moved a man into her home? Into her life? Her bed? I wanted to lie down on the floor and moan, but I managed to keep it together. I'm pretty sure I lost color.

"Roommate? Who is he?" Might as well tackle it head-on and tame the beast rising inside.

"He? Not a he. It's one of my friends from LA via Philly. She's come out to Vegas and has been staying with me till she gets on her feet. She had to take a quick trip back to LA to tie up a few loose ends, but she's due back any minute. Her flight's landed."

The relief that washed over me was staggering.

What in the actual hell?

"Oh," I replied weakly.

She didn't notice my relief and continued speaking while she printed out more photos.

"Her name is Daria, and she's moving not only because she was planning a new start, but also because she found her worthless boyfriend *in flagrante delicto*," Robbie air-quoted while waiting for some prints, "and bounced the hell outta there. She was hoping to move out here eventually but hadn't talked to Mr. Asswipe about it yet."

Oh great. Another ain't-shit dude happy to tarnish Robbie's already less-than-stellar opinion about men. I sighed.

"Daria called me a few weeks ago, and I helped her plan," Robbie cackled, cutting a quick glance my way. "She had packed everything because they were going to move in together. She already gave notice to her apartment before she left and had to go back to oversee her stuff being shipped to storage here."

Robbie paused to look at one print in particular. Her printer could print poster-size images, and she held one in front of her. She nodded as if answering an internal question and continued to print.

"So what about the boyfriend?" I had to know. So I'd know what not to do in the future.

"Well, from what I understand, and this may not be exact, she was supposed to have breakfast with him at his place. She used her key to let herself in, but he wasn't waiting for her. So she went into the bedroom to wake him up and caught him fucking a ratchet she guessed was his ex. Not that it matters. She left the breakfast, the key, and a note explaining that she didn't want to disturb him with his thot of the day, and left.

"Daria figured it would take him a while to tame the shitstorm he'd have with the ex and her questions about why *another* woman brought breakfast into his apartment. That gave her enough time to pull everything together and roll. That was two weeks ago."

"Do you have to pick her up at the airport or anything?"

"Nah. She said she'd just Uber or Lyft back home." Robbie chuckled. "I offered, but since she's staying here for free, she didn't want to bother me any more than necessary."

After disconnecting her phone from the speaker system, Robbie gathered several images that met her approval and walked toward the door. "C'mon," she said, "I'm starved. Let's see if we can scrape together something to snack on while we go over these pics."

I followed her out of the studio, admiring the play of her firm, round ass cheeks in her jeans. She stacked the photos on the kitchen island and headed toward what I assumed was her room to get her iPad.

"I've never gotten the tour," I offered hopefully. She glanced over her shoulder and beckoned to me to follow. I walked with her into the family room. Like the front of the house and the kitchen, it was light and airy, with warm, pale gray walls and dark wood floors. In one corner stood a classic floor-to-ceiling fireplace of dark lava rocks, which showed this was a vintage mid-century Vegas house. She had a dark gray area rug in front of the fireplace, which had a conversation area of two linen loveseats facing each other over a massive, free-form wooden coffee table.

Moving past the dining room, we walked down the hallway where we passed her secondary studio and a small bathroom. Family photos of her, her parents, and various family members hung on the walls. We went into her bedroom at the end of the hall. I had expected light and girly, but it wasn't. The walls were painted a soft blue-gray color with a darker accent wall that backed a king-size platform bed with a tall, linen-covered headboard. I was surprised to see original and numbered print artworks by other artists hanging on the walls. Two doors indicated what I guessed were closets. She was chatting all the while, and I was absorbed in the care she had taken to make her home beautiful.

We walked into the master ensuite, and I was greeted by another light room. The large shower had an unusual stucco finish. "Tadelakt plaster," Robbie informed me. "It's Moroccan." There were several showerheads, and the pale gray vanity sported a marble countertop. A large soaking tub had its own place of honor by the window of the roomy bathroom.

"I could live here," I murmured to myself. Robbie gave me an odd look, and after picking up her iPad, we went back down the hallway. Instead of stopping in the kitchen, she went down another hallway where there were other bedrooms. She showed me the largest of the guest rooms where Daria was staying. It was surprisingly spacious, and it had its own ensuite. There were two other bedrooms, besides. Each one had a queen-sized bed and access to the hall bath, another spacious and airy room.

"What's upstairs?"

She grinned at me. "My sanctuary." She led me up the stairway which ended in a loft. I climbed the stairs behind her, my mouth watering over the sexy globes of her ass.

This room was considerably darker than the rest of the house, which was painted in light, neutral colors. The loft's walls were a dark ocean blue-green, including the ceiling. Dark fabric draperies covered one wall. Thick, off-white and teal flecked shag carpet covered the floor. The room was quiet, muted. Very relaxing. The furniture was sparse. There was a small bar with a fridge along one wall. A charcoal-colored microfiber sectional faced the fabric-covered wall. A low entertainment shelving unit held a stereo system, and there were several speakers mounted on the walls. She had framed and autographed jerseys from the Las Vegas Raiders, Vegas Golden Knights, the Aviators, the Vegas Aces, and the old 51s and Wranglers. A real hometown girl.

Robbie smiled at me and walked toward the draperies. She pressed a rocking lever on the wall, and the draperies hissed open.

Wow!

This was one of the best views of the Strip I'd ever seen. Although Robbie's house was some distance from the Strip, it had a postcard-worthy view. Every mid-Strip casino stood out in sharp detail through the floor-to-ceiling glass walls. It was breathtaking.

"Sometimes I feel I could sell tickets for New Year's and the Fourth," she chuckled. "Everything about this house was perfect for me, but this room sealed the deal. This is the first room I renovated. This is my sanctuary. And the fireworks are awesome."

We started down the stairs, this time with me in the lead.

"This is a big house for one person."

"Yeah," she agreed. "When Mom and Dad come down to visit or have a date night, sometimes they'd rather stay here than drive back up to Calico Basin. When my grandparents visit from Cali, they have a place to stay if they decide to hang near the Strip. My house is closer than the folks'. The other bedrooms are for any random person or if I have a houseful. I use the upstairs room for overflow. As long as I have my privacy in my bedroom, I'm good."

We spent the next couple of hours noshing on a few leftovers she found in the fridge and sipping on a nice but overly oaky Napa Chardonnay. Her concept for "The Mural," as I'd come to think of it in my head, was perfect. It fit the style I wanted and would blend into the restaurant's dark woods and warm colors. And this amazing woman was right. Her idea was way better than mine.

"What was the picture you were looking at that you seemed to like?" I asked. She smiled shyly at me and plucked one which wasn't in the mural design pile. The photo was me.

She had framed me looking at her from a three-quarter position. She had caught me laughing at something she said while the sun danced on my hair and clothing. I looked like a man who was flirting with a woman he loved.

Shit.

"This is my favorite of you," she said. "I'm going to do something with this after we're done with the restaurant. I have a couple of ideas."

So do I, dear. So do I.

While she was smiling at the photo, I approached her. I took the picture from her hand and placed it on the island countertop. She looked at the photo and then up at me, at first startled. Her expression changed when she realized I was there for another reason.

I caressed the side of her face with one hand and leaned over to catch her lips. One, two, three feathered kisses. And then I lingered on her mouth, opening her for my tongue, and amid her breathy gasps, she gave back. She slowly wrapped her arms around my neck, and I ran one hand down her back to her buttocks and pressed her against me. She felt my now pulsing erection, but this time she didn't try to escape. I pulled back to look into her eyes, which had turned smoky with need, and then went in for another searing kiss. She arched against me, her moans stoking my fire.

And then the doorbell rang.

Fuck!

Chapter 11

Robbie

REMIND ME TO PAY whoever invented doorbells lots of money or put them in my will. Because the ring of the bell saved me from doing something foolish.

We kissed, lips touching softly. He looked at me as if making a decision. He then came in for the most searing kiss I've ever had. All of my inhibitions, cautions, fears, and anxieties fell away as if they'd never even existed. His eyes blazed with golden fire, and his passion washed over me like a river. I threw my head back, and his lips were on my neck, suckling gently down my throat, drawing shocked cries irresistibly from my lips. When he pressed me against his erection, I didn't pull away this time. My breasts were aching for him and my body arched against his of its own volition.

And then the doorbell rang.

Dammit! Hallelujah! It saved me from myself.

I leaned against Rogan, and he held me tightly, fighting for control.

"It's okay," he breathed. "We have time."

I walked shakily to open the front door and there stood Daria. Thank goodness.

"I forgot my key," she said sheepishly. Thank goodness for that, too.

Daria and I had met in a local hoagie shop in West Philly. The shop was tiny, with just a few small tables along one wall. I was diving into a cheesesteak hoagie when I saw a pretty, brown-skinned woman looking for a place to sit. As always, the shop was packed, so I waved her over to take the seat across from me at my table.

Daria was graduating from the University of Pennsylvania. She was impressed that I was graduating at such a young age from Moore. We chatted like we'd known each other forever. We exchanged information and the rest, as they say, is history. We stayed in contact during the last few years, talking to each other at least seasonally. We celebrated when she moved to LA. And now, even though it was under unhappy circumstances, I was celebrating her move to Vegas.

She stood there, a half-smile on her face as we looked at each other. Then we were hugging and almost crying. In my peripheral, I saw Rogan shaking his head with a smile.

"It looks like you survived," I told her. "Everything must have gone okay. You look free!"

And she did. She looked like she'd shed a ton of emotional weight.

I consider Daria my sister from another mister. We are about the same height, but that's more or less where the similarity ends. Daria's skin is almost chestnut in color, and she has the blackest eyes I've ever seen. Her smile is full and white, *sans* braces, and her lips are plush. She has a button nose, high cheekbones, and a stylish natural haircut. She has a killer figure, with full breasts, tiny waist, and lush hips. Honestly, if I had the curves that she does, who knows where I might have ended up!

She was dressed in jeans that accented her curves, a loose, bright red top, and a sweater draped over one arm. She walked into the foyer, pulling her carry-on behind her.

"Maybe I should go..." Rogan began.

"You can't. We still have a lot of work!"

"Yes ma'am!"

"Daria, this is Rogan. Rogan, Daria." They shook hands, smiling genuinely. Good.

"I haven't slept in four days," Daria said apologetically. "I didn't get a single wink on the plane, and I'm so tired I'm shaking. Unnecessary drama fatigues one."

"I'll walk you to your room," I replied. We headed down the hallway together. When Daria first arrived a couple of weeks ago, I gave her the guest room with the ensuite.

"Moving and dealing with shit-for-brains was exhausting." She smiled. "He's still 'confused.'"

I chuckled. "You go ahead and get some sleep. Rogan and I still have some loose ends to tie up on his project."

"Yeah, about that. That's Rogan?" she asked, eyebrows raised. "He's lovely. In a way, he sorta reminds me of Jason Morgan, except with long hair. You know who he is, right? Male model? Yummy? Beauteous? GQ? Plus, it looks like he has a touch of honey in there somewhere, too."

"His mother is from Spain," I confirmed. "That's why his skin is so warm, even with freckles."

"And those yellow *Witcher* eyes are somethin' else! And he sure does like you!"

I felt my face heating. "We're just friends," I lied.

"Uh huh," Daria replied skeptically, lips pursed. "Well, anyway, you go out there with your 'friend' while I clean up and take a nap. The last couple of days have been, well, eventful."

"We'll talk and drink ourselves into oblivion later. So get comfortable, and if you need anything, just holler."

She nodded, chuckling, and waved me away. I walked out of her bedroom and closed the door.

"Talk about timing," Rogan smiled ruefully when I returned to the kitchen. He'd been rummaging through my wine fridge and found a bottle of Sonoma Coast Pinot Noir. He lifted an eyebrow as he held up the bottle.

"If you don't mind," he said, "the Chard was a little too oaky for me."

I nodded and went to my overhead cabinet to snag a couple of Burgundy Riedels. He poured a little wine into one and handed it to me for tasting. I sniffed, swirled, sipped, and then smiled my approval. Delicious.

"I'm blown away by your ideas for the murals," he commented as he returned to the barstool. "It's almost as if you crawled into my unconscious mind and found what I didn't know I wanted." He frowned. "Does that even make sense?"

"Makes perfect sense," I replied. "Don't tell anybody, but that's been the secret to my success. I can 'see' what people want in their space. It's a gift. Most successful artists have it."

"Are you in a relationship?" Rogan asked.

What? That was random.

"No. Why do you ask?"

"I'm trying to figure out the playing field," he replied. "You're a beautiful woman, and I'm trying to see how many men you have on speed dial."

I chuckled and looked at him fondly.

"Well, I don't, and there's a reason for that," I answered, sobering. "Rape has a way of changing your opinion about men and makes you avoid relationships."

At first, he was stunned. And then Rogan's face turned into a mask of red raging fury. His eyes blazed dark gold, and I swear that his hair was stirring as if in a hot wind. He stood up and grasped my arms in his hands.

"Someone hurt you?" he growled.

"No, no. It didn't happen to me," I quickly reassured him. "But it happened to a friend of mine when I was in Philly. Her boyfriend took her V card and then let a few of his friends sample the goods. When they drank themselves into oblivion and passed out, she was able to escape. She called me to come and get her, and while I was helping her into my car, a couple of the dudes came to and ran out to grab us." I suppressed a shudder.

"I barely escaped but was ready to run over all of them. I took her straight to the hospital while I called 911 and made a report. And then I called Dad, who almost lost his shit because it was *my* voice saying something about rape." I could still feel his panic.

"Once I calmed him down, he made some calls to Philly to make sure that she wasn't put into a pile of unprocessed DNA kits or onto the DA's back burner. I stayed at the hospital with her even after her parents arrived. She had to be placed in a medically induced coma. It was that bad."

I looked up at Rogan, still feeling the pain in my chest. "I never saw so much blood before," I whispered. "They had torn her up. She had a sheet wrapped around her body that was soaked in her own blood and vomit. She was the sweetest girl, and they went crazy on her."

I closed my eyes at the memory, shuddering. "They tell you that rape can damage a woman for life. But they don't tell you what it can do to close friends and family. After that incident, I swore off men.

"But to tell the truth, I haven't really thought about relationships for a while, at least not entirely because of that. That incident has faded in its intensity since then. It's been a few years. It's the whole 'time heals all wounds' thing. For me, at least, even if not for her."

Although still angry, Rogan was no longer raging. He didn't look like an avenging angel anymore, and he'd loosened his grip from my arms. He took a deep breath and looked at me with an unreadable expression, eyes still glittering. Enveloping me protectively in his arms for a very long moment, he kissed my forehead.

"So I don't have to go to Philly and fuck somebody up."

I laughed. "No. For once, in no small way thanks to Dad, who's from Philly and 'knows people,' the system worked. Most of the perps are behind bars. I think each one was sentenced to 30 years. Hopefully, they'll serve their full sentence."

"I want you to spend some time with me."

I blinked at him. "Spend time?"

"Yes. We've known each other for so long, and I've liked you from the beginning, even when you were this weird genius androgynous nerd thing. I didn't even know that I liked you. You were a kid, so there's that. Who knew that despite your baggy clothes and crazy hair, that there was actually a girl beneath it all." He looked into my eyes with affection, lips twitching.

"Now I more than like you," he continued. "As a man, I'm very attracted to you, and I think I've shown just how much. I think you're attracted to me, too, if your response is any indication." He grinned as I felt frissons of heat tickle my cheeks.

"I want us to spend a weekend together and see where this goes. I have a feeling that this is more than just a surface attraction, but I want you to give the go-ahead."

The butterflies in my stomach turned into F-16s flying in formation. This man was asking me to spend time with him. I was floored.

"Spend a weekend with me. Not as my date, per se, but as someone who wants to be with me as much as I want to be with her." He motioned between the two of us. "I think that this is something we can plan for the long haul. So let's see if I can help you put that incident behind you and you can see that some men are good guys."

There were a couple of beats of time while confusion blanketed my mind.

"You okay? You look surprised." He was fighting a smile. He knew he'd shaken me.

Bastard.

I opened my mouth and then closed it again. I gave my head a shake.

"I'm surprised. I feel like an idiot for saying this, but even now, I never thought you were even remotely interested in me. I figured you always saw me as Janina's nerdy, artsy-fartsy, tag-along little friend. That you kissed me out of curiosity. I'm still surprised you even see me as a girl."

Chapter 12

Rogan

"... I'M STILL SURPRISED you even see me as a girl."

I don't see you as a "girl," my love. I see you as a woman. A woman of intelligence, character, and honor who grabbed my heart and has held on to it ever since. All I can think of is you, having you in my arms, in my bed, and by my side. You've grown into a woman of incredible strength and beauty, and you don't even realize it. My god, Robbie, I want you so much it hurts.

Instead, I said, "Let me give you my sales pitch." I looked at her puzzled expression, my smile in place. Might as well go all in.

I twirled the stem of my glass before bringing my eyes back to hers. "I'm single and never married. Honestly, I haven't had time for a serious relationship. I'm an entrepreneur, investor, and restaurateur. Because of Dad's guidance, I have interests in financial sectors that count, and frankly, even if I never worked another day in my life, I could live quite comfortably and," I paused, "have and support a family." I smiled and continued.

"That said, I learned to cook early in life, which led the way into my becoming a successful chef, and the combination of all of those ensures that I will always work. Being productive is in my DNA."

I set the glass down and took her hands in mine.

"I have no diseases, but I'll get tested if you want. I've been told that I'm a good lover. In my entire adult life, there's only been one woman who's ever come close to touching my heart, and she's right here, now, holding my hands."

There. I just declared myself as a serious contender. It's the first time I ever did so with a woman. I was shaking inside because the idea of being rejected by Robbie was nerve-wracking.

"You don't have any diseases?" she asked.

I was taken aback by that skeptical-sounding question.

"I mean, you've been around a lot, and I haven't. My last date was over 18 months ago. I'm really surprised that you don't have any infections or, at the very least, some random baby mamas out there."

She was serious. And, Robbie being Robbie, very blunt.

"No, I don't have any diseases. None. No viruses, bacteria, or anything. I've always used condoms, believe it or not. I've had long periods of celibacy after my soccer career was over. And that's because I didn't always want to hook up with every random woman who flirted with me. Sometimes even men can do the right thing."

At that moment, I randomly thought of my first visit to the gallery and how I'd allowed Hera to blow me afterward.

Yeah, well. Not my proudest moment.

"We try to, anyway," I amended.

"I've always used condoms, without fail. Knock on wood, I've never had a single failure. I've been very diligent about keeping myself safe and disease and child-free. If I'd had any babies out there, Mama, and Dad, too, I'm sure, would have made sure a shotgun wedding took place."

Robbie studied me, expressions morphing from skeptical to hesitant to humorous. What in the world was she thinking about?

She took a deep breath and hesitated, biting her lower lip. "Okay," she said, smiling tentatively. "I'm game. I'll play along."

"I'm smart," she began, "a former child prodigy. Only because I'm a former child," she chuckled at her own humor.

"I've never been with a man, so I know I have no diseases. And as far as I know, I don't have any genetic stuff going on either. It's been over a year and a half since the last time I went out with anyone. So after that particular train wreck, I decided to give myself the time to focus on my career and my future."

I stilled, blood thundering, thick and heavy. "What does that mean?"

She knit her brows in confusion. "What part?"

"The 'I've never been with a man' part."

She shrugged. "Just what I said. I've never had a serious emotional relationship, and while I've dated, I've never had a sexual relationship with anyone. I just never had the time or found anyone tempting enough."

"When you said you swore off men, you didn't already have a relationship?"

"No," she replied. "Moore's an all-female college, and because I was so young and nerdy, guys in general weren't particularly interested in me. I wasn't especially boy crazy," she continued, "and after my friend's experience, I had zero interest in any kind of relationship at all."

Robbie was a virgin? That was the last thing I'd thought of while trying to sweet-talk my way into her bed. I never even considered virgins before since I liked easy hookups with no strings. So this was a situation I was unprepared for. My cock immediately grew into the penile version of Godzilla and was hard enough to drill through concrete. "It's hard for me to believe that you've never had a sexual relationship," I stated while hoping not to pant. "I mean, look at you."

"Believe it," she smiled. "And thank you."

"You're welcome," I nodded. "Saving yourself for marriage?"

She gave a very unladylike snort.

"Hardly. But at the same time, I wasn't going to allow myself to be used for somebody's ego. So I learned early on not to tell guys I'm a virgin. It made them stupid and unappealing because their personalities disappeared, replaced by the let-me-be-first-and-I'll-be-gentle hormone."

It was my turn to snort with laughter. Guys are like that. She nailed it.

She sobered. "I had a few classmates who gave up their V card just so that they'd 'get it over with' or because they were 'in love,'" she air quoted. "And that didn't always work out well, but it gave me a great list of what *not* to do. My 'innocence,'" more air quotes, "is only physical. I've seen enough to know when it can go wrong."

She shrugged. "As it turns out, I've been too busy for sex, anyway. For me, sex means a relationship. Something of value. Something of beauty. Something that will really last, you know? And I haven't had the time. Haven't found the person. And I'm not the type to do something just to get it over with. My virginity isn't something to get rid of at the first possible convenience. It's just who I am at this point in time. When the right person comes along and we make love, then that will be who I am at that point in time."

I was speechless. I was also fighting hard to tamp down my personal version of the let-me-be-first-and-I'll-be-gentle hormone. Hey. I'm a guy.

I took a deep breath and inwardly prayed that I wouldn't insert a foot too deeply into my mouth. "Whether or not you're a virgin doesn't matter. My motivation is the same. Even if you'd told me that you'd already had sexual encounters, it wouldn't have made any difference. In fact, I figured that you'd already had several lovers. I want to make love to you, regardless. Virgin or not, experienced or not, it doesn't matter. You are who matters to me, not your past. Or lack of one, as the case may be."

I tilted my head back and continued. "But now that you've told me this, I also want to put on a loincloth, swing in the trees, and go pound my chest."

She laughed, eyes sparkling. "Whatever for?"

"Men like being first. First to discover a lost treasure. Our teams being first. Winning. That's men. And being the first man his woman has ever made love to? It brings out the inner caveman. We become primal."

"So you've been with virgins before?"

"Nope. Not even Colleen was a virgin when we were dating," referring to my high school girlfriend. "As it turns out, I was one of several guys she was 'seeing,'" using air quotes to punctuate my statement. "So I have no idea when and where she got started.

"But I was a high school jock gettin' some," I continued. "I had few brain cells located in my actual head. Like the other guys, I was thinking with my dick most of the time. It seems to be a condition that's hard to grow out of and one that's endemic among jocks."

"What about when you were playing professionally?"

"Believe it or not, I was more careful then. Even with all the groupie pussy thrown around, I realized just how I'd dodged bullets. My first coach at UNLV told us to keep our dicks in our shorts and, if we had to get some, to keep our man juice securely contained in a condom and make sure that we only fucked experienced women. No virgins. No underage. No disease. He was brutal. He told us that some modern diseases could make our dicks fall off. No cures."

I vividly remembered when Coach seemed to be laser-focused on yelling in my personal face about keeping my man meat wrapped and secure, or else it'd fall off. After his beatdown, I was traumatized for life. I didn't want my cock to fall off. I'm very fond of it.

"Naturally, with guys being guys, some of them didn't listen. Looking at the infections they got, the money they spent, the craziness they put up with, and some having to pay child support for the next umpteen years, I made sure that I was one of the few who listened. So no. Experienced only, condoms always. No virgins. No underage. No disease. No babies. And I don't regret it a bit. In fact, now that I'm older, I'm happy that Coach traumatized me."

I took a deep breath and continued.

"Actually, even before Coach scared the bejesus out of me and cemented the habit, I used condoms in high school. Mama probably would have forced me to marry any girl I might have deflowered or knocked up if she found out. Or cut off the offending body part. Painful thought at best."

I cast about in my mind for a plan to keep Robbie comfortable around me.

"Let's not plan for time together now. Let's wait until the project is done and before the grand opening. Mama's going to oversee most of the finishing processes, and that will free me up to take some time for myself. For us."

She still stood in front of me, lips slightly pursed, arms crossed, expression skeptical.

"Earth to Rob!" I softly touched her chin and lifted her face to mine.

She shook herself out of her daze. "I'm okay. Just a little surprised, is all."

I pulled her to me and wrapped my arms around her body. "I'm not interested in any other woman. I don't want anyone but you. I haven't seen any other woman since you came back into my life."

I still can't believe I put myself out there like that. I pulled back and looked into her stormy eyes before leaning over and giving her another light kiss on her forehead. "You are my project."

Her face dissolved into a smile. "Okay. You have a deal. But by the end of the project, you may think I'm the most temperamental, self-centered, argumentative, hot-headed, unpleasant bossy prima donna bitch you've ever met. And your dick might agree and take a bye. I'm game."

She looked up at me, expression now relaxed and friendly as she settled in the circle of my arms. We both took several deep sighs, snuggling together.

"Now let's get to work," she commanded, pushing away. "These murals aren't going to plan themselves."

Chapter 13

Rogan

Derrick and I walked up to the construction tape only to be greeted by an irritated Justin Crews. Justin, the owner of Crews & Crew Construction, was the general contractor for the project. Paul Garganelli, my project manager and scion of an old Italian Vegas family, stood next to him, expression humorous.

"We have a problem." Justin pulled aside one of the construction stanchions so that we could enter the restaurant.

Alarm shot through my body. "What is it?" I asked.

Justin's scowl increased. "It's your artist. She won't cooperate."

Relief. Color me shocked. Robbie won't cooperate. Who would have guessed.

"She's here with a bunch of students. They're wearing hard hats. She won't," Paul interjected. "She told the both of us to kiss her ass."

The fleeting expression on Justin's face told me that he wouldn't mind doing just that. I returned his scowl. Paul chuckled.

"Where is she?"

"In the VIP."

I nodded and grabbed a helmet from the stack at the entrance and handed it to Derrick. I already had my own.

Derrick and I had been at UNLV together on the varsity soccer team. Because I inherited the muscular tree trunk legs of the McDonalds, I played defense while Derrick was a striker. We're both Vegas natives, Derrick from Green Valley in Henderson, and me from Summerlin in Vegas. We both had been athletic scholarship recipients. We met in Economics 101 class and became instant friends and co-conspirators. We were the same height of six three, had the lean, muscular build that's the hallmark of soccer players, and that's about where the similarities ended.

The best way to describe Derrick was as a younger, darker version of Boris Kodjoe. Women love him.

He'd acted as my wingman in school when it came to the ladies, and I acted as his. We both managed to cut a swath through the soccer groupies in the first couple of years as students, but something clicked in our junior and senior years. We grew up and focused on our academics and life goals. The girls were still around, but we weren't "playing" nearly as much. It's funny what happens when maturity kicks in.

While I'd been able to make soccer a career for a season, Derrick focused on his goal of making a career in the fire service. He spent an extra two years getting a degree in Fire Science and earned a nursing degree. His focus and physical conditioning made him almost a shoo-in during the Clark County Firefighter recruitment process. A few short years after cadet training and as a Firefighter Paramedic, he was now on track to become an Engineer with the possibility of Captain being a short jog away. All in record time. He was nearly unstoppable.

The rotating shifts gave him time to pursue his own business interests. He owned a small African arts and collectibles shop in Historic West Las Vegas. He had amassed impressive global success among serious collectors. Derrick was the whole package.

We walked through the lobby, where three helmet-wearing students were prepping the background for the design that would greet customers when they entered the restaurant. Someone had set up a cell phone and a Bluetooth speaker that was blasting rap. A young Japanese woman, a dark-haired white guy, and a young Latino man worked together, heads bobbing to the music.

I noticed a group of five students working on a larger mural near the bar. They were just getting set up, so I didn't need to see what they were doing other than to note that they were also wearing helmets.

We walked into the VIP dining area. A one-person scaffolding unit stood in front of the large wall where the beginning of a faint outline was sketched. Standing on the top level of the unit with her hand firmly gripping the guardrail was Robbie. I could tell from her posture that she was not in a good mood.

Robbie turned to look at us from her perch when we approached, and she frowned. She was dressed in her usual uniform of jeans and a loose t-shirt. This time, however, she wore a neon yellow paint-splattered snood over her locs. It fit snugly around her hairline, and she had tied a loose knot at the open end to keep her hair in check and free from paint.

She opened the hatch and climbed down from the scaffolding deck, which wasn't very tall, probably about seven feet. I couldn't help but notice that the four of us admired her curvy, jean-covered butt enhanced by the drape of the t-shirt. I frowned at the thought that the other three men would be attracted to her while not blaming them, either.

She stalked over to us and pointed to Justin. "He," she began without preamble or greeting, "must have called you. We're having a disagreement."

Damn, she's adorable, even when she's pissed off and wearing that ridiculous thing on her head.

"Actually," I began, "I came here to show Derrick the progress on the restaurant, and Justin and Paul met us at the entrance. Justin didn't call me. What seems to be the problem?"

"I can't wear a helmet at this point in the project. In fact, I won't wear a helmet because it doesn't protect my locs from the paint that I have to use because I'm doing a *fucking* mural!"

I cast a glance over to Justin, whose blond eyebrows were now furrowed into a frown. "We have rules..." he began.

"I give less than zero fucks about your 'rules,'" Robbie interrupted, one palm in the air. "I have a job to do and you're upsetting my focus."

I was torn between the two of them. I was paying Robbie a shit-ton of money to do this mural, and I didn't want her focus upset. It could get even more expensive. At the same time, I needed to make sure that she was safe and to ensure that safety laws were followed. Derrick and Paul were wisely remaining silent.

"What are the chances of something falling on her at this point?" I asked Justin.

"None," he answered honestly. "We've completed all of the tasks that require a hard hat due to falling objects. With her being on a scaffold, though, she could fall and that can be a problem. It's a liability issue. This is my company, and I want to make sure that everyone who's working in my company's area of responsibility is wearing a helmet. I hate that fucking OSHA, and I prefer to not have to deal with them. But with that so-called scaffold..."

"'So-called'? What the hell do you mean by that?" Robbie turned to Justin, lips in a vicious snarl. "It's a professional scaffold that happens to be small enough for one person. That person is me. Just because it's small doesn't mean that it doesn't do the job. Size doesn't matter." She stopped for a moment, evil sparking in her gray eyes. "But I'm sure you know all about that..."

"Okay!" I interrupted the escalating squabble, "I'll take responsibility for Robbie's safety. I need her to be able to focus on the task, and if a helmet will upset her and interfere with her progress, then we don't need it. I'll have my attorney draw up a contract that states you aren't liable for her safety because of this decision."

He nodded in understanding. I'd have to talk to my attorney anyway just to make sure that neither of us would face any consequences.

"Whatever you say, boss!" He shot another reluctantly admiring glance at Robbie's form, and he and Paul disappeared into the restaurant.

Robbie turned to me. "I said that I could be difficult. It's just that I hadn't planned to be difficult this soon into the work. It usually happens near the end of a project when I'm tired. There's too much to do and too much to concentrate on to be upset by something like a helmet. Thanks for stepping in. Now I can focus and not have to worry about arguing with the boss."

"Actually," I began, "I came to see if there's anything that you need or if there's something that you need me to do."

"Just keep Captain America away from me and we'll be just peachy," she retorted.

"I also wanted to introduce you to my friend Derrick."

I turned to Derrick. "This is Robbie," I said simply.

Derrick immediately plastered a bright, friendly, and annoyingly sensual smile on his face as his large hand enveloped Robbie's. He raised her hand to his lips and placed a kiss on it. I sent him a raised eyebrow *really dude?* glare.

"It's a pleasure." His voice seemed unnecessarily baritone in timbre as his warm, appreciative gaze lingered over Robbie's slim form. He sent her the full force of his dazzling smile and bedroom eyes.

Robbie was unimpressed and shot him an irritated look. "Nice to meet you I'm sure," she nodded, pulling her hand from his grip. And then dismissed him as she turned to me. "We need to meet later," she stated. "I have a couple of ideas that are kind of important, and I need to talk to you so that you can focus on what I'm saying."

She stopped, frowning in thought.

"What I mean by that is that it's crucial to the brand of the restaurant, and I need you to be open-minded about my suggestion."

I was intrigued, but I confirmed. "I'll call you later and we can set up a time."

She nodded, pleased. Then she dismissed the both of us by climbing onto her scaffold and picking up a thick charcoal pencil.

As we turned to leave, I noticed that Derrick sent a lingering glance back at her long, toned legs and the curvy outline under her t-shirt.

"She is one beautiful woman," he commented when we exited the front door of *Bistro Veritas* and walked down the open-air mall to PT's at the other end. No time like the present for some good bar food. Although it wasn't on the shoreline like *Bistro Veritas*, PT's was a locals hangout with good drinks, draft beer, pool tables, and hot, filling food.

After we sat down at a four-top near the pool tables, we ordered beers from the flirty waitress. I ordered the cheese curds and pretzels appetizer, and both of us ordered their "heart attack in a bun" Western Cheeseburger. That was a big, sloppy serving of artery-clogging chow if I ever saw one. And so delicious that I didn't care.

Derrick looked at me, dark eyes twinkling. "That Robbie is a dish," he grinned. "She's got that whole Alicia Keys, natural, brown skin vibe. But she sure wasn't impressed with me. I gave her the full monty, and she dismissed me like I was a first-grader at the principal's office."

I chuckled. I'd noticed that, and it gave me a huge rush of relief. Derrick was a ladies' man, and the ladies were all too happy to fall in line, vying for his attention, panties dropping at every turn. The fact that Robbie was unimpressed made me happier than I probably should have been. She hadn't slobbered over him as most women did.

"She sure likes you, though," he continued. "She was yelling at all of us, but she was giving you heart eyes."

I nearly choked on my beer. "I didn't notice."

"Yeah," Derrick laughed, "Well, I noticed. You were too busy sweating about her being pissed at us, especially you."

"Yeah, I guess you're right. I'm thinking about asking her out after she's done with the mural. I don't want to piss her off so much that she tells me to go fuck myself beforehand."

Derrick roared with laughter. "And she looks like she'd do it," he chuckled. "Seems like she's into a bullshit-free existence."

It was my turn to laugh. "That pretty much describes her. I've never met anyone so blunt before in my life."

"When did you meet her?"

"About ten or so years ago."

Derrick stared at me over the rim of his beer, mouth agape. "Damn, man! You've known a chick who looks like *that* for ten years and haven't said a word about her? What's up with that? Trying to hide her from the world so you can keep her to yourself?"

I chuckled. "First of all, when we met, she had barely turned 13 and was a child prodigy who'd been promoted into high school. Because she was so young and so tomboyish, I didn't see her as anything but a tomboy. Sometimes with the way that she looked and dressed, she could easily be mistaken for a dude. And I did, on more than one occasion. Second of all, I was 18, and gettin' some on a regular basis was new to me. I was totally uninterested in anything but easy girls with big tits. Preferably blondes. *Bouncy-bouncy* blondes in particular if you get my drift. And third of all, she's the artist of the painting in your condo. I told you that I met her, but you didn't make the connection."

I thought Derrick's heavy eyebrows were going to escape to the back of his shaved head.

"*That's* BTW? If I'd known that, I woulda taken the picture to bed and beat off to it."

I scowled at him as he laughed.

The waitress brought the appetizer and burgers, and we dug in.

"I didn't know you were into black chicks, man," Derrick commented while examining his platter of food. "I figured you were still into blondes or whatever."

"You know that I broke my blonde obsession when we were at UNLV," I replied, "and when I was on the pro circuit, there were all colors of willing and available pussy. I got to 'taste the rainbow,' my man!"

Derrick choke-laughed on a mouthful of food and quickly downed a few chugs of beer. He guffawed at my comment.

"Not that it matters," I continued. "Robbie's been in my life for so long, her skin's not even a thing. And don't forget that my mother is from Spain. I'm sure that when the African Moors invaded, they left their DNA. That means if the 'one drop' rule is still in effect, then technically, I must be black, too."

We both laughed at my quip.

"You are one crazy motherfucker," Derrick grinned after taking another swig of his beer.

"As far as I'm concerned, Robbie doesn't belong to a 'race.' She's just Robbie. With her spirit, I'd like her no matter what her color was. She just happens to be black."

All of that was true. No matter how I tried, I just couldn't see Robbie as a race, whatever that means. I only saw her as a woman. My woman.

Derrick nodded in understanding. "Seriously man," he continued, dipping a fry in some ketchup, "she's fine as fuck. I hope you're planning on moving into that, because if you don't, I'll find a way." He looked at me, expression direct and unflinching. "You feel me?"

And I knew he would try. Robbie was fine, and to Derrick, she was a target. She was a goal. For him, she'd be little more than a conquest to make. Robbie and I weren't a thing—not yet at least—and I had staked no claim on her. It was up to me to make sure that I was the only one Robbie was focused on. Because I already knew I'd kill a motherfucker who'd try to take her away from me. Even Derrick.

Let me be first and I'll be gentle.

Damn straight. And it's going to be me.

Chapter 14

Robbie

AFTER I FINISHED THE day's work on the mural, I went into the new staff bathroom and removed the yellow loc sock from my hair. I exchanged my paint-splattered t-shirt for a clean one and then zipped it and the sock into my carryall. I washed my face and hands before I put my stuff into my van, grabbed my messenger bag holding my iPad and papers, and walked across the parking lot to PT's.

I arrived before Rogan and stacked my paperwork arguments and my iPad on the four-top I'd chosen. I hoped he liked my idea.

Taking a deep breath, I felt the tension of the day drain away. There's something about the darkened atmosphere in local bars that somehow has the magical ability to suction the stress right out of you. Roy Orbison's "Pretty Woman" played softly in the background. A few scattered people conversed in hushed tones at their tables. A small cadre of friends was bullshitting each other around one of the two pool tables. The soft ringing sounds of video poker being played at the bar drifted into the air. A couple of servers had their heads together in deep conversation. The bartender hand-polished beer glasses. The *ding ding ding* of a winning jackpot filled the area 'round the bar as an older lady raised her hands in happy celebration.

Yes. The stress completely evaporated.

The progress that Rogan was making on the restaurant was phenomenal. The decor could best be described as retro without necessarily touching on a particular era. Kind of like Art

Deco meets Mid Century meets Contemporary. Smooth, clean, relaxing lines with gentle curves interspersed, and it screamed class. The dark-framed window walls were breathtaking, and the views were magnificent.

The flooring in the entryway, bar, and wine rack areas were all hand-stained, sealed concrete tiles instead of the expected ceramic or carpeting. The outdoor dining area also sported concrete tiles, but larger and with a free-form design. Both banquet rooms were carpeted in what I called "party proof" squares. I thought that was a brilliant idea just in case someone—or several someones—spilled, dropped, or vomited on it.

Plusher carpeting covered the main and VIP dining room floors and would add to the quiet and ambiance of the dining experience. I couldn't wait to see how that would look once I finished the mural.

I turned my thoughts back to the day's progress. I'd given the students working in the lobby area the day off until I spoke to Rogan about my idea. Actually, it was more of a revelation than an idea. I just hoped he liked it.

Meanwhile, the mural outline and initial background wash of paint had evolved quicker than I expected. The stylized Art Deco-meets-Vegas-meets-desert landscape concept was coming together nicely. So far, so good.

Rogan entered PT's, pushing his sunglasses over his loose hair as his eyes adjusted to the relative darkness of the bar's interior. He spotted me, grinned, and began walking in my direction. He was dressed simply in a polo shirt and Levi's. A pair of Mephisto Vilsons clad his feet. It struck me again how different he was now compared to when he was 18. He'd been a boy then, and now he was a man. A man of success, focus, and accomplishment, but who, thanks to his crazy parents, had natural warmth and a heart. My own heart skittered a bit.

I was probably grinning like an idiot when he came to the table. He smiled at me and leaned over to plant a kiss on my forehead. He hesitated, then held the side of my face with one hand and pressed a soft, warm kiss on my lips. My breath caught, although there was no tongue action involved. Just tenderness. Which, along with my heart fluttering, caused warmth to flow through my body and pool between my thighs.

"Hi Rogie," I smiled softly. "Thanks for coming."

"How could I stay away?" he replied, returning my smile. "You intrigued me. Show me whatcha got."

I picked up my iPad and brought up Illustrator. I swiped through the pages that I'd worked on and began my spiel.

"While I think that Bistro Veritas is okay for a name, I don't feel that it works with your brand. You're the winner of Top Chef, in no small part because of the Restaurant Wars, and I think you're selling yourself short."

I don't think Rogan's eyebrows could have gone any higher. "Really?" he probed. "What makes you say that?"

A waitress came to our table, and we both ordered draft beer: a Belgian White with an orange slice for me and an IPA for Rogan. I ordered potstickers and hot wings, and Rogan ordered a huge hamburger. We ordered cheese pretzels for an appetizer. It was after work, and I was tired. I wasn't going to cook when I got home, I hadn't eaten all day, and I was hungry. Bar food it was.

I didn't appreciate the fact that the flirty blonde hovered by Rogan, letting him see the cleavage leading to her substantial bosom. Besides that, she smiled and winked at him. My irritated scowl went over her head. Rogan didn't respond to her flirtations other than being courteous. Good for him.

"You used Bistro Veritas in Top Chef, right?" I asked him after the waitress had gone.

He nodded. "Yes, I did."

"Why did you pick that particular name?"

He sat back in his chair, brows furrowed in thought. "I always wanted to use Bistro in my own restaurant, and Veritas came from In Vino Veritas. I knew I wanted to focus on the wine as well as the food."

"Is there one particular restaurant that you look to as your primary influence?"

"Yeah," he replied easily. "The French Laundry."

"It's the best!" I exclaimed. "But what do you like about it?"

Rogan seemed to look through me as he pondered his answer. "Thomas Keller's focus is all about making the American dining experience better. I want to take Bistro Veritas along those lines, but more Vegas-centric. I want to see classic American dishes showcased as well as those that have become American because they've been here so long. Like guacamole, for instance. Think of lasagna and tacos. Pizza. Sushi. Soul food. Soul food has African roots. And I'll be taking them to a higher level."

I nodded. That's what I had thought. And that's why *Bistro Veritas* wasn't a good fit.

The waitress returned, bringing our beers and pretzels and promising Rogan—not me, of course—that our food would be forthcoming. She smiled flirtatiously at him again and sashayed away, swinging her hips. Geez, woman. Give it a rest.

"*Bistro Veritas* doesn't work," I shook off my irritation with her shameless flirting. "It doesn't fit you or your concept."

"Really," he replied dryly. "Tell me what your idea is."

"You need to name it after yourself."

"What? *McDonald's*? I think the name's already taken."

I laughed at his unexpected quip and looked at him affectionately while shaking my head.

"Crazy man," I chuckled. "That's not what I was thinking although *McDonald's* does have a certain *je ne sais quoi*." I did a chef's kiss with my fingers, and it was his turn to laugh, his gaze tender.

Suddenly parched, I chugged half of my beer and licked the suds from around my lips. Rogan's pupils dilated as he watched my tongue action. Hm. I know what he's thinking.

"Actually," I said, biting back a knowing grin, "I was thinking of something along the lines of using your first name."

"How would that work?" he asked, interest piquing.

"It has to be something very American. The name, I mean. Here, let me show you." I woke up my iPad, and as it was coming online, the waitress arrived with our food. As expected, she pretty much just dropped my dishes in front of me and then fluttered around Rogan. Only this time, he began to look annoyed. She asked him if everything was okay.

"We're fine, thank you," he said, smiling innocuously. "Just bring my lady another Belgian White and another IPA for me if you please."

Her flirtation abruptly stopped as she seemed to notice my existence for the first time.

My Lady.

Yup. There goes that old heart-skittering thing again. I swallowed a smile and just looked at her blankly as if I'd heard nothing.

"I have two ideas to share," I began after the waitress scurried away to fetch our beers. I tapped on the screen for the first example. "You decide which one you like best. You may not like either. Regardless," I continued, "at least I was able to show you something different."

He nodded as he picked up the iPad to look at the samples.

Rogie Mac's Bistro was the first. The title was a casual script with a mid-century vibe to it, kind of reminiscent of the old Carnegie's Deli in New York. His eyebrows flew up, and his lips quirked into a smile.

"That's pretty nice," he commented. "I like it." He paused. "But is it suitable for a somewhat high-end restaurant?"

"I thought of that." I took the iPad from him and swiped to the next idea.

Rogan's: An American Bistro was the second concept. And it took his breath away. *Rogan's* was in script, and *An American Bistro*, the typeface next to it, was a sans serif style. I felt it fit in perfectly with my interpretation of the restaurant's focus.

He looked at me, golden eyes shining.

"I didn't even know I wanted this," he whispered. "It's like you picked it out of my subconscious and configured it just for me. How the hell did you do that?"

"Well," I started with a smile, "I wasn't 100 percent sure. That's why I asked you what your inspiration was and what you wanted from your new restaurant. It's all about your focus. I had figured out part of it, and I was ready to come up with another design if necessary." I patted my heart. "But I could feel you here.

"I started thinking about this as soon as we'd agreed on the final mural design." I continued. "It's too bad I'm not a graphic designer, or I would have offered a complete package at one time."

"I'll put you in contact with my designer," Rogan told me, face beaming with excitement. "You two can work on finessing the design of the logo and coming up with ideas for the menu templates and other graphic items. Tommy's a little frustrated with me because we've been trying for weeks, and I haven't been happy."

He stopped to take a drink from the fresh beer the waitress had just brought. *Sans* flirting. "I didn't realize it was because everything was all wrong. Not Tommy's fault, but mine. I felt married to the *Bistro Veritas* name and thought I'd just use it. I'll make sure you and Tommy have each other's contact information."

He looked at the rough draft and shook his head. "This is the shit! It's simple and genius. This logo is definitely up there in the 'why the hell didn't I think of that?' category. It's almost embarrassing." Rogan shook his head again and looked at me. "Yeah. I can't wait to see what you and Tommy come up with. And Tommy also works from home, not too far from you."

We clinked our glasses, and each took a swig of beer.

I was prepared for battle. After all, he had everything in place, right? Everything in place that I knew didn't fit. I had been loaded for bear and ready to brawl.

And then he happily and enthusiastically agreed with me with zero opposition. Battle mind deflated.

"I was ready for a fight and you didn't give me one," I grumbled.

Rogan cackled with laughter. "Sorry to disappoint you, sweetness," he chortled, eyes sparkling with warmth and humor. "But you're too good for your own good."

We laughed and talked while we finished our meals. I knew the fact that I hated doing murals was never going to change, but this project was special. And for the first time, I didn't regret taking the job. How could I, when this sexy, freckle-faced, golden-eyed man was looking at me like *that*?

Chapter 15

Robbie

There. I was done. I had completed the mural that somehow seemed to complete itself. I can't remember the last time a piece flowed as naturally as this one had, almost as if guided by an unseen hand.

And it was beautiful. From the gauzy images of Red Rock Canyon to the Vegas-meets-South-Beach deco stylings I'd given the silhouettes of the Strip casinos, to the shadowed images of the couple dining in the foreground overlooking the panorama through an expansive window, it was indeed my masterpiece. I couldn't add anything else to make it better. That was the key to good art, good cooking, or good anything. Knowing when it's done. And then stopping.

After signing it, I pushed my scaffold away from the wall and climbed up again. From my perch, I gasped. This was beautiful. I couldn't even begin to do any false modesty here. The mural was gorgeous.

I had finished it two weeks ahead of schedule. Yes, I'd stayed late on some evenings because I was in the zone, but still. This should have taken longer. This painting was a reflection of my soul. I still hated doing murals, but I certainly couldn't hate this. Once I finished the protective coating, it would showcase the best of my skills.

I couldn't wait for Rogan to see it.

Walking out of the VIP dining room and across the open area to the lobby, I saw Justin Crews chatting with the students applying the finishing touches on the *Welcome to Rogan's* illustration. He looked up at me and smiled in greeting.

"Is everything okay?" he asked. I nodded and motioned for him to follow me. We walked into the VIP dining room, and I asked him what he thought of the painting.

Happily, he was thunderstruck. His mouth dropped open and his eyes bugged out.

"*This* is what you've been working on?"

"Yes. This is why you haven't been able to get into the dining room. You can in a couple of days after I've applied protectant and it's had time to cure. But what do you think of the painting?"

"Fuck!" he exclaimed. "This is awesome!"

"Thank you," I replied and smiled at him. At this moment, I didn't even hate him anymore. Even though I'd ultimately lost the hard hat battle and had to wear one anyway. PLUS a visibility vest.

Fucking lawyers.

"You're welcome," he said with a smile. He looked at me and hesitated for a moment before extending his hand. "Truce?"

I laughed as I took his hand and shook it. "Truce!"

"I don't know how people will be able to sit in here and just eat," he commented. "There's so much to see! This will take you away from the food and bring you into the soul of Las Vegas. I hope I don't sound like a simp, but this is spectacular. I'll be bringing a date here."

"I need 48 hours for the paint to cure before I add two layers of protectant," I told him. "After the weekend, it will be finished."

Justin, aka Captain America, smiled at me in approval. "This puts us ahead of schedule, and that's all good."

"I have to contact Rogan," I said to him, grabbing my phone from my back pocket. "He hasn't been here to see the mural in quite a while. I hope he'll be as impressed as we are," I chuckled.

Justin nodded. We smiled at each other, genuinely this time, and shook hands again. We'd never be homies, but at least I didn't hate him anymore. Justin then snagged his phone, which had beeped. "Gotta take this," he said as he put the phone to his ear and walked out.

I took a deep breath and texted Rogan.

I'm at the restaurant. Please come. Now, if possible.

Rogan and Mama were busy with staff. They were training, creating menus, cooking, tasting, and all the other stuff you have to do to launch a successful restaurant. Rogan and I had spoken maybe three times in the last four weeks and texted nearly every day. Mostly along the lines of "how ya doin'?" and not much else.

I'll be right there. Give me 20-ish.

Good.

I'll be in the break room.

I went into the staff break room, removed the helmet and sock, and shook out my locs. Next, I shed the visibility vest and sat down to eat the peanut butter and jelly sandwich I'd prepared in the morning. I hadn't been eating and figured it was quick and easy enough to hold me over until dinner. I drank a bottle of water and stretched out a bit. While I was musing, Rogan came into the room and sat on the chair across the table from me. Wow. That was quick.

"What's up?"

I smiled at him and replied, "Boy, do I have a surprise for you!"

I balled up the pb & j-stained paper and threw it into the bin. We both walked out of the staff room into the restaurant. We went into the VIP dining room, and I gestured toward the mural. I looked at him closely and was very happy with what I saw. He was, as the British say, gobsmacked. His mouth flew open and stayed there.

He sauntered to the mural, one hand on his face at first before he put both into his front pants pockets. He examined the details, and when he reached out to touch it, I yelled at him.

"Don't touch it yet! It's not cured."

"Did it have a disease?"

I laughed. "I just finished the last stroke less than an hour ago," I explained. "Some of it will still be tacky. I'll need a few days for the paint to cure before I add the archival sealant. And a couple of days after that before it's safe to be around the painting. Then, after the weekend, it'll be fine. Just not now. I already told Justin."

"You finished early. Way early."

I nodded. "Yeah, I know." I pondered for a minute and then looked up at him. "I can't explain it, Rogie. It just flowed. It was like I didn't even have to think about where to place the paint. Where to place the stroke or the color. Everything just fell into place. This mural painted itself. I was just the catalyst. I've never had anything like this happen before."

He turned to look at me.

"It almost felt as though someone or something else was using me as a conduit, even though everything was my idea." I shrugged again.

"I feel like I just robbed you," Rogan stated, eyes clear and bright as he gazed at me. "I've really been into your work for the last few weeks, and I swear that this is the best you've ever done. Maybe it's because I'm a Las Vegan, and the painting touches me in a way that it wouldn't if I were from, say, Dubuque, but that doesn't matter."

He took my right hand and placed it on his heart. "I feel you."

I lost my breath for a hot minute.

"Now I have to put cones around it to make sure nobody comes in and starts putting their nasty fingerprints all over it. I'll be back in a couple days to roll on the first coats of sealant. I'm sleeping in tomorrow!"

Rogan smiled. "I have a couple of things to ask you."

"Yeah?"

"One, why don't you stop by one of our staff training sessions? We're currently at an events company whose kitchen is similar to ours, and we're paying for the use of the facilities. Just stop by to see what we do."

I nodded. "That would be fun! And what's the other thing?"

"Remember when you said that you'd like to go out and have some mindless fun?"

I nodded and felt my face warm a little. If I recall correctly, that was when Rogan and I had our first kiss.

"Then let's go out. Maybe dinner and a club? Reserve a table and bottle service? You invite Daria, and I'll invite Derrick, and the four of us can dance till we can't move."

I laughed. "Yes! That sounds great! That also means that I'll have to wear something besides jeans, won't it?"

"Yeah, I think so. But don't go crazy. Just wear something that's not a t-shirt and jeans. Or sweats. Let's plan on something during the next week or so, and that'll give me time to put everything in place. I know people who know people." He gave me a conspiratorial wink. "You'll have the time of your life. I promise."

I playfully scowled at him over the jeans and sweats comments but agreed. I'd told him I wanted to have some mindless fun and going out clubbing with friends sounded like a good way to start.

"Okay," I replied. "I'm game."

ONE WEEK LATER

After I finished the last coat of sealant, I turned the mural over to Rogan, who was ecstatic over the results. Unsurprisingly, he was also over the moon about the others. The *Welcome to Rogan's* lettering in the lobby had been completed at about the same time as the primary mural. The students and I put the final touches on the Art Deco bar painting, which had a smoky bar slash romantic drinks vibe.

I hadn't seen Rogan since he'd given approval of the murals. And that was just fine. I felt I needed some distance while I tried to sort out my feelings. I simply texted him when each of the other paintings was done.

Tonight, however, we were going to go out to some random nightclub to just have fun. And I was more than prepared.

I seldom wear makeup other than lip gloss. I was blessed with good skin and naturally thick lashes, so I don't need to compensate for anything lacking. Plus, since I work in solitude, who would I be trying to impress?

Just because I never wore makeup didn't mean that I didn't know how to use it. After all, my grandparents and Mom had been successful photography and runway models. Grams and Mom both taught (brainwashed) me how to use makeup. Plus, with Mom's makeup and personal products company, I sure as hell better know how to use it. I'd be disowned if I looked like something from a clown car.

After showering, I spritzed on a little Aromatics cologne. I figured while it wouldn't make much difference in a nightclub, it was still worth the effort.

With my locs tied up out of the way, I began my transformation. Naturally, I used Mom's products. I used a bronzer on my cheeks and applied smoky eye makeup. I started with my eyebrows, giving a little additional arch using a microblading brush. The eyeliner and mascara were black, and the eye shadow deep charcoal. The shadow had to be used carefully to make my eyes look sexy, not like I was in the first stages of a zombie transformation. Finally, I used a touch of silver frost to bring out the gray of my eyes. Several coats of mascara later, and my makeup was complete. Yeah. He'd be stunned.

One reason I'd opted to wear dreadlocks instead of natural, straightened, or weave hairdos was because of the ease of care. Locs could be challenging now and then, especially when soaking wet. It was a price. For tonight, I'd already figured out how I wanted to style them. I took a few strands from around my hairline and pulled them up into a ponytail, leaving the rest of the locs free. I carefully pinned the ponytail into a small bun at my crown. I clipped some brass filigree cuffs on a few strands to cascade over one shoulder. The rest I let drape down my back.

I slid into rose-gold metallic Helmut Long leggings, which I pulled up over my new Victoria's Secret thong. Uncomfortable but necessary. Regular dainties weren't practical because panty lines would be gauche. The leggings' shimmery metallic fabric almost looked as if someone had painted the color on my legs. I slipped the creamy silk Ramy Brooks halter top over my head and let it drape over my hips. The low-cut V-neck of the halter top teased the view of my small mounds, and my back was completely bare. I slipped on a couple of my beaded gold bangles and rings, a chunky gold necklace, and dangling gold hoops. A pair of Jimmy Choo wedge sandals completed the look.

I stood in front of the full-length mirror, giving myself a critical once-over, the way Mom had taught me before she threw her hands in the air over her bohemian tomboy daughter. She'd despaired that I'd ever have even a touch of femininity. I took a picture of myself in the mirror and sent it to her. She'd probably faint.

The woman looking back at me in the mirror was tall, sexy, and had a set of legs and an ass that just wouldn't quit. I adjusted the front of the silk halter top to ensure a random nipple wouldn't expose itself. This top was made for someone who was more endowed than I was, but I could still rock it. I nodded in satisfaction. If he reacted the way I thought he would, all of this would be worth it.

I do clean up well, thank you very much.

The doorbell rang, and I heard Daria's voice drifting down the hall in greeting, followed by the deep timbre of the men's voices. It was time. This was literally the first time Rogan would see me dressed up in something other than jeans, t-shirts, cargo shorts, sweats, or anything boho. I hope he likes it.

I took a deep breath, grabbed my small sparkly clutch, opened my bedroom door, and stepped into the hallway.

This was it.

Chapter 16

Rogan

EVERY TRAINING SESSION TO prepare for opening a high-end restaurant is, essentially, a dress rehearsal. Mama and I worked side by side while training our sous chefs, chefs de partie, garde mangers, pastry cook/bakers, multiple commis, and the rest of the BOH staff on *Rogan's* processes. Despite her arguments to the contrary, eventually I wanted Mama to return to her consultations, which were her paying jobs. However, she refused to allow me to pay her for her time. I yelled (sort of yelled) at her to please take my money, but she'd just smile at me and pat my cheek.

Nevertheless, I wanted to hire a Chef du Cuisine slash Head Chef to take some of the load from her so she could do what she loves. Even if it means staying with me, I guess.

Sigh.

But tonight, anything related to the kitchen was far from my mind. I'd be going out with friends, Robbie included. Although she's not just a friend, I had yet to figure out where she was in my life outside of my fantasies. And tonight, we were going to have mindless fun at a nightclub. Robbie had mentioned a few months ago that for once, she wanted to have some fun just because.

I had driven the Range Rover over to Robbie's, and we would take a Lyft Lux from there. That would allow us to have fun without worrying about a pain-in-the-ass DUI. I parked under the porte cochère, and Derrick and I strode up the walkway. I wore a white, long-sleeved Zegna dress shirt untucked, Burberry black dress slacks, and black Johnston & Murphy Winston Moc slip-ons. I had slicked my hair back into a low ponytail. Derrick was similarly dressed, *sans* ponytail, of course, but somehow looked sharper. How was that possible?

Daria opened the front door just as we arrived, and Derrick and I both whistled. She was dressed in a blood-red, off-the-shoulder bodycon dress with matching stiletto sandals. Her lush figure was, as the girls say, bangin'. Her tapered natural hairstyle now showed geometric lines sculpted around her nape. Large gold hoops in her ears and a rhinestone choker completed the picture. Derrick and I both admired the stunning view.

"*Shit*, girl," Derrick smiled. "Hot."

Daria laughed, her dark eyes lighting up at the compliment.

"You're looking pretty good yourself, sir," she replied. "You clean up well!"

We all laughed as we headed to the kitchen.

I'd introduced the two of them when Derrick and I went to our favorite bar close to *Rogan's*. She and Robbie stopped by after they'd finished a day of errands (code for shopping). The two had hit it off, with Derrick using his signature overly baritone voice to impress her. Because Daria was a lot like her friend, she'd tilted her head slightly to give him a *really dude?* look, rolled her eyes, and we'd all laughed. This evening would be their first date. More or less chaperoned, I guess.

"Where's Rob?" I asked. I was eager to see her. I figured that she'd wear her signature bohemian style but would make it sexy.

"She'll be out in a minute," Daria replied with an inscrutable smile and a wink. "She's finishing up her ensemble and makeup."

We heard a door open down Robbie's hallway and waited for her to appear. She turned the corner from the hallway, and we all went silent.

Is it possible to have your mouth go bone dry *and* drool buckets at the same time?

While we were all gaping at her, she strutted toward us in perfect runway style. Painted-on, shimmery leggings showed off every curve of her long, toned legs from her shapely calves to her curvy thighs, the feminine swell of her hips, and the perfect globes of her ass. She put one hand on a hip and slowly twirled around before lifting her head alluringly.

She radiated pure sex. The sultry looks she gave me, along with a hidden smile through softly parted lips, had my cock growing like a titanium tree inside of my slacks. I felt my face heat up.

"*Fuuuuck!*"

Three sets of eyes turned to look at me in amusement. Had I said that out loud?

"Can I get anyone something to drink while we're waiting for our ride?"

I blinked out of my stupor and looked at Daria.

"You knew I'd lose my mind, didn't you?" Daria laughed in delight and nodded.

"We both wanted to make sure that you'd see her in a different light. I think it worked!"

You know that thing where you're supposed to lose your hard-on when you get embarrassed? Yeah, well, *no*. Although I knew my face was probably glowing red, my cock was greedy and begging for Robbie. And showed no signs of receding. I was glad my shirt was an untucked style. I would have been even more embarrassed than I already was.

"Yeah, I need a drink."

I reached for Robbie, and she came into my arms and gently kissed the hollow of my neck. I inhaled her sexy, exotic cologne. This was not going to be an easy night. If circumstances were different, I'd tell Derrick and Daria to go ahead and take the Lyft, have fun, it's all on me, and then I'd drag Robbie to her bedroom so that I could sink inside of her sweet heat.

Let me be first and I'll be gentle.

Robbie and I stood there in one spot, holding each other, smiling into one another's eyes. This succubus in front of me was taking me apart, molecule by molecule, and she didn't even know it. Just by breathing, she was branding me as hers.

Then she patted my cheek and went into the kitchen to help Daria serve up four Nick and Nora martinis.

"Who are you, and what have you done with my Robbie?" I asked when she handed me my drink. Silvery eyes, surrounded by smoke, sparkled at me fondly.

"Welcome to Robbie 2.0," she answered huskily, smiling. She reached up and brushed her lips against mine, wiped off the lipstick she'd left, then demurely smiled as she sipped her drink.

Derrick spoke up while looking at his cell. "The Lyft will be here in four minutes," he declared. "Let's get ready to roll."

Chapter 17

Rogan

I DON'T LIKE STANDING in lines if I don't have to. The four of us walked to the front of the "hopeful" line, which snaked almost to the casino floor. The beefy security guy, who was at least four inches taller than my six-three height and at least double my weight, greeted us. His short blond hair was slicked back over his broad skull, and although his facial expression was steely, his bright blue eyes turned friendly when he spotted me.

"Rogan," he nodded as we shook hands. "Tiny," I nodded back, wondering how the massive Bulgarian got his nickname. Even though he had nothing to do with the reservations I'd made, I slipped a Benjamin into his palm. It's the Vegas way.

We entered the glass elevator that would take us to the roof of the Vegas Strip's newest casino, *The Obsidian*. Its flashy rooftop nightclub, *Noire*, had already garnered wide international acclaim. Its design and focus were targeted toward a more mature, over 25 crowd who, theoretically, would know how not to be stupid in public. That remained to be seen.

The mind-blowing sight of Vegas neon spread like a twinkling carpet below us as we shot upward. Robbie's eyes were enormous, and she looked like a kid seeing a Christmas tree for the first time. I felt like a hero.

The host greeted us and led us to the booth I'd reserved for the evening.

Make no mistake. Nightclub table service in Vegas is not cheap. The closer you are to the DJ in the better clubs, the more it'll cost you, even up to a high five-figure amount. I believe in some places it's more, but I don't indulge enough to care. That eye-watering amount depends on the casino and the popularity of the nightclub. This type of table service is popular among attention-seeking celebrities. Because I wanted as little attention as possible, I opted to be above the dance floor far from the DJ. Which meant our table was a relative bargain price of $8,000.

Our location ensured we'd be able to converse in relative comfort and enjoy each other's company. We were still close enough to get to the dance floor easily if we desired but would not be interacting with the DJ or the crowd.

I had also reserved a bartender-server. This bartender was a flirty blonde. I'd requested security so that if we all wanted to go onto the dance floor, the ladies could safely leave their clutches. Or if the random Food Channel fan recognized me and wanted an autograph or to talk. Our security guy, Damyan, was much smaller than Tiny—who wasn't—and took his responsibilities seriously. I would compensate him well at the end of the evening.

I asked our bartender to serve Cristal Rosé Champagne. She brought the flutes to us and did not hesitate to display her cleavage to Derrick and me. After she winked at us and sashayed back to her service bar, I excused myself and went over to her. Her eyes widened and warmed at my approach, and her smile curved upward.

I smiled back and extended my hand, which she grasped and held onto lingeringly, flirting with me under long false lashes.

"Hi..."

"Cassie," she answered breathlessly.

"Look, Cassie," I said to her. "Do you see that beautiful black woman who's sitting next to me?"

Cassie nodded, eyes wide.

"Well, she's my lady. I'm not interested in making any other 'acquaintances.' She's mine and I'm hers. While I appreciate that your flirting would be fun if I were single, I'm not. So I want to cut this before she decides she's had enough and snatches your face off. *Capishe?*"

Cassie's eyes got even wider if that was possible. I saw her cut a quick glance at my bare ring finger, and the wheels started turning in her head.

"Don't even think it," I interjected, my voice now cold. "If you don't conduct yourself professionally, I'll have you replaced by someone who will. I won't disrespect my lady for anyone."

I sent her a humorless smile. "I hope that we have an understanding."

Cassie, obviously disappointed and a little flustered over her lapse in protocol, nodded again.

"Good."

I returned to my seat next to Robbie and took her hand and kissed it.

"What was that about?" she inquired, shooting a lethal glare in Cassie's direction.

"I had to let her know I didn't appreciate the fact that she seemed to think I'd disrespect you by flirting with her. So I told her to cut it out, or I'd have her replaced."

She reached one ringed hand to my cheek, eyes softening. "Thank you."

Suddenly, the DJ's scream of "Old School Disco!" and the beginning chords of Trammps' "Disco Inferno" had both Robbie and Daria shrieking. The crowd started jumping with enthusiasm, and the next thing I knew, I was being dragged to the dance floor.

Mesmerizing.

Robbie moved like her body was liquid, her motions fluid and supple. She spun as I held her hand and let her twirl. I brought her body against mine as we rocked disco-style to the music. The song went immediately to "Hot Stuff" and then into "Don't Stop Till You Get Enough." We never let go of each other, our hands clasped as we danced to the music. Next, the DJ launched into a set of *Saturday Night Fever* tunes from the movie, and we did the *Saturday Night Fever* disco thing, hips gyrating while we laughed. I will readily admit to not being the best dancer in the world, much to my Spanish mother's shame, but Robbie somehow made me better.

After dancing to several other songs, the DJ ended the disco set with "Love to Love You Baby" by Donna Summer, and we brought our bodies together in a sensual beat. Ultimately, I couldn't help myself. I leaned over, stroking her sweat-dampened back, and caught her lips in mine. Her arms went around my neck as she welcomed my kiss. Our tongues dueled with each other, igniting fire. We slowed our dancing to almost nothing while our kiss deepened even more. Right there. On the dance floor. We finally ended the kiss, our eyes never leaving each other.

Let me be first and I'll be gentle.

The DJ changed up the beat to Electronic Dance Music, which blasted through the enthusiastic crowd who roared in approval, and we retired to our booth, laughing. We glimpsed Derrick and Daria, still dancing and laughing together.

This was a damn good DJ. One of the best I've seen work. The music was good, and he kept the crowd entertained and engaged. He wasn't afraid to play old-school music, which had even more people dancing and laughing. I'd have to follow up later and get his information. You never know when you might need someone competent for an event in the hospitality industry. Especially in Vegas, where wannabes were everywhere.

After a few songs, I saw Derrick and Daria making their way back to our table, and I nudged Robbie. She raised an eyebrow when she saw them walking hand in hand. Hm. Maybe my dude is smitten. I waved over to Cassie and asked her to keep the Champagne flowing. She nodded at me, flirtation-free, and began pouring when Derrick and Daria sat down.

"I have to use the restroom," Robbie whispered in my ear. She looked around me at Daria and quirked her head. Daria nodded back, grabbed her clutch, and they both walked off together.

"How in the hell do they do that?" I asked Derrick, who snorted with laughter.

"You mean the silent group bathroom break code thing?"

I laughed back. "Yeah. That's the one."

"Hell if I know!" he chuckled.

After what felt like hours later, I watched as our ladies made their way back to our booth. A hand shot out and grasped Robbie's arm, stopping her in her tracks. An older man of indistinguishable ethnicity looked her up and down and began talking to her. She frowned, shook her head, and then attempted to pull her arm from his grasp. As if to emphasize his interest, he held on and grabbed her other arm to bring her body closer to his.

Rage, seething and hot, coursed through me, and I rose to address the issue. I realized as I got closer to the struggling pair that he was drunk.

"Let go of me before I hurt you!" Robbie cried, her voice lost in the din. She didn't sound like a frightened woman, but like someone who was giving a don't-fuck-with-me warning.

The man laughed lecherously, his eyes still glittering over her slender form. "And just what can a pretty thing like you do to me?"

In real life, with just about any other woman, he would have had a point. He was a big man, and it took little effort to hold her. I noticed people were moving away from the wrestling match, and I hoped to make it in time. For his sake.

Uh oh. Too late.

A yowl of pain, and the man dropped to his knees, releasing Robbie's arms and cupping his groin. Then Robbie grabbed his head and kneed him in the face, which jerked his head back as he hit the floor, nose gushing blood. One final blow to his midsection tore a gurgled shriek from him, and she was done just as Damyan, Derrick, and I arrived.

"Pushy motherfucker!" she snarled through gritted teeth, leaning over his moaning body. "I told you to leave me the hell alone!"

Security rushed in through the crowd, and the witnesses began telling them what happened. Mostly in tones of admiration. I was still boiling, as enraged as I've ever been in my life. Robbie had imprints on her arms where he'd grabbed her, and I wanted to stomp on the fucker. But he had his own set of problems now.

A couple of floor managers came over to us to take a report, noted the marks on Robbie's arms, and took our names and contact information.

Oh, and the music and dancing never stopped. What happened with Robbie was just a microcosm of activity and brought little attention to that corner of the club. That made me happy because I was hoping to continue our evening. And, surprisingly, so was Robbie. As a trained martial artist, she wouldn't let this incident disturb her focus for the night. I increasingly hoped her focus would include me.

When we returned to our booth and began talking, I noticed Cassie in my peripheral vision. She was looking at Robbie with something resembling terror. Good. Now she understood why I told her to back the hell off. My woman brooked no nonsense and no disrespect.

Derrick leaned over and looked at Robbie.

"Girl, *what*?"

Robbie laughed; her anger dissipated. "Krav Maga," she answered. "I'm not quite a black belt, but all I have to do is to test. I warned him, and he didn't listen. I was just trying to get back to my guy here," she smiled as she patted my thigh.

My guy.

I kissed her, just barely skimming my lips on her cheek. She laid her head on my shoulder and nestled into my body with a sigh.

Let me be first and I'll be gentle.

I need her. We have to decide what our next step will be and how we're going to move forward. I want her badly.

Virgin or not.

Chapter 18

Robbie

SEVERAL HOURS AFTER THE kneeing event, we left *Noire* and took the glass elevator down to *The Obsidian's* casino floor.

Rogan generously tipped our wide-eyed bartender and the security guy before we left. We talked to club security, who had helped the guy I'd temporarily disabled. They told us he'd been hitting on women for a couple of hours and was continually rebuffed. He was on probation, more or less, and had been warned to behave himself before he got ejected. Apparently, he'd decided that I was "the one," and of all the women in the place, I was his worst possible choice. Unfortunately for him, my reaction to his pulling me close to his body and ignoring my "no" had not gone well for his genitals or his face. I'd put him down in about five seconds and stepped right into Rogan's arms. He and the security guy appeared just as I'd given the bastard a final punch in the gut. Rogan's face had been a raging mask of pure fury.

I'd gotten pats on my back and murmurs of admiration from several women, and men looked at me askance. Good. Leave me the hell alone.

I sat snuggled close to Rogan for about half an hour before feeling relaxed enough to dance again. The four of us went to the dance floor, and I rid myself of any lingering stress. Along with the EDM, hip-hop, and old-school dance music that had people jumping, the DJ began spinning several versions of "Cha Cha Slide," and Daria and I screamed as we jumped into the group to dance. Both Rogan and Derrick begged off while Daria and I Cha

Cha slid with a group on the dance floor. We hopped, stomped, took it back, turned it out, Charlie Brown'd, and got funky with it.

I'd learned how to do the Cha Cha Slide in Philly when Daria tried to get me out to loosen up a bit and to teach me some street smarts. Which, as the overprotected prodigy in a crazy family, I was very sadly lacking. She also taught me street slang and the proper use of a large variety of cuss words. I'd had a blast with the lessons. With some fake ID and enough makeup to make me look plausible at the nightclubs even at 18, I learned a lot. I was forever indebted to her.

The DJ changed up into a slow music set, and Daria and I returned to our table, laughing and sweaty. I looked at Rogan as I slid into the booth, and he wore an inscrutable expression.

"What?"

He said nothing but kissed my bare shoulder. Our eyes locked, and I could see the heat rise in his. He licked the damp skin, and the heat turned into an inferno. He closed his eyes as he kissed my shoulder again. A couple of beats, and when he opened his eyes, the heat had been tamed. Not cooled. Just slightly banked. And, just like that, my leggings were drenched.

Derrick looked at his watch and leaned over to whisper something to Rogan. Rogan looked at his own watch and nodded.

"It's almost 2:00 a.m. Ready to go?"

I nodded and looked over at Daria. "Let's bounce!" she cheered.

We left *The Obsidian* and headed to the rideshare area where our Lyft Lux was waiting for us.

When we arrived home, we went into the house, exhausted and happy.

"Anyone want a snack or some coffee?" I asked. Everyone mumbled in the affirmative, and I went to the fridge to grab a container of half and half for the coffee and a snack tray that I'd prepared earlier in the afternoon. I started the coffee and then excused myself to get comfortable. I'm pretty sure Rogan was hoping for more, but tonight would not be his night.

It took me about five minutes to put my hair into a regular ponytail, scrub off most of the makeup, put on a t-shirt, and put my aching feet into my comfy bedroom socks. I still wore the leggings since they were comfortable. Besides, I didn't want anyone to feel awkward because I'd changed into scruffies while they were still in their party clothes.

When I returned to the kitchen, the coffee was ready, and everyone was around the breakfast table, snacking and laughing.

When Rogan saw me return, his face softened. I'd fully expected a look of disappointment since I was closer to my everyday look, but that wasn't the case at all. Instead, he warmed to the familiar me.

I opened a cabinet, grabbed a tray, and set it with four coffee mugs, the coffee carafe, and a bowl of sugar along with the half and half and some spoons. I brought it to the table and sat between Rogan and Daria.

"It was worth it," Rogan was saying. "Every single minute. From the table, to the dancing, to the drinks, to the castration attempt. It was worth it."

We all burst out laughing. "You so crazy," Daria laughed.

After about an hour, fatigue hit me like a bomb. I must have looked pretty bad, because Rogan smiled at me before he nodded at Derrick. It was time for the guys to go. Rogan tossed his fob to Derrick. "Give me a couple of minutes."

Rogan took me aside into the living room.

"I want to spend time with you," he said, restating what he'd requested weeks ago. "I can find some time for us if you'll have me," he continued. "I know this is a big deal for you, but believe it or not, it's a big deal for me, too. I can't explain the feelings here," he continued as he patted his chest, "but I know I can't let it go by."

He stopped long enough to press his lips against my forehead. His arms wrapped around me and pulled me to his muscular body. I wrapped my arms around him and reveled in the feeling.

"Okay," I replied. "I think it's something we need to talk about."

"I gotta get Derrick home," Rogan murmured in my ear. "Let's talk in a couple of weeks. Will that be okay? I still have a lot to supervise and a TV interview slash demo in a few days. I'm still swamped."

I nodded. I couldn't read the emotions that chased over his face. He kissed me lightly on the lips and headed toward the front door. I followed him as Derrick met him from the kitchen, where he'd been talking to Daria.

After the guys left, Daria looked at me speculatively.

"Just friends?"

"Oh shut up," I retorted, but couldn't hide the grin. "He wants to be more than friends, I'm sure," I continued.

"No shit," she replied. "Rogan did everything but mount you on the dance floor. And that kiss y'all had hardly looked 'friendly.' I was fanning my face lookin' at that one. Ooo chile!"

I laughed. "Tonight was a one-off. When he's not so swamped, we're going to be talking about what comes next in our friendship. Or whatever this is."

Daria gave me a quick hug and a speculative smile before she trudged down the hall, stilettos in hand, to her own room.

I washed the mugs and carafe, and after wiping down the table, cut the lights as I made my way to my room. I undressed and padded to the bathroom to take a shower to remove nightclub funk from my body. Frowning, I rubbed the bruise on my arm where the creep had grabbed me and wouldn't let go. And then smiled because I'd forced him to.

After I got out of the shower and dried off, I donned my sleep bonnet and crawled under my sheets, naked. I never slept naked, but it seemed to fit tonight. The touch of pajamas on my skin was too much for me when the reality of making love to Rogan was so close.

Chapter 19

Rogan

I SMILED POLITELY AT the two women on either side of me in the TV studio kitchen. An electric burner and a few ingredients for whipping up a quick dish or two to showcase some recipes from *Rogan's: An American Bistro's* menu sat on the countertop. A makeshift oven was behind us with a dish ready to serve. I'd arrived earlier to do some prep work and precooking ahead of going on air. I had also brought some items that were mostly ready to serve. All I had to do is to put on the demonstration.

The improvised kitchen was ready and stocked with the food items I'd be using. Two young lifestyle reporters flanked me while we waited for the director to give us our cues.

"Rogan," greeted the young black woman to my right, "I'm Natalia and so happy to meet you." I smiled in response as we shook hands. She was about five-six and wore a long weave. She had milk chocolate skin and sported the requisite layers of studio makeup. Natalia seemed to be genuinely pleasant and excited about our upcoming cooking demo.

"I'm happy to meet you, too. I'm Abby," smiled the blonde to my right. She was about the same height as Natalia, and her hair was sprayed beyond movement. She, too, wore layers of studio makeup.

"You're becoming quite a celebrity," Abby gushed. She moved almost imperceptibly closer to me, invading my space, smiling flirtatiously.

I didn't move from my spot but gave her a look that took my warmth down a degree or two. I knew what she was doing. But after reconnecting with Robbie again, I was uninterested in Abby or her flirtation. My abrupt coolness caused her cheeks to flush as she stepped out of my space.

I'm used to being in front of the camera. After being a judge on *Chopped*, beating Bobby Flay, and triumphing on Top Chef, I'd grown adept at ignoring cameras and the people around them. So I was happy to do a little public relations push for *Rogan's* to local news stations. The excitement of this venture was buzzing through the culinary cognoscenti of Las Vegas. This news interview was designed to both market the restaurant and foment temptation. It was one of the last planned promotional pushes before focusing on the job of the grand opening.

Danny, the director, stood in front of us to get our attention. He was young and rail-thin, with wild, curly dark hair and thick "Poindexter" glasses. "Don't forget that we have to do this in about four minutes with not much flex. And we start in five...four...three...two...one." He pointed at us, and we began.

After introducing me and giving a ten-second spiel on the restaurant, the interview began.

"What made you decide to open a restaurant in Vegas?" asked Abby, the blonde.

"Homesickness," I answered. "Believe it or not, it's as simple as that. Except for mosquitos the size of small helicopters and air humid enough to swim through, Florida was wonderful, but it wasn't home." I gave her what I hoped was a perfect PR smile and began to put together the ingredients for my macaroni and cheese dish. "So when I sold my restaurant interests in Tampa, South Beach, and Miami, I took the first thing smoking back to Vegas."

"Why did you name your restaurant *Rogan's: An American Bistro*?" asked Natalia.

"Well," I quipped, "I couldn't very well name it *McDonald's*, now could I?" Both women laughed with me. "I have to thank my friend Rob for the idea. The feeling was that our original name was a little too stiff. We were looking for something unique and warm. Like me!"

More laughter.

"*Rogan's* focuses on classic American dishes, with some surprises thrown in. I call it American Plus. For instance, I use six kinds of cheese in one of our favorite mac and cheese offerings," I continued. "Cheddar, Gruyere, Fontina, Feta, Eastern European Farmer's cheese, and a special secret ingredient."

"What's the secret ingredient?" asked Natalia.

"Well, if I tell you, it won't be a secret anymore, would it?" I quipped as I mixed the roux with pre-measured bowls of various shredded cheeses. "But if you must know, it's Velveeta."

Both reporters lifted their upper lips in a disgusted sneer.

"Velveeta!?" they chorused in horror.

I laughed at their scandalized expressions. "Don't knock it till you taste it!"

Natalia remarked after squinting suspiciously into my pot, "I noticed you don't smoke. Every chef I know smokes. Why don't you?"

"I've played soccer since I was a toddler, thanks to my European parents. I was an athlete through high school and college. In fact, I received an athletic scholarship from UNLV. You can't be a smoker and expect to be a successful athlete. A year in MLS showed me that smoking was a horrible idea because I saw its effects on teammates. Any professional athlete who smokes is asking for big trouble and a very short career.

"Plus," I shrugged, "I was never interested in starting the habit. I like my tastebuds, and I firmly believe that smoking can damage your sense of taste and smell. That said, more younger chefs are non-smoking, so there's hope."

"What makes your mac and cheese better than homemade?" asked Abby.

I whisked the roux as I added the cheeses to make a thick, creamy mornay sauce. "Nothing's better than homemade," I responded, "but we have an advantage. We make our own pasta in-house using bronze die which make the pasta more textured, which allows the cheese to stick, and you never lose a single bit of flavor. Besides, we can make different shapes of pasta, not just macaroni.

"We can also get cheeses that are difficult or impossible for the home cook to find. That said, there's nothing better than a pan of good old-fashioned homemade mac and cheese!"

"Some would say that your mother's importance and visibility in the culinary world would give you an advantage in the Vegas marketplace," Abby stated.

"'Some' would be wrong," I replied. "I worked every position in the kitchen as a kid. Even when I finished culinary school from CIA in Napa, I started as a grunt, peeling carrots and potatoes despite my education and experience. When I returned to work at the family business and restaurants, my parents never handed anything to me. I had to earn my way up the ladder. I worked hard in other restaurants as well as the family's, and Mama's a hard taskmaster."

"CIA? Are you a secret agent or something?"

I laughed. "No, not that lucky. It stands for Culinary Institute of America. It stands head and shoulders along with Le Cordon Bleu, Julia Child's culinary alma mater."

"What's that you're doing here?" asked Natalia, watching as I added seasonings.

"I'm adding in some spices as well as one other secret ingredient."

"What would that be?"

"Nutmeg."

"Nutmeg?" asked Natalia. She and Abby looked at each other, mirroring surprised expressions. "Isn't that for pumpkin pie?"

"Nope. Adding nutmeg to the cheeses brings out their umami flavors. It makes this mac and cheese a perfect pairing with rich red wines, such as a Napa Cab or Washington Syrah. While some mac and cheese dishes are casual, I have a couple intended as standalones to pair with our finer wines. Our seasonal truffle mac and cheese, for instance, is designed to pair with some of our vintage Pinot Noirs from Oregon or Sonoma. And for those who don't drink wine, craft beers such as Porters or Stouts."

"Wow."

They both watched as I scraped the pasta and the mornay into a long pan.

"We serve five different styles of mac and cheese, and we design most of them for the adult palate. This particular one is a little nod toward childhood," I winked. They both laughed.

"So you've bought one of the most iconic restaurants in Vegas, and it's not on the Strip," said Abby. "What is it, and why did you do that?"

"*Chez Dionysius* owners were retiring, and I'd been lusting for a restaurant in that area for a long time. I jumped on it the nanosecond it went on the market, and now I'm renovating it. I didn't want a restaurant on the Strip because of what many casinos are charging for parking, resort fees, and other nickel-and-dime BS that I think is a disservice to customers. They're also charging ridiculous rents to the restaurants, which means they're operating on less than a shoestring budget.

"As a result, the prices of the meals are too high for people to afford. Especially locals. I mean, I guess it's okay when people are vacationing and have the disposable funds to overpay, but the locals are ripped off if they want a nice Strip dinner. I resent that. I want to make sure locals know they can come to a restaurant with Strip-level quality, reasonable prices, and still have a world-class experience. As a native, that's been my focus and my passion. I feel that locals and tourists alike who find *Rogan's* will love it."

I grinned as I prepared to take the pan to the oven. "Excuse my soapbox. And sorry about your advertisers."

Natalia opened the oven as I placed the pan inside. Then, I came back to the table for the lamb chops.

"I enjoy being innovative when it comes to lamb chops. I avoid clichés such as mint jelly. Although I don't know anyone who uses mint jelly nowadays, to be honest."

"So what do you use?" asked Abby.

"When I sous vide my racks of lamb, I add dried herbs and seasonings such as mint, pepper, coffee, and a few other secret things in the sous vide pouch, which make the chops an ideal pairing with Syrah or Cab. Or a good IPA."

I removed the rack from the sous vide bath where it had been immersed, cut open the vacuum-sealed bag, and strained the juices into a saucepan. I added a splash of Syrah into the pan and watched as it simmered.

"Always use the best wine you can afford for cooking," I said. "If you reduce a bad wine, you'll have concentrated nastiness."

I patted the rack of lamb dry and placed it into a hot cast iron pan for searing.

"You have to sear meat that's gone through sous vide," I chuckled as I worked. "Otherwise, it looks pretty unappetizing."

I placed the pan onto the shelf underneath the burners and brought out an already-finished dish where I had sliced the rack into perfect, medium-rare chops. I continued to answer their barrage of questions while I drizzled the wine sauce over the chops. Then, I gingerly removed a hot pan of mac and cheese from the oven. I scooped some onto the plate with the chops, added some vegetables I'd previously sautéed, and motioned to the women to taste.

"Oh my god," they chorused through mouthfuls of food. "This is so good!"

I nodded and smiled. I already knew that.

"Tell us something else about your restaurant that's unique," Natalia said, smiling at me. I liked her. She seemed genuine.

"The menu isn't fixed and will change according to the season and ingredient availability. We source from all over the local area. Of course, 'local' for Vegas means from here to Overton and Utah in the east and California to the west. With the occasional surprise, of course. We'll always have some things that are standard, such as bread, pasta, and beverages, but when you go on our website, you won't see a static menu, but a seasonal one."

"That sounds fascinating," Abby commented, "and like a lot of hard work."

I laughed. "It is. But when your mother is a world-respected chef and the head of your kitchen, the standards have to be high."

"And that's about it, everyone!" declared Abby, facing the camera. "Be sure to visit *Rogan's: An American Bistro* when it opens in just a few weeks! And don't forget to visit the KNNV website for more updates."

"And that's a wrap." Danny nodded toward us and smiled. "That was nearly perfect."

I smiled and rolled my shoulders. These TV news interviews were brief, intense, and necessary. I was pleased with how smoothly everything had gone, and, as expected, the food was spectacular. The studio staff would be ecstatic when they finished the leftovers.

After the lavalier mic was removed and I made my goodbyes, I packed my materials into my roller cart. Walking toward the Green Room, I pulled the chef's apron over my head. I preferred to wear an apron over my chef's jacket whenever possible. I felt that it allowed me to enjoy the give-and-take in the kitchen with the line staff. Besides, Mama would be wearing the executive chef jacket for the time being.

"Oh, Rogan!" Abby's chirpy voice brought me out of my reverie, and I turned to watch her trotting to catch up to me.

"I'm really impressed with you," she said invitingly. "Do you have someone special in your life?"

I immediately thought of Robbie, and our new, albeit delicate, more-than-just-friends fledgling relationship.

"Technically, no."

She brightened.

"But the potential is there with someone special," I continued, "and it's a relationship I want to pursue."

"Really. Are you open to talking to other potential 'relationships' in the interim?" she asked.

"No." My answer was curt and brooked no argument. I knew her type. Just like most fuckboys, I'd be little more than a notch on her "famous people I've slept with" bedpost. I would lose the opportunity to secure a relationship with the woman who had zero tolerance for any bullshit.

I stopped walking to look at her. Her eyes met mine, challenging and flirtatious.

"I'm not interested in one-night stands, friends with benefits, side chicks, or anything else. There is the potential for a once-in-a-lifetime relationship, and I won't fuck it up by fucking you." I gave her a mocking smile. "I think we're done here."

She was startled at my blunt response to her advances. I wasn't interested in pissing off Robbie because I was wishy-washy with some rando.

"Alrighty then," she said. She regarded me reflectively. "Well, if you find yourself without that once-in-a-lifetime coming to pass, just look me up." She looked around, encompassing the area where we were standing. "You know where I am." She winked, flipped blond hair over one shoulder, and turned on her heel to strut down the hall toward the studio.

I sighed, shook my head, and continued to the Green Room. There was still bullshit to take care of with my Hera situation. I don't need another insane woman in my life. And Abby radiated high maintenance loco. No thanks. I was done dipping my cock into crazy.

Chapter 20

Robbie

THE PHONE RANG ONCE. Twice. And unlike in the olden days when a ring was just a ring, a full symphony played instead. I reluctantly opened one eye and looked at my iPhone charging clock.

5:00 a.m.

A frisson of alarm shot through me. Who'd be calling at this hour? It can't be good.

I grabbed my phone and saw that Rogan was calling. What the hell?

"What?" I cranked when I answered the phone.

His deep chuckle rumbled into my ear. He was cheerful. I wasn't.

"Hi, sunshine! Wakey wakey!"

I hate cheerful and perky. Especially at o'dark thirty when the sun hadn't even made an appearance yet.

I snarked something rude into the phone, only to be greeted with more soft laughter.

It had been a few days since we last spoke, and I figured he was too busy to call. I wasn't upset, though. After finishing the mural and completing a couple of commissioned works for other clients, I was taking some needed time off to relax, refuel, and sleep in. With the emphasis on sleeping in. This meant that being awakened at 5:00 a.m. was not in the plans.

"I'd like to have you at the restaurant this morning," he was saying, interrupting my morning fog, "I'm doing the punch list, and I want your input."

Another groan and a curse. *What the hell is a punch list, anyway? I guess I'll find out.*

"I don't feel like it, but what time?"

"How soon can you be there?"

"Noon."

More laughter.

"Can you be there in about an hour? About 6:15?"

"No. More like 6:30. Maybe 6:45. I need a shower and coffee."

"That'll work. See you then. Wear work boots." He clicked off, and I glared at the phone. What the hell had just happened? I rubbed sleepy eyes. The temptation to just roll over and bury myself in my sheets and surrender to sleep was almost overwhelming. Instead, I forced myself to get up.

I plodded into the kitchen and started the coffee. Maybe I'd pick up a breakfast sandwich somewhere, but truthfully, I wasn't hungry. Instead, I poured a glass of OJ and took my morning vitamins. I headed back to my room to shower.

After showering and wanting to sleep while standing up, I toweled off and dressed in my usual jeans and t-shirt uniform. Because they'd gotten a little damp, I let my locs hang loose. I slipped on a pair of hikers. A slick of lip gloss, which I'd doubtless lose on my coffee cup, and I was done.

Back in the kitchen, I poured some coffee into my travel mug, pumped a shot of Torani caramel syrup and some half and half, and headed to the door.

A sleepy Daria was standing in the hallway, brows furrowed, eyes questioning.

"Rogan," I answered her unasked question. "If this isn't worth it, I hope you have bail money. I may need it," I groused.

Her expression softened in humor, and she waved as she trudged down the hall back to her room.

I yawned my way in the early morning light while I drove to the restaurant. I parked the van, grabbed my coffee, and walked toward the entrance, eyes widening in wonder. It'd been a minute since I was last here, and this was the first time seeing it without construction stanchions and warning tape. Rogan, Justin, and Paul stood at the entrance, the three of them grinning at my expression.

Bastards.

"This better be good," I grumped. "If not, Daria's scraping together bail money."

They laughed. Apparently, my early morning mood was comedy. I wasn't feeling it.

A white Mercedes C350 drove into the nearly empty parking lot, drawing our attention. Out of the driver's side, an older woman just a few inches shorter than me, stepped out, casting her eyes in our direction. She brightened when she saw me, and after locking the car, she rushed over to me and enveloped me in a big hug.

"Robbie!" she exclaimed excitedly in a slightly accented voice, "it's been such a long time since I've seen you! You are just as beautiful as ever!" This beautiful, friendly woman was Maria, Rogan's mother, and I'd only caught a glimpse of her a couple of times when I was working on the mural. She'd been in deep conversations with Rogan and the construction crews during the building phase, and we'd missed each other every time. I hadn't seen her at all once Rogan began staff training off-site.

I'd first met her during one of the times when Janina had taken me home when we attended Palo Mesa. Maria had thought I was adorable but skinny and always tried to feed me. Hey. She's a chef. Chefs feed people. I'd thought she was beautiful then, and my opinion hadn't changed one iota ten years later.

She was originally from Spain or Catalan—I know there's a difference, but I forget—and has a flawless olive complexion. Mama wears her incredibly glossy, silver-threaded dark hair medium-short with a signature headband, a la Susan Feniger, to keep the curls out of her face. Her eyes are large, friendly, honey-colored, and as clear and sparkling as amber. Her lips are full and always turned up into a smile. I hate the fact that they are naturally rosy. No lip gloss needed. Her teeth are white and even. Like Rogan, she's not a smoker, which probably explains her flawlessness, even at 50-something.

"Hi, Mama," I beamed. "I'm so glad to see you!"

I turned to Rogan. "Why are we here?"

"Punch list time," he replied. I looked at him blankly.

"This is the final inspection of the construction before we bring in the fixtures, furniture, and people," he explained. "After that, if everything is good, we'll start stocking the bar and the kitchen."

"So why am I here?" I crabbed. "I was asleep..."

Rogan's expression turned soft. "Because you're an integral part of some decisions that had to be made, and I wanted you here to see it in the raw. If there's anything you see that's out of place, I want your feedback."

He hesitated, looking at me thoughtfully. "You're a part of the soul of the restaurant, and I really need you here."

His explanation warmed me, flattery notwithstanding, and I removed homicide from my to-do list. Instead, I smiled at him warmly. "Thank you."

In my peripheral vision, I could see Mama looking at us speculatively and with an approving smile.

The three men had construction tablets of some sort, and they began the process. The first thing I noticed as we stood in front of the building was the large sign mounted on the wall to the right of the double door entrance. *Rogan's* was in the cursive font that Tommy, Rogan's graphic designer, and I had chosen. The sign background was a matte pewter-colored metal, which made the smooth, clean lines of the almost-golden brass script shine. *An American Bistro* was a sans serif, Art Deco-esque font in shining chrome. I nodded in approval because the sign had turned out so well.

The front doors were an ornate wrought iron design over heavy frosted glass. The doors looked like they weighed a ton. I was pleased to see that the doors were assistive, which were in keeping with ADA guidelines. Justin opened one of the doors for us with barely a touch, and I walked in, mouth agape.

You would have thought I hadn't even seen the inside of the restaurant before. And in a way, I hadn't. When I was working on the murals, I had tunnel vision after I began the project. I was focused and only saw the art. Once I was done, I hadn't returned. Most artists rarely follow their art once it's completed and sold, and I knew I would see it when I visited for dinner at some point. So today, I get to see it through fresh eyes.

The lobby was gorgeous, and the *Welcome to Rogan's* mural that the students had completed behind the hostess desk was beautiful. I looked at Rogan with a smirk. I'd told him the students would do a standout job, and they hadn't let me down. He winked at me in silent confirmation, and we continued.

I was in awe of the spacious dining room. To the left was the bar area, with a large, U-shaped bar. The back bar sported glass shelves, and bar-to-ceiling mirrors etched with the *Rogan's* logo.

To the far right, we entered the kitchen door. When Rogan bought out the business next door, it was to expand the kitchen into it. As a result, he had trebled the kitchen's original footprint. Justin, Paul, and I stood quietly while Mama and Rogan discussed everything in an interesting combination of Spanish and English.

We walked through the cavernous kitchen, peeked into the walk-in, and I drooled over the appliances. Too bad these weren't allowed in a home kitchen!

After exiting the kitchen, we walked through the double door on the window wall to the outside area, taking the concrete tiled steps down to the lakeside seating. There was a wine bar chiefly for the outdoor customers, which would make it easier for the servers. A miniature stage looked ready for a small jazz band. To the far left were the entrance doors to the banquet rooms. They weren't very large and were meant for smaller gatherings. *Rogan's* was, after all, located in a residential community.

We walked up the tiled steps back into the main restaurant, where Rogan gave me an odd, cryptic look. We all followed him as he took a hard right into the VIP dining room. I stumbled to a stop and gasped.

My mural stood out in almost bas relief, illuminated by gallery lighting, and it seemed to glow with an inner light of its own. I stood there, gaping at my own work when Mama gave me a warm hug.

"It's beautiful, *Mija*," she whispered to me.

Stupid me. I began crying. I was touched by the term of affection and the acknowledgment of my contribution to the building of such a beautiful restaurant.

Rogan smiled at me. He took me in his arms and just let me cry. Mama wrapped her arms around me, placing her head against mine.

"I contacted Doris at the gallery to help me with the lighting," Rogan murmured. "And she guided us to properly showcase this painting. It's beautiful, and now, with the lighting, we get to see just how beautiful it is."

He smiled down at me. "She loves the painting, by the way."

I ugly cried for a while, eventually dissolving into hiccups. Justin smiled at the three of us and left to get toilet paper from a restroom so that I could dab my eyes and blow my nose. I was overwhelmed with the beauty, not only of the painting but also of everything in the room.

Of the restaurant.

Of Mama.

Of Rogan.

Chapter 21

Rogan

PUNCH LIST DAY WAS pretty insane. More than I'd thought it would be, to be honest. With Justin, Paul, and I all being borderline OCD types, we picked out a few things that had been overlooked or ignored by a subcontractor or two. Thankfully, nothing major had to be addressed, but there would be a few phone calls to get everything right. We were running far ahead of schedule, so there was no panic.

Justin and Paul took care of assorted details while Mama and I drove off to training. The banquet facility that I'd rented had been more than adequate for our needs. The use of the kitchen had been invaluable, and both my trainees and the facility staff had been happy with the culinary results. Today, however, we wouldn't be using the kitchen. Instead, this was a sit-down training for both the front of house (FOH) and the back of house (BOH) staff. We'd be reviewing the procedures that would keep them out of trouble and me out of court.

The meeting was mandatory and had been arranged two weeks prior so staff could deal with any pain-in-the-ass scheduling conflicts. A simple roll call, and I was happy to see everyone was in attendance. Each person had brought his or her own employee manual. With the restaurant opening being just a few weeks away, the excitement level was high.

One hour later, after I'd gone over the things that mattered most to the restaurant, to me, and their interactions with customers and each other, Mama took the BOH folks into the kitchen to review appropriate procedures. Then, the

FOH consultant I'd hired, Maybelline *don't laugh because my mother named me after her favorite cosmetics* Wiggins, a lively, 30-something black woman with impeccable grooming and smiling brown eyes, took the service staff to another room for additional training. That I hired industry training professionals spoke to my high expectations for my very well-paid staff.

I stood up and stretched while the two women took over. After next weekend, we'd be at *Rogan's*, conducting on-site training, doing actual "dress rehearsals," and planning the grand opening.

Out of the corner of my eye, I saw a person sitting in the back of the large room, apart from everyone. My head whipped around when I realized it was Robbie. Where had she come from? She'd left shortly after the mural reveal, and because she'd crabbed at me for waking her up so early, I thought she'd gone home to take a nap.

"Hey Rob," I said affectionately as I grabbed a chair and straddled it in front of her. "What are you doing here?"

"Well," she began, "you invited me to see a staff training one day, and since I was already up," she scowled at me pointedly, "I thought I'd take you up on it. It looks like a lot of detailed work."

"It is," I agreed. "While some restaurants have successfully started on little more than a grill, some hope, and a spatula, this is next-level stuff."

"Do you wish that you'd gone the grill and spatula route?"

"Ask me after six months," I laughed, "and I'll let you know."

"We'll open a diner, and I'll be your waitress," she cackled. "I'll chew gum and call everybody 'Honey.'"

We laughed together, and I glanced at my watch. It was just about noon. I looked at Robbie and raised an eyebrow.

"Want to go to lunch? My treat."

"It's the least you can do after waking me up at the butt crack of dawn," she remarked dryly.

"Let's go to Maggiano's," I suggested. "It's quiet, and we can relax."

"I don't feel like Italian, at least not for lunch. Since I didn't have breakfast, I'm feeling like Phỏ. I'll meet you at my favorite place."

Thirty minutes later, we'd both been lucky to find parking in the restaurant's minuscule parking lot just off Spring Mountain. I looked askance at the old building and the squeaky double doors when we entered.

And then the mouth-watering aromas of herbs, aromatics, and spice hit me. The fragrance was almost heady. Since it was lunchtime, the little Vietnamese restaurant was busy. Steaming bowls of Phở were on nearly every table, and the air was full of the hum of voices. I also noticed we were just about the only non-Vietnamese people there. That's a great sign of good food.

In many venues, both on and off the Strip, I could flex a little influence simply by walking in. Getting the best seats was a given. That wasn't happening here. These people didn't know jack about me and couldn't care less. Robbie and I were just like everyone else as we waited our turn to be seated. An impossibly petite young Vietnamese woman beckoned us. She led us to a table by a window overlooking Spring Mountain and handed us menus. Perfect.

I was looking through the somewhat battered menu and noticed that Robbie had closed hers, and she'd folded her hands.

"You know what you want?"

She nodded.

"Then I'll have what you're having."

She laughed.

"I don't eat enough Vietnamese food to be all that familiar with it. We studied several Asian cultures' food in culinary school, but after that, I haven't dealt with it as much."

Robbie nodded and gave our orders to the young man, who collected the menus before departing.

"What are we getting?"

"One order of spring rolls which we'll split, beef Phở with tripe, tendon, brisket, raw beef, an extra side of tendon, and a pot of tea."

I nodded. Sounds delicious. I'm an offal kind of guy, and I was pleased that Robbie was, too.

"I want to spend time with you, Rob."

Her eyes met mine, and I sensed her inner turmoil.

"I'm hoping that you want to spend time with me, too," I continued.

"I do."

"We're getting close to opening *Rogan's*, and thanks to Mama, Paul, and Maybelline, I'll be able to take some time off. And because you finished the mural so early, I should be able to take off at least three days. Maybe more."

I stopped as our server placed a dish with two rice paper-wrapped spring rolls and a small bowl of peanut sauce on our table. He also set down two larger plates, one for each of us, of Thai basil, bean sprouts, jalapeño rings, green onions, lime wedges, and raw beef.

"Your Phở will be here soon," he stated in a slightly accented voice before walking away.

"I always use fingers."

Robbie picked up one of the spring rolls and dipped it into the peanut sauce. With their wrappers, the spring rolls looked like small translucent burritos filled with shrimp, strips of pork, lettuce, and noodles. I followed her lead and did the same with the other roll.

Delicious!

The rolls were small and I finished mine in about three bites. It was perfect timing because the server arrived with two fragrant bowls of Phở. He placed a separate saucer with extra tendon next to each of our bowls. A carrier with three small covered ceramic pots of various condiments completed the setting.

I followed Robbie's lead in preparing my Phở. Raw beef went in first to cook in the steaming, aromatic broth. Then the bean sprouts and the rest of the garnishes. Stir with chopsticks. Ladle soy sauce, hoisin sauce, or chili oil from one of the containers. Eat with chopsticks and a faux ceramic spoon. When we dug in, talking ceased. There wouldn't be any kind of conversation happening now.

About thirty minutes later, we were winding our way through the tables and out of the exit. I was fully satiated. I'd passed by this hole in the wall dozens of times but had never stopped in. Who knew!

We had parked our cars side by side when we arrived. Robbie stopped at my driver's side door and looked up at me, a little nervous.

"Come by the house. Let's talk then."

I nodded and took one of her hands in mine and kissed it. Then I gave her a hug and kissed her on her forehead.

"See you in a few."

She smiled and went to the other side of her van.

About fifteen minutes later, I parked under the porte cochère behind her Odyssey. I took a deep breath before walking up the brick path to her door. Like the first time I visited, she opened the door before I rang the bell.

I walked in and followed her to the kitchen. But instead of sitting on the barstools at the island as we usually did, she grabbed two wine glasses and a bottle of Pinot Noir. We went into the family room and I made myself comfortable on one of the loveseats. She connected her phone to her Bluetooth speakers and started playing some OG music. Stan Getz, I think. To my surprise, she sat close to me before pouring each of us a glass of wine.

I began the conversation. This was unfamiliar territory because I'd never been with someone who stoked my fire and emotions the way Robbie did. I was as nervous as she was.

"I want you," I murmured, after taking a sip of the Pinot. "And whatever it takes, and however long it takes, I want you to know how important you are to me. I think we're ready to spend time together. Even though our history is a little disjointed," I smiled, "there's still history, and I think we have feelings for each other, no matter how fledgling they are."

"I'm on vacation," Robbie replied. "Just taking a break from everything. That means that my calendar is free. So any time you have to spend with me, I can spend with you. But I have a few conditions."

"What are they?"

"We can't be here, on the Strip, or at your house."

"Okay. Why not?"

"Call me a pessimist, but if we made love here and then split up, I'd feel squicked out in my own home. I've worked hard to make this my zen space, my sanctuary. I think that if we broke up, there would be bad juju, and I'd lose my serenity. The Strip is, too, well, cliché. And for us locals, maybe just a little cheesy. And I won't sleep in a bed where you've had other women. Particularly Hera. More bad juju."

I grunted. Robbie was as frank as ever, and I wouldn't argue with her logic or feelings.

"Okay. That's all fair." I'd tell her later that I have a new bed because Hera had violated it the last time she was there. I had to get around to telling her why she had been there in the first place. Ugh.

"Anything else?"

"No condoms."

I sat up. She had my full undivided. Except for maybe the first time or two when I was a stupid kid, I'd never had sex without a condom. I had been certain Robbie would insist that I use them. In fact, considering her earlier crack about diseases and baby mamas, I was surprised at her requirement. I shook my head in disbelief.

"What? Why not?"

"I had always promised myself that when I made love for the first time, there'd be no barriers." Her voice was soft, almost a whisper. "Because when I did, it would be because I wanted to feel everything with that man. I want nothing artificial between us."

She hesitated for a moment and pursed her lips. "I still want test results, though. I'm not stupid."

I laughed. "Of course, sweetness. But what about birth control? Especially if we're going to be spending time together soon. Doesn't it take a month or more to take effect?"

I watched her cheeks flush pink under her caramel skin. Fascinating.

"I've been researching different types of birth control." Of course she has. This is Robbie. "And I can get a shot that will take effect pretty much right away, so long as it's within a certain number of days around the start of my period. It'll cover me for about three months."

Oh. There's a shot that does that? Who knew.

"Since my period is due by the weekend, all I have to do is to contact my OB/GYN and go in."

She hesitated. "There's not a shot in the world that can take away the nervousness, though."

"Actually," I drawled, "there is. But the jail time ain't worth it."

We both laughed, breaking the tension.

Let me be first and I'll be gentle

I will be loving her first. And it's up to me to make sure that everything I do will show her how much I cherish her.

Let me be first and I'll be gentle

And I'll be her only. There's no way in hell that I'm letting this woman out of my life. There's no way another man will touch her once I've made her mine.

Period.

Chapter 22

Robbie

I HAVE TO ADMIT it surprised me that Rogan didn't push back against my requirements. He accepted them all without hesitation and in total agreement. It's almost as if he had taken residence inside of my head and understood my reasons for everything I asked.

The only thing that rocked him was my desire for no condoms. At least from my girlfriends' perspectives, I know it's usually the guys who balk at condoms. And for stupid reasons, in my opinion.

"I can't feel anything with a condom."

"I'm too big. They won't fit over my dick."

"I'll pull out in time."

"If you love me, you won't make me wear one."

"I'm clean. Trust me."

Or my favorite, *"I want to feel all of you, baby. You know I love you."*

Bullshit. All of it.

There are more excuses, but it comes down to their wanting to fuck without barriers and not giving a damn about babies or disease. And that happened to more than one girlfriend back in college. How I sat and held the hand of a crying girl who was aborting the baby she would have craved if things had been different and if she hadn't fallen for a fuckboy's lies. Those girls who found out that the disease they had was only treatable, not curable, and still possibly life-threatening.

HIV, anyone?

And those who found out that the disease they had was now cured but had destroyed their ability to bear future children.

Unfortunately, many ladies were needy or "in love." They compromised their values to those lying emotional vampires who bounced anyway after hitting the new pussy. They left the girls broken, having lost far more than they gained. And the girls never gained anything. They had to deal with the consequences alone. Kind of what happened to Mom and *my* sperm donor. I guess that's why I'm far more cautious than the average young woman. I know what emotional devastation looks like, and I'd rather avoid it, thank you very much.

A husband and family were my future, and if it meant keeping my legs crossed for a while longer, then so be it. If it meant pushing even Rogan away permanently, then so be it. My standards are my standards, and sharing my life with a man who disrespects them is a non-starter. Mutual respect is crucial, and I won't accept anything less.

If Rogan had pushed back and balked at the idea of getting STD tests, then it would have been a dealbreaker. Test results were critical, as was my desire to feel everything with no fear of unintended consequences. So it's not like the fuckboys didn't have a point about "feeling." It's just that they didn't care about consequences, and consequences are a *very* big deal to me. The difference is that I want to feel everything with my first, and hopefully only, lover, and that has nothing to do with making a conquest.

We sat on the loveseat looking at each other, and I'm sure we were both sharing the same emotions. He reached over and took me into his arms. I wrapped my arms around him, reveling in the feel of his lean muscularity. I swallowed a moan. There was nothing better than this. I felt at home in his arms like this is where I'm supposed to be, you know? I closed my eyes and melted into him, inhaling his masculine scent, wine and music forgotten.

I felt one hand on my locs, smoothing them away from my face. The same hand caressed my cheek, coaxing my head up to face him. My eyes opened to meet his, which were warm with affection.

"I wouldn't expect anything less than your terms," he murmured. "Because if you'd jumped into this without them, I'd wonder what happened to you. Where in the hell is my Robbie?"

That surprised a smile out of me.

Rogan was a successful, mature, and intelligent adult. As an adult, he understood the need for compromise, and in his eyes, my demands were reasonable. Grownup to grownup, we respected each other as adults capable of making the right decisions, hormones notwithstanding. He respected my terms, and I appreciated that. It bumped him up even higher in my estimation.

I smiled up at him, happy and confident I'd made the right decision. He kissed my forehead, drawing out a sigh. Then he kissed my cheek. My heart started skittering.

I watched him watching me, his eyes golden with warmth. He leaned over to take my lips, and I opened for him in welcome.

What was it? That we already knew we'd be making love soon? Or was it because we had dismissed the awkwardness and had approached it head-on? Or was it because we'd been hungry for each other from the beginning?

Whatever it was, he pressed the kiss, our tongues meeting, dueling in the spreading flame. My nipples hardened, and my panties were immediately drenched. A moan escaped as he moved his hand to the back of my head, grasping my locs and deepening the kiss.

"Oh, baby," he rasped.

His large hands went under my t-shirt, and he lifted me up to straddle him. We were core to core, our mouths locked with each other. I couldn't help my hips from rolling against the thick ridge in his jeans. He groaned, grabbed my hips, and held me still.

"You keep doing that, Rob, and I'll have to go home to change my underwear."

My chuckle turned into a moan when his hands went from my hips to under my shirt, skimming over the bare skin of my back. My body curved against his, and he deepened the kiss. I wrapped both my arms around his neck, losing myself in the heat of his mouth. Of his touch.

Rogan's full lips left my mouth, and he trailed small drinking kisses down to my neck. His other hand cupped one breast over my light sports bra. I placed one hand over his, a whispered gasp escaping my lips.

Rogan pulled my shirt over my head, leaving only my bra in place, which he swiftly unsnapped and removed. He took off his polo shirt and drew me close to him, the shocking intimacy making me gasp. I placed one hand on his chest, and I clutched the soft dusting of hair covering his golden-eyed wolf tattoo. He moved my hand and hugged me even closer, and suddenly I was shaking. I wrapped my arms around his neck again, and I pressed my face against his beard, my trembling unabated.

We held each other, our rasping breaths blending together. Rogan whispered into my hair and continued to kiss my neck and along my shoulders. I cried out and arched against him when he caressed my breasts and suckled my nipples, bringing them to stiff peaks.

My hips began rolling helplessly over him again, seeking release, which brought him back to his wits. He grabbed my hips to still them.

Golden eyes hot with molten fire, he lifted me from his lap and set me down on the seat next to him.

"Whenever I'm around you, my control is shaky at best. Having you half-naked close to me is flirting with the limits of my sanity. If we continue, there will only be one of two outcomes."

I lifted a questioning brow.

"I'll either throw you down and take you, consequences be damned, or I'll come in my pants." I smiled at his chagrined expression. He enveloped me again in his arms and plopped a kiss on my cheek. I quickly, and with no little embarrassment, donned my bra and shirt.

He slipped on his polo shirt, taking a deep breath. His breathing slowly ticked back to normal.

"I'm leaving before I do something I'm not supposed to." His smile gleamed as he waggled his brows.

When I closed the door after he left, I leaned against it, once again feeling that Rogan had invaded my body and left his mark. He'd branded me as his.

Yeah. I need to be honest with myself. There is no other man for me. There is only Rogan.

Chapter 23

Robbie

"The door's unlocked!"

Rogan opened the front door and sauntered into the house. He was here to get me so we could spend the next few days together. I was packing bottles of water and wines into my soft-sided cooler.

"I brought a couple of wines, too," Rogan commented, eyes sparkling. "Just wait till you see."

I grinned at him, enjoying his warmth and humor. This is the man I'd be loving tonight. After years of single-minded celibacy, this man is the one I'd be loving first.

After zipping the cooler, I gave it to Rogan to take out to the car, and I grabbed my suitcase. I texted Daria to remind her I'd be with Rogan for the next few days, but it was okay to call in case of an emergency.

Otherwise, I wrote, **consider me totally out of pocket!**

Daria replied immediately: **Have fun! ;-P**

Rogan held the door to the Range Rover and helped me in. He'd already placed the cooler and my suitcase into the back.

"Where are we going?"

Rogan smiled at me as he turned out of the driveway.

"Lake Las Vegas."

"Wow."

Lake Las Vegas is a master-planned community in southeastern Henderson. It was originally a resort community. Because it turned out to be a magnet for retirees, celebrities, and all manner of monied people, it quickly established itself as a desirable residential area. Many homes, shops, and new schools later, it became a great, if expensive, place to call home.

"I rented a penthouse condo in the North Shore area," he continued. "It's large and has more bedrooms than we need. One of Dad's clients owns it. It's one of his winter homes, and he was more than happy to let me use it." He sent a warm smile my way. "I think you'll love it."

We rode in companionable silence until he turned onto Lake Las Vegas Drive. It was almost noon when we reached the condo community entrance, where he punched in a code and drove through the open gate. The homes were breathtaking.

"Believe it or not, these are all condos," Rogan told me. We drove up to what looked like a massive three-story home and parked in one of the three garages. We removed our belongings, and I followed Rogan to the elevator entrance to the garage. He inserted a card into a slot, and the door opened.

The elevator door whispered open into a spacious, beautifully appointed condo with vast expanses of honed travertine flooring. The walls were sand-colored, and the furniture was tastefully conservative, mostly Traditional, in style. What caught my eye was the wall of French doors that displayed beautiful views of Lake Mead through the covered balcony.

The elevator door closed behind us, and Rogan's deep chuckle brought me back.

"Meet with your approval?"

"Yes," I whispered. "This is beautiful."

Did I just see a wash of relief flit over Rogan's face? I knew that he'd spent some time pulling this together, and I appreciated it. I reached up and gave him a kiss on his bearded cheek.

"Thank you for being so considerate," I said to him.

While I wheeled our bags into the spacious master bedroom, he began emptying the cooler I'd brought. Then, after a few minutes, he came into the bedroom, opened his bag, and took out a bottle of wine.

"This is for later," he grinned. "I wanted something special for us."

He left the bedroom, and moments later, he returned, face somber, body language tense.

"Babe, I have something to tell you," he said tentatively. "And it's not going to make you happy."

A frisson of unease danced down my spine.

"It has to do with another woman."

My breath caught, and I looked away from him. He grabbed my hand and held it loosely.

"I've been dealing with this for a while, and the longer it sits on my mind, the harder it is to be with you on an honest level."

"Is it Hera?"

He nodded. "Yeah."

I pulled my hand out of his and crossed my arms, dread snaking its way through my body. He placed his hands on my shoulders, and I flinched away. No. Now is not the time to touch me. I had to brace myself for what was coming.

"Let's sit down."

I followed him to the plush microsuede sofa in the living room and sat down on the opposite end. I like to think of myself as someone who has well-honed bullshit detection skills. I don't like it when people underestimate me. The expression on Rogan's face wasn't shady or guilty, but direct. That was good. We'll see.

"You remember when I first came to the gallery and Hera was with me?"

I nodded. Of course. Her silicone preceded her.

"Well, and this is the key to everything. I didn't invite her that weekend. She'd shown up literally as I opened the door to leave for the gallery. I'd planned to stop seeing her because of her fakery and general lack of intelligence, but just hadn't gotten around to it yet. Mainly because I never thought about her. Out of sight, out of mind. So it was a surprise when she showed up. Not a good surprise, and I wasn't happy. I should have sent her back right away, but I was in a hurry to get to the gallery and knew there'd be a fight I didn't have time for."

He closed his eyes and pinched the bridge of his nose.

"I don't know if you could tell that I was irritated with her when I was there."

I nodded again. The fact that she seemed so out of place in his presence and how she treated Doris and me told me a lot.

"Well, after I left the gallery, we went back to my condo. After our little spat, she'd gone to the beer garden and had a few, so I couldn't responsibly let her drive back to California in that shape. When we got home, she started chugging my vodka. I think she was doing it on purpose because she knew how I felt about drunk driving. It was her way of staying overnight with me."

He looked at me, eyes direct. "And then she attacked me."

Foreboding weighted my heart.

"I foolishly allowed her to give me head, right there in my living room. I let her do it because I let my imagination take over. In my mind, you were giving me head, not her." His face reddened. "It sounds like bullshit, but it isn't."

What? I swallowed the lump in my throat and didn't react. I didn't know what to think.

"But I wouldn't fuck her. Couldn't. I just wanted to be left alone. For what it's worth, I felt disgusted with myself. I apologized for not wanting to sleep with her despite the blow job, but it was a no-go on sex.

"Geez," he said, sitting back on the sofa. "That really makes me sound like an asshole."

I'm not sure what expression I had on my face, but he looked concerned even though his direct gaze never wavered.

"I let her sleep in my bed. Alone. I slept on my sectional in the living room. Not very well, but that's where I stayed. I didn't even want to be in the same room with her.

"Sunday morning, I got up about five and checked in on her. She'd gotten sick overnight and had thrown up all over my bed. Apparently, the combination of vodka and beer wasn't a good one. Even if it's a quality craft beer and a $5,000 bottle of Stoli Elit.

"It was a stinking mess. She still had on the same clothes she came in, believe it or not. I made her change, took her to breakfast, and when we got back to the condo, we had a huge fight over her place in my life. I told her she didn't have one. She finally left after slapping me in the face."

By this time, I was engrossed. And relieved, I might add. If this Hera drama had happened, say, a week ago, I'd be outta here, even if I had to hitchhike back to Vegas.

"After she left, I pulled the sheets from the bed. I saw that her vomit had soaked through to the mattress. So I said fuck it and called a haul away company first thing Monday, and they hauled the entire bed away on Tuesday. I bought a brand new king bed, mattress, new bedding, everything."

He looked over at me, his expression indecipherable. His cheeks had regained their normal color.

"I'm the only one who's slept in the new bed. Alone."

Imagination is a funny thing, isn't it? As soon as Hera's name had come up, I was sure he'd tell me that while he was waiting for me to be ready for him, he'd slipped into some familiar pussy. And his conscience wouldn't let him have sex with me until he'd told me he'd slept with her. Using a condom, of course. So I'd be safe.

We weren't even together when his little scenario took place. I guessed it wouldn't have happened at all if she hadn't invited herself to his house. I figured she'd be hopping mad that he didn't take her up on the fucking part.

"How did she handle not being able to sleep with you?"

Rogan's face was awash with relief. I'm pretty sure he thought I'd tell him to go fuck himself. And I would have.

"I told her, and this is pretty much verbatim, that I wouldn't be fucking her again. Ever. If she didn't remember that we'd both agreed this was an occasional booty call and nothing else, then I didn't know what to say. I'd been very clear when we first hooked up. And at the time, she was okay with it."

He looked at me with a pleading expression.

"After meeting you again and plotting to get you back into my life, I made the decision that there was no other woman who'd be in my bed except for you. And it hasn't been difficult at all. I'm not some crazy horndog. You've been my only focus."

"Plotting?"

His lips twitched. "Yup."

"As far as I'm concerned, everything that happened before our first kiss doesn't matter. Even then, I thought you were just curious or something. Like along the lines of 'can the tomboy kiss?' kind of thing."

He moved over to my side of the sofa and enveloped me in his arms. He kissed my forehead, closing his eyes.

"I should have told you sooner," he murmured, "but I was afraid that you'd either think I was crazy..."

"And I do."

"...or you'd tell me to fuck off. And I don't know if I could handle that. And I guess that's why I waited till now. To give myself time to win you over so you wouldn't kick me out of your life. To forgive me."

"God, Rogie, there's nothing to forgive. We weren't together. I looked at our meeting as a happy accident and looked forward to working with you, but nothing more. As far as I was concerned, you were with your woman, so it didn't matter how I felt or what you did." I hesitated. "I appreciate you telling me about the bed, though. Now I can see myself in it with you."

I felt the tension leave his body.

"Thank you," he breathed into my hair.

We sat like that for a long time, in each other's arms, just savoring the connection.

I finally murmured into his chest, "I want to go in the pool, but should we get some food first?"

We chowed down on sandwiches and salads we'd brought and avoided the topic of sex. The tension was there. We just didn't talk about it.

"Ready for the pool?" Rogan asked. "A little sun, a little hot tub, and we be chillin'."

I laughed, and while Rogan put the leftovers into the fridge, I went into the bedroom to change into my swimsuit. I dressed in the bathroom, and when I came out, Rogan was wearing board shorts. When he saw me in my skimpy crocheted ivory bikini, his eyes gleamed and his shorts tented. Oh my.

I'd found this little treasure in a funky shop in Pismo Beach the last time I visited California. When I tried it on, the clerk in the store said that it looked like it had been custom-made for me. It did! The triangles barely covered my breasts, and the bikini bottom rode high on my hips. The ivory yarn was lined with fabric nearly identical to my skin color, teasing anyone who cared to look.

"I'll kill a motherfucker who looks at you too long."

"You mean like *you're* doing?" I laughed when he scowled at me.

The swimming pool was one of several dotted throughout the community. There was an outdoor shower and a jacuzzi for residents. We each took a thermos of cold water, several beach towels, and lots of sunscreen. We wouldn't be out long because even the late afternoon summer sun could be brutal in this part of the valley. Fortunately, today's weather was a mild 99 degrees. It's a dry heat.

There were several people by the pool who nodded our way when we went through the gate. Rogan scowled at one young man who was ogling me.

We found a couple of chaise lounges and spread our towels on them. Along with my thermos, I had a bottle of nuclear-grade sunscreen. Of course I'd thought of Rogan's freckled skin when I bought it. I didn't want him to turn into a pomegranate.

After I shed the beach tunic I'd donned in the condo, I had Rogan stretch out on his stomach on the chaise, and I rubbed the sunscreen on his back. I felt his breath hitch as my hands smoothed the lotion over his neck, shoulders, back, arms, and legs. Then, when I applied it to the inside of his muscular thighs and along his shapely calves, he didn't even try to suppress a groan.

"You're killin' me."

I chuckled.

"Turn over."

Chapter 24

Rogan

"Turn over."

My cock was already hard enough to drill through the pool deck, and I didn't need to turn over and show everyone my current state. No bueno.

"Hand me a towel first."

Robbie reached into her bag for a spare towel and handed it to me. I bunched it up and placed it over my midsection when I rolled over.

Her lips twitched as I adjusted the towel, camouflaging my situation as much as possible.

"No need showing the whole world," I grumped. Her expression softened with affection, although her eyes were twinkling with suppressed laughter.

She smoothed the sunscreen over my face, neck, and shoulders while I laid there, eyes closed, reveling in the feel of her hands gliding over my body. Next, she applied the lotion down each arm and the back of each hand.

I was limp *and* stiff at the same time.

When Robbie started down my chest and stomach, it got worse. The feel of this beautiful woman's soft touch on my body almost had me groaning out loud. She was astute enough to know that she had to stop at the top of my swim shorts. I had the towel there for a reason.

She lotioned each leg, taking extra care of my scarred right leg. When she stopped, I opened one eye and looked at her. She lifted my leg and gently kissed the scars, causing my breath to hitch and my heart to expand even more.

This woman.

She handed me the sunscreen and then turned, offering her back. I shakily reached for her, lifting her locs over one shoulder. She was sitting at the foot of the chaise lounge, shoulders slightly hunched. I squirted some sunscreen in my hand and, after a brief hesitation, began to rub it on her back.

Fuuuuck!

I got so hard from touching her silky smooth flesh that it was almost painful. She lifted her head and practically purred with pleasure as I swiped the lotion on her back. I reached around her, applying more to her shoulders, chest, and stomach.

"Thanks, Rogie," she murmured. She took the bottle from me and sat down on her chaise, lifting one shapely leg after the other while she smoothed lotion down their endless length.

I smiled at her, heart pounding. I stretched out on my chaise, towel carefully in place. I tried to relax. From the corner of my eye, I saw the dude was still ogling Robbie. A couple of others had joined him in his gape-fest, including an old guy whose wife smacked him on the arm when she realized what he was doing.

I chuckled to myself as I dispatched the towel and dove into the deep end of the pool. There's nothing like being doused with cold water to deflate an overly hard cock. It was exactly what I needed.

And then Robbie stood up and stretched. Then, with her shapely, mouthwatering ass in my direction, she bent over to grab a scrunchie. She turned as she put her locs up into a loose bun at the top of her head and then walked to the pool. I deliberately watched the dudes around the pool. Because they sure as hell weren't watching me.

All eyes were on Robbie's graceful figure as she tiptoed over the hot pavement. She stepped gingerly into the cold water, pretended to shudder, and gradually submerged herself. I swam over to her, and she wrapped her arms around my neck. I planted a big one on her lips. She laughed happily and hugged me closer.

That whole cold water equals soft cock thing is largely horseshit, by the way.

We floated lazily for a while, me on my back with her arms still loosely draped around my neck. Gazing at each other, words were unnecessary. We floated by the side of the pool, our faces this close. She placed both hands on either side of my face and kissed me softly on the lips.

I wrapped my arms around her and deepened the kiss and followed up with a kiss on her forehead. I saw all the dudes—there were only about six, to be honest—looking at us. Or, more accurately, looking at Robbie with longing and at me with envy. I'm good with that. However, it annoyed me that they didn't even try to hide their gawking.

The main jacuzzi was located under the overhang of the pool building. Robbie gave me a quick smack on the lips and climbed out of the pool to tiptoe across the hot concrete. The jacuzzi timer was on the wall, and she set it before tentatively touching her toes into the water.

The ogling motherfuckers were still gaping at her. If it were legal, I'd punch every single one of them for coveting what was mine. And glaring at them did no good since they weren't looking at me. At all.

Robbie was oblivious to the hormonal havoc she was causing in the poolside male population. She settled into the Jacuzzi's roiling water with an audible, satisfied sigh. That did nothing positive for my libido and caused at least a couple of the dudes to make adjustments if you get my drift.

I mentally shook my head and did a few laps since she was relaxed and enjoying the spa. The pool was on the small side, which meant that my laps were short by necessity. But it gave me room to think.

When in the hell had I become so possessive? So crazy? So *unglued*? I have never gone Godzilla over any woman, not even my high school girlfriend, Colleen. She'd been my first, but I wasn't hers. But I'd been too hooked on the idea that I was gettin' some to care.

I'd had a couple of close relationships through the years, of course, but they didn't last for more than a few months. Other than what happened in bed, there had been no real connection. They'd scratched my itch for pussy and female company, and then it was done. Don't get me wrong. I liked them well enough. There were a couple I actually had feelings for and was pretty upset when we broke up. But the fact is that when we did break up, there was no real sense of loss. It was time to move on because that particular chapter was closed.

And then, from my deep past, Roberta Thornquist Wilkes entered my life. All whiskey skin and sueded locs. Eyes the color of liquid mercury. A sweet, husky laugh. A sexy body and a mind like a well-tuned engine. And a soul and straightforward honesty like I'd never experienced before. No deception. No gold digger aspirations. A genuine, independent, accomplished woman who, despite her strengths, liked me anyway. A woman whose look and touch easily sent me into hormonal King Kong mode, pounding my chest and protecting her against all comers.

Let me be first and I'll be gentle.

And tonight, I will make her mine.

Chapter 25

Robbie

WHEN ROGAN SMOOTHED THE sunscreen on my back, I could feel and hear the catch in his breath. Yeah. Well. Me too. My own breath had stuttered when I rubbed the lotion over the muscles of his back.

We spent the greater part of the late afternoon drenched in sunscreen and enjoying the pool, spa, and each other. When early evening approached, we rinsed under the outdoor shower, and laughing, we dried each other.

We entered our condo doorway and headed to the elevator. My nerves were brittle. I know for a fact that if had it been anyone else, I simply would have taken a bye.

Who am I kidding? If it had been anyone else, I wouldn't be there. Period. Rogan was my only.

When we entered the elevator, Rogan took my hand in his and looked at me sharply.

"Nervous, Rob? Your hands are freezing."

I nodded. "I thought I'd be chill, but I'm pretty much a wreck."

He smiled and kissed my icy hand. "I care about you too much to hurt you," he assured me as we stepped out of the elevator. "I hope you believe me."

I nodded again, wanting to believe. I wrapped my arms around his neck and gave him a big kiss on the lips. Then I danced away, removing my tunic and grinning back at him.

I swallowed at the fierce heat that appeared in his eyes. His gaze went from my feet, up to my body, and finally to my face.

His eyes were like burning lava, and I heard his breath hitch from where he stood.

"Damn, girl."

"Just stop," I scolded. "You've looked at me all afternoon. Time to behave."

He howled out a wolfish laugh before grinning at me and winking.

I gave him a scowling smile, which only made him laugh harder, and I rummaged through my suitcase. I grabbed my oversized shower cap because locs can be a pain in the ass to dry. I found my special bottle of lavender shower gel and walked to the bathroom.

I squeezed a bit of gel onto the washcloth and began to wash my body, starting with soaping my face. My eyes were closed when I heard the shower door open and felt Rogan enter and stand behind me. He reached around me to wet his hands under the spray and then glided them down my back. I gasped and trembled at his touch but didn't pull away. I heard the bottle of gel being squeezed, and then his large hands were massaging me all over.

He began at my neck and smoothed the soapy gel over my shoulders. I felt him tug at the washcloth that was now dangling uselessly from my hand. He used it to soap my back, my butt, and the back of my legs. He stood up, reached around my front, and gently squeezed my breasts before sliding down my belly, triggering a gasp.

My stupid body was responding even if my brain was frozen.

He washed my front down to my belly and stopped. I realized that he was rinsing the soap from the washcloth, after which he helped the water remove the soap from my face and my eyes, which were still closed. He was still behind me and had begun softly kissing my neck and shoulders.

He brought the now well-rinsed washcloth to my triangle and gently coaxed my legs apart. I submitted, spreading my feet to allow him access. He tossed the washcloth aside, replacing it with his fingers.

This was real. This was intimate. I gasped a small cry as his fingers gently grazed and then stroked my folds.

"Oh baby, you're so slick," he rasped into my ear. He pulled my body to his, and I jumped at the feel of his erection pressing into my back.

"Oh god," I gasped. My emotions were all over the place, and I felt as if I were melting.

After removing the handheld showerhead from its mount and rinsing my body thoroughly, he rinsed himself before turning off the shower and stepping out. I watched him, gaping stupidly through water droplets while working overtime to avoid looking at his, um, *member*. He grabbed a towel and wrapped it around his middle. He helped me out of the shower and wrapped the other towel around my body.

The man was perfection. His hair was damp and fell over his shoulders in water-darkened waves. He was slim, but hard, athletic muscles flexed underneath his golden, sun-toned skin. His chest had a light dusting of hair that thinned as it drifted toward his stomach, which was bare except for a thick trail of red-brown hair that went from his navel down the center of his well-defined adonis muscle. With the towel wrapped around his hips, all I could see below it were his strong athletic legs. I tried not to look at the *very* tented area in his middle.

My eyes rushed up to meet his, which were twinkling. He stepped close to me and removed my shower cap. He let his hands run down the length of my loosened locs and sucked in a sharp breath as he nosed them and inhaled.

"Damn, girl."

He removed my towel and turned me around. He pushed my locs over one shoulder and patted down my neck, my back, and my waist. He crouched behind me and kissed and nibbled my butt cheeks.

"You have the best ass," he murmured.

He turned me around to face him, flipped my locs behind my shoulders, and began to pat down my front. He stopped at my breasts and I could see the fire. He licked one pebbled nipple and then licked and suckled the other, drawing a cry. His kisses followed the towel downward until he was kneeling in front of my core.

He lifted one of my legs and let it rest on one muscular shoulder. I stared down at him as he placed one hand around my ass and then fingered my pussy with the other. I cried out again, clutching his hair and arching helplessly against his probing fingers. His mouth replaced his fingers and I thought I was going to die. He gave my clit a lick and a little suction. He caught me as my knees buckled. How could something so small feel so intense?

He growled, stood up, picked me up in his arms, and strode to the bedroom.

He stood me on the floor by the bed before palming my face, his eyes searching mine. His amber eyes were golden fire as he smiled warmly at me.

"It's going to be okay, sweetness."

I nodded, still shaking like a leaf. He kissed my forehead, my nose, my cheeks, and then he took my mouth in a lingering kiss. I hesitated only slightly as I felt his tongue against my lips, coaxing them open, persuading my tongue to respond. I gladly gave in to him, and once again felt my body liquefy under his touch. His hands moved over me with a sense of masculine ownership.

Suddenly he stepped back, breathing heavily and with an odd expression on his face.

"Let's relax for a while," he said. "Do you have another robe or gown or something?"

I blinked, completely confused. My body felt bereft. "What?"

Rogan gazed at me fondly, a soft smile on his lips.

"Don't get me wrong," he smiled. "I want to throw you on the bed and ravish you." His expression grew serious. "But I can't. You are important to me, Rob, and this is important to us. I want to relax a bit, snack on leftovers, have a little wine, and then we can make love the way we want, when we want. We have time."

I smiled at him, my heart full and appreciative. I should have known he'd be that considerate.

That loving.

"Yes," I said. "I'll get it." While I rummaged in my suitcase, he found a pair of cotton shorts and dropped his towel to put them on. I got a glimpse of his beautiful ass cheeks and then shrugged on my linen dressing gown and tied the belt around my waist.

He took my hand as we went through the balcony doors. I settled down on one of the wicker reclining chairs and he disappeared inside. He returned with a platter of leftovers, two wine glasses, and a bottle of 2015 Leflaive Puligny Montrachet 1er Cru Les Pucelles. Oh my. This was way better than Champagne!

He splashed a tasting pour of the Leflaive into one of the glasses, sniffed, swirled, and tasted. He nodded to himself and poured both of us a glass. I took mine by the stem and settled into the chair.

We sat quietly for a while, enjoying the view of the lights on the lake and watching as yachts navigated their way into their berths. I began to unwind and relax. I didn't even realize I'd been that tensed up. Relaxing like this was a very good idea.

"Why art?"

I'd gotten that question many times. I mean, after all, who could possibly make a living from fine art, right? The big boys were few and far between, so how could I possibly have thought that I'd make an impact in the art world?

As it turns out, I *am* one of the big boys.

"I used to model with Mom," I began. "Mother and daughter matching outfits, photography sessions, runway stuff. I really didn't like it. Especially since some of the photo sessions could be hours long and really boring.

"One day, I think I was about five, six, or so, I found a pencil and paper and just began drawing. There was a pretty model with long hair who was sitting on a stool because they wanted closeups of her face. I drew her face."

I stopped to take a sip of the incredible wine. Leflaive is my spirit animal.

"While the model was getting her makeup refreshed, the main photographer started talking to me and saw my picture. While it had obviously been drawn by a kid, apparently it was good. He called Mom over and asked her how long I'd been taking art lessons. Mom told him that I hadn't.

"The photographer was surprised and somehow was able to arrange for me to get lessons. It cut into my modeling career, but I didn't care because I didn't like modeling much. After about six months, he showed some of my work to somebody at Bravo who was working on a documentary about child prodigies. I was featured as a gifted creative, and the rest is history."

I turned to look at him. "I love art way more than I ever tolerated modeling. I did modeling because it made Mom happy. She seemed sad a lot. It wasn't until later that I learned it was largely because of my sperm donor. But that's a whole saga in itself."

"So," I said. "Who's your favorite chef, other than Mama?"

"Jon Favreau."

"Jon Favreau isn't a chef!"

"He played the chef in the movie *Chef* a few years back. It was fun enough that I briefly considered getting a food truck. We'll have to Netflix and chill it one evening," he grinned wickedly, waggling his brows.

"Anyway," he continued, "After the movie, he renovated his home kitchen to look like a restaurant kitchen. I admire that kind of dedication."

I smiled and motioned towards him with my glass. He poured more of the Leflaive for both of us. I was enjoying this quiet time with Rogan more than I expected.

Because you love him even if you won't tell him so.

Our balcony was near the pool, and the sounds had long since faded. It was nearly nighttime, and the lights barely illuminated our sitting area. Beyond the pool, the lake had darkened in the twilight.

We snacked and sipped our wine in companionable silence. I was smiling inside, feeling relaxed and at ease. I looked over at Rogan. He was twirling the stem of his glass and seemed at least as calm as I felt. He glanced at me, and the warmth in his gaze made my breath wobble and my heart skip. What a beautiful man.

He smiled and said, "hold that thought."

He rose from his seat and went through the balcony door into our room. Rather than worry about what he was doing, I relaxed in my chair. I finished my glass of wine and sighed.

The sound of the doors opening made me turn my head. My heart skittered.

Rogan stood in the doorway, chestnut red waves falling around his shoulders. His hand was extended toward me. I blinked but had enough presence of mind to take his hand as he helped me out of my chair. I stepped over the threshold, and he reached behind me to close the doors and draw the draperies.

The overhead lights were dimmed, and the soft, smoky vocals of Anita Baker crooned serenely in the background.

We moved together in time with the music before he stopped and looked down at me. I reached up and tangled my fingers in his silken mane. He stroked my locs, still gazing at me with that look that was making my heart do somersaults. Then he leaned over to kiss me.

His first kiss was gentle. He kissed me again and coaxed my mouth open, which I gladly gave to him. I felt a rumble as he deepened the kiss, his tongue stroking across mine, first softly, then with increasing fervor.

Both of his hands gently caressed my face as our kisses intensified. I pulled away to gasp, eliciting a chuckle. He continued to stroke my hair as he looked down at me, eyes bright with arousal. He tugged the tie around my waist, and I allowed him to slip the dressing gown from my shoulders. He gathered me into his arms, carried me to the bed, and placed me on the sheets.

After adjusting the bedside lamp to dim, he stepped out of his shorts and climbed into bed with me. He pulled the top sheet over us and encircled me with his arms.

Ohgodohgodohgodohgod...

The shocking intimacy of his body against mine fueled my desire while sending me into a state of surreal yearning and some fear. Our lips met, greedily drinking in each other's mouths, our tongues dancing fire. I was moaning again, making sounds I couldn't stop.

His mouth left mine and moved to my jaw and then to my neck, lightly kissing and nibbling as he made his way down to my shoulders. He found my breasts, this time sucking in earnest. I cried out again and again as his mouth danced over my nipples, making my blood roar.

"Oh baby," he groaned, "Your body was made for me."

I let my hands drift over his hair, gripped its silken length in my hands, and held him as his lips flickered gently over me.

I trembled as he took me in his arms and pressed our naked bodies together. My nipples pebbled against the soft hair on his chest. My belly quivered at the shocking feel of his body against mine.

I reached for his face and kissed him again. His kisses were hard, intense, and I returned them with my own fire. His hands possessively explored my breasts, my belly, and the curves of my thighs. As one hand went between my now open legs and began to fondle my dripping folds, I gasped into his mouth. He gave a primal grunt and deepened the kiss.

He broke the kiss and feathered his mouth down to my belly until he got to the apex of my thighs. I felt the warmth of his breath just before his tongue touched my clit. I gasped out a moan which turned into a cry as his lips and tongue touched every spot of my core. My body was writhing of its own accord, my hips bucking toward his mouth.

He deeply suckled my now-throbbing sensitive clit and curved a finger into my channel.

I gave a small grunt of pain at the intrusion of his large finger, and then there were explosions. I don't know what kind of sound I made, but I'm sure I was noisy as wave after wave washed over me. He followed my every move, his mouth never leaving my core as I drowned in ecstasy.

He didn't remove his finger as he made his way up my body to give me another crushing kiss, this time seasoned with my own essence. He broke the kiss to look fondly into my eyes, his hair curtaining our faces. His lips grazed my cheeks, my neck, and my shoulders.

And then his hands were gently gripping my thighs. He settled between them, tenderly pulling them around his hips.

I felt the blunt head of Rogan's erection at my entrance as he guided his hardness into place. I sucked in a gallon of air and squeezed my eyes shut.

This was it.

Chapter 26

ROBBIE. MY ROBBIE.

This woman was melting in my arms, returning kiss for kiss, touching my body with a confidence I didn't know she had.

I was shaking with anticipation. Not because I was nervous about sex, but because of my need to be connected with Robbie. She's not some random chick I can nut and forget. Robbie was already inside of everything that I am, and I knew that this was special. I just had to make sure that it was special for her. Deep down, I knew we'd both be irrevocably changed after this night.

Need.

I was overwhelmed by her response. She was anxious, but her pleasure and anticipation seemed to tamp down her fear.

Her body had a life of its own as she moved against me. I made my way down her neck, marking her with small, drinking kisses which sparked breathy moans. I kissed her delicate breasts and reveled in her soft cries as I sucked and nibbled on her sensitive rosy-brown nipples, my hands holding each mound as I took my pleasure. I wanted... no, *needed* to taste every single inch of her. To put my hands, mouth, and body where no other man's had ever been.

Possession.

I moved down her body, past her navel, and down to her juncture of neatly trimmed curls, licking, sucking, and tasting every inch.

Delicious.

I spread her thighs with my hands, and after I parted her folds, I sank my face into her sweet, innocent warmth. I inhaled deeply before I stroked her clit with my tongue. Her gasping, shocked response let me know that I'd touched a sexual nerve. I kissed and licked her core, using my lips and tongue to savor her now-drenched slit. Of its own accord, her body arched against my mouth, her soft, sexy cries nonstop.

I curved a finger through the delicate tissues covering her entrance, which drew a sharp cry from the unexpected breach. Her tight muscles clenched around my finger as I probed her G-spot and suckled her clit.

Holy shit.

She exploded like a thousand July fourths. Her hips undulated under my mouth, her thighs shaking, and her murmured moans became cries of surprise as the orgasm had its way with her. Her body poured its release into my hand and I continued to stroke my finger into her folds, then brought it to my mouth to taste her juices.

Sweet. So Sweet.

I crawled my way up her body, tasting and licking every inch of skin as I settled back to face her. Her hands feathered over my arms and my back and pushed back my hair which curtained our faces. She kissed me with ardor, with passion, and I plundered her mouth, reveling in her response. Her soft murmurs and sighs were making me harder than I've ever been in my life. I needed to be inside of her. Now.

Our eyes locked as I moved my body between her silky legs. I grasped her thighs and let her feel my erection against her entrance. Her silvery orbs slammed shut. She opened them and her emotions changed from fear and reticence to desire, and yearning. She wanted me.

Let me be first and I'll be gentle.

"Look at me, sweetness. There's no turning back after this. Are you sure?" Even though it would kill me to do it, I would pull away from her if she decided that she couldn't go through with this after all.

Her eyes were smoky and heavy-lidded. She nodded, never breaking her gaze.

My eyes held hers as I began to press into her. As her membrane started to give way, she let out a shocked gasp and shot a hand against one thigh as if to push me away.

"It's okay." I grasped her hand, kissed it, and brought it up to my shoulder. I wrapped my other hand around her hips to steady her. By slow degrees, I pushed into her, rupturing her delicate, virginal folds. I caught her sharp, sobbing wail in my mouth as the head of my cock fully breached her entrance. Her body writhed beneath me, unsure of this invasion. Her soft cries of confused pain and pleasure echoed in my ears.

Ah, Sweetness.

I pulled back a little and then pressed forward again. Damn. She was tight. I pulled back again, and thrust further with a small rotating move, my cock stretching her sheath to accommodate my girth. I continued to do this dance of degrees as her body adjusted to this alien intrusion, her soft moans gasping in my ear.

One sharp, final surge, and my hips were nestled in the apex of her thighs and I was encased. I was almost dizzy because the effort to remain still was almost too much for me to handle. I instinctively wanted to piston into her till I came, but I held back while she accommodated the invasion of my body within hers. My lips rested in the hollow of her neck and shoulder. I was fighting for control.

"Ohgodohgodohgod."

Robbie's gasping breaths echoed in my ears as she held onto my back and shoulders. I whispered encouragement to her as I began to move in short, gentle, rotating thrusts to lessen her pain. I gradually moved with smooth strokes that promised my too-quick release as our bodies tuned into each other and our hips rocked together.

Her pussy was tight, hot, and slick, and her inner muscles quivered around my cock.

Fuck!

I knew I wouldn't last long. Her soft cries and moans, her quivering thighs and her clenching walls completely undid me.

And then I came, hot and raw, in thick, pulsating waves. I spilled into her, helpless and throbbing, without holding back, and with the most intense pleasure I'd ever experienced. With every beat of release, my groans were guttural and deep until I was depleted. I collapsed, completely spent, over her still-trembling body.

I rolled to my side, still connected, with her in my arms. We looked at each other, panting heavily from the exertion.

Her eyes were wide and stunned. I smiled tenderly at her.

"You okay?"

She nodded, unable to speak.

"Does it hurt?"

"Yes," she breathed. "A lot at first. More than I thought it would. Now a little but it's fading." She snuggled her face into the hollow of my neck and gave my skin a soft kiss. I closed my eyes at her touch.

This woman.

As I began to soften, I dragged myself out of her. Her quavery "oh!" touched me because I knew she was sensitive. Our fluids streamed from her as I withdrew completely.

I wish I could say that I felt some guilt at hurting her. But I didn't. Don't get me wrong. I didn't want to hurt her at all. But this was just the rite we needed to write the next chapter of our friendship. Relationship? All I know is that I didn't want to be anywhere else or with anyone else than at this place and with this woman. This woman who'd connected with me a decade ago and who was now wrapped in my arms. This woman who gave me—ME!—a priceless, irreplaceable gift.

"I thought I knew what was going to happen and how I'd feel. I had no idea," she whispered. "This was..." she trailed off.

"Yeah. I know. I thought I knew what was going to happen, too. I was totally off base. This was more than anything I imagined."

I pulled back to peer tenderly into her eyes. "Because it's you."

I held her in my arms for a while longer and then decided that we needed to clean up. I swung my legs over the edge of my side of the bed and walked to the bathroom, where I grabbed a hand towel to rinse. I used one end to sponge myself and noted the presence of her virginal blood streaked along the length of my cock. I took a deep breath, closing my eyes, leaning against the countertop, and drinking in the moment. I had never expected to experience anything like this in my entire life.

After I finished cleaning myself, I walked back to the bedroom and sat on the bed at her feet.

"Here, babe. Open your legs."

She acquiesced, and I dabbed between her thighs, cleaning her juices, her blood, and my cum. I dabbed at the sheet which held her virginity stains on its whiteness.

Oh. My.

I don't particularly consider myself a praying man, but I sent up words of thanks for this gift from this incredible woman.

I finished the cleanup and returned the towel to the bathroom. I got back into bed and gathered Robbie into my arms. *Shit* this felt good.

Throughout my entire adult life, I had always felt that the idea of being the "first" lover for a woman was moronic. I mean, who really cares, right? What horny red-blooded man wouldn't prefer a willing, experienced woman with a freaky streak who'd be down for whatever. No strings. Just fucking. That had always been my choice, all through high school, college, and in my professional life, both on the soccer field and in the kitchen. All I needed was condoms at the ready. My latest mistake, Hera, had been a prime example of my usual preference for a woman. Good looking and freaky. Nut and go.

That was before Robbie. Before my heart was involved. Before this woman wormed her way into my soul, without even realizing she'd done it.

I looked down at her face. She was staring at me, unsure of what to say.

"What are you thinking?" I murmured as I stroked her locs, relishing in their feel and texture in my hands. I smiled at her, looking into her luminous eyes in the lamplight.

She smiled softly. "I don't know what to say. This was the most amazing experience of my life. And I know this sounds cheesy, but I'm so happy that it was with you."

I'm her first. And dammit, I will be her only. She needs to know that she's mine alone.

I'll be damned if another man gets to touch her. No other man will experience lovemaking with her. No man will take my place between her thighs or in her life. The very thought of another man making love to her triggered something crazy in my mind.

I kissed the top of her head and squeezed her tighter as she snuggled trustingly into my body. I was soon rewarded with soft, whispery snores as she fell into a deep sleep. I didn't want to let her out of my arms. My breath hitched when she murmured in her sleep and snuggled more deeply into my body. And as I began to drift, a voice as clear as morning echoed in my head.

God I love this woman. With everything I am.

Wait. What? Where the hell had that come from?

Chapter 27

Robbie

I woke up to a still-darkened bedroom. I reached for Rogan, but his side of the bed was bare. The pillow held the indentation of his head, and the sheets were still warm. Then I heard the water running in the bathroom and sighed.

Can he tell?

I don't know a lot about men aside from what Papa and Dad had told me, which was along the lines of "keep your legs closed because men are shit," so this was unknown territory. Being the youngest in high school didn't help much since I was a very late bloomer and usually dressed like a boy. I was pretty androgynous, which meant I was way at the bottom of the interest totem pole for guys. And then I spent my college life in an all-girls school that didn't allow males anywhere close until graduate school. When my friend Nikki was raped, I cut dating to focus on my goals. My life and career became the things to be concerned about.

Rogan is a sexually experienced man, and I don't know how that affects his mindset. So, although he couched it with sweet words, I couldn't help wondering if this was just another sexual conquest for him. Because for me, this has brought me to my knees.

Can he tell how I feel? Can he understand what making love to him has done to me? Does he love me? Can he ever?

I closed my eyes to my jumbled thoughts, remembering last night. In the shower while he touched my water-dampened body. The tender glow in his eyes as I touched him back. There was the heat as we moved together, learning each other's bodies through our caresses and kisses. His gentleness even with the sudden, searing pain and surreal feeling of his entering me. And then there was the look in his eyes when he had fully cradled himself between my thighs. Was that love? Affection? Conquest? My mind had been too blurred by emotion and physical impact to tell.

These broodings and more were a Rubik's cube of confusion inside my head as I tried to bring my thoughts together.

What am I going to do now?

The water had shut off in the bathroom, and shortly, Rogan walked out, holding a hand towel as he dried his hands. He peered at me and asked, "You wake?"

I mumbled something that sounded vaguely like "yes," and he turned to open the room-darkening curtains. I squinted when the sun invaded the room.

Rogan's back was facing me as he shook the curtains open. His back was brawny without bulkiness and watching the rippling muscles underneath his sun-kissed golden skin stopped my breath. He had a flawless athlete's ass, the cheeks rounded with striated muscles. His long legs were powerful, with sinewy thighs and thick, muscled calves covered with fine hair. Only the surgical scars on the outside of his right leg marred the perfection.

He turned toward the bed, and in that slow-motion moment, I watched the early morning sun cast a brilliant scarlet halo around his long, red-brown waves. His eyes glowed like sunlight through amber and blazed at me with golden fire, matching those of the wolf tattoo on his chest. He had little hair on his muscular stomach, but a thick trail traveled from his navel to his trimmed pubic hair, which surrounded his...Wow. No wonder it hurt so much. Are they even *supposed* to be that size?

He was beautiful. And, at least for today, he was mine.

What time was it? I sat up to reach for my phone to check the time and let out a gasp of pain.

Rogan darted to the bedside, alarmed.

"You okay?"

I nodded, but I felt like every muscle below my waist had been through a war. I was sore in places I'd never been sore before. I'd been flayed. Impaled. I flopped back down on the bed with a shuddering groan. My eyes watered.

"I feel the way a beer-can chicken looks," I gasped. His amber eyes glittered, and his lips twitched as he fought back a laugh.

"Let me help you." He bent over the bed and swept me into his arms. He took me to the bathroom, and while I was using the toilet—which burned, by the way—he started the shower. While I should have demanded some privacy, it was obvious he wasn't having it.

When I flushed the toilet, he picked me up again and stepped into the shower. I said something about my hair, and on the counter, he found a scrunchie that he'd used and caught my locs in it. My shower cap had disappeared. He grabbed a washcloth from a towel bar, used my bath gel from last night, and began to wash me from head to foot. When he got to my legs, he coaxed them apart and cleaned up any remaining fluids from our lovemaking. I couldn't read his expression, but his dick was clearly enjoying his ministrations as it began to rise and thicken.

My word. Wasn't it large enough already?

When he finished caring for me, he gave himself a quick rinse and stepped out of the shower.

"Don't move," he told me as he dried himself and wrapped the towel around his hips. He fetched another towel and helped me step out of the shower. He dried me off, wrapped the towel around my body, and swept me up into his arms again as he carried me back to the bed and stood me on my feet.

"Is there anything you need?"

"Yes. My lotion." I was trying hard not to giggle at his intensity.

He fished it out of my bag and handed it to me after flipping the cap. I began rubbing the lotion over my arms as he snagged a pair of shorts from his bag and stepped into them. He picked up my towel, checked my locs for dampness, and took it back into the bathroom. He came out and watched me, eyebrows furrowed, as I continued to rub lotion on my body. Rogan took the bottle from me, squeezed some into his hand before handing it back, and lotioned my shoulders, back, butt, and thighs. His expression was earnest and determined.

"Rogie, what's up? Why are you being so weird?"

He regarded me with a warm but otherwise unreadable expression. "You don't understand. I'm trying to be a human being," he said.

"What does that mean?" I asked, perplexed.

"After last night, I feel very male, and I'm not sure how to act. It's taking everything I have not to throw open the balcony door and go all silverback. Pounding my chest. Howling at the moon.

Swinging through the trees. Peeing on a branch. I feel like I've got extra testosterone and need for it to go somewhere."

He looked at me, lips in a half-smile, eyes warm and affectionate. He moved close to me and held my face with one gentle hand. "You don't know what you did to me last night, babe. You took me to a place I've never been before. That said, if I go running through the streets naked and bellowing, I hope you have bail money."

I burst out laughing. I stopped and looked at him fondly, holding my bottle of lotion to my heart. "You are a crazy man."

"Yeah, I've heard," he replied, sending a look in my direction. "I know I'm crazy about you."

You love him. You always have. Now what?

Chapter 28

Rogan

I WOKE UP BEFORE Robbie and didn't release her from my arms. She was cuddled against my chest, sound asleep. I still reeled from my final thoughts last night.

I love her.

I accepted the emotion. And until now, I never thought it possible. Between playing major league soccer and my appearances on TV, there were always women available if I wanted, and I didn't have to deal with useless emotions or romance. All I had to do was to wink and crook a finger at the woman of my choice. That said, I didn't always think with my cock. My recent celibacy periods were because I didn't want to take the time. I was focused on my business legacy and career, and I didn't feel like dealing with drama.

Cue Hera. Right? Easily one of the biggest mistakes of my life. All because I wanted a body for a change instead of my hand. I hadn't planned on the psycho that accompanied it. I didn't want a relationship with her, but she did her damnedest to try to make one. That's what I get for dipping into crazy.

And then Robbie happened. Sweet, warm, *delicious*, Robbie. And for the first time in my life, I made love and understood what it meant. Not fucking. Not just nutting. It was something else that called to a part of me that had never surfaced before. Her body responding to mine, her sounds of joy and pain, her core enveloping and loving me, took me to another place.

Last night had been incredible. This may sound strange—blame it on my romantic European mother who propagandized me throughout life—but I felt like we had connected. Bonded. And not just physically. We had moved together like we had been designed for each other, two puzzle pieces interconnecting perfectly. Yes, she gave and I took, but afterward, we touched and kissed and loved like our spirits were one. I was inside of her body, and she returned the favor by crawling inside of my soul.

It had been the most intense sexual experience of my life. This was more than the actions of my body. I could have taken care of any urges with a bit of hand cream and rubbing one out in a warm shower. Making love to her enveloped not just my body, but my heart and my mind. Her responses to me were unexpected. There was no fakery. There was no artifice. Only a passionate woman's sounds, actions, and responses about the man she was loving. And that man was me.

Robbie murmured and sighed in her sleep and curled away from me. I took the opportunity to roll out of bed to go relieve myself. After I was done, I turned on the faucet to wash my hands, rinse my mouth, and splash water on my face and beard. I looked at myself in the mirror, and I couldn't put my finger on it, but I looked changed. I felt changed. I wanted to make love to her again, but not until she was ready. Naturally, I was ready. My body was already craving hers.

When I finished drying my hands, I heard her gasp of pain when she woke up and tried to get out of bed. I rushed to check on her to make sure everything was okay. She told me that she felt like a beer can chicken, and I chuckled at the word picture.

She thought I was crazy for sweeping her up into my arms, taking her to the shower, helping to soothe her sore, torn tissues, and carrying her back to the bed. I helped her dry off and smooth lotion onto her body. I felt like a conquering Viking. A silverback. Primitive, protective, possessive. I am her first lover, and I will do everything possible on this earth to make sure that I remain her only lover. The idea of another man making love to her triggered something a little psycho inside. No one else would have the experience I had with her last night. She's mine, and mine alone.

I hope she's good with that.

After she finished with her lotion and tossed the towel aside, she stood naked in front of me.

"Love me again, Rogie."

I hesitated for a split second, and then my lips met hers in a crushing kiss. Our tongues dueled with one another, stoking our fires higher and higher. I tore my mouth away from hers and trailed kisses down her neck, her shoulders, and to her beautiful rosy-brown nipples.

I took her in my arms and placed her gently on the bed. After stepping out of the shorts I'd donned, I climbed into the bed and hovered over her, both hands on either side of her head, and took her mouth again. Robbie writhed beneath me, and her legs opened and encircled my body.

Our eyes met, and I caught my breath at the raw emotion in hers. I claimed her with another searing kiss as my fingers found her core and I began to drive her over the edge. I whispered encouragement to her and watched her undulate against them, her arousal drenching my fingers.

"It's okay, baby," I whispered, "come for me."

When my thumb flicked her bud, she came with a gasping cry, the waves pulsing through her. Robbie's silvery eyes were wide in disbelief as ecstasy tore through her body.

Before she came down from her orgasm, I held her hip with one hand and entered her in one smooth thrust. Our movements together were frenzied, and she went shattering over the edge again. Her body reached up to mine as it found its pleasure, and I groaned my own release, moaning her name as if in prayer.

It was Robbie's first orgasm with me inside of her. I found her eyes and gazed at her with smiling encouragement. My hands held onto her thighs, allowing her to relax into my body.

Our breathing slowly returned to normal. She pressed her hands against my chest and rained light kisses across my skin.

This woman.

"I never knew sex was like this," Robbie sighed.

"Babe," I interrupted. "Sex is never like this."

She gave me a quizzical look. "What?"

I propped myself up on one elbow, my eyes traveling along the length of her body. Our legs entangled with one another's, skin contrasting in the early morning light.

"I've been around a bit for a few years," I began, using my free hand to air quote "been around," "so I consider myself to be a somewhat experienced man." Then, I paused for a moment to weigh my next words.

"In all those years, I've never had an experience like this. Not once."

She stiffened a bit, her expression turning guarded. I figured any discussions on my past sexual experiences were difficult for her to hear.

"This is not sex," I continued, waving my hand over the length of our bodies. "This is some next-level shit that I can't even wrap my brain around. I've never felt like I was losing my entire body through my cock. Or like my soul was owned by the woman with me. Or like my heart was involved." I hesitated. "Not even close."

I brushed her locs behind one shoulder and stroked her hair for a moment before I rested. My thoughts were chaotic.

"All I know," I smiled, "is that this is the best sensation I've ever had. You've brought something out in me I can't describe, Rob. Stuff I've heard about, but thought wouldn't exist for me."

I stopped, willing her to look into my eyes.

"You are the most special woman in my life. I think I knew that when you were standing in front of me at the gallery. When I saw you there, it felt like someone had drop-kicked me in the gut. And when you told me who you were, and although I didn't realize it then, it was meant to be. There's a reason why we were brought together again after all these years. And I'm not a mystic kind of person. But this feels real."

She smiled as she reached for me, and this time when I growled my release into her, I held onto her trembling thighs, chanting her name.

Ultimately, I didn't throw open the balcony doors and beat my chest or go running through the grounds naked, letting everyone know that mine is the biggest. But, I wanted to because I felt like a conqueror and protector who would kill a son of a bitch who tried to do anything to or with my woman. My woman.

So yeah, Tarzan, it's time to step aside. There's a new king of the jungle in town.

Chapter 29

Robbie

THE HOLMENS CALLED ME Saturday morning to cancel our appointment set for later that evening. They'd forgotten, they told me with regret, about a restaurant grand opening they'd been invited to. I grinned because it was for *Rogan's*, and their cancellation freed me up to attend. Rogan knew I had a meeting with established customers and wouldn't be able to make it. Well, that just became a moot point.

I dressed in beige boy shorts with a matching strapless bra and silky nylons with garter-style tops. I slipped a one-shoulder ivory sandwashed silk dress over my head and savored the feel of the layers of soft airy fabric resting on my skin. The waterfall hem settled just above my knees and dropped to mid-calf in the back. Bare shoulders and loose fabric were as sexy, in my opinion, as something skin-tight and suffocating. I felt sexy, and the dress had the bohemian look I prefer.

Because the weather was warmer and I was wearing such an airy and beautiful dress, I decided to use a light touch on my makeup. After using light powder and a bronzer, I added fringy false lashes to enhance my eyes and because they're fun. I completed the look with a deep rosy lipstick. I usually just wear a tinted gloss at most, so this change really enhanced my lips.

Looking good!

After clipping a couple of brass cuffs on a few locs, I braided the others into an intricate French braid style, weaving an ivory ribbon among the strands. Even braided, my locs were nearly to my waist, and I nodded in approval. I fastened large gold hoops to my ears, which was a change from the tiny moissanite studs I usually wore.

I finished the look with a pair of strappy white wedges. Not stilettos, because I hate them, but sexy nevertheless. My polished toenails looked great after the pedicure I'd given myself. My fingernails were short and plain with clear polish. That was enough.

I climbed into my minivan and headed for the restaurant. Twenty minutes later, I finally found an open parking spot. The parking lot was close to overflowing, and it looked like the place was jumping. Information about the invitation-only opening had been seeded in local publications and websites, and I knew that many elite types would be there. Rogan's recent TV interview had brought even more attention to *Rogan's*.

A Latino-looking bouncer dude stood by the door, dressed in a two-piece black suit. He looked me up and down as I approached, and it was apparent—even to me—that he approved and liked what he saw. He looked at my invitation and asked for my ID. I showed it to him, and he waved me in.

The restaurant was crowded. People were seated indoors and many more were in the outdoor areas. I wandered through the restaurant and peeked into the VIP. The lighting around the mural impressed me again, and I finally headed outside. A five-piece jazz band played covers on the small stage. A few people stood around the bar enjoying wine tasting, and others marveled at the view across the lake. I went back inside and hoped that I'd see someone I knew.

I didn't see Rogan anywhere, so I figured he was in the kitchen. His sister Janina and I spotted each other at the same time and squealed and hugged one another. My de facto protector slash sister was a sight for sore eyes. She was a feminine version of Rogan, with red and chestnut-colored hair and olive skin, *sans* freckles and golden eyes. She was blessed with their father's sky-blue eyes and their mother's smooth, freckle-free skin. She was almost my height, but with more curves, and her smile was warm and welcoming.

"Little sis!" she exclaimed. "How the hell are you?"

I laughed in greeting. She was one of the few in my small cadre of friends. It had been a couple of years since we'd last seen each other, but that didn't matter. We could pick up just like a day hadn't passed since the last time we hung out.

"I love you!" I exclaimed. "I've missed you so much! It's been a long time! And you look exactly the same! Do you even age?"

She blushed and said, "You were always good for my ego. I knew I missed you for a reason!"

I snagged two tulip glasses of sparkling from a passing server's tray and gave one to Janina. The newspapers' society pages were in full force, apparently. Somehow I found myself posing with celebrities whose names escaped me. A couple of men propositioned me and I waved them away. Where was a "taken" sign when I needed one?

Janina and I walked toward the VIP dining area, where my mural stood out in its glory.

"I wish you could have been here last week when I first saw this," said Janina with a grin. "I was blown away. This is gorgeous! When Rogan told me that you had painted it, I screamed!" she laughed. "But I wasn't surprised. I remember how good you were as a kid."

I grinned back at her. "Thanks!" I chuckled. "If this were on watercolor paper, I could have sold it for maybe a couple hundred grand, possibly more. Rogan's lucky I didn't charge him at least that much."

Janina gave a long, low whistle. "Does he even know how valuable this is?"

"Not really. He was just happy that I did it. I know what it's worth, but I gave him a crazy discount because I'm foolish."

"You're a hoot," Janina laughed. "I don't know where my brother is. I can't believe that he'll be in the kitchen all night."

A photographer for one of the local gossip papers asked us for our names. I guess we looked famous or something because his face lit up when Janina told him who we were. He took several photos of the sister of the chef, but I wasn't left out. Janina pointed out that I was the artist responsible for the murals and he asked me to pose next to my VIP room showpiece. Which I gladly did, posing as BTW.

I joined Janina again, feeling stoked. Grinning at each other, we continued our way through the crowd.

"Is anyone else here?"

"Dad is here," she laughed and nodded toward the main bar. Angus was there, a glass of Scotch in hand, laughing with a couple of other men.

"Dad and Uncle Hugo, Mama's brother, have been tight forever. Of course, Hugo wasn't going to miss the opening of his favorite nephew's restaurant! Uncle Hugo is a chef like Mama and has about five restaurants in Spain. He's good!"

I nodded, impressed. I'd go over later to say hi to Angus and meet Uncle Hugo.

Justin Crews, aka "Captain America," stopped us, his eyes on Janina. Well, well, well. We all spoke for a couple of minutes before Justin engaged Janina in conversation. Hm. Looks like he's interested in little sister. And from the way Janina was smiling, she was returning the favor.

Despite Rogan's busyness, we had still managed to snatch some time together at his condo. I didn't mind spending time there since it was closer to the restaurant, and I scheduled my own time as it suited me. I was learning about the realities of a relationship and about sex. Under Rogan's gentle tutelage, my natural reticence and inhibitions were falling away when I was with him. Every night I spent in his arms bonded me closer to him and him closer to my heart.

And then I saw him. He had finally been able to get away to mingle with the guests. I figured Mama and his sous chefs had everything under control so that he could come out and do a little one-on-one PR. He'd tied his signature black-printed white bandana around his head, and his hair was in a low, out-of-the-way bun. He wore a white chef's coat, dark slacks, long white apron tied at the waist, and black combat boots.

Because of his old leg injury, he preferred the boots over the omnipresent Dansko clogs. I asked about them one morning when he was getting ready for a "dress rehearsal" at the restaurant. He smiled at me and said that they helped support his old injury and were very comfortable. "They're waterproof, slip-resistant, durable, and steel-toed. After all," he quipped, "if they can support our troops through fucking *war*, they can hold up in a kitchen."

I started toward him, hoping to surprise him before he returned to the kitchen. That proved to be impossible. Everyone from simpering teenagers to local celebs and politicians to aggressive reporters wanted to speak to him. He was talking to everyone, including a trio of teens who wanted selfies with the hot chef. I smiled to myself at the girls. Their eyelashes were batting furiously as they twirled their hair, hoping that their flirting would get at least one of them asked out on a date.

Not a chance, jailbait. But it was cute. They all squealed and feigned swooning when he elegantly kissed each of them on the back of the hand and stood for selfies. They were fans for life, no doubt. I rolled my eyes and smiled.

A hand on my shoulder made me turn around to face Daria, whose radiant face told me that she was enjoying a date with Derrick. Daria wore a colorful two-piece African print dress that displayed her stunning curves to the max. Derrick was simply dressed in dark linen slacks and a lightly woven chambray dress shirt. They looked good together, and I grinned in approval. Introducing them to each other had been perfect.

"Daria, if I had your body," I began, feeling envious. As always, my friend was stunning, even if she was too shy to admit it. Derrick was grinning at her, smitten. Hm. Could our favorite playa be thinking about going all-in with one woman? In my opinion, he'd be a fool if he let her go.

Daria laughed. "Look at you!" she exclaimed. "You look like an angel."

"Both of y'all look good enough to take home," Derrick drawled, waggling his heavy eyebrows. We both laughed, and Daria smacked him on the arm before giving him a kiss on the cheek.

"You are so good for our egos!" she chuckled. She turned to me. "What are you up to, and what should I know?"

"Well," I began, "I've been here for a while, and I've been trying to get close to Rogan. He came out of the kitchen about a half hour or so ago, but I can't seem to catch even a second to see him. He always has a crowd of reporters and stuff around him, and he doesn't know I'm here."

Daria looked around at the cheery multitude of people. "Good luck with that! We're going to explore and we'll see you later," she smiled.

I found Rogan talking to a reporter with a microphone. Maybe a podcaster? People were milling around him, but politely keeping their distance. His back was to me, and I cautiously approached, waiting for an opportunity to let him know that I had been able to attend after all. He nodded with a final comment, shook hands, and the happy reporter left him as several other people gathered around him to ask questions and share comments.

And then I stopped. A woman's hand was around his waist and rubbing his lower back while he talked animatedly to a small group of people. That seemed like an awfully intimate gesture, and I frowned. She put one of her hands on his butt, pulling him close to her. Rogan's body language told me that he was either oblivious to the woman's presence or so intimate with her that this was an everyday thing. Could it be one of his kitchen or wait staff? He laughed goodbye to the group he'd been talking to and turned toward the woman whose arms were now draped intimately around his middle.

Hera's face appeared from around his front and her eyes locked with mine. She sent me a sneer and then, never breaking her smug glare, wrapped her arms around his neck and pulled his head down so that she could reach his lips. And just like that, he was locked in a kiss with that fake woman. The one he was supposedly done with. He certainly wasn't fighting her.

What in the actual hell?

Photographers were taking pictures of the kiss when they broke it, and the small group applauded. She seemed to slither her body against his, and even though I couldn't hear it, I knew she was purring. Her eyes met mine again, and she waved at me, a smirk on her face. Did she just get her man back?

Everything blurred. The earth tilted. I couldn't breathe. I began to back up, seeking an escape. How could I have been so foolish? This was supposed to be an invitation-only event, personally curated by Mama and Rogan. He had invited *her*? Because I know Mama sure as hell wouldn't. Rogan knew that I wouldn't be able to attend this function. Was that an excuse to have her here to take up the slack just in case? A body to warm his bed in my absence? After all, if I wasn't supposed to be here, he might as well fill the void with something else in celebration. Familiar pussy, I guess.

Daria, who was walking toward me with Derrick, looked at me curiously. She hadn't seen the kiss. I looked at her and said, "I can't do this. I have to leave."

"Robbie, wait!" her cry hit my ears as I turned to leave. My heart was pounding, and I ignored her. I had to get out of there.

Daria caught my arm just before I ran out of the front entrance.

"Robbie, what happened?" she asked, concerned about my stricken expression.

"He was kissing her. He invited her. She was all over him." I stopped, gasping, trying to get my breath. "I mean nothing to him," I whispered. "I need to get out of here!"

I wrenched my arm from a stunned Daria's grasp and ran.

As I left, the bouncer guy asked, "Leaving so soon?"

"Yes," I replied, fighting tears. "Something came up."

I ran across the parking lot, jumped into my van, and tried not to peel away in this quiet neighborhood. My hands were shaking, and my chest was tight. Once I had gotten a few blocks away, I pulled over so that I could breathe. I fought back the sobs that rose in my throat. Several deep breaths later, I focused on driving home. At the last minute, I changed my mind and decided to go to Mom and Dad's instead, and made a quick call.

I should have known better. He let her touch him. Hang on to and fondle him. Kiss him. I can only imagine what he was going to let her do to him later. I felt like a fool. I had believed that he cared. He was just another fuckboy.

They say a picture is worth a thousand words. Well, not quite. Witnessing something so up close and personal is worth even more.

Chapter 30

Robbie

I DROVE WEST ON Charleston to Mom and Dad's spacious home in Calico Basin. I navigated my way through the rustic side roads before arriving at their gated entrance. When I keyed in my personal code, the gate's iron doors swung inward, and I piloted my way up the long driveway.

When I pulled over for a gasping moment, I had called Dad to tell him I would stay overnight. I gave him the short version of what had happened, and he was sympathetic. I needed to disappear from Rogan's life since he'd shown me and the world what his preference was. Being played wasn't in my life plans.

I parked my van in front of the garage and ran to the front door. I rang the doorbell, and Dad opened the door right away. He took me into his arms, giving me the bear hug I so desperately needed.

He guided me into the family room and straight to the plush loveseat.

"Let me get us a bottle of wine," he said. "That'll be a good start while you give me the whole story."

I curled up in the corner of the loveseat, my dress a cloud around my legs. I heard him fiddling around in the kitchen, and he walked back into the family room with a bottle of Pinot Noir and two Burgundy Riedels on a tray with some pâté and crackers.

Judson David Wilkes is not my biological father. He met Mom when I was about ten or so years old, and they married only months after meeting. My sperm donor, who fertilized Mom when he was an up-and-coming rapper, had nothing to do with my upbringing. He hung around long enough to give the illusion of caring and then disappeared, chasing groupies and a rap career. So I hadn't known how having a father figure around would impact me until Judson came into my life. Then I learned what a real man and a proper father were. I loved him more than anything.

Dad completed the adoption process just before I graduated high school at 15. Initially, my sperm donor didn't want to give up his parental rights. He disrespected Dad even though he never paid a dime of child support. Since he was being a son of a bitch, Dad asked a few "people" from Philly to "talk" with him. After that meeting, my sperm donor eagerly signed the necessary papers so Dad could adopt me. Did I mention that Dad was an attorney for one of the "families" in Philly? I guess they made sperm donor an offer he couldn't refuse. So to speak. It was the best thing that ever happened to me.

Dad was home alone when I arrived because Mom hadn't returned from an international personal goods conference. She would be home on Sunday since the conference activities ended too late to take the red-eye from New York.

"Where's Zion?" I asked.

"He spent the day with his buddy Carter across the road," Dad answered. "When he came home after dinner, I made him shower, and he crashed.

"Now tell me what Rogan did. I couldn't understand everything because the reception was bad, and you weren't coherent. Do I need to fuck him up?"

Dad's voice is striking. If James Earl Jones and Barry White had a son together, it would have been Dad. His voice is rich, buttery, deep, and sonorous, a pleasure to the ears. He easily could have been a voice actor if he wanted. Still, after working so hard as a young lawyer in Philly and then moving across the country to Vegas, he decided this was an excellent time to enjoy the fruits of his labors.

When he was an attorney in Philadelphia, Dad had been incredibly successful. With his employer's guidance, he made targeted real estate investments in Las Vegas when the recession hit. When the turnaround came, those investments made him wealthier than he already was. He started a small real estate law firm, and he only worked a few days a week. He was now semi-retired and didn't mind playing the part of househusband when needed.

Rogan and Mama had invited my parents to the opening, but Dad had opted out because he didn't go to social events without his wife by his side. "It's unseemly," he always said. The way Dad treated Mom, Zion, and me was my model, my plumb line about how to be treated by the man in my life. He set the "real man" bar high, and I had no reason to expect anything less.

"Rogan didn't know I was going to be there," I began. "And his most recent ex was in attendance."

Dad nodded. "And?"

"She was all over him. Her arms were around his waist, she was rubbing his butt, and," I stopped to swallow the lump in my throat and take a deep breath, "she was kissing him. On the mouth, with her arms around his neck, in front of the entire crowd. I couldn't handle it, so I left."

Dad grunted. "Have some wine."

He poured the glistening red into both glasses and spread some pâté on a couple of crackers. Delicious.

"I made the pâté myself," he said. "You like it?"

I nodded and gestured for another one. I just realized I hadn't eaten all day and snacked on only a few of the passed hors d'oeuvres at the restaurant.

"So. What are you going to do about it?"

"Do about what?"

"Rogan and that woman."

"Nothing."

"Do you think that's wise?"

"Dad, I saw them kiss. Her arms were around his neck, and that was after she patted and rubbed his butt. So what am I supposed to do? Go ghetto on him?"

He chuckled.

I looked at him, scowling. "I swore ages ago that I'd never fight another woman over a man. Not ever. And if he didn't want to put me in the position to decide how important he was in my life, he shouldn't have let her kiss him. Or he shouldn't have kissed her."

Dad nodded, never breaking his gaze. He twirled the stem of his wine glass and inhaled the cranberry-and-earth fragrance of the Oregon Pinot. He took a contemplative sip and tilted his head.

"If I were a lawyer, and I am," he said enigmatically, "I'd need a closer examination of the evidence."

"What do you mean by that?"

"I mean," he continued, setting his glass on the coffee table and leaning forward, forearms draped over his knees, "that not everything may be what you think it is. There may be a plausible explanation for what you think you saw."

I was aghast. *What the hell?*

"So I'm supposed to believe some random explanation instead of my own lyin' eyes?"

"I know how that boy feels about you," Dad rumbled, "and I think there's more to the story than what meets the eye."

I started a retort when he held up one large hand. "Don't forget that along with my other duties, I was also the defense attorney for people who'd been accused of some pretty heinous stuff. Eyewitness observations can be very unreliable.

"I'm not telling you to confront him now. But after you've had some time to cool off, to vent, and to put some time and space behind you, revisit the situation.

"Although," he mused, "I have a feeling the boy will track you down. If he's the man I think he is, he will do the 'ends of the earth' thing to get you back into his life."

I shook my head vigorously. "I don't think so. I shouldn't be surprised that after he got what he wanted from me..."

Oops. I hadn't meant to confess that.

But Dad looked at me fondly. "Finally did it, huh?"

I felt the heat rising in my face. I was so embarrassed that I began to sweat and my eyes watered. I couldn't remember ever feeling so mortified.

He chuckled, watching me with affection. At least, I think it was affection. I was so flustered I couldn't even see.

"Robbie, baby, it's okay. You're a grown woman. You decide your own fate. I know that once you decided to love a man, you didn't make that decision lightly. I've been in your life too long, baby girl. All that being said," he smirked, "if I find out he intended to use you and drop you, I can take care of things my own way. But I don't think that's the case at all."

He tilted his head again. "My gut tells me that he cares for you more than you think he does."

"If he did, then he wouldn't have kissed that fuck doll of an ex." Teary again. "But he never said he loved me. I made assumptions. And you know what they say about assumptions."

"You're not an ass, baby girl," Dad replied gently. "You're a woman in love. We've all been hurt at some time."

I looked over at him, my expression clearly skeptical. What stupid woman would break *his* heart? Dad was astute, handsome, educated, cerebral, and *my oh my* between the sheets, according to Mom. Ew. Some things you just don't need to know, amirite?

He smiled. "Even me. And now, I couldn't be happier. Because those relationships made me grow up and be the man I needed to be when I met Molly. She's the undisputed love of my life, and I thank God every day that she's mine.

"But I had a couple of serious relationships that, whether I broke it off or the woman did, left me devastated." He placed his hand over his heart. "So I know what heartbreak is."

"It hurts," I muttered.

"Yes, it does," he agreed. "Like your life is ending. Like you want to die."

He stood up and walked into the dining room. He returned and tossed a key chain my way.

"Go to Cambria," he said. "Spend a few weeks unwinding and decompressing. Sometimes you just have to get away from a thing in order to address a thing with a clear mind. And that's what you need right now.

"Don't worry about your house. I'll take care of security. Let your friend stay there and let her know that she'll be safe."

He crouched down in front of me, dark eyes full of compassion. "This, too, shall pass. And whether it's the worst thing that could happen or if everything turns out okay, you'll be fine. Time heals. Life goes on. Wounds fade. And you survive. Through all the pain, you survive.

"And if the worst happens and you never get back together, you now can restart from the point of experience and newfound maturity. That's not a bad thing. And no matter what, I got you. Never worry about that. I got you."

He stood up, gazing down at me with a hint of a smile on his face, and cleared his throat. "And, your honor, I submit that the empirical evidence will demonstrate beyond a reasonable doubt that the defendant has been falsely accused and that the so-called eyewitness evidence is unreliable and circumstantial at best. Accordingly, I shall ask and expect you to return a verdict of not guilty. And then jump his bones."

I burst into helpless, watery laughter. Okay. We'll see. But tomorrow I'm outta here. I'm leaving Vegas. To find some solace for my heartache.

Chapter 31

Robbie

I TURNED INTO THE driveway of our Cambria house and sighed. I had been driving since o'dark-thirty this morning and, except for a break for junk food and gas at the truck stop at Kramer Junction, drove non-stop. To escape. To escape the pain and humiliation.

Leaving Las Vegas had been easy. Once I told Dad what happened, he let me stay overnight in the big house. I woke up early and drove home, and instead of parking in the driveway like I usually did, I parked the van in the garage. If by chance Rogan came by with some bullshit excuse why he had been playing tonsil hockey with the thot, he didn't need to know I was here. I was in no mood to talk to him.

I had half-heartedly begun to pack, but I didn't leave on Sunday. Although I was eager to get to Cambria, I was too drained, hurt, and sad to make the long drive. I couldn't. Besides, the Sunday traffic on the I-15 to California was always a nightmare, and I didn't need the extra stress.

Daria and I had lunch at Applebee's on Monday, where we talked about the situation. How had everything turned upside down so badly? Would he ever have told me he kissed her? Or was I another conquest, and he didn't have to tell me shit? Did he take her back to his condo to "celebrate" a successful opening since I wasn't around? After all, we hadn't seen each other or spoken much for at least two weeks.

When we left the restaurant, we spotted the new copies of the *Vegas Weekly Tea* in one of the magazine racks in the foyer. Rogan was on the front cover, standing proudly in front of *Rogan's* with a toothy grin, luxurious mane around his shoulders, and his arms crossed in front of his muscular chest. My heart skittered just seeing him.

Maybe I was a little hasty.

We eagerly opened the magazine to the article, gasping at the coverage and the photos. A photo of me in front of the mural made us both smile. We were jumping up and down at the picture's quality and the caption underneath, *Roberta Wilkes, Vegas' Own Residential Artist, Displays Her Masterwork*. So much for BTW. Oh well.

And then, we turned to the center of the magazine, which was the showcase of the article. And there were Rogan and Hera. She had arched her body sensually against his, flung one arm around his neck, and the other hand was holding his head as their lips met in an open-mouth, tongue-heavy kiss. The caption read, *Is Rogan McDonald, Cooking Network Judge, Top Chef Winner, and New Vegas Restaurateur, Reconciling with Ex-girlfriend, Hera Byrnes?*

That sound of a wounded animal? That was me.

I felt like a fool.

I don't remember much other than Daria holding on to me as we walked to my van. She had to go back to school, but she was worried enough to ask me if I was okay. Once I could breathe and focus again, I nodded.

"I'm leaving first thing," I told her. "And I'll be fine. I'll finish packing and taking care of a few things tonight, and I'll probably be gone when you leave for school. I can't handle this."

Even though she'd been at the opening with Derrick and had only heard from me what Rogan had done, Daria swore on the heads of her future children that she wouldn't tell him where I was going. Oh, *hell* no!

Daria had continued to live at the house at my insistence. This would make it easier for her to save money for classes and her own place without being saddled with high rent. Besides, I liked her company, and knowing that someone would look out for me was reassuring. I could leave my house in good hands.

I spent several hours packing everything I'd need for a month away from home. I went online and forwarded my mail to Mom and Dad's. They'd send anything important to the Cambria house. I let my bank and credit card companies know that I'd be in California for a month. There were other loose ends to tie up before I hit the road. Maybe after a month, the hole where my heart used to be would be healed. If not, I'd just stay another month. Or longer, if necessary.

Seeing Rogan with that woman had, as the British say, gutted me. She was hanging all over him, and he was letting her. She kissed him, open-mouthed and tongue deep, and except for pulling back after a second too long, he seemed to let her. Why had he done that? Why did he let her put her hands all over him, kiss and swoon over him? And the smirk she sent to me was the equivalent of a middle finger.

I guess I shouldn't have been surprised that even someone like Rogan, who always swore he was one of the "good guys," would slip. And that was a major slip. He'd allowed that woman to touch him in ways a committed man should never let a random woman touch him. I dedicated myself to him, and there's no way I'd allow any other man to grope me like that.

But he didn't commit, did he? Yes, he said he cared for me, I was his woman, blah blah blah, but that was as far as it went. He'd never told me he loved me. We'd never talked about a future together. So I suppose he really didn't commit to or love me. I guess that as long as his fuck doll ex-girlfriend was still open to him, then he was open to her.

The real-life visual of him kissing her, coupled with my imagination's picture of him touching, licking, and fucking her, sent a slash of pain through me. In my mind's eye, I saw his glorious body connecting with hers, doing to her what he'd done to me, giving her that intense pleasure I thought was mine alone. It sent a shard of pain through me that was so intense that I sat in the driver's seat gasping, waiting for the anguish to pass.

The prickle I'd felt when he talked about the women he'd been with in the past and how he no longer had anything to do with them wasn't a prickle anymore. Instead, it was a blown-out rupture in the middle of my soul. Is this what they meant by being heartbroken? Because while it was apparently still beating, it felt like it was beating in a hollow space lined with shards of glass. I leaned back against my seat and closed my eyes as I tried to let the wash of pain melt away.

Through all the pain, you survive.

I pressed the button on my garage door opener and rolled inside. Once parked in the spacious garage, I turned off the engine and began removing my belongings from the van to store away. I planned to be here for a month so I could heal. Maybe more. It may be months before I make my way back to Vegas, but for the time being, I needed the solace and restorative power of solitude and the sea.

First, I wrestled my electric bike out and rolled it into a corner of the garage near my punching bag. I needed the bike to travel into "downtown" Cambria for meals and shopping. I refused to tackle the hills on foot, particularly if I carried anything. Shopping was way too easy to overdo in Cambria, and lugging shopping bags back up to the house was not my thing. And I certainly didn't want to drive my van every day. So my bike was it.

I rolled my two carry-ons through the house garage door. After dropping them into the master, I returned and arranged my art supplies on the garage shelves. I hadn't brought much. Only a couple of watercolor palettes, graphite pencils and blocks, a box of pastels, colored pencils, inks, and lots of paper. If I needed more, I could drive to San Luis Obispo for extra supplies.

I took my fabric drop cloths to the second bedroom and laid them on the floor. This would be my makeshift temporary studio if I did any art. I had also brought my Sony mirrorless. Photography was another comfort.

Opening the heavy Igloo cooler, I took out the foods that I'd packed. I made several trips to the kitchen, but I had enough to last me a few days before I'd have to go shopping. Fortunately, daily farmers' markets were available along the Central Coast, so I'd never run out of fresh food.

I went outside to the front of the house, walked down the driveway, and smiled. This was a lovely neighborhood with small homes, friendly neighbors, and lots of quiet. Our beach house looked like a regular house you'd see anywhere, with clapboard siding and asphalt shingle roof. Most of the homes looked like middle America. Very un-Californian.

I walked back into the garage and pressed the wall button to close the door. I locked the van and went inside the house.

A spacious living room slash great room with a large fireplace was just off the kitchen and dining area. My folks recently renovated the kitchen and installed natural hickory cabinets with off-white quartz countertops. Ocean-colored subway tiles covered the backsplash, and the appliances were stainless steel. The peninsula jutted into the compact dining area right in front of one of two sets of French doors.

A sofa and loveseat covered with white-on-white patterned canvas duck sat in the living space. A huge, burled wood coffee table invited wine glasses and foot propping. I knew from experience that the massive stone fireplace could warm the entire space on cold California nights.

The wraparound deck went from the dining room around the corner to the master. Two other bedrooms were a little small and didn't have doors to the outside. The one I was using as a studio had a Murphy bed, which gave me enough room to do some artwork or invite a guest if I felt so inclined. Bedroom three was an office with a built-in desk, bookshelves, and computers.

The master bedroom was spacious, with two large windows and a set of French doors leading out to the deck, perfect for morning coffee or evening wine. The dual walk-in closets were way more than I needed since I'd only brought jeans, t-shirts, shorts, several summer sundresses, and a couple of bikinis. You can't be blocks away from the Pacific Ocean and not indulge! Besides, the ocean is what I came for. Even though I'm a desert rat, I feel the pull of the water when I'm stressed. And stressed doesn't begin to describe how I'm feeling.

I turned on my Apple Radio station to listen to music while I got ready to put my stuff away, and a few bars of "What Becomes of the Brokenhearted" filled the space.

I snapped off the station with a sob. I couldn't think about broken hearts or departed love right now. Instead, I had to focus on myself.

I love you, Jimmy Ruffin, but not today. Not now. I just can't.

After taking a deep, cleansing breath, I hung up my jeans and dresses and folded my t-shirts, underwear, and swimsuits in the drawers of the massive dresser. After stashing my toiletries in the bathroom, I trudged back into the kitchen.

I stood in front of the refrigerator, door open, trying to figure out what to have for lunch. Everything I'd brought would have to be cooked or prepped, and I didn't feel like it. I was too tired to either cook or go into town to get something to eat, and I'd had enough snacks on the road to constipate me for a year. I grabbed a small bottle of Pellegrino, sighing. Looks like I'd have to go shopping anyway.

The doorbell rang. What? I wasn't expecting company.

I opened the door to a tall, handsome man with skin the color of freshly brewed coffee. Except for short bouncy locs caught up in a ponytail at his crown, his head was shaved bald. Onyx-dark eyes gleamed at me, and full lips smiled, showing off a meticulously groomed goatee and ridiculously perfect teeth. Dressed in jeans and a branded t-shirt, he stood there in all his glory, quirking a grin my way.

"I thought I heard your raggedy-ass van pull up a while ago."

"Lonnie!" I laughed and threw myself into his arms. We rocked back and forth, hugging each other like there was no tomorrow.

"What the hell are you doing here?" I demanded, grinning.

"I'm on vacation. And what better place to spend a vacation than at the beach in California. I can't go anywhere else and get what I've got here, and this is as far as I want to travel. You know how it goes. If you can't make it there, you can't make it anywhere."

Alonzo James Jenkins had been a friend of the family for years. Older than me by at least a decade or so, he'd taken on the job as my protector and guardian whenever I came to the beach house alone. Yes, he knew I was Krav Maga trained and had a carry permit, but his basic protective instincts didn't care. He was the drop-dead gorgeous older brother who had girlfriends clamoring to get to know him.

Lonnie was a founding partner of a successful sports and entertainment law firm in LA, and he had a spacious luxury apartment in the city. He only worked four days a week, only when he wanted, and spent the rest of the week in his house next door to ours.

He looked at me closely, one eyebrow raised. "How are you?"

"I'm fine," I lied.

And then I crumbled. The tears I'd been holding back started streaming down my face, and I broke.

Lonnie wrapped muscular arms around me and walked me into the living room. I cried as I'd never cried before in my entire adult life. I sagged to the floor in front of the sofa, sobbing, surrendering to the pain and heartbreak, trying to hold the hole in my chest together while Lonnie patted my back and just let me cry out my despair. After a while, when all I had was hiccups, he got up and went to the hall bathroom. He handed me a box of tissues, which I took and sent him a smile paired with my watery, bloodshot eyes. I was so drained. I felt so empty. So desolate.

"If nobody's dead, the only reason someone cries like this is if there's heartbreak involved," he said. "Is this because of a man?"

I nodded. I couldn't cry or speak anymore, but he understood.

"You're in love?"

I nodded again, feeling tears well up despite trying to will them away. I wanted to curl up into a ball and rock back and forth, holding what's left of my heart inside. Wallow in my misery.

"It's my own fault." I hiccuped, letting the tears fall. "It's not like Rogan ever told me he loved me. He didn't. I thought he did until I saw him French kissing his ex-girlfriend. So I left."

"Damn!" Lonnie exclaimed, looking at me disbelievingly. "I can't even wrap my mind around the idea that someone would do that to you, li'l sis. You're a jewel."

Lonnie rubbed my arm. "Come on over for lunch. You look hungry, and I know you don't feel like fixing anything. There's plenty. After all, I'm on vacation, and we gotta eat."

I smiled at him in gratitude. "Thanks, Lonnie. Let me change into something that doesn't have road funk on it, and I'll be right over."

Lonnie smiled at me, still concerned, and nodded, softly patting my cheek. "See you in a few. If you don't show up, I'm comin' back to get you."

After he left, I went into the master bath and was shocked at my appearance. My face was splotchy and my eyes were puffy from crying. My nose was red, and I looked, well, more than sad. Oh well. I can't pretend to feel something I don't. I'm not built that way.

After splashing my face with some cold water, I changed into a pair of baggy cargo shorts and a t-shirt. Then, carrying an old pair of Keens sandals to the front door, I picked up the house key where I'd dropped it on the small table in the foyer. I looked around and nodded in satisfaction. Yes. This was going to be very good for me. It had to be.

I closed and locked the front door, slipped on my sandals, and trudged next door to Lonnie's house.

Chapter 32

Rogan

It was early Tuesday afternoon. I sat in a booth below Robbie's *Magnum Opus* a couple of hours before restaurant opening. The bar had opened at noon, and a few patrons were joking with each other and enjoying glasses of wine. In the background, Premier League soccer played on the mounted TVs.

I had some paperwork to finish and was typing somewhat distractedly into my laptop. No matter how I tried, I couldn't focus. I was a steaming hot pile of misery.

Probably acting out of pity because of my downturned face, one of my new wait staff brought me a bottle of Acqua Panna and a glass of clear ice.

"You okay, sir?" he asked.

I smiled at him. "I didn't know it was showing, but I'm fine. Just preoccupied. Thanks for the water."

He nodded and left the VIP room.

Mama had started prep hours ago and didn't need my help. Hell, she didn't need *me*, period. She had seen the photo of Hera kissing me and had immediately gone into "you ain't shit" mode. Mama had courtesy hard-wired into her DNA and treated me accordingly, but she was upset and fuming.

That she had thrown the *Vegas Weekly Tea* at my chest, swore at me in Spanish about the *puta*, and then turned on her heel and stormed away, gave me some indication that maybe, just maybe, she was ticked off with me. I could tell.

When Mama had done that, I had no idea what had happened. Then I saw the mag opened up to the half-page photo of Hera deeply French kissing me along with a blurb about how I, the up-and-coming Vegas restaurateur, had reconciled with my ex-girlfriend, Hera Byrnes.

Oh. So that's her last name. Not that it matters because we sure as hell ain't "reconciling." Oh, *hell* no.

If Mama had seen the photo, then Robbie probably had too, because she had ghosted. I tried to call and text her after the opening had ended, but it was a fruitless effort. After about the fifth call, she blocked me.

Daria had ripped me a new one about Hera. I think she had seen what Robbie had apparently seen and looked at me with such feral hatred that I almost feared for my life.

After opening night, I went straight to Robbie's when staff had finished cleaning and the restaurant shuttered. Her courtyard gate wasn't locked, but no one answered the front door. The house was dark, and my ringing the bell and pounding on the door resulted in nothing. There were no signs of life whatsoever. Apparently, she'd gone somewhere else to avoid me.

Dammit.

I went home to grab a few hours of sleep before I had to be up early to prep for family meal and brunch service on Sunday.

I stopped at Robbie's house on my way to the restaurant and was surprised to find the courtyard gate locked. Someone had unlocked it last night, which told me that Robbie was still around but wasn't interested in speaking to me. I pressed on the ringer, but there was no response.

Cursing, I got into my car. I swore and left for the restaurant. I felt helpless. I needed her.

I drove to *Rogan's*, seething. I shook my head, trying to straighten myself out before going in. My personal problems couldn't be a part of my working day at the restaurant.

Foodservice ended at nine, and the bar remained open an extra hour for a few lingering patrons. I stayed till final closing and went to Robbie's house. The courtyard gate was locked, but I tried the ringer again to see if anyone was home. To my surprise, there was a faint buzz, and I opened the gate and ran up the courtyard to the front door. My heart was pounding.

The door opened, but instead of Robbie, Daria stood in the entryway.

"Is Robbie here?" I hoped I didn't sound as desperate as I felt.

"She's not available."

"Not available? What does that mean?" I'm not a frantic type of person, but I felt my anxiety rising.

Daria closed her eyes and took a deep, dramatic sigh.

"She's not available to *you*," she declared flatly, face expressionless. "I suggest you leave. She's not interested in speaking to you or communicating with you in any way. Sorry."

I was trying not to lose my shit.

"I'll let her know you stopped by." She fake smiled and shut the door in my face. The decisive snap of the deadbolt on the other side punctuated her statement.

When I got back to my car, I roared at the top of my lungs and pounded the dashboard.

Even though the restaurant was dark on Monday, I still had staff training and product ordering to do. Unfortunately, Monday was when the public edition of the *Tea* dropped. On the front cover was a photo of me standing at the restaurant entrance with my hair around my shoulders and arms crossed. I had dressed in casual clothing and looked happy. The picture looked pretty damn good, even if I say so myself. I usually hate getting my picture taken, but this had turned out great.

In the middle of the article was a photo of "the kiss" with Hera. She had encircled one arm around my neck, and the other held the back of my head as she pressed her overdone body against mine, giving me a deep, intimate kiss. Therefore, it was the centerfold of the *Tea*. And that's why Mama had thrown the paper at me.

Shit.

If Robbie saw the photo, that would destroy her. A lasting reminder of my inattention was now permanently in print.

I was thinking about my next step when Derrick walked in and stood over me. "You look like shit, man."

I looked up from my paperwork and snarled at him. Tell me something I don't know. I hadn't eaten much besides tasting food while in the kitchen with the sous chefs, and sleeping was just an abstract theory.

"You talk to Robbie yet?"

"No."

"Man, she must be pissed."

I pinched the bridge of my nose, shaking my head. "I know she is. She blocked me on her phone, and she's ghosted. Daria won't tell me a damn thing. She looks at me like I'm Hannibal Lecter,

Norman Bates, and Lucifer, all blended together into a steaming pile of shit."

I could feel the emotions welling up in me. We'd be opening in an hour. I had to keep it together.

Derrick slid into the booth next to me, turned his baseball cap backward, and gave me a long, assessing look.

"What?"

"I gotta ask, man. You sure you done with Hera?" he probed. "That kiss looked awfully legit."

"Fuck you."

Derrick chuckled, dark eyes twinkling. Then he turned somber.

"It was bad enough that Robbie saw you in person kissing the woman that you swore you were done with," he began, "but then she saw it in print."

"We don't know that."

"Yeah, we do. Daria told me that she saw it yesterday when they were out together. They'd had lunch, and when they were leaving the restaurant, they picked up a copy of the *Tea* from the foyer rack.

"They picked it up because you and the restaurant were on the cover. So they opened it up, and there you were in the centerfold during 'the kiss,'" he air quoted, "and Robbie lost it."

Fuck.

I could feel a headache coming on. This was not going well.

He asked me again, this time with zero humor, "You sure you're done with Hera?"

I met Derrick's eyes, giving him a glare. He was my best friend, but the way I was feeling now, I had no compunction about punching him if he continued talking shit.

"Why do you keep asking me that, man?" I hotly returned. "Just to be clear, I never did like her for anything more than a random nut. I was ready to end it way before I ran into Robbie again."

Derrick looked at me challengingly. "So why didn't you?"

I felt foolish as I answered, "She was a mindless distraction when I was in the first stages of putting this place together. Plus, she swallowed."

Derrick let loose a roar of laughter. "Man, you crazy."

He gave me an all too probing look, suddenly serious again.

"This is a personal question, and it may seem beside the point, but did you ever have oral sex with Hera?"

I looked at him, raising an eyebrow. What does that have to do with anything?

"Yeah," I stated. "At least at first. Not so much during the last few weeks we were seeing each other, which was less than four months total, if you remember. She's a loud faker in bed, and it got old. After a while, I couldn't stand her smell, her taste, or her noise. Or much of anything else about her. She's way more drama than I want in life."

"But you didn't mind that she swallowed."

I felt my face turning hot with embarrassment. He had me there.

"That's true," I replied, "but I sent her on her way when I found Robbie. I knew then what I wanted and that having Hera around was a waste of time and a complication I could live without. The only reason she was with me at all is because she'd invited herself and had just randomly shown up when I was leaving for the gallery. No notice. No phone call. As far as I was concerned, I was done, and I let her know that. So I haven't been a total ass."

"I have something to show you," he continued. "I did a little bit of investigating and found something, um, interesting. Have you ever heard of Trezura Mapps?"

I shook my head and shrugged. "I don't even know what that means."

Derrick sent me an enigmatic look as he swiped through his iPhone. Then he handed the phone and earpiece to me.

"Press play. But first, you need to know that this was dated about six months ago. So it was around the same time period you were seeing her. Maybe a little after."

I looked at him with a raised eyebrow and then pressed play.

What? Why is he showing me a porn site?

The scene started. Slinking to the middle of the large room, clad only in a practically invisible thong and stupidly tall platform stilettos, was Hera.

Trezura Mapps.

She smiled saucily at the camera and undulated while running her hands down her body. Then she lifted both fake tits and ran her tongue around her own nipples.

One man, dressed only in jeans, walked into the scene and began fondling her. She gave him a brash smile as they started kissing, and she began unzipping his pants. She dropped into a squat and started giving him a loud and sloppy blow job. Two more men, already naked, entered, fisting themselves as they felt her up and stood around her to be serviced. She went from one hard cock to another, slurping and gagging the entire time, letting drool roll down her chin.

I swallowed, staring in disbelief. My stomach roiled. I'd been on the receiving end of that mouth more than once, so it wasn't because of the act. But hell. Hera is a porn star? As the men started fondling her and slapping her ass, she started making the sounds that had always made me roll my eyes. I'd thought she was acting like she was auditioning for a porn video. I didn't know that it was dress rehearsal.

Derrick took the phone from my hand and swiped to another spot in the video. He handed it back to me, still silent.

In this scene, two of the men had her sandwiched between them and were ejaculating inside of her, accompanied by her shrieks of ecstasy. One guy waited until the others were done. Then he jacked off on her face and into her mouth as she licked her lips and smiled into the camera, rubbing his cum all over her face while she showed what he'd unloaded into her mouth. The next shot showed how the other two men had emptied their loads into her holes as she dipped into a squat and showed off the dripping semen. They laughed and high-fived each other, all while encouraging her to "push it all out."

Nausea hit me like a cannonball. I tossed the phone to Derrick as I slid out of the booth and ran to the men's room, where I lost what little breakfast I'd had this morning, the sandwich I'd had later, as well as every meal I'd consumed in the last year. After I'd finished dry-heaving, I washed my hands, rinsed my mouth, and splashed cold water on my face.

"Wow, man. You're really green," Derrick commented when I returned. I knew I was. I hadn't been this sick since I was a kid with a nasty case of the flu. He poured some Acqua Panna into my glass. "You look like shit."

"At least I always used condoms. Every single time. But I put my mouth on that." I placed my hand over my belly as my stomach threatened to revolt again. I took a few gulps of water, which helped to quell the nausea.

I looked at Derrick and said, "I don't think there's enough toothpaste or mouthwash in the world to get this feeling out of my mouth. Mama always hated her. Called her a *puta*. I wonder how she knew what I couldn't see?"

Derrick looked at me, incredulous. "You jokin', right? With all that makeup and silicone, she looked like a factory fuck doll. She has more miles on her than the I-15 at rush hour, man. If you'd been thinking with your big brain, you would've seen that." He shook his head. "You're crazier than I thought."

This was the worst possible thing that could have happened. If Robbie ever found out that Hera's a porn actress, then it's definitely over. She already thinks that men are shit and that I'm fascinated by Hera and her ilk. This little revelation would send her over the edge because she's sexually inexperienced and hasn't built up a lot of confidence with me yet. In her eyes, I'd be the king of ain't-shit men.

I said as much to Derrick, who nodded in agreement.

"She may kick you to the curb for real for real, man. Your last girlfriend is someone who fucks men and women for a living. And Robbie was a virgin?"

"Yes," I quietly replied, reliving that night with Robbie. "She was."

Derrick shook his head, passing one hand over his bald head while looking at me with a combination of irritation, envy, and disbelief. "You went from a woman who's trash to one who gave you what most grown men nowadays only dream about and never get. I hope for your sake that she forgives you."

I don't think that I've ever felt so miserable in my entire life. Not even when the car accident ended my soccer career. At least then, there was another career that I loved and happily jumped into. But there is only Robbie. There is no other woman.

Derrick continued, "I don't think you appreciate the gift you have in Robbie. You love her?"

"Yes." No hesitation.

I love her.

"Have you ever told her you love her?"

"In so many words."

He stared at me in disbelief. "'In so many words'? What kind of motherfuckery is that, man? That's bullshit. What you holdin' back for?"

I opened and then shut my mouth. I realized I didn't have an answer. Robbie was a total 180-degree contrast from Hera. She wasn't a gold digger, a halfwit, or a manipulator. She wasn't whiny, entitled, or self-centered. Focused, intelligent, and successful, she's the consummate professional with an obsession for her work.

Robbie is natural and beautiful. Inside and out. What's more, I knew she loved me. She loved me with an openness and unrestrained passion that I'd never experienced before.

I'm an idiot. And truly fucked for life if she didn't come back to me. Oddly, at that moment I began to understand how someone could become a stalker.

"I have to find her and tell her everything. She needs to know how Hera came on to me. Tricked me. And her." I stopped, feeling too hollow inside to continue.

"Hopefully, including telling her you love her. Robbie's bona fide, man. You can't lose that. I can tell you that if quality men find out that she's single, always on her grind, and looking for a social life, they will line up. Talk about a catch. She's a real *Jessie's Girl*, and some men appreciate the gift of a solid woman."

I didn't miss the mockery or the pointed nature of his comment. My gut still felt murky, and Derrick's remarks weren't helping. The thought of Robbie with another man made me sick inside and almost murderous.

"I hope you get this taken care of soon, man. Daria is standoffish because of your situation with Robbie. You get that fixed, and maybe I can have a chance with her. Right now, she's putting me in the same ain't-shit category with you. I'm the real deal, and I'm catchin' feelings for her, but with the mess that you, Robbie, and 'Trezura Mapps' are in, she's figuring I'm a cheatin' SOB just like my homie. Let's just say that you aren't her favorite person right now. Or mine."

I just nodded my head, not disagreeing. I had to find Robbie.

Where was she?

Chapter 33

Rogan

Three Weeks Later

Sunrise was brightening the sky when I returned to my condo after an early morning run. I'd started when it was still dark because I needed to work out some of my stress. I'd even been going to the condo community gym at 2:00 a.m. several times a week to hit the weights.

I chugged a pint of lemon water and headed for the shower. While leaning against the tile walls with my head hanging, I let the hot water cascade over my aching body. No matter how hard I tried, my brain wouldn't stop thinking about Robbie. I desperately missed her and hated the idea that a skank like Hera could break us up. While I didn't like Hera before, now I despised her with the heat of a thousand suns. Between what she had done to break us up and her porn career, there was no way in hell she'd ever have any chance of being with me again. She was, without exception, the biggest damned mistake of my entire life.

After rinsing, I stepped out of the shower and grabbed one of my bath sheets. Tossing the towel aside, I went to the sink to get my deodorant and grooming supplies. I squinted at my face in the mirror and shook my head. I looked like shit. My eyes looked hollow, my cheeks looked gaunt, and my face projected misery. Geez. Pathetic.

Where was she?

Robbie's family was keeping her location close to the chest. While I think I could have gotten it out of Zion—if he even knew, that is—there were probably legal repercussions to harassing a minor. So I'd better not. I'm not built for prison.

Daria still wasn't speaking to me. I was pretty sure she knew where Robbie was, but she was keeping it firmly zipped. I'd been to the house a few times. If Daria was there, she was coldly polite but uninterested in conversation. I begged her to tell me where Robbie was, and she told me bluntly she'd only tell me if Robbie said it was okay. She left the comment hanging, which meant Robbie was *not* okay with me knowing where she was.

Shit.

I'd be doing family meal today and wanted to get to *Rogan's* early enough to finish other tasks. Mama wouldn't be in till afternoon, mainly because she still couldn't stand to look at me. I got a chance to tell her what happened, but she made it clear she didn't care. After all, I'm the one who'd hooked up with the *puta* in the first place and didn't have the sense *Dios* gave an insect to hurt a wonderful woman like Robbie. *Estúpido.*

Fuck. My. Life.

Even my usually super-courteous mother was done with me.

Sighing, I got dressed. On its charger on the nightstand, my phone started ringing. It was awfully early for someone to be calling me. I picked up the phone without looking at the screen.

"This is Rogan."

"Hi, Rogan. This is Natalia from KNNV."

"Hi, Natalia! How's it going?"

"I'm great! Sorry to call you so early in the morning."

I waved away her apology. "I've already started my day. What's up?"

"KNNV is doing a special on new and upcoming businesses in Vegas, and *Rogan's* is included in the proposed lineup. It's a project the Lifestyle folks have wanted to do for a while, and so far, it feels like fun."

I grinned. More PR! And for free, no less!

"That sounds great!" I exclaimed. "How can I help with the project?"

"Since we're the news," she replied, "we can pretty much say anything we want."

"Tell me about it." I thought of the line about Hera and me "reconciling." Anything they want.

"That being said," she continued, "the Lifestyle folks want to do our best to showcase Vegas. So I wanted to give you the opportunity to review some clips and photos we'd like to use. We have videos of the exterior, some exterior and interior shots, and a few clips of dinner service and your grand opening."

"I'd love to see them. Naturally, I want *Rogan's* to be showcased in the best light. When can we make this happen?"

"We have a deadline we're kind of up against. What's the soonest you can come to the studio?"

"I can't," I confessed. "We're swamped, and I have to be there the greater part of the next week, from prep to cleaning after we close. I have a bunch of 14-hour days ahead of me."

"Okay," Natalia replied. "Can I meet you at the restaurant, then? I have everything on my laptop, and it will save you a trip."

"Today?"

"Yes. I can meet you at noon-ish. Will that work?"

"Perfect."

We clicked off, and I felt better. This was just the distraction I needed to take my mind out of my personal hell.

The staff was digging into family meal when Natalia arrived. I smiled when I saw her without the layers of studio makeup. She looked like a young college student dressed in jeans and a patterned blouse.

We shook hands and took a seat at the bar. Sergio, the day shift bartender, asked if we needed anything to drink. I ordered sparkling water and lime, and Natalia requested a plain iced tea.

She took her laptop out of its sleeve and set it up on the bar.

"I want to show you the pictures first," she began. "And then we can look at the clips. I hope you can see it the way it's intended. They look much better on the studio monitors."

No doubt.

She tapped on the laptop touchpad and opened up the Photos app. Next, she went to a folder marked *Rogan's* and opened it.

The first few photos were glorious. They had taken the exterior pictures in the evening during "golden hour" when the setting sun washed the stucco with a warm glow. There were several interior photos when the restaurant was empty, and one of Robbie's masterwork. My heart thudded. Natalia explained the rationale behind each shot and how they'd be used in the *Rogan's* portion of the TV special.

One particular photo caught my eye. It was of me standing in front of the restaurant before opening. It looked like the same cover photo on the *Vegas Weekly Tea*. I looked at her quizzically and wondered about the similarity. She told me it wasn't exactly the same photo, but it's one that wasn't chosen when the photoshoot took place. The *Tea* was a subsidiary of KNNV. Who knew.

I asked about other opening night photos, and she scrolled through the bunch of them, and lo and behold. The Kiss. I asked her how she ended up with that one. She looked at me and said the photographer thought it was a great one of my girlfriend and me. She hesitated. Apparently, I looked outraged.

"What's wrong?"

"That is not my 'girlfriend.' In fact, that kiss is why my actual girlfriend is pissed at me and has ghosted."

"Oh. I'm sorry," she apologized.

I couldn't be angry with her because she was just a part of the machine. I had emailed the *Tea* to request a retraction stating that Hera Byrnes was *not* my girlfriend. Evidently, the Lifestyle team hadn't gotten the message.

I asked Natalia to scroll to the VIP page. She did and found the photo with Robbie standing in front of her *Magnum Opus* with a dazzling smile. The ivory dress she wore showed off one naked shoulder and drifted like a cloud around her. Her eyes sparkled with pride. She was beautiful. I sighed, looked at Natalia, and said, "This is my girlfriend."

Natalia's eyebrows shot up.

"*She's* your girlfriend?"

"Yeah. At least she was before the picture of the kiss went viral. Despite how it looks, it was totally involuntary on my part. Hera caught me by surprise, and I was a very unwilling participant. I used to date that woman, but she turned out to be a manipulative gold digger. And batshit crazy."

"Huh. Interesting. In that case, I have something to show you. I've looked at all the videos, and there are a few we're not going to use. A couple were weird, and I knew we wouldn't use them, but now that you've told me what's what, this may be important. Now, this makes sense."

She opened up another folder titled R *Videos*. When she opened it, she told me these were just raw clips, and they'd leave most of them on the cutting room floor, so to speak.

She scrolled through the videos and stopped at one. I watched it play out and realized that this was my vindication. This was the proof I needed to bring Robbie back into my life. If it's not too late, that is.

I'm sure my eyes were brimming when I turned to Natalia. I gave her a huge hug of gratitude and asked if it was okay to provide me with the video clip.

"Since it's too disjointed to use, I'll send it to you now," she replied. My phone pinged in my pocket, and I opened the video. While I wanted to jump onto the bar and beat my chest, I knew that would be, well, undignified.

"Wait," she said, bringing up a few other short clips, "I'll send you a couple more. They're kind of funky, and now that I know your situation, I'll make sure they're not used."

We spent the next hour choosing the best photos and video clips to use in the special. Natalia told me only a few would make it into the program since we'd only have about five or so minutes in the scheduled half-hour. I didn't care. I appreciated the more-or-less free PR, but I was more eager to find Robbie so I could be exonerated.

When Natalia left after another hour, I was flying high. Now all I had to do was to get my ducks in a row. I had to clear my name and find Robbie.

My first task was to stop by Robbie's house and give Daria my phone. And cross everything that's crossable and hope she'd finally share the secret of Robbie's location.

Chapter 34

Rogan

AFTER PICKING UP A rental car at the San Luis Obispo Airport, I punched the destination into the GPS. I was heading toward Cambria on the 101, sweaty palms and all. I hoped Robbie wouldn't turn me away. We needed to talk. She had to understand that I hadn't cheated on her and never intended to make it appear that I was interested in any other woman. Much less Hera.

If she didn't believe me, I had a piece of evidence to show her so she would see with her own eyes that I had been framed, for lack of a better word, into making it appear that I wanted Hera. There was only one woman for me. And I hoped Robbie didn't hate me so much that she'd tell me to go fuck myself and turn me away for good.

I started searching for the address once I turned onto Burton in Cambria. Quaint, beautiful homes lined the streets, and I was smiling despite my anxiety. Everything looked so peaceful. Very Americana.

I found the address on a small, taupe-colored home with white trim. There was an electric bike with a girly-looking basket parked in the short asphalt driveway. I hoped this was the right house. I sat in my seat for a while, gearing up for what was ahead of me. Girding my loins, so to speak. I thought of what Derrick had said and kicked myself again for not telling Robbie that I love her. I hope it's not too late.

I walked up the pathway to the front door, stepped onto the porch, and took a deep breath. After ringing the doorbell, I stood back, silently rehearsing the spiel I was going to give to Robbie when she came to the door.

All of it vanished when a tall, elegantly handsome older black man, dressed in sweats and a wife-beater, opened the door. The man was as tall as me, with coffee skin and onyx-dark, discerning eyes. Except for a crop of short springy locs pulled together at his crown, his head was clean-shaven. A short, neat goatee, lightly sprinkled with gray, framed his full lips. His arms were muscular, and a tuft of tight curls appeared at the neckline of the shirt. His gaze was all too probing, as if he were a human bullshit detector. I guessed he was about 40. Mature. Experienced. Worldly.

Fuck.

I swallowed the baseball-sized lump in my throat and shifted uncomfortably. After less than a month, had Robbie already moved on? A dismal pain coiled and snaked through my heart and gut. How had I allowed it to get this far out of hand?

After a stupefied moment, I found my voice.

"Is Robbie here?"

Before he could answer, Robbie's voice echoed from somewhere in the house. Relief. At least I'd found the right place.

"Who's at the door, Lonnie?"

Lonnie pulled the door open wider, muscles rippling subtly under espresso skin. When Robbie appeared at his side, her face transformed into a wall of shock. Then annoyance. Then fury.

"What the hell are you doing here?" Her voice was low, growling, raw, and laced with pain. Pain I was responsible for.

My eyes shot to Lonnie and then back to Robbie.

"I came to talk to you."

"Why?" She was fuming. Angry. Her caramel cheeks tinged pink, her teeth clenched, and her silvery eyes squinted into dark, smoky slits. If her expression was any indication, I figured that if she'd had her Smith & Wesson on her, I'd be full of inconvenient smoking holes about now. I had to fix this quick, but what to do about this other man standing here?

"Because I love you and I need you back," I stated matter-of-factly. "And I'm not leaving until we have talked this through."

Once again, I shot my eyes quickly to Lonnie, just to gauge the other man's reaction. I didn't want to fight, but if I had to fight for my woman, I would. Unconsciously, I straightened up and rolled my neck. I did that to tamp down the pain and rage of the thought of Robbie—my Robbie—being bedded by this man. I can't describe the anguish or the anger. And, if I could only get her back, none of it mattered.

Lonnie watched the two of us verbally spar with interest, arms crossed, his head going back and forth as if he were at a tennis match. There was a hint of a smirk on his lips, apparently finding humor in the situation. Was he so self-assured that he knew he didn't have to fight for her? The sorrow coiled in my heart a little more.

"It looks like I'm gonna need some popcorn and a glass of Chardonnay to enjoy this little battle," Lonnie chuckled, his deep voice amused.

Robbie regarded me for a long moment as if debating whether she'd even let me into the house. She seemed to come to a conclusion, and with a glance toward Lonnie, she nodded. Lonnie opened the door and gestured for me to come in. I pushed out a relieved breath and stepped over the threshold.

I followed them in silence. We passed what appeared to be a master bedroom where the bed was neatly made. I released another breath. Tangled bedding would have gutted me. We turned the corner into a bedroom that had been transformed into a makeshift art and photography studio.

A photography backdrop stood in a corner, along with camera-topped tripods, reflectors, and softboxes. In front of the backdrop was a barstool of plain, bare wood. A man with shaggy dark hair looked up as we entered the room, eyebrows shooting up in surprise when he spotted me. He was adjusting the cameras and tripod heights. Lonnie took a seat on a chair next to the doorway, and I stopped, a little confused. Lonnie motioned to a folding chair a couple of feet from him, and I sat down, still not knowing what to expect.

Robbie turned and shot me a look of defiance and slipped the beach robe she was wearing from her shoulders.

She was nude.

My breath hitched in my chest, both from the sight of her breathtakingly beautiful body, and anguish at the thought she may have allowed Lonnie to use that body. I could feel the dueling emotions of rage, jealousy, lust, and pain course through me. I was struggling.

She turned and walked to the barstool at the photography setup, picked up what looked like a satin throw, and pulled it over her shoulders. The other man walked over to her, and they made eye contact for a long moment.

It occurred to me that maybe Lonnie wasn't the one I had to worry about. Maybe it was this Italian stallion-looking dude. Maybe I had to worry about both. A flash of Hera simultaneously fucking several men went through my brain, but I couldn't connect that to my Robbie. She had too much dignity and self-respect. Unless she hated me that much.

The other guy started adjusting the throw over Robbie's slim shoulders. While he was changing the lighting setup, Lonnie gestured to me. I moved my chair close to him and nodded.

"That's Nico," Lonnie said in a low voice. "He's an architectural photographer but has been wanting to do Robbie for years. She finally said yes."

I nodded again, not knowing how to reply. I didn't know the dynamics of this little group, and while breaking into Godzilla mode for my woman would be easy to do, I'd rather not if it meant making a fool of myself. Looking like an idiot was way at the bottom of my to-do list. I needed to tread carefully here, and as the saying goes, discretion is the better part of valor. Besides, Nico wanting to "do" Robbie probably meant the same as it did when Robbie wanted to "do" me months ago.

"They're just about wrapped up," Lonnie continued. "We've been here all morning." He looked at me, raising one eyebrow. "You must be Rogan."

Surprised, I nodded. Unthinkingly, I shook Lonnie's extended hand.

"I figured you'd be here sooner or later," Lonnie said. "Robbie and I have argued about it a lot. But she'll fill you in."

I looked at him, baffled.

"Things aren't always as they may seem," Lonnie said cryptically with a smile. "Just hang on."

Nico was helping Robbie with her beach robe, photography session over. They spoke in whispered tones to each other before Robbie threw her arms around his neck and gave him a big hug. He dropped a kiss on her forehead, squeezed her once, and they parted. Nico began packing up the photography gear as Robbie approached Lonnie and me.

"How are you feeling, love?" Lonnie asked her.

"I'm okay. I think." She shot an unreadable glimpse at me.

Lonnie spared me a glance before focusing on Robbie. "I'm going to help Nico get some of this stuff cleared out of here. Give us a minute."

Lonnie strode over to where Nico was dismantling the softboxes and began removing the cameras from the tripods. The two of them rolled up the backdrop, and in a few moments, they had packed away everything in their respective cases. They stacked them in a corner of the room, and both men walked toward us.

Nico was of some sort of Latin descent, with olive skin and hazel eyes. He had shaggy dark hair that appeared to have a mind of its own. He wasn't as tall as Lonnie but was just as solidly built. The two of them looked as if they spent some quality time at the gym.

"Rogan, this is Nico, my husband," Lonnie introduced, expression bland.

Wait. What? *These* dudes are gay? I can't even begin to describe the staggering wash of emotion in discovering this bit of information.

Nico and I reached out and shook hands.

Things aren't always as they may seem.

Indeed.

"We'll leave and get the gear later. I think you guys have a lot to hash out, and the sooner we're out of here, the sooner you can talk."

"Nice meeting you, Rogan," Nico said. "Hope to see you around again." His voice was well-modulated as if he'd been a singer at some point. Neither of these guys fit my version of the "gay" stereotype. Coming from a testosterone-fueled sport where being openly gay wasn't necessarily safe, and from a kitchen career where many gays were often flamingly so, they were an anomaly for me. And I was grateful for it.

Lonnie placed two fingers on his brow for a mock salute goodbye, and the two men exited the bedroom studio. Robbie and I continued to stare at each other until we heard the front door slam.

When Lonnie and Nico moved the photography backdrop, it revealed some artwork hanging on a clothesline or leaning along the wall.

A largish drawing looked like a study in pencil and color wash. It was Robbie. The background was dark, and she was completely nude. She was on one haunch, eyes focused on the viewer. Her eyes were rimmed with tears, and there was a trickle on one cheek. She was holding a signature glass of white wine. The expression of profound grief was unmistakable. Though her lips were closed, anguish was written in their set. One breast was partially bared, exposing part of one nipple while her locs covered the other. The wine glass, held in one hand on her thigh, discreetly covered her shadowed mons. Next to her curled form stood one leg, a man's leg, and it was mine. How do I know? Because it was a right foot and leg and had my scars on it. The leg stood over her as if in heartless domination. In cruelty. In dismissal. The title of the piece was clipped to the watercolor paper.

Heartbroken.

The work was wrenchingly exquisite. And ripped me to bits.

Mounted with bulldog clips to a masonite backer board was a painting of...me. Clipped to an angled draft table, it was done in layers of watercolors, and it was me. My image was asleep, in repose, mouth slightly open, hair disheveled, and sheets tangled around my waist. Everything was perfect, down to each freckle and each strand of hair on my torso. She hadn't painted the sketched-in wolf tattoo, but the work wasn't quite complete. It was a picture of peace, serenity, tranquility.

Only someone who had total intimacy and adoration could have created my features so perfectly in slumber. It was a picture of love. Of tenderness.

I turned around to face Robbie. "Thank you."

She looked up at me, and except for a glimmer of pain that flashed in her eyes, her expression was unreadable.

"You're welcome." The response was toneless.

"I can't let you go. You can't leave me."

"And yet, here I am." Her expression was closed. Her voice, flat. She took a deep breath before continuing.

"You never committed to me. So I shouldn't have been surprised you didn't care if that woman hung all over you, fondled you, kissed you, or whatever. I can only imagine what you two did after I was out of the picture. I never would have left you. But I was not going to be publicly humiliated. Not by anyone."

She straightened her posture and lifted her head proudly, eyes glossy with unshed tears.

"I won't be second to anyone. I won't be anyone's afterthought. If I'm not the only one, then I'm nothing. I told you a long time ago I'm nobody's side piece." She was now close to breaking, and she bared her teeth to hold the emotions in. She prepared to unleash the weeks of heartache.

"You used me, knowing all along there was someone else you preferred more than me. But it's not like you ever told me you loved me. That you were committed to me. But it looks like you didn't value me in the least. So the only person I have to blame, I guess, is myself. I was expecting something you couldn't give."

"Stop. Just stop." I leaned over enough to put my face close to hers. "There's an explanation for everything, and I need you to hear me."

Glowering, Robbie crossed her arms after wiping away one errant tear, waiting, body erect and proud.

"That nutjob is not my girlfriend, there's no reconciliation of any kind, and I sure as hell am not hooking up with her. It was an unbelievable series of bad events that made me look guilty, and I didn't even know it had happened."

I ran my hands through my hair and exhaled.

"That's what I wanted to tell you. She's turned out to be something like a sociopath at best, a psychopath at worst. She's crazy. And you need to know that I did not, and would not, touch her. Not ever."

"I don't understand." Robbie's anger seemed to be tempered, replaced by wary curiosity.

"She didn't have an invitation, but she finagled her way into the opening by finding someone who *had* been invited, and she tagged along as a plus one. She wasn't on the invite list. I didn't want her there. I didn't even know she was there.

"Once she got in," I continued, "she went out of her way to make it appear that we were together. That we were being 'reconciled.' People who knew we'd dated jumped to the conclusion that we had kissed and made up. It was embarrassing, mainly because I was so focused on a successful opening that I missed her scheming behind my back. It just never occurred to me that someone would work so hard to mess up someone else's life for their own gain. Especially since they have zero chance of being the replacement. *Hell* no.

"Even before the opening and before I came up here to reclaim you, I had told her she was not invited to anything connected with me and she needed to stay the hell out of my life."

"Reclaim?"

"Yes. Reclaim." I looked into Robbie's beautiful eyes and took a deep breath. "I hope you didn't think that I could possibly continue my life without you."

I hesitated. Here it goes. I was going to lay everything on the table. If she rejected me, I didn't know what I would do. I steeled myself against the gathering heartache if she said no.

"I love you, Robbie. With every fiber of my being, I love you. When I first saw you in the gallery, I was gut-punched. The emotions were crazy then, but I stupidly tamped them down. I knew I loved you when we first kissed in your kitchen. I loved you when we first made love, and it hasn't diminished one iota.

"My biggest mistake was not telling you I love you. That no other woman, *especially* Hera, has a chance with me. I swear on the heads of our future children that I have not touched her or any other woman. No one else has any chance to hold my being, my body, or my soul, Rob. All of me is yours for as long as I live. For as long as you want me.

"You activated my inner caveman, and he's never gone away. You stole my heart, and I don't even want it back."

Chapter 35

Robbie

"...You stole my heart, *and I don't even want it back.*"

Damn him! Damn him! Damn him!

And just like that, the walls that I had constructed around my heart began to crumble. I looked into his eyes and realized that his reflected my pain. He was hurting as much as I was.

"Please," he whispered, placing one warm hand on the side of my face.

I began to cry again, and he reached out and enveloped me. His powerful arms cradled my body against his own, and I heard his pained murmur of relief as he held me close.

If he's the man I think he is, he will do the 'ends of the earth' thing to get you back into his life.

And I lost it.

I felt like I had come back home. I grasped the front of Rogan's shirt and laid my head against his chest. He was whispering in my ear and holding me as if our lives depended on it. I sobbed my grief. Grief over the loss of so much time. Grief over the pain that we had suffered together. And sorrow and anger that someone had schemed to hurt us and keep us apart.

I don't know how long I stood there in his arms, against his body, inhaling the essence that was Rogan. I looked up at him and almost broke again at the sight of his red, watery eyes.

"Do you have a way I can get rid of the tears and snot?"

I burst out into teary laughter, and we went to the bathroom to rinse our faces. We were both blotchy messes.

"Ah, sweetness," Rogan breathed, taking me into his arms again. "Please believe me when I tell you I love you. I'm ashamed for not telling you the second I knew it."

I looked at him, and although his eyes were still red-rimmed, they were bright and clear. I felt him. Here.

We went into the kitchen, where I grabbed a couple of bottles of water from the refrigerator along with a bowl of fruit.

"Let me show you something. I know that the kiss with Hera looked bad. But that wasn't the whole story."

Rogan took out his iPhone and swiped through it. He brought up a video.

"Watch it all the way through and be sure to keep your eyes on the background of each clip."

They were clips from KNNV, the station where he'd had his successful interview and food demo.

"They're putting together a local special on several new Vegas businesses. One of the lifestyle reporters showed me these clips from our opening night."

I nodded and tapped play to watch. It looked like a montage of short video clips from the grand opening. The first clip was of Rogan being interviewed by some random reporter. Several people had stopped, smiling, and watched Rogan answer questions. The following clip showed him answering more questions, but this time, Hera was in the background, looking at him speculatively, eyebrows furrowed. The video camera moved slightly, and that's when I saw myself smiling, just feet away from Hera. She spotted me, and her expression changed to a sneering one.

What? I had been that close to her and hadn't even realized that she was there? I gasped.

The short clip that followed showed him talking to a local podcaster. The station's camera caught the caster's enamored image as he spoke to Rogan. In the background, my smiling image was trying to inch closer to him, respecting the fact that he was occupied with the interview.

Hera came into view from the side, and she sidled up to him, completely unnoticed. Rogan was oblivious to her presence. She moved closer to him, patting his butt before draping one arm around his waist. He moved away slightly but didn't break his focus from the podcaster. She wrapped both arms loosely around his waist while he was listening to a question. I was still behind him, my expression confused.

Because I was behind him, I hadn't seen the annoyed glare that he sent to Hera while he was trying to answer the reporter's questions. She waved her fingers while sneering at me. I looked stricken. Rogan shook hands with the reporter at the end of the interview, and a small crowd gathered around him. While trying to speak with them, he sent Hera an angry look. Ignoring his glare, she swiftly moved in front of him, arching her body against his. She threw one arm around his neck and the other hand in the back of his head and pulled him down for a kiss, her mouth opening for his. His mouth opened in surprise, not in greeting. There were the sounds of cameras clicking as they captured the scene and some people in the crowd cheered.

My image looked shattered. After Rogan broke the kiss, his expression was furious. Hera, with her back toward the camera, waggled her fingers at me once more, and I turned and ran.

What happened next is what I had missed.

Another video clip, this time with discernible sound, showed Rogan shoving her away from him.

"What the hell are you doing here?" He was livid.

"I've missed you, but I'll see you later," she purred and patted his chest before sauntering off. Before ending, the clip showed Rogan following her with his eyes, his expression a mask of baffled fury.

He hadn't seen me. He hadn't seen her waving at me. He hadn't even known she was there. He hadn't known I was there.

If I were a lawyer, and I am, I'd need a closer examination of the evidence.

Dad's words once again echoed in my head. He was right. How did he know?

"I have one more." Rogan took the phone and scrolled to another clip.

I pressed play, and on the screen, Rogan wasn't even being interviewed. Some random local celebrity was. Then I looked at the background where I saw Rogan finishing up yet another quick interview, where he laughed and slapped the reporter on his back. The reporter left, and Janina, Daria, and Derrick immediately surrounded him. I couldn't tell what they were saying, but all three of them were upset. Daria said something to him and then turned on her heel and stormed away from all of them, furious. Rogan looked stunned and began to look around. I can only guess that he was looking for me. But I had long gone.

His expression was decidedly unhappy, but the camera swung in another direction, following the reporter who started interviewing someone else.

So he knew right away. And I had disappeared, not only from his sight but from his life.

"When I saw the photo they published in the *Tea*," Rogan was saying, "I was pissed. I contacted their editorial department and threatened a lawsuit if they didn't print a retraction. I let them know in no uncertain terms that Hera and I were *not* reconciling. Period."

"A couple of days after that, I learned something else." His expression was more than unhappy; he looked agitated.

"It's something about Hera."

I looked at him, raising one eyebrow.

"She's a porn actress."

My mouth flew open.

"She's a *what*?"

Before I could say anything, he placed one hand over mine.

"I found out the Monday after you left," he said quietly. "I hadn't even known. Derrick showed me a video of her, um, *working*, with several dudes, no less, and I got sick. I'm talking about *The Exorcist* head-spinning, eyes bulging, blowing green stuff sick. I threw up because I'd allowed myself to get involved with her. And the things she was doing..." He had an unseeing expression on his face, lips turned down in unhappy self-loathing.

"You don't have to take my word for it. Ask Derrick." He turned his golden eyes toward me. "I'm glad that I always used protection, but if I'd known what she did for a living, I never would have touched her. At that time, I thought she was just someone who did plastic surgery for a hobby. That I was just a rest stop in between sugar daddies."

While Rogan was sometimes absent-minded when it came to our relationship, he had never lied to me. That he had spent so much time tracking me down to declare himself said something about his heart. We were meant to be, and for once, it felt as if the universe was tilting in our favor. I looked into his eyes, took a deep breath, and made the decision of my life.

I reached out and put one hand on his bearded cheek.

"Whatever she's done means nothing to us. As long as we're together, she doesn't matter. I can't hold something against you that you didn't do. I love you."

He reached across the barstools and hugged me so tightly that I squeaked. He looked at me again, eyes glowing with gratitude.

"I will never deserve you."

"I know," I replied with a shaky smile.

He slid from his barstool and stood between my legs. He caressed one side of my face and leaned in, his glance asking for permission. I nodded.

His lips touched mine softly at first, as if seeking to recapture their feel. I sobbed, remembering and feeling his touch. It had been so long. I began to tremble.

We touched again, and I parted my lips as Rogan pressed against mine. I wrapped my legs around him and drew his body to my core and was rewarded with a deep, masculine groan.

"Oh baby," he whispered.

"Take me to the bedroom," I whispered into his neck. "Please." A hitch of his breath, and then he scooped me up, turned around, and stopped.

"It's to your right," I murmured. I felt his bearded grin under my face as he started toward the master bedroom. After entering, he stood me in front of him and reached for the tie around my robe. He looked at me, one eyebrow raised.

I nodded, and he loosened the tie, allowing the robe to fall to the floor. His gaze traveled over my body, expression heated.

"I never thought I'd see you like this again," he rasped, voice gruff and emotional.

Our lips met again, and this time, the kisses were hot and deep. He stepped back to pull off his polo shirt and to step out of his jeans and boxer briefs. It was then that I noticed—really noticed—how haggard he looked and how his body looked thinner than it had before. Almost gaunt.

He's been suffering as much as I have.

We sank onto the bed together, our mouths clinging to each other, our hands rediscovering the feel of one another's body.

I missed him. Oh, god, I missed him so much. I missed his body against mine. I missed this exquisite pleasure. I missed everything about Rogan, and I knew I couldn't let him go. He was mine. And those sunlight-and-amber golden eyes were telling me I was his.

"I need to be inside of you," he rasped.

His kisses went from my mouth to my jaw, and down to my breasts. I moaned as my body filled with liquifying heat, and I drenched the fingers that had found their way through my folds.

I grasped his length and relished the feel of velvet over steel. I guided him inside of me and gasped because it had been so long since I'd felt the fullness of his girth. He eased himself inside and slowed while raining kisses on my face, my neck, my mouth.

Rogan's hips moved with smooth strokes that caught me up in his intensity, and I matched him with my own. I greedily surged against each rhythmic beat of his body while I reached higher and higher to join him in ecstasy.

It didn't take long. It seemed only a few short moments before I was crying out his name, the pleasure rocketing through my body as the orgasm tore through me. Rogan's strokes were deep and long, and he was quickly reaching his peak. A roar of release, and he was rhythmically jetting inside of my quivering channel.

And before I surrendered myself to the encroaching darkness of sleep within the comforting circle of his arms, one thought glued itself in my mind.

I can't ever be without this man. I love him more than life.

Chapter 36

Rogan

I GAZED AT ROBBIE, who was still sound asleep. It was barely dawn, and she was wrapped in my arms, her hair bonnet askew, and her locs splayed everywhere.

Adorable.

Last night had been incredible. Once she understood that the whole Hera fiasco had been a malicious ruse, we'd ended up making love (makeup sex) throughout the night.

I explained to her how the *Vegas Weekly Tea* had printed a retraction over the misleading photo the very next week and apologized for any misunderstanding or inconvenience. The video evidence I showed her had cleared up all loose ends. And Robbie, being Robbie, had thrown her arms around me. The rest, as the saying goes, is history.

Robbie loves me. Loves me more than I probably deserve, but I'll take it. She'd long since been added to the very short list of people whose lives I'd protect with my own.

Evidently, I'd fallen asleep again because when I opened my eyes, Robbie was gone. I stretched, yawned, and swung my feet over the side of the bed. After using the restroom and washing my hands, I slipped into a pair of shorts and a t-shirt from my overnight bag and headed toward the kitchen. I heard voices as I approached and was surprised to see Nico sitting across from Robbie at the breakfast table. They each had a cup of coffee and looked up in greeting as I slouched in.

Robbie smiled at me with affection and gave me a peck on the cheek when I dropped onto the chair next to her. She got up to fetch me a cup of coffee, whose fragrance I greedily inhaled before sipping.

"Hi Nico," I finally said.

Nico chuckled, hazel eyes congenial and friendly. "I know I just met you, but you look like shit."

I grunted at him, not disagreeing.

"Lonnie'll be over in a few," he said. "We always have breakfast with Robbie whenever she's in town."

I looked around. Breakfast? Except for the coffeemaker, the kitchen was pristine.

"No worries," Robbie chuckled. "I ordered breakfast sandwiches and OJ from Soto's, and they'll be delivering it any minute."

There was a noise at the front door, and Lonnie sauntered in with a smile of greeting. He walked over to the coffeemaker and poured a cup before taking a seat next to Nico.

Lonnie directed his gaze at me and grinned. "So, how're you feeling this fine morning?" His eyes twinkled knowingly.

"Satiated," I grinned, which earned me a smack on my arm from Robbie. We all laughed.

"I hate all y'all," she huffed. We laughed even harder, and I leaned over and gave her a sloppy one on her blushing cheek.

Lonnie looked at her with a smile.

"Didn't I tell you?"

"Shut up."

More laughter.

"I know how much you love her," Lonnie said to me. "She talked about you and the things you said and did, and that particular incident seemed to be too much of an anomaly. It was such an outlier that I disagreed with her. We've spent the greater part of the last month arguing about you and about that little incident."

He sent a look of affection to Robbie's faux-scowling face.

"She just can't stand the fact that I was right," he finished with a grin. "Right, sis?"

I chuckled and looked at Robbie. Our eyes met, and I watched hers warm with affection. Yes. She loves me. And her love is a treasure. I grabbed one of her hands and squeezed it with a smile.

In the corner of my eye, I saw Lonnie and Nico exchange approving glances.

A ring of the doorbell and Nico jumped up with a wave for the rest of us to sit. He came back with several sandwich boxes and a half-gallon container of juice.

We ate our breakfast in companionable silence, only grunting now and then. The sandwiches were delicious. I made a mental note how great these would be on a brunch menu.

After draining the last of his OJ, Nico gave his stomach a satisfied pat. He sent me an unreadable look.

"You're invited to my exhibit this afternoon," he smiled. "Robbie will tell you about it." He picked up the discards before taking them to the trash. Lonnie stood up and gathered his items as well.

Nico winked at Robbie and exited.

Lonnie chuckled. "Please come and see it, and when you do, don't forget our dynamics. Remember what I told you yesterday. Things aren't always as they may seem." He gave Robbie a wink and followed Nico out of the door.

I looked at Robbie, baffled.

"I'll tell you everything at the exhibit," she commented enigmatically. "You'll understand the explanation then."

The stubborn set of her jaw told me that any argument would be futile, so I just nodded my head. We cleaned up the last of the breakfast discards, wiped down the table, and cleaned the coffeemaker.

I took her hand and did my best Groucho Marx eyebrow waggling impersonation.

"Come into the shower with me, sweetheart, and I'll show you my etchings."

A FEW HOURS LATER, after driving south on the 101 in my rental, we pulled into the microscopic parking lot of a small art gallery in West Hollywood. The lot was overflowing, yet somehow the universe had provided a spot for us.

We walked into the nondescript gallery, stopping to read the sign in the front.

Black Love in Black (and White)
a photographic study
Nico Contreras

Interesting! But he's an architectural photographer.

Robbie stopped me just inside the lobby of the gallery and reminded me, "Things aren't always what they seem." She sent me a cryptic smile, and we continued in.

There were quite a few people in the gallery, looking at works either hanging on the walls or placed on stands. The people, it seemed to me, were a little on the snooty side. I was a bit irritated until Robbie pointed toward Lonnie and Nico, who were in deep conversation with a couple of older guys.

Robbie and I settled in the first row of folding chairs facing a dozen fabric-draped easels standing on a low staging area. I figured this must be Nico's exhibit. A tall, dark-haired man stood in front of the easels and tapped on a microphone.

"Hello ladies and gentlemen," he began. People stopped whatever they were doing and milled about, each one looking for a seat. After some of the hubbub died down, the man smiled at everyone and began speaking.

"Hi everybody! I'm Lawrence, but you can call me Lare," he lilted. "While I could talk for hours about the exciting photos we're about to see, I think you'll be happier hearing from the photographer himself, Nico Contreras. Nico!"

"Thank you. Thank you," Taking the mic from Lare, Nico spoke to the audience through the applause.

"This photoshoot was special to me," he began, "because one of the models had been very reluctant to pose. Fortunately, my charm and good looks won out, and she finally agreed." Laughter rolled through the audience.

"First, I'd like to thank my husband, Lonnie, for his patience and cooperation. And of course, Robbie, who brought her own special charm and exotic looks to the collection."

Nico turned his head and nodded at Lare. "Ladies and gentlemen, *Black Love in Black and White*."

Lare and Nico removed the fabrics from the easels, and my breath slammed into my chest.

Things aren't always as they may seem.

All of the photos were larger than poster-sized and gorgeous. And jealousy hit me like a javelin.

Robbie and Lonnie were the models. They were both nude and in various positions to reveal a loving couple. While there was no overt sexual contact, the implied intimacy and eroticism were unmistakable.

One photo was of Robbie alone, arms crossed over her breasts, and one leg positioned to shadow her mons. There was a similar photo of Lonnie, standing strong and muscled, with a towel hanging low around his hips. Every subsequent photo had the two of them together in one embrace or another. A couple of the photos revealed Robbie's breasts, but that was it. There was another of Robbie straddling Lonnie, her head thrown back, with Lonnie's lips between her breasts. It was sensual and erotic, but somehow not overtly sexual.

Another had them both on their knees facing the photographer, Robbie in front of Lonnie. He had one large hand over her mons and one over her breasts. Her head was thrown back, her mouth open in ecstasy, while one of her hands lay over his hand on her pubic area. His mouth was hovering in the hollow between her neck and shoulder, his eyes devouring her as if waiting for her to finish an orgasm.

I'm glad I know Lonnie is gay. Or else I'd be murdering his ass in front of eyewitnesses.

There were twelve photos in the entire collection, and they were true art. The attention to detail was breathtaking. And I wasn't the only one who thought so. The audience exploded into applause and gave Nico a standing ovation.

"If you have questions about the art, please see me, and I'll be happy to answer them. Any inquiries regarding acquiring the original signed collection or copies can be directed to Lare," Nico said after the noise had died down. "But before that, I'd like to introduce you to the models. Alonzo Jenkins and Roberta Wilkes."

Robbie stood up and turned toward the audience with a big smile. Lonnie walked over and stood next to her after kissing one hand.

Once again, the applause was deafening. After a bit, Robbie took her seat next to me and held on to my arm while Lonnie joined Nico in the staging area. They both bowed and left the stage, and Lare invited everyone to take a look.

Robbie and I joined Lonnie and Nico near the easel area, and I shook hands with the guys.

"I'm completely and totally blown away," I said. "The collection is fantastic, even though I'm raging with jealousy."

The three of them laughed at my expense. I looked at Robbie and asked her the question in the back of my mind. "How did you like modeling with Lonnie?"

She looked at me, surprised. "Ew."

I laughed. "Why?"

"How would you feel posing like that with Janina?"

"Ew."

Everybody laughed, and then patrons showed up and started asking questions of the three of them. I excused myself and wandered over to a corner niche to watch them handle the questions and comments from people.

Robbie was an introvert's introvert. She preferred her small circle of people and avoided crowds. But here she was, just as she was the first time I saw her at the gallery in Vegas, smiling, laughing, answering questions, and enjoying every minute. She's the consummate professional.

I watched as she fielded questions and turned away the flirtations of several people, some of whom were of indistinguishable gender. And I felt no jealousy whatsoever. It's as if the jealousy gene of my psyche had been put to rest. Robbie and I were connected, and this crisis, this separation, had bonded us closer.

A few hours later, as we headed up the 101 toward Cambria, she explained how the photo collection project came about.

"Nico had been asking me for years to do a nude photoshoot. I'd always been too shy and always turned him down. This time, when I was struggling so badly with my emotions, he asked me again. This time, I said yes.

"I felt safe doing the photoshoot with the guys. I didn't feel as shy."

She hesitated, and I cut a glance toward her in the passenger seat. Her hands were fidgety as she weighed her next words.

"Why the change?" I asked gently.

"I was feeling bolder. I was feeling beautiful and free."

She raised her eyes to catch my glance.

"Because my body had been loved."

My eyes turned back to the road, and I felt my breath catch.

Not just your body, my love. But all of you.

Chapter 37

Rogan

AFTER SPENDING TWO DAYS, um, *reconciling* with Robbie, I finally had to leave the comfort of her arms and head back to Vegas. She'd be returning within the week but had some local commission work to complete before leaving the house.

It was just about twilight when the plane circled in for a landing at Reid International. I loved looking at the Strip during this time. It was the golden hour, that time between daytime and night when casino lights were just flickering on. The combination of the setting sun's rays striking the casinos just when the lights were coming on always drew gasps from people who were obviously visitors. I smiled to myself and simply enjoyed the view.

About an hour later, the shuttle dropped me off at long-term parking, and I strode purposefully to my Range Rover. I threw my bag into the back, and once plopped in the driver's seat, I made a phone call.

"Hi. Yeah, this is Rogan. Will you be around for a while? I have something that I need to talk to you about."

I nodded as the voice on the other end replied.

"I think it'll take me about an hour, give or take, to get there. I haven't even left the airport yet. Long-term parking is pretty packed, and everything is backed up. See you soon."

About 45 minutes later, I was at the far side of Charleston. After entering Calico Basin, I drove up to a security gate that encircled the spacious property. I punched in the temporary code I'd been given, and the gates swung open to let me in. I parked next to an E-Class with California plates and trotted to the front door.

The front door opened after I rang the doorbell, and the young boy standing there grinned. Zion Anthony Wilkes is Robbie's little brother. His father is Robbie's stepfather, but that doesn't make a difference. Robbie and Zion are as thick as thieves.

Zion's skin is a little darker than Robbie's, and he doesn't have her gray eyes. His eyes are the same color as his warm brown skin, and like Robbie's, are large and expressive. Also like Robbie, he has a dimple on his left cheek. His hair was in a short afro, and he wore the typical tween uniform of baggy jeans and an oversized branded t-shirt. Naturally, he was wearing Jordans that looked to be about size 50. I held in a chuckle as I looked at the boy, who, even though the coloration varied a little, had such a resemblance to his sister.

My beloved.

He sent me a big, braces-covered grin. "Hi, Rogan! Dad said you were coming over!"

I stepped into the house and was greeted by Judson, Robbie's stepfather. Or I guess actual father since he adopted her. I'm not sure how all that works.

"Rogan," Judson's deep, rich, full-bodied voice greeted me as he extended his hand. I swear his is the only voice that could make Barry White sound like a soprano.

We shook hands, and Judson's eyes sparkled.

"This is kind of unexpected," he commented. "What's up?"

"Is the young man here?" A slightly accented male voice echoed from another part of the house, and we were joined by someone I could only assume was Robbie's *Morfar*. He was tall and lean, with incredibly pale skin. His short blond hair was heavily frosted with white. When I looked at his face, I saw Robbie. Those eyes. His eyes were such a pale gray they were virtually translucent except for a ring of darker gray around the iris. They were large and expressive, just like Robbie's. Her eyes are also silver and ice, but a little darker than her grandfather's.

Feminine voices floated into the front room. Two women, Robbie's mother Molly and a darker older woman I figured was Robbie's grandmother, walked in, looking at me curiously.

I was beginning to sweat.

Molly, Robbie's mother, is a taller version of Robbie. At just shy of six feet, she was striking, with high cheekbones, flawless café au lait skin, dark, wildly curly, silver-streaked hair, and a model slim figure. Her eyes were the same color as her father's, and I could see why she'd been such a successful model. Like Robbie, her gray eyes stood out in arresting contrast to her warm skin.

Grams, Robbie's grandmother, was also tall, about five-ten, and had features that would leave no doubt that she, too, had been a successful model in her day. Her eyes were as dark as her French Roast colored skin, and she wore her hair in a short, silvery gray afro. Her smile displayed a surprisingly square jaw and nearly perfect white teeth.

"Can me and Carter go over to his house to play video games?" Zion piped up as he and another kid skidded to a stop in front of us. I looked down and saw a boy with pale, freckled skin and riotous strawberry blond hair dressed in the same uniform as Zion.

"Yes," Molly replied, waving her hand toward the front door. "Go. But only for three hours. Take your cell."

"So, Mr. McDonald," Judson began after the boys had stampeded out, "what brings you here?"

I took a deep breath and called on every nerve I still had left.

"I have something I need to ask you. And my entire future depends on your answer."

Chapter 38

Rogan

MY BEDROOM WAS BRIGHT with early morning sun when I finally dragged my eyes open. Squinting, I realized that I'd slept way past dawn, which was rare. But today, that was okay.

Robbie and I had been making love until we crashed about 3:00 a.m. Every muscle in my body ached. Robbie's soft and loving sexiness had me staying hard all night. I couldn't get enough of her. We'd had a sexual marathon, and I was completely drained.

Why, then, was my cock stirring against her butt cheeks as she lay sleeping, spooned against me? I never thought that I would be ready and able to have sex all around the clock, but with Robbie, damn. She made being a sexual Superman possible.

She'd grabbed her satin bonnet before falling asleep, but it was askew, and her locs splayed everywhere. The crooked bonnet and the tousled locs, along with her peaceful, sleeping face, softened my heart even more. She looked so damned adorable.

I love her. Period.

After our heart-to-heart in the house by the beach, I was all in. I hope she understood that.

Robbie loved me like no woman in my life had ever loved me. The superficial nature of every relationship I'd had before became clearer every time I was with her. Robbie was solid. Robbie was real.

What's more important is that I loved her back. Her open frankness, her smarts, her heart, her beauty. Hell, her *everything* is why I've fallen so deeply and can't imagine my life without her. I was foolish not to have told her I loved her the first time we kissed, and I almost lost her because she had no reason to trust me or my heart. And she had every reason to put me in the ain't-shit category of loser fuckboys.

I'd left her hanging with no proof that I loved her. I said all the right words and did all the right things except to tell her I loved her. Which made Hera's little stunt so effective. Planned or not, she'd played on Robbie's insecurities and almost won her little effort to break us up. But, even if she'd succeeded, there was no way that she'd ever have me again.

Last night had been another eye-opener. While I was sure that Robbie would refuse to do some of the things that I wanted to experience with her, she was actually all in. Her plush lips, warm, loving mouth, and gently stroking hands had me groaning in ecstasy more than once.

When I sat propped against my headboard, she straddled me, her warm, wet pussy enveloping my cock. I held the sexy globes of her ass while she rode me, the sensations piercing and exquisite. I whispered my arousal to her as I stroked inside of her body, her channel holding me in a tight, quivering grip. Her slick walls pulsated while the portal to her sex clenched and tore my orgasm out of me in thick, groaning waves.

And that's how it had gone all night, as we caressed and loved each other until morning.

My woman. Everything we did together was her first, and my King Kong soul was reveling in that knowledge. I'd branded her as mine. And no one else's.

While I was reflecting on my feelings, she stirred against me, murmuring in her sleep. I smiled and removed her bonnet while burying my nose in her neck, inhaling her early morning fragrance.

"Rogie?"

"Umm?"

"Why is it called 'sleeping together'? We didn't do much sleeping." Her voice was still gravelly with sleep and laced with humor.

"I have no idea." I chuckled and pulled her closer.

"I love you," I whispered into her ear. She sighed, eyes still closed, and allowed herself to be enfolded in my embrace. My little head responded with enthusiasm and hardened between her cheeks.

"Seriously, dude?"

"Yes. He knows I love you and can't help himself. He loves you, too," I laugh-murmured in her ear.

"You so crazy." Her throaty voice held a chuckle.

She wriggled her ass cheeks against my cock, turning my laughter into a groan. Her answering giggle didn't help much.

"I gotta go pee," I muttered as I rolled out of bed. "That's cruel and unusual punishment."

Robbie's laughter followed me into the bathroom. Smiling, I relieved myself after I'd deflated some. I splashed water on my face and beard, washed my hands, and rinsed my mouth thoroughly. I padded back into the bedroom just as she sat up and swung her feet to the floor. She was smoothing her locs and nodded, "Me too."

As I slipped into some sweatpants, she stood and stretched. "Ow," she groaned. "I'm sore all over." She sent a scowl my way, and I could only laugh. I guess our bedroom acrobatics had affected her, too.

"Sorry, babe," I replied. "I couldn't get enough of you."

"I noticed." Chuckling, she made her way to the bathroom as I stood there admiring the perfect globes of her ass.

Damn.

"Dat ass, tho."

"Lech," she laughed in reply.

"I'm going to start breakfast," I called to her. "Mama is opening this morning, and I don't have to be in till about three. She's doing family meal and brunch, and I'm expediting dinner service."

"Okay," she garbled through toothpaste.

While she was washing her hands, I put on an old t-shirt and slipped on a pair of Mocs. Leaning into the bathroom, I gave her a juicy kiss on her forehead while she brushed. She rewarded me with an affectionate, foamy smile. I waggled my brows at her, pulled my hair back into a messy ponytail, and headed off toward the kitchen, phone in hand. I was half tempted to try to coax her into a little morning delight, but I was starving and needed some energy. Morning delight would have to wait till after refueling.

I grabbed my apron hanging on its hook on the side of my stainless restaurant shelving unit and slipped it over my head. While yawning and stretching in front of the fridge, I tried to figure out what to make for breakfast. Ah. I'd found some Iberico bacon online and decided that this would be the perfect morning to cook it. Duck eggs were next. A unique twist on bacon and eggs, but I didn't win Top Chef by making oatmeal.

I turned on the oven and started the coffee, deciding that regular drip would be okay for today. After the oven had finished preheating, I put strips of bacon on a sheet pan lined with a Silpat® and slid them in. I figured that fluffy biscuits, cultured butter, and artisanal blackberry jam would be fine additions to our fancy little breakfast. While I was opening the flour canister, the doorbell rang. I wasn't expecting anyone, but I went to the front door to open it, wiping my hands on the towel tucked into my apron strings. Robbie had sauntered into the kitchen, looking fresh and well-rested, considering. She looked at her watch and raised an eyebrow.

"It's not even 7:30. Expecting company?" She poured a cup of coffee, splashed in a bit of half and half, and padded over to the breakfast table. She sat on one of the chairs, curling her feet underneath her.

"No," I answered. "I never get company this early. Maybe it's Mama, but she would've called. Or it could be Derrick, here to mooch breakfast. That's not unusual. I don't know what his schedule rotation is this month."

I opened the front door, and my jaw nearly hit the floor. After all the drama, destruction, heartbreak, and near ruination of my life, this was the last person I expected to see.

Hera.

Chapter 39

Robbie

"WHAT IN THE EVER-LOVING hell are *you* doing here?"

Rogan's voice was as thunderous and as angry as I've ever heard. But this was not an annoyed voice. His voice was vibrating with rage.

"Oh, calm down," a female voice replied flippantly. Oh. This definitely wasn't Mama. Or Derrick. But I had an idea.

"I'm here to spend some time with you since you're free," the voice continued. "A man like you can only go so long without some, well, *entertainment*." A devious chuckle. "And I'm here to provide it."

Before following Rogan out of the bedroom, I'd donned a pair of yoga pants and slipped into one of his t-shirts, which swallowed me. After pouring a cup of coffee, I'd curled up on a chair at his small dining table in the breakfast nook while he prepared our morning meal. I didn't have a line of sight to the front door.

I heard heels tapping on the tile floor as the woman entered the condo. She strolled her way to the island and took a seat with an air of entitled familiarity. She looked like a fuck doll, or, as Mama put it, a *puta*.

It was Hera. No surprise there.

No one else would be this brazen. I suppressed a snarl and kept still. Ripping her face from the front of her skull and hocking a loogie into the empty sockets would probably be frowned upon by the authorities. Crime of passion defense notwithstanding. Instead, I decided to sit tight to see how this scenario would play out.

Rogan followed her into the kitchen, fury clearly etched on his handsome face. Wow. He was pissed.

"Now, since you don't have your scrawny little plaything around," Hera chirped nastily, "I figured you'd be wanting a real woman to, how should I put it..." she wiggled her butt in the barstool while she pretended to think, "... *alleviate* your stress and tension. I have ways to help take the edge off." Good for her. She learned a word that has more than one syllable. And from the sound of it, she apparently knows what it means.

She flipped satiny dark hair over one shoulder and crossed her legs as she faced Rogan. I could see the tight blue dress she wore ride up, exposing miles of creamy thighs.

Bitch.

Rogan sent me a look, face dark with anger. I smiled, nodded, and put a finger in front of my lips. He visibly relaxed. I had picked up on her agenda. She came to claim Rogan, but Rogan was mine. She would have to find out the hard way. But first, I wanted to see how far she would take her little stunt before I announced my presence. I sat silently sipping my coffee and observing the drama.

"Even if you think you haven't missed me, I know you have," she whispered. "I've missed you."

"No, you haven't," Rogan replied. He measured flour in the glass mixing bowl he'd set on the countertop. Next, he added microplaned shreds of frozen butter. "You were hoping to be the main squeeze of the hot new Vegas chef," he continued before raising one eyebrow. "Or am I wrong?"

"I've been busy, but I've missed being with you. People need to see the type of woman you like, and that I'm the only one for you. Since you're a celebrity, you need someone sexy, glamorous, and white. I'd look better on your arm. No offense."

Really, bitch? Fuck you!

"None taken. But delusions of grandeur aside, aren't you supposed to be spending some time in front of a camera or something? Is this your day off?" Rogan quirked a questioning eyebrow, barely addressing her last comment.

From my perch, I saw her shoulders go rigid. He'd hit a nerve.

"What do you mean?" Her voice wasn't quite as breezy and confident as it had been when she first strolled in.

I figured she didn't know he'd learned about her line of "work." This was a bowl of popcorn moment. I had a feeling this was going to be epic.

"When we first met," Rogan remarked off-handedly as he added whipping cream into the flour mixture, "I thought you were just a sexually experienced woman looking for entertainment in between sugar daddies. I also thought," he said as he turned the soft dough out on the marble slab and began pulling it into a ball, "you understood what I said. That I was only looking for a random hook-up, not a relationship. In fact, I'm pretty sure I used those exact words. To tell the truth, if we'd only been a one-night stand, that would have been fine. The first time we did it pretty much took care of my celibacy problem."

He had relaxed, and I could practically see what was coming. Yes, popcorn would be perfect right about now.

"I told you then, and I'm telling you now. I don't want a relationship..." he stopped as he patted out the dough, looking pointedly into her eyes. "... with you. Not then, not now, not ever."

"And why not with me?" Hera demanded, whining like a toddler. "I thought we were good together."

"'Good together'? We fucked. I came. That was as 'good together' as I wanted. Any woman could have scratched that particular itch. I certainly didn't need you specifically. If I knew then what I know now, 'we' never would have happened. Period."

Rogan cast an eye at her while he used his tall biscuit cutter to punch round circles of dough and place them in a circular cake pan he had buttered and floured.

"One question I never asked you," he drawled conversationally, "that I'm curious about now. I didn't ask before because it didn't matter, and frankly, my dear, I didn't give a damn."

"So, what's your question?" Her voice was no longer sultry and seductive but sounded pissy.

"What do you do for a living?"

The aroma of bacon wafted through the kitchen as he looked at her, expression unreadable. Hera's shoulders stiffened again. She stuttered before answering, "I'm a, um, adult entertainer."

"Uh-huh. Really. And what kind of 'entertaining' do you do?"

She was silent for a few moments while, I guess, she tried to formulate a plausible lie.

"I already know the answer, *Trezura Mapps*," he stated flatly before she could come up with an answer. He took the bacon out of the oven and slid the biscuits in. "I wanted to see if you would tell me the truth about your so-called career."

Oh snap.

She gave half a shrug before she answered. "I don't know why it's so important. As long as I'm making a lot of money and I look good on your arm, what difference does it make?"

"The difference it makes," he began, "is that I take pride in the fact I'm usually circumspect. That means I'm careful, in case you don't know. I avoid risks, especially with sexual partners. When we met, I wasn't as cautious as I should have been, obviously. Old-fashioned? Okay.

"Now that I know what I know about you, I'm glad I always used protection."

"What if I told you I was pregnant?"

A chill shot up my spine. *Oh hell no!*

Rogan sent her an outraged glare. He had the avenging angel look he got when he was seriously pissed.

"It sure as hell wouldn't be mine because, one, my condoms never failed. And two, it's been months since we last hooked up. It could be one of the ten thousand men you let dump their loads inside of your pussy, though. And we both know you're lying, anyway."

Rogan smirked at her as he removed the bacon from the baking sheet and placed the strips on paper toweling to drain. He set a timer, and while wiping his hands on a bar towel, he eyed her with contempt.

"In a way," he continued, "I'm glad you stopped by. Even though uninvited. Again." He hesitated and seemed to weigh his next words while looking at her under his lashes. "You need to understand that if I'd known what you do for a living, I never would have had sex with you. Not with my worst enemy's cock. Not with a titanium condom."

He braced his hands on the counter and got into her face. "Before you," he snarled, "I'd never been with someone who'd fuck anybody for money for millions to beat off to, which is what you do. A friend showed me one of your videos. You wanna know what I did when I saw it? I vomited. A lot. I *Exorcist* projectile vomited knowing I'd shared my body and put my mouth on you."

Rogan's anger escalated because she was here and because he'd had her.

"When we first started seeing each other, it didn't take me long to realize you weren't my type of woman. But it didn't matter because I wasn't in it for your brain. I wanted pussy, and you seemed to know what you were doing. At the very least, maybe you'd be someone who one day could transition into a friend with benefits. But, to put it bluntly, you're crude, not very intelligent, and a faker in bed. Add to that your porn career, and it's a dealbreaker."

He stopped, looking at her thoughtfully, frowning. "The thing that has pissed me off more than anything else is your habit of driving all the way to Vegas when I hadn't invited you. What's that all about? If I'd wanted you here, I would have asked you to come. Instead, just like today, you showed up and to hell with my plans or desire to see you. Which is less than zero."

"Well, for your information, I tried to let you know I was coming. I couldn't get through," she pouted.

"That should have been a hint that I blocked you and wanted nothing to do with you. That maybe you had become even less than an afterthought. If there's a question, the answer is that I don't want you in my life. Not even a little.

"So, with all that being said, you can leave now. We have nothing more to say or do with each other. And if you come here again, I'll get a restraining order against you."

Hot damn.

"How about one more round just for old times' sake?" she purred seductively as she slipped off the stool to approach him. "At least it'll take the edge off."

How stupid can you be? He told you to get lost. So get lost, bitch!

"My 'edge' is extremely well taken care of," he scoffed. "In fact, it's nonexistent."

His face relaxed into a blissful smile.

"Isn't that right, Rob?"

My cue!

"That's right, my love," I answered from my perch on the chair.

Hera whirled around to find me looking at her, smirking grin in place. I waggled my fingers at her. Couldn't help myself.

Ah. Karma. Gotta love it.

"You little bitch!" she shrieked and stomped toward me, fists balled.

Oh lord. Someone needs to stop this woman before I kick her fuck doll ass.

Chapter 40

Rogan

WHEN HERA SPUN AROUND and stalked toward Robbie with her hands balled into fists, I found myself torn in that split second. Should I yell at her to stop and get out of my house, or should I let her get up close and personal with Robbie's Krav Maga skills? I've seen what Rob can do. It ain't pretty. At least not for the other guy.

I decided to split the difference.

"Hera! You have no business insulting or attacking my *invited* guest!" Okay. It was a lame, fake-sounding warning. But at least I made an effort, such as it is. There was a big part of me that wanted to see Robbie take her down. Then I had the bright idea to begin recording this little interchange with my iPhone. I had a feeling that this might be one for the books.

Hera turned her head and shot a furious glance my way, eyes narrowed, blue eyes blazing. I shouted at her again to leave because she hadn't been invited and wasn't welcome. Repetition? No. *Evidence.* I wanted my voice on the recording. Just in case.

I didn't dare touch her or physically stop her because she was batshit crazy enough to try to figure out a way to have me arrested. I was more than sure that Metro would get involved if I put my hands on her, even though she was basically a trespasser. I wouldn't it do anyway because I don't put my hands on women. That said, the situation had the potential of being disastrous.

Watching Hera's heated response to Robbie's presence told me that she had no sense of self-control. If she had, she would have left instead of thinking that she could accomplish anything by fighting Robbie.

She looked at me with something akin to hatred because I'd thoroughly dismantled her plan of seduction. She was just now figuring out that I wouldn't touch her ever again. My days of dipping into crazy were forever over.

Hera turned and stormed toward Robbie, apparently ready for a catfight. Robbie stood up to face her and briefly closed her eyes in resignation over the inevitable. She didn't do catfights. As Hera reached her and swung her fist, Robbie easily dodged it, her movement practiced and fluid. Hera came at Robbie again and tried to punch her. Robbie deflected the attempt and slap-punched her with one hand before giving her a stiff-armed palm strike in the middle of her face with the other. If I'd blinked, I would have missed it. Just like that, Hera was on the floor, yowling in pain while holding her suddenly very bloody nose.

Smirking, I ripped several paper towels and handed them to Robbie over the counter. She tossed them to Hera.

Robbie dropped into an easy crouch and shoved her wrathful face directly in front of Hera's bloody one. Robbie's expression was one of ice-cold fury, brooking no nonsense from Hera.

"Listen, *bitch*," Robbie snarled, her words tight and feral, "lucky for you, my man would never put his hands on you. Me, on the other hand, would get great joy in givin' your fake 'ho ass a beatdown. Nobody asked you to come here. Rogan doesn't want your poison pussy, and I have no problem in kickin' your ass while I *personally* throw you out."

Robbie, my educated, well-spoken, introverted artist, businesswoman, and Ninja, had just gone full ghetto. Good for her. Thanks, Daria!

Robbie straightened to her full height and watched Hera as she staggered to her feet in her ridiculous shoes. I noticed that Hera's free hand was still fisted. It appeared that her interaction with Robbie's skills had taught her nothing. I started to warn Robbie. It wasn't necessary.

"If you even think about trying to hit me again," Robbie hissed just as Hera was ready to swing, "I will punch the taste right out of your mouth." She got into Hera's face and space, practically snarling. Hera's heels put her at the same height as Robbie, so she got an up-close-and-personal view of pure, barely controlled ferocity. And wisely took a few stumbling steps back.

"You do not want to mess with me because I will Fuck. You. Up."

Wow. My girl was lit. Her eyes were blazing, and her head was rolling. I was, unsurprisingly, thinking about popcorn. I knew that

Hera would suffer a soul-destroying beating if she persisted in trying to fight Robbie. I also knew that Robbie was holding back. For now. Hera had no idea just how lucky she was not to be a laid-out bloody mess already.

"I'll go to the police and tell them he beat me up," Hera taunted, pouting like a child.

"I'm taping everything," I replied with more than a little relief that I'd decided to record the whole thing. "Go ahead. I'll have this vid uploaded on YouTube and sent to the cops before you can blink."

Hera glowered at me and then turned her malevolent glare to Robbie. Her eyes were red, and her nose was bruised and still dripping blood. Robbie was laser focused for anything that Hera thought that she might do.

"I don't fight over men," Robbie snarled, "But if you think that fighting me will get you Rogan, then you're welcome to try to see how far that gets you. I will have so much fun just kicking your ass. Not over Rogan. Just kicking your sorry ass."

Hera turned again to look at me for help, only to see that I was still recording her confrontation with Robbie. I waved at her from behind the phone.

"I saw Robbie drop a six-foot man and almost cripple him in about five seconds," I remarked. "Just imagine what she can do to you."

Hera's eyes widened as she sent a stunned look to Robbie. I saw the second that she decided to back off after struggling between her emotions and what little common sense she may have had. Good. Although I'd readily admit a bit of disappointment in not seeing Robbie deliver another smackdown.

"You need to get out," I told her. "You haven't been welcomed here in months. Get a clue and leave."

She stormed over to the bar, grabbed her purse and sent me an "I hate you!" shriek. Robbie unceremoniously "escorted" her to the front door and put her out. I finally turned off the video. Evidence. Just in case.

As soon as the door slammed behind Hera, the oven timer chimed, and Robbie returned to the kitchen, grimacing and shaking her head. "What a psycho bitch! What the hell were you thinking?"

I took the pan of biscuits out of the oven and placed them on the counter.

"I wasn't," I answered, embarrassed. I hadn't been thinking. "Between leaving Florida and getting everything set in Vegas, I'd been celibate for months. So when we met, I talked myself into thinking that this was okay for immediate gratification. The first weekend wasn't too bad because I was able to scratch that itch with a warm body instead of just my hand. The second weekend was when she went all porn star on me, and her fakery started to turn me off."

I looked into Robbie's eyes, willing her to feel my emotions. "I only saw her a few times after that because I realized I didn't even like her. Hera's not particularly intelligent, but she's scheming and devious. When I met you at the gallery, she'd done the same thing she did today. She showed up uninvited just as I was ready to leave for the exhibit. She was with me because I was in a hurry and didn't think to just send her right back to California. She is the biggest regret of my life because she managed to make me hurt you, and that's the worst thing I've ever done."

Robbie made her way around the counter to drape her arms around my waist. We exchanged looks and hugged, kissing and rocking back and forth.

"I love you," we exclaimed to each other. And then laughed.

"That was a real eye-opener," she said softly. "I think I get it now. Do you think you should take out a restraining order anyway? She seems a little mental to me."

"Give me a minute," I told her before answering her question, "I need to upload this to YouTube to time stamp it so in case she does something stupid, I have proof that this is unedited. It'll be private so no one can see it unless and until I make it public."

That took all of five minutes to complete.

"And I agree with you," I continued, looking down at her soberly. "I think she's more than a little unhinged. I have no idea why she became so jealous and focused on me. I didn't like her fakery and the fact that she couldn't hold a conversation with a pair of tweezers. I swear that I never gave her any indication I wanted a relationship with her. We weren't a thing. Ever. I didn't find her to be likable, so it was goodbye for me."

"Maybe," Robbie speculated, "that's why she became so obsessive. You weren't groveling at her feet and worshiping her genitalia. I bet she has a big porn following, and you weren't falling into place. Maybe she saw you as a challenge."

I shrugged, loosening my arms from around her so that I could get the duck eggs scrambled.

"What I don't get is why she'd drive all the way from California," Robbie mused. "There's something creepy about someone who'd do that. It feels almost stalkerish. At the same time, I really think that she believed that I was old news. That you'd be so hard up she could just walk in and take over."

"She had no idea the lengths I'd go to ensure that you were in my life," I replied. "I'd move heaven and earth to make sure you were mine, and that means she has a snowball's chance of getting close to me."

I plated the Iberico bacon, the fluffy whipped cream biscuits, and creamy scrambled duck eggs. Robbie set down jam, cups of coffee, and glasses of fresh orange juice after placing the silverware. Then she gave me another hug.

I wrapped my arms around her so tightly that she gave a little squeak. I looked into her glowing eyes and started to feel the whole silverback, chest-pounding, howling at the moon Tarzan thing coming back. Me Tarzan. You Jane. A Jane who can kick some serious ass, but my Jane, nevertheless.

I dropped a kiss on her forehead.

"Let's eat."

Chapter 41

Robbie

IT WAS EARLY AFTERNOON when, overnight bag in hand and still dressed in yoga pants and Rogan's t-shirt, I let myself into the house. I toed off my Keens at the door and left them next to Daria's sandals. As usual, I dropped my keys and purse on the side table.

"Hi honey, I'm home!" I yelled as I walked toward my room.

"I'm in the kitchen!" Daria called back.

"Okay! Let me drop off my stuff," I answered as I made my way to my room. I dropped my overnight bag and trudged back to the kitchen. Daria was sitting at the island with a platter of cold fried chicken, macaroni salad, olives, and watermelon chunks. She was sipping a glass of white wine and reading a Real Estate textbook.

"Behold the box," she quipped as I opened the fridge and poured myself a serving from the box of Black Box Chardonnay she'd purchased. Hell, I didn't care. It's decent stuff and I'm no snob. I sat on the barstool next to Daria's and snagged a drumstick.

"So," Daria began with a twinkle, "how was your overnighter?"

I felt my face go warm as Daria cackled. "That good, huh?"

"I may never walk again."

Daria chortled. "I'm so glad you guys got everything worked out. To think that you almost split up because of that thot."

"Speaking of that thot," I began with a grin and told her about the morning's events.

"Hm. She sounds deranged," a concerned frown flitting across her face. "Is Rogan going to get a restraining order?"

"We talked about it, but she lives in California, so we're not sure how that would work. He doesn't know where she lives or where she may be 'working' so that may be more trouble than it's worth. Serving her on her job might stir up a bunch of problems that don't exist now, especially relating to his personal PR brand. He's going to get his gate code changed and her name removed from the visitor list just to be sure that she can't just randomly waltz in again. He'd pretty much figured that after everything had gone down, she'd go along her merry way and he forgot about it. He didn't count on her being batshit. As for me, I'm willing to leave well enough alone. The less we have to deal with her, the better."

Daria nodded. "I get it. Maybe it's nothing. At least I hope it's nothing. Maybe she'll find herself a sugar daddy and get some more 'work' done."

"After this morning," I laughed, "she'll need a new nose job."

Daria nearly snorted her wine through her nose, her dark eyes twinkling in amusement. "I know that's right!" she laughed. "Nobody told her that sista girl got skills!"

We laughed together and I grinned at my friend with affection as we high-fived.

"So," I began, scooping a forkful of salad, "how's everything going with tall, black, and yummy?"

"Better," Daria replied, her face morphing into a soft smile. "I'd said a few things that are hard to take back, but because of the circumstances, we've been talking through them. It took me a while to understand here," she patted her heart, "that Derrick isn't Keenan. Derrick's for real, and I have to get through my trust issues."

I looked at her, partly in understanding, and partly in friend-girl mode. "You walked into an apartment where the man you were going to be living with was booed up with a rando. Trust issues, hell! Any so-called 'trust issues' you have are totally legit. I hope he realizes that."

"Oh, he does. And because he's so perceptive, he realizes that when I was yelling at him, I was actually yelling at Keenan. And Rogan. Even I thought Rogan was being a fuckboy."

She paused, looking at me with a twinkle. "And speaking of Rogan? How's he treating you?"

"I pity the fool who tries to come on to me, hurt me, or whatever. They'll have to deal with Tarzan of the Jungle. I swear, every time we're together, it's like I can feel him morphing into King Kong, Godzilla, or something."

Daria laughed merrily. "Hah! I knew dude was into you from the first time I met him. You were so blind!"

"Not as blind as you may think," I replied, face warming again. "When you met him, he'd just laid one on me that almost had me ready to give up the goods. You were a godsend. Your timing was perfect."

"So he really wasn't just your 'friend,'" Daria laughed.

"Rogan is not a man you can friendzone if he doesn't want to be friendzoned," I answered dryly. "Even before the big PDA at the nightclub, he was determined to have me, and nothing was going to stand in his way. The problem was that he didn't tell me how much he really cared for me until it was almost too late. That said, the time we spent apart really impressed upon him that if we were going to be together, there could be no messing around with our feelings. We have to be honest with each other. The fact that he lost me for a while really shook him. Hard."

I shrugged, taking another sip of wine. "I'm happy we worked everything out. He doesn't let a chance go by without telling or showing me how much he loves me." I looked at Daria frankly. "I have my own trust issues, too, even if I wasn't the one affected. The whole situation around Nikki still echoes inside of my brain and causes the occasional nightmare. That circumstance is why I'm so focused on self-preservation and self-defense. And you should be, too!"

"You keep saying that," she remarked. "I was looking into Tai Chi. Why didn't you choose Tai Chi instead of Crave Magoo?"

I laughed. "Krav Maga," I corrected. "Because Tai Chi is a beautiful, rhythmic, and graceful dance of self-defense. Krav Maga is used by the Israeli army to kick the shit out of the person attacking you, disable them as much as possible, stomp them into the dirt if you can, and get the hell outta dodge. You saw it. There's something about that violence factor that speaks to me." I popped a couple of olives into my mouth and looked at her innocently.

Daria howled. "Okay! I think I'll go with you one day."

"What I did to Hera this morning was Krav Maga 101. I blocked her when she tried to hit me and then did a slap and a palm strike to the middle of her face. Laid her out. It's one of the first things you learn when you start taking classes. She was ready to throw hands and I threw fists. I wanted to take her out so there'd be no question as to whether or not I had the skills. I needed to diffuse home girl in a way to show her that I am *not* the person with whom to fuck."

Daria's eyebrows flew up before she burst out laughing.

"Okay. I'm definitely going to look into Krav Maga," she chortled.

"Well," I said as I slid from the barstool and finished the last of the glass of wine, "Thanks to Rogie, I need to take a long, hot shower. My lady parts are gooey and need to be scrubbed."

"Eww!" Daria laughed as she wrinkled her nose, then asked, "Is Rogan working tonight?"

I nodded. "Yeah. Mama started early for family meal and brunch and he's expediting dinner service. That's why we were able to spend so much time together this morning."

"Let's have dinner there," Daria suggested.

"Good idea," I nodded. "Let's go. With any luck, the thot has gone home to sunny California, and we can enjoy our meal. I'd prefer it if Rogan not know we're there so we can enjoy ourselves like regular customers. If he knows we're visiting, he'll drive the wait staff crazy as usual."

Daria laughed. "It's a date! I'll make the reservations."

Chapter 42

Rogan

WHAT IN THE ACTUAL *hell just happened?*

Service had finally ended, and we were wrung out. There had not been a single minute to breathe from the first service till closing.

When I checked with Sharita Jones, our head hostess and scheduler, she informed me that we had been completely booked for the entire day, from brunch through evening service. Every available seat had been reserved, and there was no room for walk-ins. All of the bar stools had people sitting, waiting expectantly for their drinks and food.

What the hell. This was a Sunday, and while it was a day when we were always busy, this was nightclub-on-a-Saturday-night busy.

Mateo Garrido, my new executive sous chef, had brought a copy of Thursday's LA *Times* with him. "Look at this," he said as he handed the *Food* section to me.

One of their food critics had been on a weekend getaway to Las Vegas with friends and family and had eaten at *Rogan's*. Like most people, he'd taken a few photos, and had submitted his observations after returning to Los Angeles. Under the picture of the entrance to *Rogan's*, the headline promised an outstanding review.

Neighborhood Gem Explodes Vegas Stereotypes
Top Chef winner brings world-class cuisine to his Sin City

hometown.
And no, folks, it's not on the Strip!

We'd been reviewed and had somehow missed it. And because it was the *Times*, the review would be seen worldwide. This was a level of credibility and publicity we couldn't buy.

I asked the entire staff, both front and back of house, to stay after closing for a brief, impromptu meeting. Although it was late, I knew they wouldn't mind.

The doors were locked after the last patron left, and we gathered in the main dining area. I first thanked Mateo for the heads up and then read parts of the *Times* article to the staff. I smiled inwardly at the excited saucer-sized eyes.

"I hope you're happy that you accepted your position here," I told them, "because it looks like we just hit the big time. The *Times* gave us an in-depth review before the *Review-Journal* has, and the *RJ* will now have to play catch up."

I smiled at the group. This was my staff, and so far, I didn't have a single regret at choosing every one of them.

"At least for the time being," I continued with a chuckle, "expect to be slammed."

I turned to Sharita. "What do our reservations look like?"

She grinned widely before answering. "We're totally booked through the next two weeks, and the VIP Room is booked three months out."

I turned to the wait staff who were standing together in a small group. "How were your tips?"

They all started excitedly chattering at once, clearly ecstatic over the amount of money they'd earned.

"That's wonderful news, and I hope it's just the beginning. If we get more recognition, then it could be even busier. And don't forget to tip out the barbacks, bussers, and runners." That was the extent of tip sharing that I required from the FOH staff, and it was based on the honor system. If someone was found to be holding back, they'd be terminated after only one warning. I had a waiting list of people who wanted to work at *Rogan's*, and I didn't have to tolerate bullshit.

I glanced over at Mama, who was clearly fatigued, but whose eyes were sparkling with excitement. She'd worked the pass since afternoon, expediting for the busy servers and runners.

"If you need to take a day off this week," I informed everyone, "please email in the leave request by noon tomorrow. That said,

I need each and every one of you for the next two weeks. I have a feeling that this is just the beginning. Everybody is important. Everyone counts."

I stood up from the stool I'd been resting on.

"Thank you for your work and dedication. And thank you for a great service. See you Tuesday, and don't forget to punch out after cleaning."

The chatter continued as everyone went to finish their different tasks. The bartenders and barbacks started cleaning the bar area, the servers wiped down the tables and placed the soiled table linens in the laundry area. The sous and commis worked on cleaning the kitchen stations.

Technically, as the owner, I didn't have to do much more than oversee and manage, but that's not how I roll.

The first thing I did was to help the dishwashers. I concentrated on making sure that the glasses were clean and free of pain-in-the-ass lipstick marks. I helped with pre-rinse as the crew stacked the plates, glasses, and silverware into the dishwasher.

I helped store, label, and refrigerate the leftover sauces and foods that would be added to family meal the next working day. I helped with the stock pots' cleanup and finished mopping the floor after I'd made my exhausted staff punch out and go home.

After everyone had left and I was going through the restaurant double-checking everything, I knew I had to find a way to get rid of the stress that was thrumming below my skin.

I needed Robbie. That wasn't something I even had to think about. I needed her.

It was hard to believe that just a couple of years ago, I'd hang out with the other kitchen workers at a place like PT's after work. I'd drink till dawn, eat greasy bar food, play some pool, gossip, and ultimately go home to have meaningless sex with some forgettable woman.

That's not me anymore. The same backhanded slap of maturity that hit me when I was a junior at UNLV hit me again when I decided to leave Florida. As the owner and executive chef of my own eponymous restaurant, hanging out like a dudebro was no longer in the cards.

This adulting stuff could be a pain in the ass.

I jumped in my Range Rover and told Siri to call Robbie.

No answer. I looked at the dashboard clock and realized that she was probably in bed. Although we'd closed at 9:00 p.m. with the last patrons finally exiting after 10, it was now nearly 1:00 am. The busyness of the service had substantially extended the evening.

I'd call again after I arrived at her place.

About 15 minutes later, I pulled into her driveway and parked behind her van under the porte cochère. I told Siri to call Robbie again.

This time, her voice, sounding worried, echoed from the speaker.

"Rogie? Everything okay?"

She didn't sound particularly sleepy or tired, but that may be because she was alarmed. I mean, who calls at 1:00 a.m. with good news, right?

"I'm beat, I'm stressed, and I'm outside right behind your van. Can I come in?"

A gasp of surprise, then a moment of shocked silence.

"Come in!" Her voice vibrated with happiness.

I slid out of the driver's seat of the Range Rover, chef's apron slung over one arm and phone in hand. I trudged up the walkway of her courtyard toward her front door. Halfway there, the door opened, framing her silhouette in soft light.

Man, I'd never been happier to see someone before in my life. I jogged the last few steps up to her door and walked into the welcoming space.

I knew. I just knew. Even though she'd told me more times than I could count, I could feel this woman's love. Despite the day that I'd had, I knew in a way that I couldn't explain.

I have no idea where that random thought came from other than her glowing eyes as she looked at me, a tired, stinking mess. She was welcoming, and her eyes reflected concerned tenderness.

My lips found hers before my arms could embrace her.

Suddenly, she pulled away from me, nose wrinkled, eyes squinting.

"You smell."

Chapter 43

Robbie

I FINISHED THE 11TH of the twelve paintings for my calendar project. Tommy, Rogan's graphic designer, and I were collaborating on the project together. Tommy was designing each month's calendar while I did the coordinating watercolor. The painting I'd just completed was the Rainbow Vista rock formation at Valley of Fire. I used my photos as my references, and the results were beautiful. The project's working title was *Beyond Vegas*, a series of atmospheric watercolors showcasing sites outside of the familiar scenes of the Strip and Downtown. Tommy's detailed calligraphy and linework was a perfect foil against my watercolors of landmarks, known and little known, throughout Southern Nevada.

After turning off the studio lights, I locked the door and headed back to the house. I stretched and rolled my neck because sitting in one spot for hours can make one creaky and cramped. I looked at my phone. Hm. Almost midnight.

Once I got to my room and stripped, I took a long, hot shower. I washed my locs every Sunday and had taken care of that in the morning. After the shower, they felt a little damp, so I just wrapped a microfiber turban around my head. *Good enough for gubmint work.*

I slipped on my shorty pajamas and a pair of fluffy socks and decided to treat myself to a glass of wine before hitting the sack. Halfway down the hallway, I heard my phone ring. I ran back to my bedroom, alarmed. It was too late for someone to call with good news.

Rogan's face and number popped up on the screen.

"Rogie? Everything okay?"

"I'm beat, stressed, stinky, and parked right behind your van. Can I come in?"

I was flabbergasted, which was an understatement. Rogan had never come to my house after work.

I opened the door when he was halfway up my walkway, looking pretty disheveled. I felt sorry for him and, at the same time, was glad to see him.

For some reason, he seemed to look at me with an intensity I'd never seen from him before. It was as if he were seeing me for the first time. Very strange.

But he looked like shit.

His face was smeared with something undefinable, his eyes were bloodshot, his hair, although pulled back into a tight bun at his neck, looked greasy, and his chef whites were stained.

He came into the house and shut the door behind him. He immediately leaned over me, his lips touching mine. And I took a deep breath.

I smelled grease, onions, fish, garlic, spices, man sweat, and busy kitchen.

I pulled away from him. "You smell."

A slightly wounded look flitted across his face before he grinned at me sheepishly. "I know," he replied with a twitch of his lips, "I was hoping you wouldn't notice."

"Come with me," I said to him, "but leave your boots outside. We'll hose them off in the morning."

He didn't say a word but did as I asked. He followed me down the hallway to the laundry room.

I opened the door and grabbed an empty laundry basket. I dropped it in front of him.

"Strip."

Humor flickered in his tired eyes. A touch of lechery danced across his lips.

He fished his chef bandana out of a pocket of his apron and tossed both into the basket. His chef coat, undershirt, pants, compression socks, and underwear followed. I reached up into one of the cabinets, grabbed a fluffy bath sheet and washcloth, and gave them to him.

"You know where my shower is," I said to him, fighting a smile, "take your time. There's plenty of soap and shampoo."

He nodded and left the laundry room. I put all of his smelly whites into the washer and made a mental note to set the soak cycle later in the morning.

I walked into my room to hear moans coming from the bathroom. I peeked in and saw Rogan leaning against the wall under the shower, letting the massage selection of the showerhead cascade down his neck and back.

I removed my pajamas, socks, and turban and placed them on the vanity. I found a scrunchie for my locs and opened the shower door to step in behind him. I picked up a bar of African black soap and the washcloth, which had fallen to the floor. After liberally soaping the washcloth, I began to wash his back from his neck to his butt, massaging the suds into his skin while his moans of pleasure became louder.

"God, babe," he wheezed, "that feels incredible!"

I smiled and made my way from his butt to his thighs and used the washcloth to massage his calves. The noises he made were somewhere between pleasure and pain. I reached over him to take the handheld showerhead, made sure it was on the highest massage level and rinsed his back. After I adjusted it back to normal, I shampooed his hair, smoothing in the suds and using my short nails to massage his scalp. He leaned his head back as I rinsed out the lather and applied the conditioner.

"Turn around," I ordered.

He did, eyes still closed and a whisper of a smile on his face. I washed his neck, shoulders, chest, wolf, and entire torso, gingerly avoiding his now-pulsing erection. I washed the front of his legs but couldn't resist landing a soft kiss and an open-mouthed swirl of my tongue around the head of his crown, turning his soft moans of pleasure into a groan of need.

I placed the washcloth into his hand and stepped out of the shower to dry myself. After washing his face and beard and giving himself a full-body rinse, Rogan stepped out of the shower into the bath sheet that I held open for him. He gave me a look of gratitude as he used it to dry himself. He dried and combed his hair with a comb I'd left for him and pulled it back loosely into a ponytail with a scrunchie. After he tucked the towel around his waist, he brushed his teeth and rinsed his mouth. When he was done, he turned to me, but before he could do or say anything, I took his hand and led him to the bed. I pulled the quilt and top sheet down and took his towel.

"Lay on your stomach."

I squeezed some body butter into one hand, rubbed them together, and began to knead one calf and then the other. Using my thumbs and palms of my hands, I massaged them deeply, releasing the tension from his tight, aching muscles.

"Oh babe," he moaned, "that feels so damn good even if it hurts." I spent at least five minutes on each leg, making a mental note to repeat in the morning.

Rogan rolled over and reached for me, and I melted into his arms. He kissed me lightly on the lips before turning his still-fatigued eyes to mine.

"Thank you, love. I didn't realize how much I needed that pampering."

Then his lips were on mine, his tongue seeking entrance to collide with my own. He rolled me over so that his body covered me. We sank together into the comfortable recesses of my bed, our mouths never breaking contact. My body was singing everywhere that our skin touched.

Rogan was ravenous. He was thirsting for me. His lips left mine and landed where they wanted on my body, ramping my heat up to unbearable levels. It was my turn to cry out in exquisite pleasure, helplessly responding to every touch of his mouth, his hands, his body. My nipples seemed to be seeking him and had pebbled even before his tongue swirled around each mound.

"I can't get enough of you," he groan-whispered as he moved downward. After he feasted on my breasts, his mouth feathered over my belly, and when his hands opened my thighs for access, his warm breath had me arching up toward him. His tongue licked and snaked over my already drenched folds. And when he swirled his tongue around and suckled my bud, I cried out in rapture.

And then he was hovering over me, one arm on each side of my head.

"I need to be inside of you now, sweetness," he gasped. Our lips met, and when he entered me, my legs wrapped around his body of their own accord. My body surged against his, welcoming him back into my soul. He pistoned inside of my sheath with deep, rolling strokes, and I came violently, suddenly, with a searing intensity that had me crying out his name.

I wrapped my arms around his neck as he growled his release.

The room was filled with our harsh breathing as we struggled for control.

"I'm in the wet spot," I complained.

Rogan laughed into the pillow before raising his head to look at me, eyes sparkling with humor. He wrapped his arms around me and rolled over so that he was in the wet spot.

"It's the least I can do after that wonderful massage and lovemaking," he quipped. Then he added, "Rob?"

"Mmhm?"

"Marry me."

Instantly awake, I sat up and stared at him.

"What?"

"Let me give you my sales pitch..." he began with a chuckle.

"Oh stop," I laughed. "What did you just say?"

"Marry me. It's okay with your folks. My folks, especially Mama, are wondering what has been taking me so long to ask.

"I love you. I'm a good provider and I understand that I'm pretty good in bed," he winked. Then he hesitated.

"Words I never thought I'd say, but I want a family, too. You're the only woman I want to have a family with. It wasn't until you came back into my life that I realized that. Even if it took me a minute."

Now serious, Rogan sat up, the faint light from my bedside lamp our only illumination.

"We love each other. I mean, we *really* love each other. We love each other enough that even I know that this isn't something that happens every day. This is special, and I feel it. I've already seen our children in my mind's eye. Scared me shitless.

"But we can't get to that point without each other. Marry me, Rob, so that we can get started on the rest of our lives."

He reached up and closed my mouth, which was agape.

"Everybody thinks it's a good idea," he continued, lips twitching. "Judson, who I guess I'll have to call Pops or something, thinks it's a good idea and what the hell took me so long to decide to make an honest woman out of you. Molly actually gave me a hug and started crying. Which freaked me out. And Grams and Papa congratulated us. Zion thinks I'll make a cool big brother. That was a while ago, and I hoped to have some sort of flash mob, 'will you marry me' thing. But we're both really busy, and it's taking too long to get to that point.

"So here we are. You just loved me more than I've ever been loved in my life. You care for me." He was again serious. "And I can't imagine life without you and our family. You are mine, babe. No matter how busy I am, you're the one who's always with me. Here." He patted his heart. "You're the only one who brings out my inner caveman." He hesitated a moment before chuckling, "Even though I know you could kick my inner caveman's ass.

"You already know that the restaurant is my life. Restaurant work is crazy, and owners put their entire lives into it. I won't always be home at a decent hour because this business is insane. Especially in Vegas. Random things happen. The LA *Times* reviewed us a couple of days ago, and all hell broke loose, but in a good way. That's why I was so late. If you can love me through that, I know that we'll be perfect.

"So. Will you marry me?"

Tears streamed down my face as I held the top sheet up to my chest.

"Of course I'll marry you, crazy man," I replied through a watery smile. "On one condition."

"What's that?" His eyebrows lifted in surprise.

"Figure out a way to do the flash mob thing anyway. That way, you already know that I'm saying yes, and it can still be kind of a party."

He howled with laughter, eyes shining even in the lamplight.

"You, my lady, have a deal."

Chapter 44

Rogan

"TILL DEATH DO US PART..."

It sure as hell is gonna have to be that way because I'll be damned if I'm doing this again. This whole engagement slash wedding stuff is a pain in the ass.

First, there was the "official" announcement.

Robbie and I decided to have a little get-together at her home because she has a spacious patio, outdoor kitchen, and entertainment-worthy pool. Mama chose the menu with paella and gazpacho being the main events. After I set up the temporary paella grill on the patio, I'd be working on the gazpacho. Everyone else would bring potluck items.

"Everyone else" consisted of all the parents, Robbie's grandparents, Zion, Janina, Derrick and Daria, and Derrick's older brother Cortez. Justin, Paul, Maybelline, and a few from the restaurant staff also attended, their significant others in tow. The overseas extended families couldn't come, of course. The Wilkes family couldn't make it on such short notice since this was a last-minute get-together.

This was the first time that the "second shift" would run the restaurant, but I had complete faith in Mateo and his crew. I had cherry-picked the best for a reason.

Everyone was milling about on the patio and in the kitchen, oohing and aahing over the huge paella pan that Mama had going. I heard the doorbell ring and told everyone that I'd get it. I laughed evilly to myself as I went to open the front door. There was a small group of fifteen people, and I invited them in.

We walked out to the patio, with a few curious people following us from the kitchen. Robbie and Mama looked up, surprised.

"I have something I want to share, and my friends here are going to help me," I announced. Out of the corner of my eye, I could see that Robbie knew what this was and was fighting a grin.

The group spread out in the middle of the patio and one of them started their Bluetooth speaker.

When the first stanzas of "When I'm 64" by the Beatles started, everyone started roaring with laughter. They knew.

I danced with the group. It's a catchy tune that even I can look good dancing. Besides, we hadn't rehearsed all that much.

As the words to the last stanza trailed off, I dropped to one knee in front of Robbie. She was laughing and crying at the same time.

"You know I love you with every particle of my being. Marry me, Robbie. My inner Tarzan desperately needs your inner Jane. I can't imagine going on in life without you in it. Let's make this a beautiful story to tell our children."

"Yes, crazy man," she tearily exclaimed, "you know I will!"

I took her left hand and under thunderous applause, slid a ring on her finger. Gasps went all around, but I wasn't paying attention. I was looking at her. Our eyes never left each other's, and just like a couple of weeks ago, I knew. Just knew. I stood up, cupped her face gently in my hands, and leaned over to kiss her. After a stage-whispered recommendation that we get a room, everybody laughed.

My flash mob group bid their goodbyes and were invited to stay, but they had to leave for another gig. I would tip them generously later. They'd put in extra effort to teach me steps, and I wanted to be sure to reward them.

When I asked the family's permission for Robbie's hand in marriage, Molly warned me about diamonds. *Consider a quality simulant or an alternate stone. Robbie won't have anything to do with blood or conflict diamonds,* she'd said. *No diamond at all is better than a conflict diamond as far as Robbie is concerned.*

With Dad's help and connections, I found an incredibly rare deep pink cushion-cut flawless diamond sourced from Australia, and that was "the one." No blood. No conflict. I'd rather not have someone's corruption tainting the symbol of what was up until then, the best day of my life.

I'd commissioned a local jeweler to set the beauty into a custom platinum setting. The diamond looked as if it were floating in the metal. This ring would suit my bohemian goddess perfectly.

Later, after everything had settled down a bit and while we were still snacking, somebody asked about the date or wedding plans. I said something about doing a quick wedding as soon as possible, maybe at the courthouse. A small party afterward, perhaps. Then we could start our married life right away.

Cue record screech.

Except for Robbie, every woman was glaring at me like I'd just curb-stomped a puppy. Mama, Molly, Janina, Daria, Grams, Maybelline, and the other women stared at me in horrified disbelief.

"What?" I demanded.

Mama came up to me and yelled at me first. She used an interesting mix of Spanish and English with the word *loco* thrown in liberally. She was pissed at me. Again. After she finished chewing my face and stormed back to tend to the remaining paella, Molly came up to me. While she wasn't upset as Mama was, she still had plenty to say. I think she realized that I was just a dumb guy on a new adventure.

"This is my only daughter," she began, patting my cheek, "and she's not getting married in the courthouse. Or in a chapel. Or by Elvis. We will be having a wedding. A big one. Period."

The only thing I wanted was to marry Robbie. I figured as long we got married, why should the size of the wedding make any difference? I said as much out loud and got the same stomped-a-puppy glares. Ultimately, the women kicked me out of the room, so to speak. The men invited me to sit down, put my feet up, have a beer, and shut up. Wedding planning is women's work, according to them. All I had to do is to show up and say I do.

Deal.

A couple of days later, Robbie and I met the parents at *Rogan's* shortly before opening. Judson, Dad, and the moms talked to me about how much time and money would be spent on the wedding. It was apparently going to be one of those E! Channel-worthy events. Dad and Judson would be paying for everything with an unlimited budget, which surprised me, considering Dad's frugal (cheap) nature. The guest list would be extensive, and Robbie and I would be pampered.

Dad said it was important that we not have to worry about the budget. He and Mama had to scrimp when they were married. Judson and Molly nodded in agreement. Their wedding had been kind of traditional, but far from extravagant. Mama and Molly talked about the most important things to them and were happy that those things wouldn't be a worry for Robbie.

"I want her to be a beautiful bride free of stress on her day," Molly smiled.

Robbie and Molly interviewed wedding planners, and we met with Yael Guggenheim, the planner they'd selected. During the meeting, Robbie and I shared our wants for our wedding day. Which was too far away in my opinion, but whatever. Yael, whose specialty was high-end luxury weddings, scheduled *The Obsidian* country club venue. The casino where we'd had our first real date also had a country club. While that's not unusual, it was unexpected because it was such a new casino.

The Obsidian had reached out to us some time ago, offering to comp us for any needs that we had. Robbie's little altercation made them nervous, especially when they learned that I was the son of the CEO/Owner of AIMM International, and it was my date who'd been accosted. We happily passed that information on to Yael.

Yael gave us a list of items that would have to be scheduled. I marked the appointments in my calendar, shaking my head at the craziness. Who knew you'd have to schedule an appointment to taste cake. *Cake!* Anything else having to do with wedding planning I left in Robbie's hands, because all I wanted was to be married to her. I didn't care about the details.

Dad and Judson kept me sane and laughing by reminding me to show up and say I do. All the rest was just fluff.

Chapter 45

Robbie

STANDING OVER THE COUNTER-HEIGHT table in my studio, I stared at the painting I'd started of the Kraft Mountain Loop Trail near Red Rock. I'd taken a boatload of photos when I'd hiked the trail in early spring on an overcast day in March.

Las Vegas isn't known for fog—an understatement if there ever was one—but occasional low-lying springtime clouds could give the appearance of fog. Mom had called to tell me that there were clouds, and I rushed up Charleston in the Odyssey. I found a place to park near the end of Sandstone in Calico Basin, not too far from Mom and Dad's house.

I had my Sony and an extra lens, and I spent the morning in the three-and-a-half-mile loop, taking photos of the hovering clouds and the brilliant red rock formations. It was time to go home after the clouds had lifted and the only pictures I could take were of a blindingly bright blue sky.

Now I stood in front of the stretched paper, which had the first layer of watercolor. I was very pleased with the progress.

There was a chime from my Ring doorbell, and I picked up my phone to see who was at my front door.

An older black man stood on my front stoop, a few feet away from the door. He seemed to be just under six feet, had a medium brown complexion and black goatee. He sported an embroidered Kufi on his head and was dressed simply in a sports jacket, dress shirt, and jeans. His posture was relaxed while waiting for a response.

"Can I help you?"

"Yes. I'm here to speak to Roberta if she's available."

"This is Roberta. How can I help you?"

"Hi, Roberta. I'm Robert, your father, and if possible, I'd like to talk with you."

How could I go from pleased to pissed in less than three seconds? This man, who abandoned Mom and me, had the nerve to show up at *my* house? I tamped down the wash of rage and headed toward the house.

"I'll be there in a minute."

When I got to the front door, all of my home training vanished.

"What the hell are you doing here? And how did you find me?"

"Your fiancé told me."

Wait. What?

"Rogan? He doesn't even know you."

"No, he does not," Robert concurred. "But he likes my music."

I looked at him in confusion.

"He asked for the DJ that was spinning when he went out with friends at *The Obsidian* a couple or so months ago. That DJ was me."

He was that fabulous DJ? He's the one who had us laughing and dancing? I recalled that Rogan had commented on the DJ's skill. I nodded.

"I remember that night. But I didn't think that he'd contact you without me."

"He didn't. He told y'all's wedding planner who looked me up. She had the names and addresses of the bride and groom, and I saw them. I was supposed to meet with you and your fella to set up the playlist, but when I saw your name, I had to find you and talk to you first."

"So Rogan didn't really contact you."

"He spoke with me, but he didn't know who I was to you. He wanted to set up an appointment for us, and I told him that I'd get back to him in a couple of days. I gave him some kind of scheduling bullshit reason. I knew I wanted to talk to you alone."

"Humph," I replied.

"And apologize. For everything."

I blinked.

"Apologize? Why now?"

"Because I'm overdue. I ruined Moll's life, ruined your life, and damn sure ruined mine."

I realized that this could be my only chance to find out exactly what happened between my mother and this man. Mom never really spoke about the details. I just knew that she'd gotten pregnant, he'd hung around for a minute, and then she was alone.

Mom didn't talk about him much, and at this time in her life, I guess there's no need to. I'm grown, she has a son with the man she adores, and she has a thriving business. Grams and Papa were there when she needed them most, and I never lacked for anything because they were always around. I just hated the son of a bitch because his absence scarred me.

"I want to hear the whole story," I said. "I need it."

I opened the door for him to enter, and we went to the conversation area in front of the fireplace. I motioned for him to sit down, and after he did, he removed his Kufi, crossed his legs, and relaxed. While his goatee was dyed black, his short afro was generously sprinkled with silver. The black goatee must be for his work.

He took a deep breath, but before he began, I held up a finger. "I'm going to start a pot of coffee. I think I'm going to need it. Want some?"

I returned with a tray carrying a carafe of hot coffee and stoneware mugs, a container of half and half, sugar, spoons and napkins, and a plate of wafer cookies. I placed everything on the coffee table between us. After preparing an unnecessarily decorated cup for myself, I curled up on one sofa, all ears. I waved at the platter. "Help yourself."

"When I met Moll," he began as he poured a cup of black coffee, "it was love at first sight. I mean, she was absolutely beautiful. Tall, classy, with beautiful hair and skin. And those eyes. We met at a conference for young black professionals. I had no idea what I was doing there but showed up because somebody told me to."

He stopped, his expression through his thousand-mile stare showing his feelings. His regret.

"I was real sweet on her, but she hated me immediately. And I don't blame her. She was high-class, select, educated, and I was a dude from Compton who happened to get a little luck in the gangsta rap world."

He took a long draw from his cup, expression closed.

"I had no class. And I wasn't smart enough to think that this beautiful young woman would be an asset in my life. That she was a come up. That she would make my life better. The only thing I was thinkin' was that I'd love to tap that ass.

"She was smart, though, and didn't give me any play at all."

"So what happened? What changed?"

"Me and my posse got a gig for black designers at a small fashion show in San Bernardino. They couldn't afford one of the big names, but it was a good gig and we got paid. Moll was one of the models. Anyway, we started talkin', and she didn't hate me anymore.

"About a month or so later, we played for another black fashion show just north of LA. A bigger one. We'd impressed a few important people and we got the gig, this time as the main event. Moll was there and she was, well, *dazzled*, and we talked some more. She was about 19 by then and was traveling on her own. I took advantage and managed to talk her into my room. She had no street sense and didn't know a game was being run on her."

He stopped and at least had the good grace to look embarrassed. "I didn't know she was a virgin until it was too late."

I closed my eyes. No wonder Mom had hated him so much. He'd taken her V card and then acted the ass.

"I wish I could say I was freaked, but I wasn't. Fact is, all we wanted to do was hit as many pussies as we could, and if there were cherries to pop, even better."

Ugh. He was blunt.

He tilted his head back, his stare full of self-loathing.

"We saw each other quite a bit from that point. I wasn't famous enough to make it onto the tabloids, but she was a fine woman to have around. When she told me she was pregnant, I was chill. I told her to take care of it and I'd square with her after she got it done. She slapped me so hard that she loosened a tooth. And then she left me."

Robert took a sip of his coffee. "I caught up with her again when she was modeling maternity wear. Let's face it, your moms is beautiful. She could strut a burlap sack and make it look good.

"I apologized and tried to stay around until after you were born. I knew I'd blown it. She never looked at me the same again. And then the drugs and shit I was involved in caught up to me. I was spending a lot of time tryna keep my ass out of trouble and I didn't have time for a baby. I always had time for pussy, but never a baby. Not that it mattered. She never gave me any more play."

I felt a dragon inside of me uncurl and want to strike this son of a bitch down. Apparently, I was little more than an annoyance to be sucked out of my mother's uterus. My fury was barely controlled. Thank goodness for my Krav Maga training, or I might have slapped him like Mom did. I tamped down the anger with a cleansing breath.

Bastard.

"And one day I couldn't find her. Nowhere. She just disappeared. I didn't know that her folks had upped and moved out of California to Vegas, so I lost track. And because I was in such deep shit, I didn't look. I could have hired a PI to find y'all, but I had too many problems. I was 'rich and famous' for a minute which meant that users, drugs, and women were easy to get. I had no discipline and not a lick of sense.

"You're my only child," Robert continued, sad eyes meeting mine. "A few other girls got knocked up, but they went ahead and got them taken care of like I told them to. I couldn't be bothered wearing a rubber because it would make me less of a man. That was the general thought that we had. And somewhere among all the fuckin', somebody gave me a case. Messed up my swimmers. Nothin' fatal, but I wasn't gonna be makin' more babies.

"When your stepfather found me..."

"He's my dad," I interrupted.

"When Judson found me," he continued, "I had pretty much hit bottom. I didn't want to give up the only thing that I knew was mine, but he made it difficult for me to say no."

"Dad mentioned that he had a few friends talk to you," I smirked.

"Yeah. He did." Robert chuckled. "They used the line from *The Godfather.* Either my signature or my brains would be on the release form. That was, no pun intended, a no-brainer."

He sighed. "After that, I really lost track of you for a while. Then I found out how successful you were in school and with your art, and I knew that I'd done the right thing. I never woulda been able to give you the life you have now. You woulda been surrounded by users, thugs, drugs, and living the high life. For a minute. And then been at the bottom of the barrel along with me. Moll and Judson did okay. Better than okay."

"They did," I agreed.

"When I finally got out of prison..."

Whoa. I didn't see that coming.

"...I was surprised to find out that you still lived in Vegas. I'd come here because I needed a fresh start. I began DJing and found that I had a natural gift and shot to the top. I've been doing national gigs for a few years now. When *Noire* wanted me to be their main DJ, I jumped on it."

"You were in prison?" I was stunned. After all, I hadn't exactly kept close track of his life.

"Yeah," he answered, head tilted as he regarded me from under his lashes. "I had a temper problem and a drug problem. A charge of domestic violence and possession with intent as well as punching an officer can mess you up. Five years. I've been out and clean for seven."

"Wow." For a minute I forgot to be angry.

"The bottom line, though, is that I got convicted and sent to prison for being stupid. There were crimes involved, yeah, but it all comes down to being fuckin' stupid. When I got out, I decided it was time to stop being stupid and start being a grown-ass adult."

I chuckled against my will.

I had to admit that Robert was interesting. Despite his previous issues, he was still handsome and spoke bluntly, which I appreciated. He'd probably never be able to shake completely free from his roots in Compton or the thug life. I appreciated that he was trying to be respectful of Mom and Dad's place in my life. Which was only right. After all, he'd been the fuck up. Not them.

"Not contacting you or your moms for all of these years is just another example of being stupid. I want to say I'm sorry. Sorrier than I have words for. I had a chance, and I blew it. If you decide that you don't want me to DJ at your wedding, I understand."

For once I was speechless. What was the etiquette in a situation like this? I took a deep breath and decided to just wing it.

"Actually, I'll be okay with it. I won't know if Rogan is because he doesn't know who you are. Just like I didn't know. But he likes the way you spin and your music sense. But it's not just us. There's Mom and Dad. Your history with them is more complicated. Frankly," I continued, "I don't remember much more than Mom seemed sad a lot until Dad came along."

I didn't regret in the slightest the expression of pain that briefly flitted across his face.

"I think it's important for Rogan to know, and I'm pretty sure he'll leave it to me to make the final decision. That said, I need to talk to Mom and Dad to get their input. No one else needs to know, but I think we'll have to tell Grams and Papa at some point. They had to take up your slack, after all," I said pointedly.

"I don't think anyone will be able to tell we're related. Or even care, to be honest. We don't need to broadcast it if we don't have to."

Robert nodded before standing up to leave.

"I'll have my assistant James call you and that fella of yours and set up an appointment in my office. I think it's important that you, me, Moll, and Judson talk about it. I have a feelin," he patted his heart, "that it'll be okay."

We walked to the front door together. We shook hands, and just like that, he was gone. I watched as he climbed into his BMW 840i. He's doing very, *very* well now, I see. That's good.

I leaned against the closed door and just stared into space. I had a potential mess on my hands. Suddenly Rogan's idea of a courthouse ceremony and party didn't seem so bad after all. I was in the middle of this and had to be the mediator when I still wasn't too sure of my own feelings. Rogan would be fine. Mom and Dad? That remained to be seen.

Chapter 46

Robbie

IT WAS LATE MORNING, and I'd been working on my latest piece since about 5:00 a.m. I desperately needed a cup of coffee. I made my way into the house and started up the coffeemaker. I was tired, but I was in the zone. It was time for a break.

While I was pouring myself a cup of caffeinated goodness, Mom, Dad, and Rogan entered the house. I had lost track of time and had forgotten when they were coming to pick me up. We would be meeting Robert ostensibly to talk about music for the reception, and we were going together. After doing a mental facepalm, I hurried to my room to change.

Rogan excused himself from the folks and walked into my bedroom with me. He came behind me and kissed the back of my neck, which made me respond to him. Of course. My body has a mind of its own when it comes to Rogan.

"Let's elope," he whispered into my ear.

I laughed and turned to face him. Although he smiled back, I could see that he was semi-serious. My expression gentled and I held his face in both my hands.

I love this man so much.

"All of this planning crap is way more work than I'd figured it was going to be," he complained. "I've attended my share of weddings, but I never thought about the work involved. I was always a guest." He looked into my eyes, his lips downturned. "I just want to be married to you, Rob, as soon as possible. Just us. All of the other stuff is a pain."

I smiled before giving him a big hug.

"First of all, my love, we live in the elopement capital of the world. So where would we go?"

He laughed, grinning back at me. "You may have a point."

"This wedding," I sighed, "isn't for us. It's for our folks, our extended families, our friends, their friends, blah blah blah. It's for memories we can share with our children. It's for the pictures and videos we'll be watching when we're old, and the kids will be laughing at how old-fashioned we look. The folks are beyond over the moon paying the ungodly amount of money this wedding costs. We are normal people with crazy parents. Let them be crazy. Why hurt them by telling them we don't want this?

"Honestly, I don't mind that they're over the top with this whole thing. I'm willing to go along with it to make them happy and give us memories. Even if it takes longer, I want to be your wife more than you can imagine."

"You don't know how much imagination I have," he replied with a grin and waggling brows.

We laughed together.

"Let's give the folks their time. This will pass soon enough, and we can begin our lives together with wonderful memories intact and no hurt feelings. Lord knows I don't want Angus or Mama mad at me."

"Gotcha," he guffawed, and then left me so I could finish getting ready.

Rogan and I were on the same page here. There's nothing I'd like better than to be married and settled. That said, I realized we needed to do the big ceremony and party for our families. Rogan, as the scion of a huge family, and I as the only daughter of mine, understood that the wedding wasn't about us, per se. It was a celebration of the uniting of two families who loved each other, as well as the bonding of two souls. Instead of getting married tomorrow, we'd be married in a few short months. Truthfully, I was okay with that.

While the siren's song of a simple Justice of the Peace wedding called to both of us, we were adult enough to make the appropriate decisions. Even if the decisions weren't convenient. Priorities and all, you know.

Robert's DJ *OG Spins* offices weren't too far from Zappo's on the second floor of a small downtown Las Vegas business complex. Yael was waiting for us as we walked toward her after we parked. Laughing, we entered the darkened offices and were greeted by a heavily tattooed young man with short, dark blond hair and sparkling brown eyes.

"Hey Yael, glad to see you again." He turned to us and introduced himself as James O'Brien, DJ OG's general assistant, assistant emcee, and all 'round gopher.

"He's wrapping up an appointment and will be with you soon," James told us. "I'll go remind him."

The windows to the front office were clad in solar window film, which helped reduce the late morning sun and warm the sage-painted walls and black ceiling. Inexpensive waiting room chairs were lined along one wall. A TV ran loops of some of the DJ's gigs, including weddings. A couple of Mid-century style floor lamps were placed in corners in the compact room.

Cozy.

While we were waiting, a bridezilla, her scowling mother, and a resigned-looking groom emerged from the back and exited. James came out of the door behind them and waved us in.

We followed him down a narrow hallway, chattering excitedly. Even though I was nervous, I had a feeling everything was going to be okay. We walked into a room outfitted for music. Large speakers were mounted on stands in the corners, and what looked like a million records were in shelves lined along two walls. The room was somewhat darkened, and a few stage lights were on stands or hanging from the ceiling. A small television mutely displayed the same video that had been running on the TV in the reception area.

I'd talked to Mom and Dad about Robert stopping by my house and introducing himself. Since he'd been Rogan's choice for a DJ, I needed to know if it would be okay and if they would meet him. While his visit had tempered some of my loathing, I was still guarded. I just hoped nobody would start a fight. I felt I'd need to keep an eye on Dad just in case he decided that Robert's life was a waste of air.

We all took a seat in cushy leather chairs, and I sat next to Rogan. He reached for my hand and then gave me a sharp look. My hands were clammy. He raised an eyebrow but said nothing.

Robert stood at the sound table, silently watching us. He was dressed pretty much the same way he was when he visited, only without a jacket. A Kufi rested on his head, and his shirt sleeves were rolled up to his elbows.

"James, Yael, can you give us a few minutes?" They looked at each other, nodded, and left the room.

"Hello, Molly. Judson." He nodded toward Mom and Dad. "Roberta, nice seeing you again. Thanks for running interference."

"You're welcome."

"Hello, Robert," Mom said. "Excuse me if I'm feeling a little awkward."

"Robert," Dad greeted. His voice, like his expression, was unreadable.

"Did Roberta tell you about our conversation?"

"She did," Dad replied.

"I like to think that I would have done this sooner or later," Robert said, "but I'm glad the young man found me and brought us together. He sped things up a little. The universe works in strange ways."

Indeed.

Robert took a deep breath, closed his eyes, and began.

"Not only do I want to apologize to you all, but I'd also like to clear the air on why I acted the way that I did. As I told Roberta, it was because I was stupid. And because I was stupid, I lost Molly and lost the daughter I'd wanted her to abort. Stupidity lost me my money, my sanity, my fertility, and my freedom. It wasn't until a small group of men persuaded me to sign some papers that I began to wake up. I didn't wake up soon enough, but it was a start. It took a stay as the guest of the state, but I made the best of my time. I realized there was nothing as important as my freedom. If I continued to be stupid, freedom wouldn't be a part of my life, and nothing would ever change."

He paused and looked at Rogan. "You did me a solid, young man. I found a way to clear the air with the people I hurt. My heart is at rest because of you."

Rogan nodded toward Robert.

"Thank you."

"I owe all of you so much," Robert continued. "And I'll never be able to repay. The years..."

He trailed off, fighting tears.

"I can't get back. There's no rewind button on life. But I've grown from the thoughtless SOB I was. I finally decided it was time to become a grown-ass adult and face the fallout. Some of that fallout ended up with me behind bars, but I could face that more than I could face y'all.

"But I can do this. No matter the cost, I will do Roberta's wedding for nothing. Considering what a piece of shit I was before I lost her completely, it's the least I can do."

"No, man," Dad interrupted, "We pay our obligations. Everything that happened, happened for a reason. You're now clean, and I have my family. You're a working man, and we pay working people.

"I want you to know I get that you were immature. And then you had some serious shit to deal with." Dad smiled. "Because of that, I have the love of my life and the daughter who's my soul. So you did *me* a solid, too."

The two men looked at each other when Dad stood up and walked over to Robert. They shook hands and did the man hug. I fought tears as the toxicity of my hatred melted away. If Mom and Dad could forgive this man, then I could, too. After all, thanks to Robert's "stupidity," they'd given me the best life ever. Dad had to deal with the crap Robert was dishing at the time, and he didn't hold a grudge. I looked at Dad with shining eyes, now really understanding why I loved him so much. He was a man with a heart who had taken me in and raised me as his own. Because I was.

Mom and I looked at each other, and her eyes were glistening. I think that we both loved Dad more at that moment than ever before.

"You don't know how what you've done has healed us," I whispered in Rogan's ear. He nodded and squeezed my hand, also overcome.

"James, Yael!" Robert called through his intercom, his voice cracking. "Let's get this show on the road!"

Chapter 47

Robbie

ONCE UPON A TIME, Rogan whispered into my ear, "Let's elope."

While I knew why that would be a terrible idea, I found myself agreeing with him more and more. After all, we live in Las Vegas. No waiting period required. We could take a quick trip to the Marriage Bureau in the courthouse to get a license on the DL. Then, minutes later, we could go around the block to the Justice of the Peace and get married. People did it all the time. The total time required, especially midweek, would be about an hour. Maybe two.

Sigh.

Oh well.

My phone buzzed when I was in my studio, and I happily answered Rogan's call.

"You busy?"

"Not really. I'm sketching out a new project."

"Let's have a date night this evening. Wear something a little dressy. I have a surprise for you. Our reservation is at six. I'll see you about five."

I glanced at the time on my phone when we clicked off. Hm. Two-thirty. I wonder what the surprise is.

Rogan and I were going out more. The outings were either hiking to places where I needed to get reference photos or, more often, to events that required a certain amount of dress-up while he promoted the restaurant and his brand. At first, I was a little starry-eyed until I realized a few of those people were, well, snakes. And the women were vipers who did nothing to hide their interest in Rogan. I was the quiet, polite fiancée until a viper got in my way. More than once, I'd snarled a quiet threat to snatch a bitch's face if they didn't back the fuck off. Rogan was thankfully oblivious. Well, he may have noticed once or twice, but he has a special glare that will chill anyone.

I had purchased several dresses for these events and decided to wear one that was form-fitting. It had spaghetti straps with a soft scoop neckline and an open back that plunged to the top of my butt. The skirt dropped to just below my knees, and a long side slit climbed up my thigh, revealing shimmery nylons. The lux dress store called the color Rose Lavender, which perfectly complimented my skin tone. A matching silk sweater and straw-colored heels completed the ensemble. I rarely wore anything that clung to my body, and it would surprise Rogan.

After I dressed and completed my makeup, Daria helped me braid my locs with a ribbon that matched my dress. We pinned the fat braid into a neat bun on the crown of my head, and the look was perfect.

The doorbell rang, and I heard Daria's and Rogan's voices drifting down the hallway. One last inspection in the mirror, and I walked toward the front of the house, already smiling in anticipation.

Wow.

Rogan stood tall next to the kitchen island and as he watched me, seemed to grow in presence and stature. He was dressed entirely in black. He wore pleated slacks, shoes, and a long-sleeved dress shirt with gold cufflinks. A silk tie and vest completed the look. His chestnut red hair was loose and flowing around his shoulders. A gemstone stud glinted from one earlobe, and a Tag Heuer graced his left wrist.

Groupie mode activated.

He smiled at me, and his eyes swept approvingly along the length of my figure. A couple of steps, and he stood in front of me, holding my chin as his warm lips met mine.

"You ready?"

I nodded dumbly.

Chuckling, he bade Daria goodbye as he took my hand, and we walked down the courtyard. My jaw dropped as a sleek vehicle the color of vintage gold came into view.

"It's a Lucid Air Dream Edition. Dad and I invested in the company when it was just a startup. After months of waiting, I took delivery just a few days ago. It's all electric.

"I thought it'd be something nice to make our nights out a bit more fun," he commented impassively as if this were the most natural thing in the world.

He opened the passenger side door for me, and I slipped into pure luxury. I groaned and snuggled into the plush leather. A click of his fob, and the door whispered close.

The driver-side door was open when he walked around and slid into the seat. He pressed on the main screen, and we had ambient lighting and soft music playing.

"I'll bring you up to date on everything when we're sitting for dinner."

While watching Rogan drive, I quietly lost my mind.

This man.

He occasionally glanced at me, smiling, while his confident, sure navigation piloted us toward the Strip. A right-hand turn, and we were in traffic on the Strip. Another right hand turn on Flamingo, and we were driving into the VIP valet parking at Caesar's next to the soaring Octavius Tower.

After we'd been seated in the low-key, classy Restaurant Guy Savoy, Rogan regarded me with a soft gaze.

"I have a lot to tell you. It's important, and I haven't tried to hide it from you. I knew it wouldn't make a difference anyway."

"Hide what from me? This isn't about Hera, is it?"

"Nope!" he laughed.

"A couple of months before I moved back to Vegas for good, Dad gave Janina and me $25 million. Each."

I stopped sipping on the beautiful Petrus he'd ordered and blinked. I probably looked like a derp with my mouth wide open.

"What?"

"Dad gave Janina and me $25 million. And that was just the down payment."

"I don't understand," I croaked.

"Because of Dad's businesses, my business and investments, and Janina's investments and work in AIMM, Dad felt that we had earned the money. We also learned that Dad's a billionaire, but because of his frugal nature, he just never shared that little tidbit with us. He didn't want us to be assholes as adults. He and Mama still live in the same house we grew up in. It's paid for, they're comfortable, and they like their neighbors, so why change."

I was stunned. I mean, I'm glad that Rogan is comfortable, but it didn't make any difference as far as I was concerned. I love him. Period. It's the whole "for richer or poorer" thing.

"But wait, there's more!"

I laughed. "Okay. What's next?"

Rogan's expression became serious, and he took my hand.

"The best thing you ever did for me was to kick me to the curb with the Hera drama. You knew my family had money, but you had the dignity to tell me to shove it. Money wasn't the reason you loved me. Money meant nothing if you thought you were being disrespected. Your self-respect didn't have a price tag. You humbled me."

He regarded me and smiled.

"All of that being said, when I turn 30, Dad will give me $250 million in currency, assets, and investments. That will be more than enough for us to live comfortably and make sure that our kids are taken care of and educated."

I almost dropped my glass of wine. What?

Rogan laughed at my expression.

"So, babe, what do you think?"

I couldn't wrap my brain around that much money. While my family wasn't poor, they were still thrifty. Dad, for instance, could afford a Bentley or an S-Class but preferred to drive his relatively unassuming BMW sedan.

"I bought the Lucid," Rogan continued, shaking me out of my speechless state, "because I wanted something to show that I was successful. Something luxe and comfortable to make the haters take notice. I wanted something to drive to events where the brazen display of shameless wealth is more or less expected. You and I know I don't ordinarily give a damn about that, but I wanted to make a statement. This is it.

"I said all that to say this: I love you. And I know you love me. That means more to me than anything material. In fact, I can't even put into words how much you mean to me."

"I don't know what to say," I finally choked out. "I love you, and the wealth part never even came into it. When I was a kid, I ignored the crush I had on you. It kinda came back when we met at the gallery, but I stayed detached because you had a girlfriend."

Rogan studied me contemplatively, swirling his glass of wine. The sommelier stopped at our table to pour more of the Petrus into my glass. Heaven.

"When I saw you, I loved you, and I didn't even know if you were a diva or not. You seemed to be real. Then, as we spent more time together, I realized that you were a WYSIWYG person. No pretense. No gold digger aspirations. No bullshit. Just a genuine, *you can kiss my ass if you don't like me* kind of person. You cracked me up from the beginning," he chuckled.

"I know we can't elope, but I want to show you my worth. What I bring to the table. And I need for you to understand that I will always protect you. I will always be faithful to you. And I will always love you."

I stared at him, speechless. While Rogan had declared himself several times throughout our relationship, somehow this time was different. Even though we'd been mingling with some of the cognoscenti of the entertainment and food industries, he never gave the vipers any indication that he wanted to be with anyone but me. He was mine. Period.

"So why are we here?"

He chuckled. "Because tonight, we're going to pretend to be high rollers. I'm going to play either craps or blackjack in the high-limit lounge, and you're going to hang on my shoulder, smiling at me and being sexy."

I cracked up. I never gamble—or "game," as the casino-speak folks put it—and didn't mind playing the part of Rogie's seductive good luck charm.

"After that, we'll go to one of the invitation-only clubs to look snooty and sip cognac. And after we're done with the fun, we'll go home, have a glass of wine, and make love."

I looked across the table at his laughing face. Smiling to myself, I agreed. We're going to have mindless fun. I didn't mind being a poseur from time to time.

After our meal—highly recommend the black truffle soup, by the way!—we walked out of the restaurant to the casino floor. We ultimately decided that going to the high rollers lounge was a little pretentious and we'd have more fun at the regular tables. We held hands while walking and I looked up to him just when he looked down at me. He stopped and leaned over to place a gentle kiss on my lips. Then I whispered into his ear, "let's elope anyway."

The End. ish. Maybe.

Afterword

"There is nothing to writing. All you do is sit down at a typewriter and bleed."
Ernest Hemingway

For years, this quote by Papa Hemingway hung on my tackboard at the "day job." I hadn't ventured into the world of creative writing because technical writing and documentation were my bread and butter. Still, Papa's exhortation was there, hovering over me, urging me to share Rogan and Robbie's story, no matter what.

Rogan and Robbie's story of love in Vegas bounced around in my mind and heart for so long that I finally had to sit down at the "typewriter" (aka keyboard) and bleed.

Now that I've shared their love story, it's time for them to make it official.

Rogan's Robbie: Ever After is in the works, and it will take you on a Vegas roller coaster ride of executing a luxury wedding in the Wedding Capital of the World, Las Vegas, Nevada!

Wedding chapels and Las Vegas go together like peas and carrots (apologies to Forrest Gump). While they range in appeal from the traditional chapels of the larger casinos like Bellagio, Venetian, or Flamingo, to regular churches (yes, we have more churches than just about anywhere else), to the super kitschy (drive-through Elvis wedding, anyone?), they have been a legendary part of the Las Vegas landscape for decades.

But even in Vegas, some weddings never see the inside of a chapel. Instead, magnificent weddings are held in venues and on budgets that are beyond breathtaking.

Just imagine what you would do if you had a wedding with no limits. And it was in Vegas!

Stay tuned for *Rogan's Robbie: Ever After* to share in their super opulent Las Vegas wedding that even Robbie couldn't resist!

Meanwhile, enjoy the prologue to *Derrick's Daria*, the second installment in the *Love Happens in Vegas* series.

Derrick's Daria

Prologue

I STOOD IN THE middle of my nearly empty apartment and nodded in approval. Marked boxes were stacked neatly in corners, ready to move. I had dismantled my queen bed and somehow managed to heave the heavy mattress, box springs, and frame against the bedroom wall. Everything would go into storage for a short time before my boyfriend, Keenan, and I moved to our new place. I had packed everything and didn't need my bed since I'd be staying with him until we moved.

We spent several weeks shopping for a reasonably priced apartment. Because it's so damned expensive in California, particularly around LA, we wanted to find a place that would allow us to save up for the dream home we hoped for in our future. After a lot of hunting, we'd finally found a two-bedroom in a new inland community near San Bernardino that had a killer starter rent special. We were going to do the walkthrough and sign the lease agreement later today. We'd both given notice to our respective complexes.

Keenan worked from home as a sports and music promoter and didn't have to worry about commuting. Since he planned to move in before I did, he'd have time to set up the second bedroom as a studio/office. Then he'd be free to help me move in my possessions. All I needed was a small corner in the office to do my stuff. He needed it to bring in income.

I'd given my two weeks to the law firm where I worked as a paralegal, and my last day had been Friday. The move would place me too far away to commute, especially to downtown LA. Spending several hours a day driving to work and back was just not in the cards. Instead, I'd find something inland and already had two interviews lined up. I was almost set.

I went into the now-empty bathroom to fluff my newly shorn hair that I'd had changed from box braids to a short afro. I'd had an undercut done, and the hair was on point. At least for the time being, I was tired of braids and weaves and extensions and just wanted to feel the wind in my own hair. I swiped on a bit of lip gloss and nodded in approval.

Lookin' good, Ms. Kioko!

When people see my last name in print, they often assume that I'm Japanese. But my father is a native Kenyan, where Kioko is a fairly common surname. I love seeing their faces when they meet me in person, and I'm not offended at all. After explaining the origin, it almost always results in a good laugh and icebreaker.

I smiled to myself as I walked out of the apartment and locked the door. I continued to smile, lost in thought while driving toward Keenan's place. I stopped at Belle's Bagels for some bagels, lox, and varying flavors of cream cheese. Then, popping into a nearby Starbucks, I purchased a cup of black coffee and one unnecessarily expensive but delicious Frappuccino. I figured we'd have a quick breakfast-type meal before heading toward our appointment.

I navigated the notoriously horrid LA traffic toward Keenan's apartment and mused on the decisions I'd made. Keenan and I had been seeing each other for about a year and a half. We had discussed the concept of marriage, and we both felt that living together for a while would either negate or confirm our compatibility. While I wouldn't necessarily call myself a love skeptic, I was still cautious enough to ensure that I had all my ducks in a row before making that deep commitment. So far in my relationships, the ducks had refused to align. They just never worked. Keenan had come the closest to my heart. Who knows? Maybe this time, the ducks would cooperate.

I found a spot in the guest parking area and locked the car door after hopping out, bagels and coffee in hand. Using the spare key, I let myself into the apartment and was surprised that Keenan wasn't waiting for me. He'd told me he'd be ready to go by the time I arrived. I sighed as I set out the bagels and coffee on the bar and went to his bedroom to see if he was even awake. *I swear,* I thought, *that boy would have slept through WWII.*

I opened the bedroom door and saw rumpled sheets.

At least he's up.

I heard the sounds of the shower coming from the bathroom, along with music blaring from his Bluetooth speaker. The door was slightly ajar, and I peeked in. I knew I wouldn't be joining him because of the appointment deadline lingering, but maybe I could reach in and grab something rigid while his eyes were closed. That'd be fun!

And then I stopped, stunned. Keenan was pounding into a naked woman who had her legs wrapped around his body. Water streamed over them as he held her slick brown thighs in place for his pistoning hips. Both of them were rhythmically grunting as he slammed inside of her over and over again.

What in the actual fuck!

I felt bile rising in my throat, and I choked back a confused cry. I stepped back, stunned. Then, tiptoeing across the bedroom, I closed the door, mind now racing, heart aching. Feeling foolish. Feeling used.

Shit! Shit!

Taking a deep breath, I decided what I needed to do. Fishing around in my purse, I found a notepad and a pen. I wrote a sarcastic note and told Keenan that I didn't want to disturb him and his "guest." I grimaced as I wrote, *Here's my key. I won't be back to give you any more pussy since you seem to be getting your share without me. I don't need you or your community penis. I'm out.*

I left the note, the bagels, my key, his coffee, took my Frappuccino, and left, not bothering to close the front door. Fuck 'em. They're lucky I didn't go scorched earth and bring all the shit down on their heads. Since I worked in a law firm, I knew better. I'm allergic to jail.

I wanted to scream, but first, there was work to do. I considered slashing the tires on his Escalade but decided that was more trouble than it was worth. Besides, I'd left the box cutter at home. I jumped into my Audi and immediately drove to a nearby shopping mall parking lot. Once parked, I blocked Keenan from my iPhone and all my social media accounts. I posted and texted our mutual friends as well as his family to let them know we were no longer together and why we were no longer together. Let him deal with the fallout. I was done.

I called the apartment complex to cancel our appointment. I told the agent to contact Keenan directly if she had any questions. Maybe he could move in with the thot.

Keenan and I had planned to open a joint bank account when we moved into our new place. I felt a wash of relief that I had found out about his cheating before that happened. If he was willing to do this to my heart, what would he have done to my money? Probably fuck that away, too.

I started the car and drove back to my apartment, where I made an important phone call. I crossed my fingers and anything else crossable and hoped my friend would understand.

"Hello?"

The voice on the other end was breathless. *Oh dear*, I thought. *I hope I haven't disturbed anything.*

"Robbie?"

"Yes. Is this Daria?" the voice replied, happiness flowing through the phone. "I ran in from the kitchen," she puffed. "I left my phone in the bedroom."

"Yeah, girl. It's me. And I have a favor to ask. It's a big one, so if you say no, I understand."

"What is it?" Robbie asked, voice laced with concern.

"Well, you know that Keenan and I were planning to move in together," I began.

"Yes."

Robbie's voice was clipped. She'd never liked Keenan. Apparently, he reminded her too much of her "sperm donor," as she called her bio father. I guess he'd been a fuckboy, too.

"Well, we were supposed to sign the lease on our new apartment this afternoon and do a walkthrough."

"Yes."

"Well, when I got to his place, he was fucking some ratchet in his shower. I think it was his ex."

"Holy shit, Daria!" A beat of time. "Did you cut his tires?"

I let out a snort of teary laughter. "No. But I thought about it. Not having a box cutter with me was why I didn't."

Robbie laughed. "Well, if you ever get a chance, do the sidewalls. And only do three, not four. Insurance will only pay for four, and cutting the sidewalls means he'll have to buy all new tires out of his own pocket because they can't repair sidewall damage. And for an Escalade, that ain't cheap. And make sure there're no people or security cameras around. You don't want to deal with any pain-in-the-ass eyewitness bullshit."

Hm. I wondered how Robbie, my sweet little nerd friend, knew all that.

"You need to come here. Get a fresh start," Robbie continued. "Ghost his ass. Vegas is the perfect place to hit reset."

"That's why I called," I replied, relieved. "Can I crash with you while I figure out what I'm going to do next with my life?"

"Girl, you don't even have to ask! How soon can you be here?"

I considered the question. Should I try to put my stuff in storage, or should I do the smart thing and just book? I still had two and a half weeks left on my apartment's 30-day notice, so there was no real hurry. I could always come back and either store everything or move everything. Or something.

"Well, all my stuff is packed. I can sneak back in a week or so and get everything moved or stored, but I feel like I need to get outta dodge as soon as I can. I left a loving note next to the bagels and coffee I'd brought. I'm pretty sure the thot he was with will be less than pleased, and he'll have a shitstorm to deal with."

There was another beat of silence on the other end. "Did you at least spit in his coffee?"

I laughed again, this time genuinely. "No. I didn't even think of it."

"Then get your ass out here now, woman!" Robbie exclaimed. "Give yourself some time to unwind and think, Ms. Kioko. *Mi casa es su casa*. Or something like that. My Spanish sucks."

"I owe you big time," I said gratefully. "It's just about 11:00 am. Depending on traffic and how long it takes to throw some things together, I should be there by 6:00 pm, give or take. I'm not worried. I'm sure he'll have some 'splainin' to do, which means he won't be looking for me any time soon."

"I'll be home all day, so take your time."

After confirming Robbie's address, *remember, if you pass the Spaghetti Bowl, you've gone too far*, I threw some clothes into a suitcase, picked up a couple of small boxes with some personal items, grabbed my laptop and chargers, and locked up. I stopped at an Arco to fill up, typed Robbie's address into Google Maps, and then navigated the labyrinth of interchanges to the I-15 North. I took a deep, cleansing breath as I steered my course up the open highway before me. I had to focus right now. There'd be time to fall apart later.

"*Viva Las Vegas, motherfucker*," I whispered.

About the Author

It all began with Fabio.

What red-blooded woman isn't swept away by a powerful, handsome man with flowing hair and chiseled muscles?

From the time she was a girl, Irene was a rabid reader and inhaled anything and everything in print. As a young adult, she learned about Romance novels from her (certifiable) mother and began a lifelong passion for the genre. Even while working at the "day job," Irene had long since decided to write the Great American Romance Novel. *Rogan's Robbie* is her debut work, and the first episode of the *Love Happens in Vegas* series.

Irene was born and raised in North Philadelphia a (very) long time ago, and after relocating several times through the American Southwest, ended up falling in love with Las Vegas and making Sin City her home. After a career built on technical writing, creating documentation, and instructing on topics ranging from real-life psychological crises to computer how-tos, coupled with a decade stint in an academic library, Irene finally decided to retire in her beloved adopted hometown. Irene has a lifetime of stories, ideas, life experiences, anecdotes, and Vegas secrets to share with anyone who is as enthusiastic and curious as she is.

Welcome to *Love Happens in Vegas!*

Acknowledgements

Many years ago, I knew I wanted to write my own book. Now that I have completed the task, I know I want to write more. But make no mistake; it is challenging work. Especially on your brain!

Anything worth doing is worth doing well, and doing anything well sometimes requires a team. On my dedication page at the front of the book, I recognized close friends and family who encouraged me. But there's more.

Self-publishing is hard work, and this process has made me respect the work of traditional publishing houses. I think it has taken me almost as long to learn the publishing process as it did to write *Rogan's Robbie*! The details of pulling everything together are not only intense, but far from inexpensive. I found that knowledge goes a long way in saving the wallet.

I learned a lot at what I affectionately call the "University of YouTube." Because once the book is written, you learn how much more there is to do. Going the regular, commercial route can be very expensive, and thanks to the UYT, I found that freelancing worked for me. In particular, Fiverr, which is a clearinghouse of freelance specialists, was invaluable to both the quality of my book and the integrity of my wallet. Please visit my website, www.RenieWritesAndWines.com for stories on my book-writing adventures.

Most of all, thanks for reading. If you enjoyed *Rogan's Robbie*, please consider leaving an honest review on your favorite online shop.

www.ingramcontent.com/pod-product-compliance
Lightning Source LLC
Chambersburg PA
CBHW032147190626
46814CB00005BA/1872